*Acclaim*

"If a TV network ran a gay primetime drama, this would be it. Like *Falcon Crest* or *Dallas,* the novel is a family saga set in the 1980s, this time on a Louisiana sugarcane plantation. Its cast of characters includes handsome heroes, a wicked Joan Collins-like villainess, and a manly yet gentle patriarch who struggles to keep his dynasty going at all costs. Fans of Ridout's *Plantation Secrets* will not be disappointed."

—Dale Edgerton
Author, *Goneaway Road*

"In the tradition of our nation's favorite nighttime soap operas, *The Man Pilot* is a multigenerational coming-out story and truly an ongoing saga. Following the lives of the Pilots, a Louisiana sugarcane-growing family, *The Man Pilot* is laden with secrets, scandals, deception, and betrayal. From the Man Pilot, the patriarch of the family, and his secret lover of years gone by, to the youngest grandchild, Number Six, this is a complex story set in the 1980s when AIDS is new and intriguing, the sexual revolution definitely has not hit Louisiana, and living as an out gay man simply wasn't done—at least not in the South.

There are so many complicated relationships and so much still left unresolved that Ridout leaves plenty of room for a sequel. With the major problems and crises resolved and the novel brought to a reasonable conclusion, readers will be anxiously awaiting a sequel to find out where the book's characters have ended up and how their relationships have turned out.

*The Man Pilot* is an entertaining read, especially for anyone who has lived through the challenges of being gay in the 1980s."

—Andrea L. T. Peterson, BA, MDiv
Freelance writer/editor

# The Man Pilot

# HARRINGTON PARK PRESS
## Southern Tier Editions
### Gay Men's Fiction
### Jay Quinn, Executive Editor

*This Thing Called Courage: South Boston Stories* by J. G. Hayes
*Trio Sonata* by Juliet Sarkessian
*Bear Like Me* by Jonathan Cohen
*Ambidextrous: The Secret Lives of Children* by Felice Picano
*Men Who Loved Me* by Felice Picano
*A House on the Ocean, A House on the Bay* by Felice Picano
*Goneaway Road* by Dale Edgerton
*Death Trick: A Murder Mystery* by Richard Stevenson
*The Concrete Sky* by Marshall Moore
*Edge* by Jeff Mann
*Through It Came Bright Colors* by Trebor Healey
*Elf Child* by David M. Pierce
*Huddle* by Dan Boyle
*The Man Pilot* by James W. Ridout IV
*Shadows of the Night: Queer Tales of the Uncanny and Unusual*
    edited by Greg Herren
*Van Allen's Ecstasy* by Jim Tushinski
*Beyond the Wind* by Rob N. Hood
*The Handsomest Man in the World* by David Leddick
*The Song of a Manchild* by Durrell Owens
*The Ice Sculptures: A Novel of Hollywood* by Michael D. Craig
*Between the Palms: A Collection of Gay Travel Erotica*
    by Michael T. Luongo
*Aura* by Gary Glickman
*Love Under Foot: An Erotic Celebration of Feet* by Greg Wharton
    and M. Christian
*The Tenth Man* by E. William Podojil
*Upon a Midnight Clear: Queer Christmas Tales* by Greg Herren
*Dryland's End* by Felice Picano
*Whose Eye Is on Which Sparrow?* by Robert Taylor

# The Man Pilot

James W. Ridout IV

Southern Tier Editions
Harrington Park Press®
An Imprint of The Haworth Press, Inc.
New York • London • Oxford

Published by

Southern Tier Editions, Harrington Park Press®, an imprint of The Haworth Press, Inc., 10 Alice Street, Binghamton, NY 13904-1580.

PUBLISHER'S NOTE
This is a work of fiction. Names, characters, places, and incidents either are the products of the author's imagination or are used fictitiously, and any resemblance to actual persons, living or dead, business establishments, events, or locales is entirely coincidental.

Cover design by Lora Wiggins.
Cover photograph by Mark V. Lynch.
Model–Ryan Harmon.

Library of Congress Cataloging-in-Publication Data

Ridout, James W.
   The man pilot / James W. Ridout.
     p. cm.
   ISBN 1-56023-460-1
   1. Sugarcane industry—Fiction. 2. Plantation life—Fiction. 3. Louisiana—Fiction. 4. Gay men—Fiction. I. Title.
PS3568.I35997 M36 2003
813'.6—dc21

2002153150

# Prologue

Julian took a stroll to his favorite resting place a short distance off the farm road to a set of feed drums that were leaning against a tired old fence. He liked to sit on top of them and gaze over the broad cane fields into the trees on the horizon. Jesse and Jay, his two oldest sons, were with him, as they wanted to spend some time with their daddy. They knew his routine and often saw him settling in on his favorite perch with a strand of grass hanging from his lips. Julian liked to end his daylight hours this way after a hearty meal at the big house, as the children had their baths and got ready for bed. The boys wanted to go with him tonight, so he allowed them, realizing that relaxation and rest were not likely to happen this evening. The boys surprised him, sidling up next to him on the cans as they watched the sun begin to set. However, it wasn't long before the boys' interest in the sunset began to wane and they wanted their daddy's attention.

"Daddy, tell us the story about how life began on the farm," Julian's oldest son Jesse requested. He was tall and slender as ten-year-old boys go, with fine white-blond hair covering his head. His skin was fair as his tan from the summer months began to fade.

"Yeah, tell us the story, Daddy," his younger brother chimed in. Jay was a year younger than Jesse and had the same build but was a shade shorter and had a head of dark red hair.

"You guys have heard this story a bunch of times. Do you really want to hear it again?" Julian asked with a chuckle as he drew them close.

"Yes, tell us again," Jesse said.

"Please, Daddy," Jay pleaded.

"Okay," Julian said, "here it goes. Let's start our story around this time of year. November is time for the sugarcane harvest season, as the growing season ends. Sugarcane is the farm's cash crop, and we transport it from the fields using large trucks with big tires forming lines coming down the cattle road to the main road, and leaving down the farm road.

"You have to remember that Grandpapa Pilot is very set in his ways. The farm runs like it did many years ago just like in the old days. Every worker pitches in to bring in the sugarcane. It's exciting to bring in the harvest and see the results of a year's worth of work.

"I can remember standing outside the big kitchen watching the trucks come in from the fields soon after I came to the farm a few years before you two were born. The trucks were moving one at a time down the farm road. As they arrived, men were quick to unload the freshly cut sugarcane from the small trucks onto bigger trucks to transport the sugarcane to the mills along the Mississippi River.

"Your Uncle Jack explained to me how the Pilot farm worked its sugarcane crop. Many sugar producers use heavy equipment to harvest their sugarcane. While machinery works fast, the quality of the sugar crop suffers. Mechanical harvesting mixes trash and dirt in with the sugarcane, which has bad effects on the refining process. Uncle Jack told me what I'm telling you now.

"There have been four or five generations of Pilots in the last two hundred years, while the sugar industry has been so important in Louisiana. A young man named Travis Pilot decided to leave northern Louisiana and set out to the Mississippi River delta region to start growing sugarcane. After a few years, there were some prosperous grinds. In years to come there would be devastating floods, diseases, and pests in the delta, where the Pilots founded their plantation.

"The sugar business became lucrative for the Pilots. To build the business, Travis took daring risks. He invested most of the family's assets in land claims. The family owned many slaves, but Travis had to convince many of the male slaves to journey with him to the river region to start a new and prosperous life. Many of the slaves did not want to leave their families, but Travis convinced them it was in their best interest to join the new adventure. He promised a better life for the slaves. If the sugarcane was successful, he promised their children would learn to read and write, and gain their freedom. The slaves trusted Travis, because he had always respected them as human beings.

"Travis held to his promise. After the farmhouse, barracks, and barns were built, the Pilot family, along with the rest of the slaves, arrived on the farm. Travis continued to treat his slaves with respect and gave them continued praise for their hard labor. He built comfortable living quarters for their families. Travis eventually gave those slaves who helped build the farm their freedom, but most continued to stay and work for wages as they enjoyed their quality of life.

"Most of the farm's families have lived on the farm since that first founding generation. Your grandpapa continues the tradition of those before him, treating the farm's black folks with respect and dignity. He never hesitates to lend a helping hand to those who wish to leave the farm to pursue their dreams and happiness. Some black folks leave the farm to pursue college educations, art careers, and other interests with the farm's help.

"The Pilot plantation continued through the years to be successful. Labor costs weren't so high as to spur the need for machinery. While other sugar producers complained of labor shortages, the Pilot plantation enjoyed a hefty supply of loyal field workers. The farm produced sugarcane second to none. The Pilot family stays loyal to the founding families who still live on the farm. They will always have a secure place to live while the Pilots operate the plantation."

"That's my favorite story," Jesse said.

"Mine too," Jay agreed.

"Daddy, why is our name Smith and not Pilot?" Jesse asked.

"My name has Pilot in it," Jay disagreed.

Sensing the beginnings of a sibling squabble, Julian quickly interceded. "You're right, Jay. Your last names are not Pilot like Uncle Jack and Grandpapa, but each of you has Pilot as your middle name. When you were born, your mama wanted to be sure that no matter where you children went after you grew up, you would always know where you came from."

Julian guessed that the three younger children had finished their baths and Emily would be waiting for these two to get themselves cleaned up before settling in for the night. "Okay, you guys, time to get back up to the big house."

"Daddy, how did you come to the farm?" Jesse asked. "Before you met Mama?"

Julian sighed as he looked into the distance. This was not a pleasant subject for him and one day he would have some explaining to do for his children. He sensed that the time wasn't right, but he didn't want to put off the question. He smiled as he started to explain. "I came on a bus one day and it let me off in town. Then I met your Uncle Jack and he said that your grandpapa might have some work for me and that I might go with him to see about it. When I got to the farm, your Grandmama Louisa, when she was living, fixed a big supper and I liked her cooking, so I thought I might stay a spell. The next thing you know, I met your mama and then the five of you came along." He saw that the two boys were content with the answer, so before they could ask another question such as nine- and ten-year-olds ask, he prompted them to get going. Yeah, someday he would have some explaining to do.

## 1

Shaun was sitting on the porch steps of the big house on the Pilot plantation. The farm was one of the larger sugarcane producers in the state of Louisiana. The man Pilot was the reigning patriarch of the place. With his guidance, the farm remained under one of the grand families of Louisiana.

The size of the place never ceased to amaze Shaun. The farm operated like a city in the center of the main farm. All the old plantations were made this way, because before cars and trucks came along, folks still needed the services a small town offered. The farm road turned off the state road through the fields to the big house where the first family lived. The farm road flowed to a T at its end. The lane leading to the big house ran to the left, while the main road to the rest of the farm rolled to the right.

Despite the farm's grand size, it replicated many of the other plantations in the region. It fronted the Mississippi River but was protected by a large dike to prevent flooding. The farms in the area flooded at times, but it wasn't the great river that caused the damage. It was the streams feeding the river that swelled at their banks and seeped into the low-lying areas. There were plenty of bayous where excess water drained, but the ground stayed wet even when it hadn't rained in a few days. Along with the summer heat, it was perfect for growing sugarcane.

Shaun gazed along the main road as he reminisced about the past four years. The barns on the left side of the main road were monsters. He remembered how awestruck he was at first sight of these grand structures. Green pastures ran along opposite sides of the barns from the main road. On the other side of the main road, the big kitchen stood across from the first barn. It was positioned next to the barracks, which sat across from the second barn up the main road. The big kitchen fed the farm people. Families living along the old quarters road, which turned off to the right of the main road past the big kitchen, ate their supper in their own quarters. However, everyone working on the farm had the noon meal at the big kitchen.

Shaun's gaze led him back to the T where the farm road ended. A few feet to the right stood a half-dozen cans where his Uncle Julian often perched, when he needed some time to himself. However, Uncle Julian spent a good deal of time entertaining visitors while leaning his back against the fence planks behind his perch. If somebody wanted to find Uncle Julian, they first looked for him sitting on the cans.

"You ready?" Uncle Julian asked Shaun as he came through the screen door from the kitchen of the big house.

Shaun was on his way to college. Today was his big day to leave the farm to go to Boston to live for seven years. He was excited, but he hated to leave. The Pilot plantation was home. It was the only place where Shaun felt he truly belonged. Sometimes the conservative bigotry in this parish was a pain, but he still loved the place.

Shaun had come to live on the Pilot plantation just over four years ago. His papa sent him to live with Uncle Julian because he found it difficult to manage a fifteen-year-old gay teenager. Shaun's papa felt Uncle Julian would help transform Shaun into a respectable young man. Uncle Julian was gay even though he was married to Aunt Emily. They had five children together. Shaun's papa believed Uncle Julian had reformed. He hoped with his brother's influence, the same could happen to Shaun.

"Yeah, I guess so," Shaun replied with a sigh. He remained seated on the steps, as he was having second thoughts about leaving.

Uncle Julian wasn't really reformed. In this backward part of the country, there were many gay men and women who were married to members of the opposite sex. Some spouses understood like Aunt Emily, while others seemed to overlook the situation. Shaun knew he would never marry a woman, but it seemed to work for Uncle Julian.

"Have you said good-bye to your aunt?" Julian asked.

"A few minutes ago, before I came out here," Shaun answered.

"Well, you'd better go in and say good-bye again," Julian admonished him. "She's good at masking the way she feels, and I know she's just sick about you going."

"Okay," Shaun said as he got back up to go inside. Julian gave him a pat on the back as he went through the screen door.

"Did you forget something?" Emily asked as she looked up from her work at the kitchen counter.

"No," Shaun answered, "I just thought I'd say good-bye again. . . . I mean for good this time."

Emily moved across the room and wrapped her arms around him. She was a beautiful tall slender woman with long limbs. Her light brown hair reached past her waist, but she always kept it styled close to her head. She squeezed Shaun even tighter. Shaun stood about five feet ten inches, but Emily was slightly taller. Her bones were delicate enough to give her a feminine appearance. His hair was a few shades darker than hers and a good deal more wavy. He wore it parted to the right and kept it longer than most young men in this part of the country. They could probably pass for kin, as he sported a similar tall slender frame. However, he had a few pale freckles, while her skin was clean of any marks.

"Well, I'm glad you did, but I wasn't going to admit it to myself right away," Emily said with a warm smile. She let him go. "Now go on," she said, shooing him away, "your uncle and Adam are waiting for you."

Shaun gave her a sheepish grin and headed out the door. Uncle Julian was loading his suitcase into the trunk of the car that Adam was driving.

Adam was the pastor of the local community church in town. It was separate from the Baptist church that most of the parish folks attended. Adam had been a great friend to Uncle Julian and Shaun. The three became close a few months after Shaun arrived on the farm when he started having trouble in school with some of the other kids. Things hit a breaking point when two boys in the school bathroom raped Shaun in an effort to teach him a lesson. After this incident, Adam helped Uncle Julian form a group at school where all youths could meet together to talk about all kinds of issues and have some fun. At first the adults sought to have the group meet at the school, but opposition from the community was too strong. Next, Adam tried to have them meet at his church, but the folks there would not hear of it. The saints at the church always were supportive of Shaun and his open personality, but they weren't comfortable with a group discussing gay issues meeting in their building. Despite the homophobia in the church, he still loved it. He got along well with the folks.

After a time, the group raised enough money to buy a small shacklike structure in town to house a youth community center. This way, they had a place to meet other than peoples' homes. Shaun spent a year after graduation getting the center underway. The building needed extensive renovation, and many of the townspeople pitched in and helped rebuild it from the ground to the top. The youth center was used for all sorts of teen groups. Now that the youth center was underway, it was time for Shaun to go to college.

"Are you ready for the trip?" Adam asked as he got out of the car. His head was covered with wavy auburn hair parted down the middle. He had a beautiful boyish face with green eyes that sparkled when he spoke. His body was slender but did not have the sculpted appearance that Uncle Julian's featured. Still, the two men were handsome together, when they stood side by side, a pair of good-looking guys in their early forties.

"I guess," Shaun replied with less enthusiasm as he got into the backseat of the station wagon.

"I thought you were so excited to go," Julian said, wrinkling his forehead while looking through the car door window at his nephew.

"I am," Shaun replied with a frown. "It's just not as easy as I thought it would be."

Shaun dearly loved his Uncle Julian. Sure, the man was his authority figure, but he was also his best friend. He was grateful to have been rescued from his parents, who lived in St. Louis.

Uncle Julian stood about the same height as Adam and Shaun. His bones looked strong and his body lean. His muscles could be seen through his loose clothes, but he was not bulky. Perhaps Shaun saw his uncle as a big man because he was his hero. Uncle Julian had blond hair that was thinning along the temples. His eyes were a soft brown like a cocker spaniel's. His eyes, nose, mouth, hands, and feet were in proportion to his body size. In Shaun's eyes, Uncle Julian was a great man.

Soon, the three men were bound down the road to the airport in New Orleans. The trip would take most of the day. Shaun would be taking a flight to Boston the following morning.

The next day, the time came for Shaun to board the plane. At the gate, he gave Adam an affectionate hug.

"I know you're going to do very well in school," Adam said with encouragement as he released Shaun from a hearty embrace.

Shaun nodded, accepting the reassurance. Slowly, he moved to his Uncle Julian. A rush of emotion came over him. He did not want to go to Boston. He wanted to go back to the farm with Uncle Julian. Still, he had come this far, so he had to make the trip. He was going to miss his uncle.

Julian's stomach was doing somersaults. Shaun was very special to him in a way that his five children probably would never share. Like himself, Shaun was gay. He was also closer in age to Julian than the children. Shaun was nineteen and Julian's oldest son ten. Julian and Adam were both forty-two.

Julian wrapped his strong arms around Shaun and held him tight while squeezing his own eyes shut. He released him and gave the young man a big smoochy kiss on the mouth. This caused a few nearby whispers, but neither man cared.

Julian was trying to keep from getting upset. "You be sure to call if you need anything. We will be far away but never too far."

Shaun put the heel of his hand to his eyes to push away tears. Quickly, he headed down the corridor toward the plane. He was glad that Adam was with Uncle Julian. The two of them got along really well. Sometimes he thought they shared more than friendship. Adam was married to a nice woman named Nancy. The only time he ever saw her was in church, though he saw Adam all the time.

The plane landed in Boston and Shaun put his homesickness aside. He was excited to be in his new home. Seven years seemed like a long time. It would take that long to finish his undergraduate and graduate work—plus he had business matters to attend to. He had inherited a fortune from his great-grandmother. It was supposed to go to Uncle Julian, but his uncle did not want to satisfy the seven-year residency in the old woman's Boston mansion stipulated in the will. Uncle Julian's mother, who was Shaun's grandmother, took care of the estate, so Shaun was able to inherit the money in Uncle Julian's place. Shaun's grandmother, Elizabeth Steele, inherited a third of the money for being the executor. Elizabeth did a superb job of making sure the conglomerate of businesses was extremely profitable. She ran the business by committee from Washington, DC, even though the company was based in Boston. She had an excellent staff working for her, which she handpicked herself.

Julian was handling Shaun's affairs while he learned to run the business. He was to receive $12,000 a year in allowance, which Uncle Julian thought to be plenty for a young man. Shaun did not think he would need that much money, but he trusted his uncle's judgment. It would all be spending money, since he would not be paying rent.

His luggage had been sent ahead of him and delivered to the mansion. He went to the cab line and gave the driver the address. Uncle Julian and he had made an earlier visit to look at the place and meet the people who would be tutoring him on how to manage Smith Power.

The dark brick house was huge, with three floors and two wings. It was much bigger than the house back at the farm. This house had a full staff to take care of it. During the day, it buzzed with housekeepers and business associates, but at night things were very quiet. There were offices in the mansion to run the estate's personal affairs, which were separate from the business.

Shaun could not believe how expensive things were. The cab ride cost $30. This was a shock, since he was used to catching a ride from the farm to town for free. The ride to this mansion was not nearly as long as the distance from the farm to town.

It was Saturday and school would be starting Monday. After sorting through his belongings in an effort to be sure that everything survived the trip, he decided to take a ride to campus to buy his books.

The cab fare was $15. Boston was a big city, and he was reluctant to use the car provided for him at the mansion. He was told the driver would be at his call, but he felt strange about making him wait at school until he was finished exploring and buying his books. He discovered that he would have to reconsider this philosophy, because with a few $15 cab rides his allowance would be spent.

He spent $400 on books and $40 for a cool sweatshirt with a bulldog logo on the front representing the University College's mascot. He spent another $12 for a late lunch, since he was hungry. In one afternoon, he had spent just about half of his monthly allowance. *Five hundred dollars should be enough for four weeks,* Shaun thought.

Shaun arrived at the mansion later that afternoon and decided to sort through his many cartons of books from home in the library. When he stepped into the room, he discovered that the books had already been placed on the shelves by the housekeeping staff. He spent the evening organizing them in the order he desired.

Monday morning. It was time to go to school. The driver dropped him off in front of the student union building. He walked to his first class, Introduction to College Life, which all freshmen were required to take.

When he got to the classroom it was nearly empty, since class would not be starting for quite some time. However, one individual was sitting at a tandem desk near the front of the classroom. Shaun froze in midstride as he entered the room. The guy at the desk was stunning. He was an exotic-looking creature with feline features, wearing a tight-fitting black sweater that clung to his thin body. His black hair was combed forward and pasted to his head with some kind of gel. His skin was a shade of coffee accented by his long eyelashes. Shaun thought he was probably a few inches shorter than himself. He looked to be about 120 pounds compared to Shaun's 140 pounds.

Shaun slid into the seat next to the man, without asking permission. "Hi," he said with a shy smile.

"Hi," said the guy, returning his attention to examining a textbook. He did not seem interested in giving Shaun the time of day.

"What do you think of campus?" Shaun asked, trying to make conversation.

The guy paused before replying, studying Shaun's smiling face. "It's okay," he answered, returning his attention to his book.

"My name is Shaun," Shaun said, extending his hand toward the fellow.

The young man paused before taking Shaun's hand. "Carmen."

"Are you excited about college?" Shaun asked with enthusiasm.

Carmen studied Shaun's face for a few moments with his topaz eyes. "Are you always so friendly?"

"Yeah," Shaun replied with a goofy nod.

"You obviously are not from around here," Carmen commented.

"No. I'm from Louisiana," Shaun answered and then added, "At least while I've been living with my Uncle Julian."

"Your Uncle . . ."

"Yeah. My Uncle Julian." Shaun felt a pang of homesickness but quickly recovered. "He is great. I went to live with him four years ago after my papa sent me to him from St. Louis."

"I see," Carmen replied.

"I live . . . or I lived on a sugarcane plantation with my Aunt Emily and him," Shaun explained.

"I could have guessed," Carmen said with a snicker.

"How?" Shaun asked, slightly bewildered.

"I hope you don't mind me saying, but you dress like you just came off the farm," Carmen stated matter-of-factly.

"Somehow, I don't think that was a compliment," Shaun said, losing his smile. He smoothed his well-worn black jeans and favorite threadbare matching black cashmere turtleneck.

"Relax," Carmen said with some warmth. "I'm only trying to help."

"Okay," Shaun said, regaining his light mood. "Maybe you can help me shop after school today. I would sure enjoy your company."

"Are you always so forward?" Carmen asked with a laugh.

"Only with some guys," Shaun said, returning his grin.

Other students were starting to filter into the classroom. Shaun returned his attention to Carmen. "What is your major?"

"I have two majors. The first one is sociology and the second is gay and lesbian studies," Carmen replied.

"Cool," Shaun said with enthusiasm. "I didn't know the university offered that major."

"They don't," Carmen said, deadpan. "I had to create it with some help from my advisor. I'll be taking classes from other schools in addition to this one. I also will have to do a lot of research on my own. The freedom may sound nice, but it's going to be a lot of work."

Shaun nodded. He was impressed.

"What's your major?" Carmen asked.

"Sociology and my other one is agriculture science," Shaun replied.

"I didn't know they offered agriculture as a degree," Carmen replied with a confused look.

"They don't," Shaun said, deadpan. "I'll be picking up some other classes across town."

Carmen laughed lightly in embarrassment as he turned his head. He returned his gaze to Shaun. "So, are you a brainchild like me?"

"Yeah. I'm pretty brainy," Shaun giggled. "And I'm also gay. Maybe you could study me."

"I figured as much, except your clothes and masculinity threw me off some," Carmen remarked.

*Me? Masculine?* Shaun started to disagree but instead protested the first remark. "Why do you keep remarking about my clothes? It's not very polite of you."

"I sense you feel the need to prove yourself. At the same time, we are gay and nobody cares about that around here, so there is no need to draw attention to yourself unnecessarily. Just try to fit in a little without compromising your values. Unless, of course, you want to be a laughingstock."

"No. I guess not," Shaun said dejectedly.

"Think of it like this," Carmen said, trying to restore Shaun's enthusiasm. "Let's say everybody knows you are gay whether or not you want them to know. Don't you want to make a positive statement about yourself in conjunction with that knowledge? What I mean is, they will say, 'He is a well-dressed gay man.' "

"That makes sense," Shaun agreed. "I'm just so used to having to prove myself. It's not so easy being a gay boy living in Louisiana."

"Well, it should be better for you here. You just have to be yourself and not come across as some weirdo."

"Okay," Shaun replied. "Thanks for the advice." He thought that he was going to like Carmen.

"Do you think you can spare me a hundred dollars until next month?" Shaun asked his business tutor at the mansion. His name was Leslie Sherman. Shaun had spent another $400 with Carmen at the clothing store and a few more dollars treating his friend to a nice supper. Managing money was a lot harder than he thought it was going to be. "I had to buy books and clothes for school and have already run out of money," he admitted with obvious guilt.

Leslie reached into his pocket, retrieved a large roll of cash, and handed it to Shaun. "Just tell me when you need money and I'll give it to you. Just don't go too crazy and buy a fleet of sports cars. Here's a charge card to use for books, clothes, and such. We have accounts set up for you at most of the large stores for your purchases, but of course you can still use cash or the card."

"This looks like a large amount of money!" Shaun exclaimed and then thought how quickly the other money was spent. Graciously, he stuffed it in his pocket. He sure had a lot to learn about finances. "I've never used a charge card, so I don't really know if I'll need it."

"You will learn soon enough," Leslie assured him. He was an older gentleman who wore an expensive suit and had slick silver hair combed toward the back of his head. He carried a few extra pounds and stood slightly taller than Shaun.

"Thanks," Shaun replied. "I think I am going to like Boston."

## 2

The chill in the November air marked the time of the sugarcane grind, but the outside temperature pushed higher than the coolness running through the master suite of the big house. The man Pilot moved to the center room of the suite that joined his chambers to his wife's. Her name was Frances Lorraine. He waited patiently for the damsel to emerge. He dreaded their confrontations, but lately they couldn't be avoided. If he had known at the beginning that he was getting involved with such a difficult woman, he wouldn't have married her four years ago. It was his second marriage. About five years before, Pilot had lost his wife of more than forty years to a bout of fever.

Pilot carried the same presence as a mountain. With his swagger and daunting appearance, he was an institutional landmark. He used his size to command great authority among his family and the townspeople. At sixty-seven years old, he stood six feet five inches and weighed a solid 280 pounds. His flaming red hair had faded to blond as he aged, and his rugged features added to his powerful presence.

Frances Lorraine came through the set of double doors sealing off their suites from the rest of the house. She was a woman of medium height with breasts the size of melons. She wore her hair long with curls draped across her shoulders. It was a rich dark brown color, contrasting with her skin, which was the same color as pure snow-white doves. Her pouty lips and innocent looks with her voluptuous curves drew the envy of the most secure women. The wonders of modern medicine had done nothing to hinder her looks, as she seemed younger than her forty-five years.

Pilot and Frances Lorraine have private quarters. They share a sitting parlor, with the entrance to Pilot's chamber to the left and Frances Lorraine's to the right. It's cozy with blue velvet wallpaper and a set of dark Queen Anne furniture spaced in front of a fireplace with a carved light wood mantel. Paintings of southern landscapes produced by a local artist cover each of the walls.

"Before you run to your rooms, I'd thought we'd have a talk," Pilot said, standing to greet his wife.

"These discussions are getting to be tiresome," Frances Lorraine replied, removing her white gloves. She set them down on a side table and proceeded to unpin her hat. She is formally dressed in a long pink dress. She didn't care much for casual attire and never left the house looking less than splendid.

"Well," Pilot started, "we wouldn't have to go through this if you would just behave yourself, Frances Lorraine. Frankly, I'm tired of having to scold you for your inappropriate behavior. I had another man's wife telephone, imploring me to have you leave her husband alone. It's one matter to give this man your affections in private, but do you have to make a public spectacle of it? Especially since he's a state senator."

"What I do is my own business," Frances Lorraine replied. "We agreed to this before we were married. You do your thing and I do mine."

"Frances Lorraine," Pilot said, "why do you make sure that everyone knows of your adulterous affairs? It not only embarrasses me, but I have lawyers and these men's wives calling me with threats. You are a beautiful woman. It's only natural for some of these men to succumb to your seductions."

"I know what I'm doing and I don't need you to tell me how to act. You do a good enough job of that with the rest of the family. Leave me alone! I've had enough of this conversation." Frances Lorraine went through the doors to her rooms. Before she had a chance to close them, Pilot was at her heels and followed her over the threshold.

Pilot began to plead with his wife. "Frances Lorraine, I know I'm not the best husband in the world. I can understand you wanting to find attention elsewhere. If you can't be happy with what I give you, can you at least practice some discretion? Can you limit yourself to one or two men?"

"In case you haven't noticed, the state and local politicians have been fleeing from your influence. Sugarcane in this state is being pushed to the back of the bus. Public officials have been placating the gambling industry. You're lucky I've been able to influence them to your advantage. I do it the best way I can," Frances Lorraine retorted.

Pilot let out a sigh. "Frances Lorraine, I'm glad you have been successful in getting political favors for the business. That's the reason I married you. You have more than lived up to your end of the deal. However, the family has become a source of entertainment for the entire state of Louisiana. I hear that horrible things are being said about us."

"I get the laws passed that you need to stay afloat," Frances Lorraine replied. "Isn't that all that matters?"

"No," Pilot answered. "I have three frivolous lawsuits filed against me on account of your behavior. One day, there is going to be one that I won't be able to defend against and it will end up costing us money. My public and business associates don't want any more to do with me, because I'm married to the state slut! Frances Lorraine, what can I do to make you happy?"

"Give me a divorce," Frances Lorraine said simply. "Give me a divorce and half of your holdings."

"There is no divorce in the Pilot family," her husband replied quietly. "You know that. We had an arrangement before our nuptials. As my wife, you would take care of the social graces that a prominent family is expected to follow. In turn, I would spare no expense to keep you comfortable."

"You preach to me about your family's fine morals," Frances Lorraine said, grinding her teeth in anger. "What I have done doesn't hold a candle to what you have going on in Seattle."

"We are not going to rehash that old argument again, are we?" Pilot said, tiring of this conversation.

"Why not?" Frances Lorraine replied. "As long as we are talking about morals."

Pilot was getting impatient. "Frances Lorraine, I don't care what you do. Just do it quietly!" He stormed from her rooms.

In the parlor, Pilot's private extension rang. He answered the phone.

"How does it look?" Pilot asked the caller.

"Not good," the man answered. "You better get up here right away."

"I just got back to the farm. I can't possibly get back to Seattle earlier than tomorrow," Pilot answered.

"Do the best you can. We'll be waiting for you," the man replied.

Frances Lorraine was right. Things were not looking good for the sugarcane industry in Louisiana. Sugarcane prices were so low that planters could no longer afford to operate. Sugarcane was being imported into the United States from poor island nations that used cheap labor. Legitimate planters could not compete with their low price levels. It was five years since the Pilot plantation had made a modest profit. The losses were beginning to mount. Fortunately, there was plenty of money in reserve, but it would not last forever.

As Frances Lorraine said, the politicians were jumping the sugar ship and looking for other revenue sources to shore up the state economy. Riverboat gambling had met with some success. Now there was a push in the state government to allow gambling in some of the larger cities. The politicians' apathy toward the Pilots may have had little to do with Frances Lorraine's extramarital affairs, but she was certainly not helping matters. For the past two or three years, most of his attention had been given to covering up the scandals she caused. These days, the Pilots were on the covers of the state tabloids each week. If it wasn't the farm, if it wasn't Frances Lorraine, it was his life in Seattle adding to his stress levels. He knew where the priority was now. It was time to get to the airport.

It was cloudy in western Washington State when Pilot touched down under the threat of rain. There was no need to retrieve luggage. He had clothes at the house where he would be going. However, he did have a briefcase full of papers.

He used his key and opened the front door to the large six-bedroom home. He went inside and ascended the steps quietly, two at a time. He gently opened the door to the first bedroom to his left. The nurse acknowledged him and promptly exited. There was a man seated in a wheelchair. He did not move a muscle when Pilot entered, because he couldn't. The man had amyotrophic lateral sclerosis (ALS) known as Lou Gehrig's disease. The illness attacked the central nervous system, robbing its victims of control of muscle functions.

Another man came from an adjoining bathroom. "Hi, Walter. I came as quickly as I could," Pilot said as he went to the man in the wheelchair. He knelt before him, but the man gave little response. "How long has he been like this?"

"Since yesterday," Walter replied.

Pilot sighed, taking the sick man's hand in his own. "Oliver, tell me what to do. If only you could."

"Let's go to the other room," Walter advised.

"You know he hates it when we talk without him present. He has a right to hear no matter how bad things are," Pilot said, pulling a chair next to Oliver.

"You are right, of course," Walter agreed. "You are also right that the prognosis is not good. The total paralysis is probably not permanent, but he will have less movement than he had even a few weeks ago."

"What else?" Pilot asked, looking at Oliver.

Walter hesitated.

"Go on," Pilot admonished him. "Oliver probably has it figured out even if he can't hear us."

"The end is coming soon, John," Walter said grimly. "Nobody knows when except maybe Oliver himself. He may regress at a slower pace than now, but we can say he won't be getting much better. The doctor wants to start him on a respirator."

"Oliver said no," Pilot said flatly.

"I know he did, John, but the doctor said he may be more comfortable with one," Walter said. He paused a few moments. "You know, things are happening very quickly. You need to decide what to do with him. You promised Oliver that you would be the one to care for him. You insisted."

"I've already decided," Pilot said forcefully. "He's coming back to Louisiana with me."

Pilot sat for over an hour next to Oliver. He had done this often over the past several months as the man's condition worsened. Usually, he read a book or studied some papers, but today, he sat quietly and did nothing. After a while he began to think of happier times. About the time they met . . .


*Pilot reminisces of a scene that took place about forty years ago.*

Pilot sat at a hotel bar in Seattle. It was the finest hotel in the city at the time. He was having a beer . . . his first beer. Alcohol was forbidden on his daddy's sugarcane plantation in southern Louisiana. But now, he was away from home. His home. His farm. His daddy and his mama had been dead for the past couple years. The time had come for the plantation to run under his leadership. The young man of twenty-five took his first sip of beer. It tasted terrible! How could anybody drink this stuff? He pushed it away and ordered a glass of orange juice . . . straight up.

The bartender pursed his lips when he served the orange juice. He was trying to stifle a grin. "Is something wrong with the beer?" He asked in a low sensual voice.

Pilot looked up into the man's face. His eyes were the color of onyx. His dark brown hair had a sheen. It was pulled back into a small ponytail at the nape of his neck. His face was clear and smooth. His torso was draped with a white button-down shirt with rolled-up sleeves, accented with a dark suede vest. His frame was slender with light definition. He was a handsome man with an air of charm.

"It doesn't taste good, but there's probably nothing wrong with it," Pilot answered. "I think I'll just stick to orange juice." He took a sip from his glass.

The bartender grinned, shaking his head. He wiped off the bar with a white cotton rag where Pilot had set his beer, then went to help his next customer.

Pilot thought it was good to be away from the farm. Sometimes he got tired of the place. Then he would get lonesome when he was away from home. His wife Louisa was visiting relatives in California, as she had done each year of their young marriage after the harvest of the sugarcane. Pilot would also feel the need to get away. This year it was Seattle. Why Seattle? Why not?

He and Louisa had four small children. He loved them all but was glad to get away a few weeks each year. He could not figure out his need to escape and his feelings of loneliness. What was the use of leaving Louisiana if he was going to be lonely?

"Where are you from?" The bartender asked. "You have a strong accent." He had finished his business at the other end of the wood-grained bar and rejoined Pilot.

"Louisiana," Pilot replied with pride.

"I've never been there," the bartender said. "Do they all talk like you do?"

"I expect they do," Pilot replied good-naturedly.

"My name is Oliver," the man said, with a look of mischief in his eye. He reached across the bar to shake Pilot's hand.

"My name is . . . eh . . . John," Pilot replied, clasping the offered hand in a firm shake. He was also tired of being called Pilot. Everyone at the farm called him Pilot, including his wife. His kids called him Daddy, which was fine. He felt that he had a first name but never got to use it.

"Nice to meet you, John," Oliver replied. "Are you with family in Seattle or are you passing through on your own?"

"I'm here on my own, but I thought I'd stay a few days. I'm on vacation," Pilot replied. "What's your life like in Seattle?"

"I work in city government during the day and bartend three nights a week in this hotel to help with bills," Oliver said. "I like social politics, so I listen and chat at the bar then lobby my bosses during the day. What's life like in Louisiana?"

"I'm a sugarcane planter. It's what my family has done for generations. It's a good life I suppose, but I get the itch to find some urban stimulation from time to time," Pilot replied.

Oliver paused a moment and then asked, "If you're not doing anything, my friends and I are going to the opera in about an hour when I get off. We have an extra ticket. Would you like to go?"

"Sure, I love the opera," Pilot answered with surprise at the invitation. "I need to change clothes. Can I meet you down here when you finish work?"

Oliver clasped the side of Pilot's brawny shoulder and gave it a squeeze. He was grinning from ear to ear. He was surprised that a man looking like he belonged on a lumberjack billboard would like opera. However, there was something very refined about the big guy. It had to do with the way he carried himself. He was groomed and immaculately dressed in expensive clothes. Although he had a strange accent, his English was very good.

Pilot felt awkward with the man's gesture, as people were usually afraid to touch him because of his large size. Oliver did not seem to be threatened by him. He stepped from the barstool. "I'll be back in a few minutes."

When Pilot returned to the bar, Oliver had changed into a handsome suit and was joined by three other men with coats and ties. The men all shook hands. "John, these are my housemates Walter, Douglas, and Eric. This is John. He's going to join us tonight."

After the opera, Oliver invited Pilot back to his house with his friends. Two other men joined them. He was surprised when they greeted each other with light embraces and kisses on each cheek. The two new men seemed to be extra chummy with Walter and Douglas. After a while, curiosity got the best of Pilot. He took Oliver aside. "Are Walter and Douglas homosexuals?"

Oliver offered a slight grin and called back over his shoulder to Eric, "Darling, do we happen to be *homasexuls*?"

"I sure hope so," Eric retorted. This brought out raucous laughter in the room at Pilot's expense. "What do you think, dearest?" he asked, glancing Douglas's way.

Douglas pondered for a brief moment. "I think we might pass." This brought another chorus of laughter. Each man increased his petting with his consort.

Oliver returned his gaze to Pilot. "You don't mind, do you?"

"No," Pilot replied. "I just never have met any before. You all seem like nice people."

"We are," Oliver said, holding his glass of wine out in a sweeping gesture to his friends. The others were drinking wine, except Pilot, who chose to have club soda with a twist of lime. "The four of us bought this house together. We are a family and have been so since college. I hope that it will always be this way. We have a great life here together."

It seemed to Pilot that Oliver, Walter, Eric, and Douglas were happy along with their mates. "I think it's great."

Mist flickered across Pilot's eye as he came back to the present. He usually was not one for tears, but the occasion for them had been more frequent since Oliver had taken ill.

"I was thinking about the evening we first met," he told Oliver. He concentrated to regain his focus. "You said that first night that you had never been to Louisiana. That, my friend, is about to change." Pilot gave Oliver's hand a light squeeze.

— 3 —

Shaun, Julian, Adam, Emily, Frances Lorraine, and Pilot's youngest son, Jack, along with Jack's wife, Marge, were waiting by the kitchen table when Pilot descended the staircase.

"Well, who is he?" Frances Lorraine asked her husband with impatience.

"Yes, Daddy, I would like to know who it is that is staying in our house," Emily said, echoing the sentiment.

"How long will he be staying? He doesn't look very well. Can he speak?" Jack asked. Jack lived on the Lamond plantation with his black mistress, Lisa. Marge lived on the other side of the Pilot plantation in a house that the patriarch and his first wife, Louisa, had given to them as a wedding present. They had not been truly man and wife for years. Lisa grew up on the plantation with the farm people.

"If you all would just give me a chance, I'll explain everything," Pilot interrupted. "His name is Oliver. He is a dear friend of mine from Seattle. Louisa and I knew him for many years before she died. I used to visit him and some other friends in Seattle each year, while Louisa visited with relatives in California. He's in the advanced stages of ALS disease. It is a slow-progressing sickness. He doesn't have that much longer to live."

"Is it contagious?" Emily asked with concern.

"No, it is not," Pilot answered firmly.

"It's him, isn't it?" Frances Lorraine said accusingly. "He may have been a friend of your other wife, but he's not one of mine!"

"He's staying and there's no discussion about it," Pilot said firmly. "If the family feels that strongly, then Oliver and I will find somewhere else to live."

"That's not necessary, Pilot. I see no reason why your friend can't stay here," Julian said, wanting to end the discussion.

"I agree as long as he can't infect anybody," Emily concurred.

24

"I guess that leaves me outnumbered," Frances Lorraine said, leaving the room.

"You're never going to get along with her if you keep blindsiding her like this," Jack said tersely. "Did you ever think to discuss it with her before you brought him here?"

"I knew she wouldn't like it, that's why," Pilot retorted. "But not for the reasons you think. She will do anything to torment me."

"I have an announcement," Marge said. The corn-fed red-haired woman saw her chance to enter the fray. "I will be moving into the big house."

"Why?" Jack whined, while Shaun let out a snicker.

"I'm still a member of this family until you divorce me," Marge said. "Perhaps I'm getting lonely on the other side of the farm and need some family atmosphere. Besides, you guys are all ganging up on Frances Lorraine, making her life miserable. I think she can use some support."

"I bet you do," Shaun said slyly.

Pilot glared at Shaun and then looked to Marge. "You're entitled to live where you want. Of course I would prefer that you live with your husband, but I see that's not going to be the case. Move in!"

"I think I'd better leave," Jack said turning toward the door. "I think I've had enough for one day."

The others were leaving when Shaun pulled Pilot aside. "I think we need to talk," he said, looking at the giant man.

"About what?" Pilot growled. His mood had turned foul. "Make it quick. I have to get upstairs."

"Well, it can't be quick, so determine a time we can talk," Shaun replied firmly. They were standing close together. Pilot had taken Shaun under his wing as a grandfather figure when he first came to the farm during his middle teen years. Pilot taught him the sugarcane farming business. They had worked closely with their heads together in his office. Shaun had kept tabs on most of Pilot's secretarial work before he left for college.

"It might as well be now," Pilot said, slumping into a chair. Shaun pulled another chair next to him. "What is on your mind?"

"Well, the farm," Shaun said, fumbling.

"Get on with it, boy! I've got things to do," Pilot said impatiently.

Shaun looked at the man in awe. His grandpapa had always been the most patient man that he had ever known. Little would fluster the patriarch, even in the most dire of circumstances. Something must be very wrong. He decided that he should get to the point; only he had wanted to spare the man's feelings. "I've been at college for two years now. Each time I come home, the farm has deteriorated more. Grandpapa, fences need mending. The buildings need painting. You have staffing problems. What has been happening?"

Pilot sighed as he rose to his feet. Shaun watched him as he paced across the room. After a few moments, Pilot began to speak. "Shaun, I have so much on my plate right now. I'm involved with one scandal after another due to my wife's sleeping habits. Sugarcane prices have hit rock bottom. Something is killing the sugarcane we do manage to produce. Now I have my friend to take care of until he dies. It seems I've handled more at times, but right now things are tough. I just have been doing a lousy job of keeping up."

Shaun pursed his lips. "You know, Grandpapa, you are getting older. In the past, you've carried burdens that no ordinary man could shoulder. Perhaps now you can only do the work of two healthy men."

Pilot chuckled. "I'm not that far gone yet." He paused to consider Shaun's words. "You know, Shaun, I am tired. I had never been tired before these past few months. Men come in tired from a day's work. I never felt that way until recently. What am I supposed to do? Your Uncle Julian and Jack have got their hands full with the other plantation. It can't be sold until the children are grown unless it starts losing money."

"I want to come back someday to help you run the place. I can't really do that until I've finished college. I wish I could do it sooner," Shaun said with disappointment.

"I think I can manage a couple more years without you," Pilot said with a grin. "I'm not ready to kick the bucket yet. Maybe then I'll be willing to turn more things over to you. I would like to enjoy life again." Pilot looked sad for a few moments. "There have been some losses in my life during the past few years and I've failed to replace them with positive things."

"Is Frances Lorraine a bad one?" Shaun said.

"I'm afraid so," Pilot agreed.

"What are you going to do about her? She's doing her part to destroy the family. She must be stopped," Shaun said firmly.

"Maybe Marge will be able to help, since she is moving into the house. Maybe she will be a positive influence," Pilot suggested.

"That lezzy!" Shaun exclaimed. "I think she wants to cause more trouble. I'm sure her motives are personal."

"Don't be so quick to judge," Pilot advised. "I've always liked the girl. Let's see what she'll do."

Then Pilot put his hands to his face. "I have the feeling my wife's going to file for divorce."

"Would she risk losing everything? After all, she is an adulteress. There is little sympathy for that in this state," Shaun replied.

"There is another variable," Pilot mused. "Oliver is here. She'll use him to get what she wants. That is, of course, over my dead body."

Shaun hesitated before asking, "Grandpapa, what is this Oliver to you? You seem so protective of him."

"Oliver is very dear to me," Pilot answered. "We're very close." He paused and then continued, "Shaun, my generation goes about things differently than yours does. There are some things a gentleman keeps to himself."

Shaun frowned but sensed he wasn't going to get anything more on the subject. "What are you going to do about Frances Lorraine?"

Pilot paused in thought for a few minutes. Shaun knew better than to disturb him. He finally answered, "You're right, Shaun. I have to learn to ask for help. I also have to do something about Frances Lorraine. There's a friend of the family from back East. I think I'll give him a call to see what he's been doing these days. If anyone can figure a way out of this mess, he can."


*A short time later.*

Dennis Jensen rolled up the lane in back of the big house. He was driving an old golf cart that his friend Billy liked to use to get around the farm. Julian and Dennis had been partners before Julian came to the farm and married Emily. A few years ago, Dennis came to the farm looking for Julian, because the two had parted company without finishing their business with each other. On the day of his arrival, Julian was charged with the murder of a prominent planter in the parish. Dennis investigated the murder and exposed the true killer. He had worked closely with Pilot, and the two had become friends. He was a colorful man and a magnet for trouble. Despite his air of excitement, he was a talented lawyer with good smarts.

Billy was in the driver's seat. Billy had helped Dennis with the murder investigation and the two of them had hit it off easily. He was a black man who had grown up on the farm and was about the same age as Julian and Dennis. Billy was Julian's first friend when he arrived on the farm as a young man in his mid-twenties.

The golf cart stopped in back of the big house, where Julian, Adam, and Shaun were standing. Dennis grinned broadly. "Julian, how did you happen to let our buddy here get so fat?" He playfully backhanded Billy in the gut. Billy smiled, feebly fending off the assault.

"That's what happens when you start enjoying your wife's cooking," Julian teased. "Also, it's what happens when you stop running."

Dennis turned to Billy. "Let's say you and I start running together first thing tomorrow. I can stand to lose a few pounds."

"What's wrong with today?" Julian asked.

"Better to have Julian run with you," Billy said.

Shaun stood silently watching the strange man. He had heard so much about Dennis and now he was finally here to meet him. Dennis was about the same height as Aunt Emily. He had rust-colored hair with a few gray strands. It had a wild and wavy disheveled look that was charming. He was broad-shouldered with narrow hips. He had the beginnings of a small paunch, but was otherwise muscled with heavy definition. He was the opposite of what Shaun thought attractive, but Shaun found him sexy. *He sure is a lot different from Carmen,* Shaun thought.

Dennis looked at Shaun and cocked his head sideways. "You look vaguely familiar." He moved his gaze to Julian.

"Dennis, this is Shaun," Julian introduced him. "He's my nephew from St. Louis."

"Oh yes, Albert's son," Dennis replied thoughtfully. "You were in diapers the last time I saw you. I doubt you remember me."

Shaun replied sheepishly, "I'm glad to finally meet you . . . I mean again." He shook hands with Dennis.

"This is Adam," Julian said, gesturing to introduce his friend. "He's the pastor of our church."

Dennis took Adam's hand in his and grinned broadly. "I can think of something else he is to you, Julian. I wouldn't have taken him as your pastor." Adam gently pulled his hand from Dennis's grip.

Julian glared at Dennis, warning him to keep quiet. Shaun noticed the exchange. *Could my suspicions be true? Are Uncle Julian and Adam more than friends? If they are, why won't Uncle Julian talk about it?* Shaun was distressed. Since coming to the farm, he and his uncle shared a special bond. They were the only two known gay males on the plantation. They stuck together and shared each other's secrets. Of course, Shaun had moved to Boston and his visits to Louisiana were infrequent. Surely Uncle Julian had to find another outlet. He felt lucky to have Carmen in Boston as a close friend as well as a lover. Still, he and Uncle Julian should be able to share things when they got together, shouldn't they? He decided to have a talk with his uncle.

After Adam had gone home and Dennis went to settle into his room in the big house, Shaun trudged over the wet ground to join Julian on his perch. "Hey," Shaun said as he bounded up onto the feed drums.

Julian smiled as he gave his nephew a hug around his slender shoulders.

"It seems we really haven't talked in a while," Shaun said.

"Really?" Julian replied with surprise, looking at Shaun. "What's up?"

"Nothing really," Shaun said, starting to feel ill at ease. "I'm at school a lot and I don't really get to see what's going on in your life. I would like to know."

"Nothing out of the ordinary," Julian replied. "What's really on your mind?"

Shaun hedged before asking, "Well . . . uh . . . what's going on with you and Adam?"

"That's what's bothering you?" Julian replied as he relaxed.

"Well . . . uh . . . yeah," Shaun said with a bewildered look. "Is there something going on that I should know about?"

"No," Julian said, "not really."

"You two seem awfully tight," Shaun commented.

"We've always been that way," Julian said defensively. "You've always been a part of it. The three of us built the youth center together and set it up as a safe haven for all kids. That project is done. That doesn't mean we all have to stop being friends."

"No," Shaun agreed. "If there was something more going on, you would tell me, wouldn't you?"

Julian sighed. "I tell you what I can tell you, Shaun."

"What does that mean?" Shaun asked with impatience. "We've never kept things from each other."

"Shaun, everything is the same between us. There are some things about Adam that I can't discuss with you unless he decides to talk to you about them himself," Julian explained.

"Why do I feel like I'm being left out?" Shaun said, getting upset.

"You're not, Shaun," Julian replied. "You'll have to trust me on this one."

"I feel like I've lost you, Uncle Julian," Shaun said, fighting back tears.

"No, Shaun. That will never happen," Julian replied with concern. "Shaun, you are so special to me. I have confided things in you that I could never do with my other children. In many ways, you've been number one in my life. Try to remember that. Okay?"

Shaun tried to feel better. He sat for a few more minutes, then excused himself. He decided he knew less than he did before his conversation with Uncle Julian.


Dennis entered Pilot's rooms on the south wing of the big house. "These are nice! It must be great to be king!" he exclaimed.

Pilot snorted, "The addition to the big house was Frances Lorraine's idea. It turned out to be a good one, since Oliver is staying with us. Actually, you're quartered downstairs on the same floor, aren't you?"

"Yeah. We aren't exactly roommates, but I do see nurses coming in and out of his room," Dennis replied.

"Have a seat," Pilot said. They were in his library off from his bedchamber.

"Are you going to tell me the reason for my visit or am I going to have to guess?" Dennis asked with amusement. "You didn't give me many details over the phone."

"I'm glad you were able to come," Pilot replied graciously. "I hope it doesn't inconvenience your schedule too much. Incidentally, I would like to put you on the payroll while you are here."

"Ordinarily I would dismiss such a notion, but the truth is I'm flat broke," Dennis said.

"Nonsense. The entire family is on the payroll. There's no reason you shouldn't be," Pilot retorted. "I thought your career was going well for you back East. How can you be broke?"

Dennis flushed. "I've never been too good with money. I spend haphazardly and forget to bill my clients. I have bounced checks, a stack of bills, and an eviction notice from my landlord. It's a good time to get out of Washington."

"I'm sorry to hear that," Pilot said.

Dennis waved a hand in front of his face. "I just have to put on paper from memory who to bill. Many of my clients haven't been billed for months. Since I won't be working, I'll have time to reconstruct my accounts and send some bills."

"Well . . ." Pilot started, "this is going to be a working vacation for you . . . that is if you agree to it."

"Ah . . . the point," Dennis chuckled.

Pilot gave his friend a frown. "I need some advice on what to do with my wife."

Dennis furrowed his brow. "Surely you didn't call me away from Washington to give you marital advice. I'm sure you remember that my persuasions lie elsewhere. I can't even manage those."

Pilot gave Dennis a hard look. "I have plenty of people who want to give me advice. However, conventional wisdom is not going to help me solve my problems. I need somebody with a creative mind to help me. Usually I do pretty well on my own, but this hits too close to home to look at it dispassionately."

"You're saying you need somebody with a devious mind," Dennis said, laughing. "I'm flattered . . . I guess."

"I made a big mistake marrying Frances Lorraine. I thought I was securing the future of this farm when we wed. She was beautiful and strong and more than able to work with my daughter Emily. We had an agreement. She would carry the Pilot name and move with the social graces that a family with this stature needs. In turn, she would live more than comfortably and enjoy all the benefits of being included among the gentry. Things started out well. I had my life. She had hers. We seemed to make a good team. Then she started getting restless and had a few adulterous affairs with married men. I suppose it was to be expected. Now I think she's using these affairs to sabotage the interests of the family. I'm up to my ears in lawsuits. She's being charged with libel against a state senator. They had a parting of ways and she's airing their dirty laundry through the tabloids and dragging the Pilot name through the mud. My legal bills are extraordinary and I'm finding it difficult to do business with my former associates. It has taken its toll on the farm. If you haven't noticed, things are not so good around here. I can't get any outside contractors to do the things needed to keep the farm properly afloat. Disease is killing the sugarcane and I can't get any government assistance that normally would be available to me. It's like the family has been shunned."

"Where is she now?" Dennis asked.

"I threw her out!" Pilot bellowed.

"Now she has grounds for divorce," Dennis said softly.

"She is the adulteress!" Pilot exclaimed.

"Yeah, but you've let your boyfriend move into the house. It can be said that's what pushed her over the edge," Dennis replied. "That's who Oliver is, I gather?"

Pilot gave no reply.

"I wasn't born yesterday and I don't think you're fooling too many others around here," Dennis said. "If you want my help, you're going to have to be honest with me."

"I don't want Oliver involved in this," Pilot said quietly.

Dennis shook his head. "I don't see where you have much choice. He's here."

Pilot paused while a wave of emotion passed. "I'll confide everything to you, but not just yet. I need some time alone right now. I'll get you when I'm ready."

## 4

Dennis went to his room. He was feeling the effects of jet lag in conjunction with the long drive from the airport. He wanted to nap for a while. The old house had been updated since he was here last. His bedchamber was large, with a high ceiling such as all farmhouses contained in this sweaty state. The temperature could be reduced by a degree or two by letting the heat rise to the ceiling then pass through the glass windowlike vent sitting above the door. Three large windows supplied fresh air into the room, pushing the stale air through the vent into the hallway. This was a moot point, since modern air-conditioning had been added. Dennis was grateful. The wood floors had been replaced with plush blue wall-to-wall carpet. This wasn't typical for old-style Louisiana, since carpets soaked up moisture from the humid air.

Soon after he placed his clothes in the bureau, there was a knock at his door. He went to answer it. When he saw that it was Shaun, he let him in and closed the door behind him.

"I know we don't know each other well, but I'd like to get your opinion on a couple of things," Shaun said, finding a chair to sit on.

"It seems I'm the giver of advice today. Maybe I missed my calling," Dennis said under his breath.

"What?" Shaun replied, confused. "I can come back later."

Dennis chuckled. "It's no bother. I actually would like to get to know you. You seem like a remarkable young man. I believe you've accomplished a great deal in your young life."

"You've done well yourself, haven't you?" Shaun replied shyly. "Uncle Julian says you defend people when they can't find anyone else to hire. He says you even manage to prove them innocent at times."

"I'm glad your uncle speaks so highly of me," Dennis said, choking down a sarcastic remark.

"He does," Shaun replied with enthusiasm. "He says you're a talented lawyer and people with your ability normally seek riches. You help the underdogs of the world."

Dennis frowned heavily. "A lot of that I've brought on myself. Despite my talent, I find it hard to keep a job. I always seem to get myself into trouble . . . unintentionally of course. The lowlifes are desperate and at times so am I. From time to time I get some good press and I get a good job . . . that is, until I blow it. My world is up and down. It's always been that way."

"You sound like you're hard on yourself," Shaun replied with disbelief. "Uncle Julian says you're a good person. I believe him."

Dennis looked into his young friend's face. "Shaun, why are you so sad?"

"That's kind of why I wanted to talk to you," Shaun replied. "It's about my Uncle Julian. Since you lived with him, I figured you knew him well. Maybe you can help me figure him out."

Dennis rose from the bed where he had been sitting across from Shaun. "That was a long time ago. He's a different man now. He's done some things these last several years that have blown me away . . . a wife . . . five kids."

Shaun nodded. "That's true, but I believe his inner fabric is still the same. I need your help. Will you help me?"

Dennis gave Shaun a pat on the back as he took a seat. "Of course. What can I do?"

"Downstairs, when you said that you thought that Adam was something other than a pastor to Uncle Julian, what did you mean?" Shaun asked.

Dennis stared at the floor. "I don't think I said it exactly like that, but I guess that is what I meant. Be straight with me, Shaun. What is it you want to know?"

"I want to know if Uncle Julian and Adam are lovers," Shaun said. "The three of us have been close and I feel I have a right to know."

"Did you ask your uncle?" Dennis asked.

"He wouldn't tell me. He didn't say yes, but he didn't say no. He said he couldn't talk about Adam," Shaun replied. "It's not like Uncle

Julian to keep secrets. I feel like he's sacrificing our relationship and compromising his own values."

"I can tell you're hurting," Dennis said gently. "I don't think it's your uncle's intention to do that."

"You think I'm right, don't you?" Shaun said accusingly. "You think they're involved."

Dennis paused and nodded. "Yes, I do." He paused a moment and asked, "What's bothering you, Shaun?"

"I would be happy for Uncle Julian to have found somebody. I know he wanted to find a companion badly. I want to be happy for him. Instead, he's shutting me out. I want to share that with him. I feel like it's a slap in the face," Shaun said, bringing his hand to his eyes.

"Shaun, I don't know why your uncle is keeping secrets from us. I agree that it's very unlike him. He used to cherish being an openly gay man with nothing to hide. Maybe he's changed," Dennis said.

Shaun shook his head. "No. Not in that way. Uncle Julian is a proud man and not a coward."

Dennis had an idea. "Maybe it's not your Uncle Julian who wants to keep a lid on the relationship. Maybe it's Adam. The last thing a churchman needs is a homosexual scandal. Things are different around here, Shaun. This is not Boston, St. Louis, or Washington for that matter. You are right. This is not like Julian." Dennis thought harder. "Keeping secrets is very difficult for Julian. I do know him, though, like you said. He would not give up his pride like this unless he was getting something just as big in return."

"What could Adam be giving up?" Shaun asked.

"I don't know," Dennis replied. "I just know it has to be a lot. It's likely that Adam and your Uncle Julian have come to some sort of agreement. It's also likely that we won't know what it is."

"I won't lose my uncle," Shaun said firmly.

"Shaun, let it go," Dennis said gently. "Your uncle had to grow up at some point. Just be happy for him. It looks like he's found his way."

Pilot was making his way to Dennis's room when he decided to stop in to see Oliver. "Nurse, I'll stay with him for a while. You go and take a break somewhere."

The nurse nodded and left the room.

Oliver had just had his hair done. Pilot made sure that it was washed and combed every day. He had beautiful hair. Despite the man's advancing age, it was still the color of chestnuts accented with long streaks of steel running through it. Oliver had preferred to style it himself, but preened like a pussycat whenever Pilot brushed it for him. Pilot displayed a mirror in front of Oliver for him to gaze upon his reflection. "You still are handsome," he said. He wondered if Oliver could see himself or hear the words Pilot would say to him. Despite just having his hair done, Pilot took out the brush from the top of the dresser and began to stroke it over Oliver's hair. He starting thinking about the first time he brushed his hair . . .

*A distant memory.*

"Johnny, it's great to see you." Oliver's welcome was warm and genuine, as he hurried Pilot across the threshold of his Seattle house. He was dressed in a soft white cotton shirt with suspenders holding up his tan trousers. "You should have called. I would have had supper fixed for you. Walter, Douglas, and Eric are out for the evening, so it's just you and me."

The sugarcane grind had ended and Pilot had jumped on a plane as quickly as possible to get to Seattle. Louisa had gone off to California to be with her people. It had been eight months since Pilot had been to his friends' house up north.

"I wanted to surprise you all . . ." Pilot started. "I wanted to surprise you, Oliver. I've missed you. Did you get my letters?"

"Every one of them," Oliver replied. "I wasn't sure you wanted answers back, so I didn't write."

"That's okay. I wanted you to know I was thinking about you," Pilot said. Last year he had spent four months in Seattle with Oliver and his friends. When he got back to Louisiana, he realized that they were the best four months of his life. He wanted his second visit to be even better.

Pilot eased into an overstuffed chair. He held his hand out for Oliver to grab. The lithe man obliged and Pilot beckoned him to cuddle with him. Although they were the same height and Oliver was not a little man, he seemed small while reclining against the big man's thighs.

"I've missed you," Pilot said as he kissed Oliver's neck. A shudder went down Oliver's spine and he did not reply. He sank back into Pilot's massive chest. "I brought you a present." Pilot reached into the bag that he had set beside his chair. He pulled out a hairbrush, comb, and mirror. They were made of silver with Oliver's monogram engraved on the handles.

"They're beautiful," Oliver marveled. He removed the band from his ponytail and let his hair fall on his shoulders. "Would you brush my hair for me?"

"Sure," Pilot replied. As he stroked, he could feel the tension release from Oliver's muscles. Soon, Oliver went limp in Pilot's arms. His head rested upon the big man's shoulders. Pilot held him for a while and wrapped his strong arms around this comely man. The warmth he had for this man was pure and gentle. There were few words for what he was feeling. He felt the need to kiss Oliver's thin lips. As he did, Oliver's eyes opened. Slowly, he rose from Pilot's lap. Pilot felt unsure of himself as a wave of emotion ran through him. Oliver started to ascend the wooden steps. Pilot didn't want to be left behind, so he got up and followed Oliver to his bedroom. Once the door closed, Pilot knew that he would never be the same man again.


There was a knock at the door. "Come in," Pilot answered.

Dennis came in. "The nurse said you were here."

"Did you have trouble sleeping?" Pilot asked, setting the silver brush and comb on the nightstand. He got up from behind Oliver where he was brushing his hair and took a seat in a nearby chair. Dennis stood momentarily in front of Oliver.

"He's beautiful," Dennis said with awe. "No. I couldn't sleep. It's probably best if I wait until tonight to go to bed."

Pilot smiled with pride. "He still looks to me the same as he did forty-two years ago when I met him."

"That's a long time. The illness hasn't done anything to hurt his looks. He doesn't even have wrinkles or that many lines on his face," Dennis commented.

"Oliver always took care of himself," Pilot said.

"Are you ready to explain some things to me?" Dennis asked.

"I suppose it's as good a time as any," Pilot sighed.

"Where do you want to go? My place or yours?" Dennis asked.

"We can talk here. I have no secrets from him," Pilot replied. "I'll get the nurse to ring for some iced tea."

"I promised Oliver I would take care of him. He owns a house in Seattle with two other men. Originally, it was three, but one died a couple of years ago about the same time Louisa left us. The four of them had been together longer than Oliver and me. I'm sure you will get to meet Walter and Eric. They should be here in a few days to visit. We are all very close." Pilot looked toward Oliver from where he and Dennis were sitting. The iced tea finally arrived and the housekeeper hurried away.

Pilot continued. He explained how Oliver and he met and the nature of their relationship.

"Did Louisa know?" Dennis asked.

"She may have had it figured out, but she never said anything. After the children came, we became more like friends than husband and wife. She seemed comfortable with the way things were. She enjoyed the time in California each year while I was in Seattle. I didn't ask what she did there and she didn't ask what I did in Seattle. However, she did meet Oliver. He would come with me to California to see her at times. The two of them got along well. He would help her with meals."

"You were comfortable with this?" Dennis asked with a twinkle in his eye.

"I don't see why not," Pilot replied. "We all had separate bedrooms. Louisa and I always had separate rooms just like Frances Lorraine and I do."

"Now we have gotten to Frances Lorraine," Dennis said. "You know, you have to get her back into this house."

Pilot frowned. "She's not helping matters around here. The business is falling apart just fine without her intervention."

"Do you want her to take what's left of things?" Dennis asked.

"Most everything is in Jack's, Marge's, Emily's, and Julian's names. Some of the family payroll is in the farm's stock. Through my lifetime, the business shifts to my children. It will be the same for their children. Frances Lorraine will get half of what little I have left. Louisa left her share to be divided among the four children who still live on the farm."

"What about your other children?" Dennis asked, puzzled. "What are they getting?"

"Nothing," Pilot replied. "This has caused a lot of strife between me and my two other sons, but it has been the way things have been for generations. To inherit the Pilot money, you have to live and work on the farm. They do work for the farm and they are paid handsomely, but they will never be vested in the farm unless they move back home."

"Does this mean Frances Lorraine is accumulating stock now?" Dennis asked.

"Yes, but not much," Pilot replied. "I don't have much anymore to distribute. She gets a modest salary like everyone else. Emily and Julian are paid dividends and receive the lion's share of stock and salary, since they live in the big house."

"This all sounds complicated," Dennis remarked.

"To put it simply, Julian and Emily are the managing partners of the farm. Frances Lorraine has little stake in it. There's not much she can do to seize a lot of money, except my personal savings."

"That may not be true. She can sue Emily and Julian for money. She is a member of this family. It is a family business. She lived in the big house and was contributing to the success of the business. She will have little trouble proving that, even if she was sabotaging it with her personal life," Dennis said.

"You can't be serious!" Pilot exclaimed. "That can't hold up in court. . . . Can it?"

"You never know what a court will do. They will probably sympathize with her. You threw her out, so you could bring your boyfriend to live with you. It doesn't paint a pretty picture," Dennis replied.

"What should I do?" Pilot asked.

"You need to get her back here," Dennis answered. "You need to try to make things work as husband and wife. Can you still father a child?"

"This is absolutely ridiculous," Pilot replied, getting up to pace the room. "I have no intention of being partnered with her. She's an awful woman."

"It will only be for a short time," Dennis said soothingly. "Chances are she wouldn't want to be partnered with you. I doubt she'll want any children. That doesn't seem to be in her plan. But, if you try these things and she files for divorce, it will not be because of neglect. You would be trying to be a good husband. Maybe she will walk away."

"What about Oliver? She knew about him before he came to live here."

Dennis thought for a moment. "I suppose it has been some time since you and Oliver were . . . close, so to speak. I mean, he has been ill for some time. It really doesn't matter what you used to do. The court most likely will dismiss any notion of homosexual involvement as long as you are trying to make your marriage work and are no longer participating in those activities. Am I assuming correctly?"

"Of course. There has never been anyone else for me other than Oliver," Pilot replied.

"It can be said then that you two are close friends and you are helping him through his illness," Dennis said.

"Then what? I make this a happy home with a loving wife who wants a baby? Then what? How do we make her leave?" Pilot growled.

"First, are you . . . er . . . able to perform with a woman?" Dennis asked, fearing the response.

"Of course!" Pilot bellowed. "I did father four children." He thought for a moment. "It's like bringing in the groceries. It's just something you do."

"You mean . . . it's a chore," Dennis commented with a smirk.

Pilot bristled. "I didn't mean to put it in such gross terms, but it can still be done. I'll have to talk it over with Oliver."

"What about your . . . er . . . age?" Dennis asked. "Will that present a problem?"

"I don't think so," Pilot mused. "I would just have to start getting plenty of sleep and rest. My grandson, Shaun, reminds me that I'm not as spry as I used to be." He paused a moment. "This will all be worth it if we can find a way to get rid of her. How are we going to do it?"

Dennis had an idea. "First, you have to make an effort to prove your devotion to her. Tell her you are willing to forgive all her past transgressions. Explain that you want to start a new family. She's a smart woman. She will call your bluff, because it wasn't part of your original agreement. However, if she wants the payoff from a messy divorce, then she will humor you for a while. After a while she will tire of you and she will resume her behavior of flirting with other women's husbands. Next is the part that will take her by surprise. You're going to be jealous!"

"You can't be serious," Pilot said in disbelief.

"Yes," Dennis said, gaining momentum. "You are going to start throwing public displays of jealous rage every time you hear the slightest rumor of her infidelity. You may even want to make up some of your own. Everyone will believe you, because she has already established herself as the state slut. Eventually, she will become so humiliated, she will beg you to give her an unconditional divorce."

"Interesting plan," Pilot said with admiration. "But I don't want her to divorce me. There's no divorce in the Pilot family. I have to do everything in my power to stay married for better or worse."

"You may have to break that family statute if you want to be rid of her. Think of the family. You have to put it ahead of your morals," Dennis advised.

"We will take this one step at a time," Pilot replied.

Marge was in her bedroom next door and heard every word of Pilot and Dennis's discussion. *It sounds like Frances Lorraine is going to need some help,* she thought. *When she comes back, she and I are going to have a little talk.* The wheels were turning rapidly in her head.

## 5

Carmen let out a gentle gasp as he released. Shaun followed as semen sprang onto his stomach. He put his arms around Carmen, as his lover slid from inside him and settled on top of his prone body. He let his legs fall to the mattress as Carmen straddled them and rested his head on Shaun's chest. Shaun wrapped his arms around the warm body.

"That was wonderful," Shaun whispered. He rubbed Carmen's back with his palms as the smaller man drowsed.

"Yeah, it was," Carmen agreed as his breathing returned to normal.

"I wish you could experience what I just felt," Shaun said, continuing to massage his lover's back.

"Shaun, don't ruin this. We just had a good time. Now hush. Let's rest," Carmen pleaded.

After a few moments, Shaun gave Carmen a gentle embrace. "I didn't mean I was unhappy about things. I was just thinking I wanted you to feel the same things I felt."

"Shaun, drop it," Carmen murmured.

"I'm not trying to start anything. I just wanted you to know that I like it now when you make love to me. I enjoy having you inside me," Shaun replied. "It just took some practice. I didn't get to this point overnight."

Carmen rolled onto his side and rested his head on the palm of his hand. "Okay, I guess you started this. Let's get it done, so we can get some rest."

Shaun tried to regain the light mood. "I was just thinking if we practiced with me being the one inside you, maybe someday you could feel as good as I do when you make love to me . . . that's all."

"We've tried, Shaun. It just doesn't work. I'm really sorry. I wish I could enjoy it when you screw me. I just don't like it. It hurts me too much," Carmen explained. "We've been over this."

"Well, whenever I do it, you shoot too fast. I think we need to slow things down," Shaun replied.

"Working myself to orgasm is the only way I can bear it in the least," Carmen said.

"If you wait a little bit longer, then I can shoot with you," Shaun suggested.

"You take too long!" Carmen replied in frustration. "I don't like it! I'm sorry! I just can't do it, Shaun!" He got up out of their bed, went into the bathroom, and slammed the door.


Dennis and Julian were sitting on the front porch when a man came out of the big house carrying a small black bag. He was wearing a navy blue suit with a dark tie and a starched white shirt. He wore his brown hair combed onto his forehead. He was tanned in rich natural tones. His dress was not the usual Louisiana style but seemed to suit his manners.

As he crossed the threshold, he stopped and turned to say a few parting words to Emily, who was showing him out. "Who is that?" Dennis marveled.

"He's the family pediatrician," Julian replied as they rocked gently in their chairs.

"Maybe I need to get sick," Dennis quipped.

"He's a children's doctor," Julian said with a smirk.

"I can be childish," Dennis retorted.

As the doctor crossed the porch to descend the steps, Dennis rose to his feet. Quickly, Julian followed his example. "Did everything go well with the checkups?" Julian asked.

"Yes, they did. You have healthy kids," the doctor replied.

Dennis cleared his throat.

"Er . . . Doctor, this is Dennis Jensen. Dennis, this is Dr. Jeffrey Martin," Julian said, introducing the two men.

Instantly, Dennis grabbed Jeffrey's hand and gave it a sturdy shake. "The pleasure is definitely mine," Dennis said with a big grin.

Jeffrey seemed startled by Dennis's enthusiastic gesture. He quickly glanced from Dennis to Julian and looked at his watch. He said softly,

"Well, I really have to get to my next appointment. I will see you and Emily in church, Julian."

Julian bid Jeffrey farewell. He sat back down in his chair, while Dennis waited for the doctor's car to pass down the road.

"I have never seen you so starstruck," Julian said as Dennis regained his seat. "I never have seen you work anyone either. Are you always so bold with your intentions? You scared the man half to death."

"Is he gay?" Dennis said, getting right to the point. "With all the people running in and out of this house, *someone* eventually has to be queer."

"I don't know about the doctor," Julian replied. "He's about thirty-two and lives by himself on a small farm outside of town. He does the upkeep on his own and stays to himself a lot. I don't know who any of his friends are."

"Sooner or later the odds have to catch up with this place. With all the people coming and going, he's the first gay person . . . possibly gay person I've seen," Dennis said earnestly. "How do you stand not having any friends, Julian?"

"I have friends," Julian said. "Just not very many. The ones I do have are very special to me."

"Gay friends?" Dennis pressed.

Julian sat silently for a moment before replying. "I have everything I need."

"Well, I don't," Dennis snorted. "If I'm going to stay here for any length of time, I need to find some people like me."

"Are you going to bug that doctor?" Julian asked.

"We'll see," Dennis replied.


"It's a nice place you have here," Dennis told Jeffrey as the doctor invited him into his house.

"Thank you. It's comfortable. Nothing extraordinary," Jeffrey replied. "Would you like some sweet tea? I just made a fresh pitcher."

The house was small compared to the other farmhouses in the parish. It was decorated expensively. Dennis noted the collection of Spanish porcelain figurines displayed by the pecan wood shelves in the living room. The heart-of-pine floors were the color of mellow gold honeycombs, unlike the traditional dark floors in Louisiana. "Thank you. That would be nice," Dennis replied.

Jeffrey set a tray of two glasses and a pitcher of iced tea on the low table. He sat on a green three-cushioned sofa, while Dennis took the matching upholstered armchair. The two sat in silence for a few moments.

"So, what brings you out this way?" Jeffrey asked.

Dennis paused thoughtfully before answering. "What made you decide to be a pediatrician?"

Jeffrey shrugged. "I feel comfortable with children. Oftentimes, they bring out the best in parents. When a child is sick or there is a concern for his continued health, the most vulnerable nature is exposed in the parents. All the barriers are down. They may be selfish in the rest of their lives, but where their children are concerned, they genuinely care. It's a child that makes an adult think of someone other than himself."

"Interesting point," Dennis replied.

"Is that why you came out here? To find out why I became a pediatrician?" Jeffrey asked.

"Yes," Dennis confessed. "Julian is a close friend of mine . . . and so is Emily. I knew him from back East."

"I see," Jeffrey said, starting to feel uncomfortable.

"The children are important to them," Dennis said. "I wanted to see what their doctor was like."

"Jesse, Jay, William, Louis, and Candy are very sweet children. They are lucky to have two wonderful parents," Jeffrey replied. "Do you have children?"

"Oh no," Dennis said, shaking his head. "I don't know what I would do with them. I'm not experienced with little ones."

"I see," Jeffrey said, rising to his feet. "I'm going to have to get ready for my afternoon appointments. I'm sure we can finish this discussion at a later date. Unless, of course, you have some other pressing need."

Dennis rose also. He knew he was getting the brushoff, but he still continued to press. "Perhaps over cocktails sometime?"

"I don't drink," Jeffrey said, showing Dennis to the door.

Dennis felt himself deflate. At least he had tried. "Maybe I'll catch you around sometime," he said as he stepped outside.

"I'll be at church Sunday," Jeffrey offered. "Maybe I'll see you there?"

"Church?" Dennis said with a confused look as he stopped to look back at the doctor.

Jeffrey nodded with a half smile as he stood against the doorframe.

"Church," Dennis said with a nod. "Okay." He gave a wave and climbed into one of the pickup trucks from the farm.


It was Sunday and time for church when Shaun arrived from Boston with Carmen at his side. They came from the airport in time to attend church, so that was their first stop. Carmen had been to Louisiana before during one of Shaun's infrequent visits. The couple was on spring break, and time off from school was mostly devoted to Shaun's company in Boston. Citing his present rift with Uncle Julian, Shaun made a promise to himself to come back more often. With the demands of a big company and a flourishing romance, the last three summers had allowed just a few short visits to the sugarcane country. Carmen was a big asset to Shaun. Smith Power had expanded its philanthropy sector to give money to those in great need. Of course, Shaun and Carmen had a dedicated interest in contributing to gay and lesbian causes. Carmen worked to find charitable organizations that would benefit from special gifts. They had a passion for making donations to grass-roots movements in need of funding. Giving money was not easy. Some clubs and organizations were not ready for large sums. Carmen was talented at deciding which groups could use specific allotments.

"You were right," Shaun said to Adam as they walked up the lawn to the church building with Carmen beside them. They were discussing the Smith Power foundation that gave to the needy. "We keep increasing Smith Power's donations to the poor, and the company just seems to keep getting more profitable."

"God makes that promise as long as we stay sensible," Adam agreed.

Shaun blamed Adam for taking Uncle Julian away from him, but it was hard not to like the guy. Adam was a caring person. He did not preach in church much anymore. He was talented in giving sermons, but new leaders had risen in the church, leaving Adam with different responsibilities. Presently, his duty called for him to visit the sick and the elderly who could not make the trip to church each Sunday. Adam and his wife, Nancy, had started the church in town after arriving several years before from upstate. Together, they worked hard to increase the spiritual strength of their followers, so other churches in nearby towns could be born. Adam's church welcomed Julian and his family when Uncle Julian's homosexuality had been exposed a few years before Shaun came to the farm to live.

Shaun saw some unexpected parishioners. Frances Lorraine must be back at the big house, because she was at Pilot's side . . . rather close to his side. His arm circled her waist. Billy was close by, pushing Oliver in his wheelchair. New Billy was tagging along close behind them. Billy didn't usually come to the service, so it must have been at Pilot's request. The blacks on the farm held their own services, but all were welcome to attend the church in town.

Dennis was with Uncle Julian and Emily. Louis and Candy had joined the other children. Jesse, Jay, and William had gone off to boarding school in late August. Their parents were reluctant at first, but they gave into the wishes of their sons. The boys didn't want to grow up to be sugarcane planters. Shaun could sense that Dennis was looking for someone. He decided to take Carmen over to introduce the two.

"I want you to meet somebody," Shaun said to his lover as they started to make their way over to Dennis. Out of the corner of his eye, he saw Marge spying close behind Jack and Lisa, who was Billy's sister. He considered it an odd sight, since the married couple didn't get along.

As they approached Dennis, Shaun gave his shoulder a squeeze to catch his attention. "You seem distracted," Shaun commented.

"Do I?" Dennis answered, obviously preoccupied. He turned his attention to Shaun and his friend.

"It's okay," Shaun replied with a gleam in his eye. "It's good to see you."

Dennis nodded and then asked, "So, who's your friend?"

As if he just remembered Carmen, Shaun drew him close to his side. "Oh, I'm sorry." He flushed. "This is my boyfriend, Carmen. We live in Boston together. We attend the same university and he helps me with my work."

Carmen was not amused, but he kept his thoughts to himself. He extended his hand to Dennis and said in a polite voice, "I've heard a lot about you, Dennis. Shaun talks about you . . . frequently."

"I see," Dennis replied. Instantly, his attention focused elsewhere. "Please excuse me. I see a friend that I'm supposed to meet." He raced toward the doctor.

It was time for everybody to file into the sanctuary to take their seats. Dennis caught up to Jeffrey before he went through the doors. "I thought maybe I missed you," Dennis said with a smile.

"Oh, Dennis . . . hi," Jeffrey replied with surprise.

"You said we'd see each other in church . . . remember?" Dennis said, trying to hold on to his composure.

"Yeah . . . I did . . . I just don't remember you coming to church. I didn't think I'd see you here," Jeffrey said with a bit of warmth.

Dennis felt a touch more at ease. "May I sit with you?"

"Sure," Jeffrey replied with a nod. "If you wish."

It would be a few moments before the processional started. Shaun used the time to see where everybody was seated. Since there was a large representation from the farm, it was difficult for everybody to sit together. Besides, church was a time for the family to visit with friends from town and from the other farms, so it made sense for everybody to mix.

Shaun saw that Pilot was seated at the outside end of one of the front pews with Frances Lorraine at his side. It looked as if he was squeezing the life out of her hand in a feigned romantic gesture. She looked miserable. Oliver was seated in his wheelchair next to Pilot and just outside the pew, in the side aisle.

"I don't understand why you had to bring him here," she whispered to her husband.

"Oliver deserves churching just like everybody else," Pilot replied.

"Fine," she said, jerking her hand from his. "You're hurting me."

Pilot gave her a serene look. "Okay, just don't look at any other men. I would be jealous."

A couple of pews back, Shaun saw Jack seated next to Lisa, and Marge was seated on his other side. Jack looked miserable.

On the far side of the middle aisle from Jack, Dennis was sitting next to the children's doctor. Dennis kept trying to engage in conversation, while Dr. Martin kept telling him to hush. Shaun smirked. Obviously, Dennis hadn't been inside a church in a while. Then his face turned thoughtful. *Why is Dennis sitting next to Dr. Martin?*

Shaun and Carmen were sitting a few pews behind Jack on the right side. Closer to the left on the same pew by the center aisle, Uncle Julian was sitting next to Aunt Emily. Sundays were days of work for Adam and he spent time with the deacons and other leaders in the church along with Nancy. Finally, the processional began.

After church, the parishioners filed from the pews to shake hands with the clergy as they emptied the church. Outside, small groups drew together and talked quietly among themselves. It was a beautiful spring day and nobody was in a hurry to leave the churchyard for home.

Frances Lorraine managed to escape Pilot's grasp and started to join a small gathering on the other side of the yard. Before Pilot could catch up with her, Marge intercepted him. "It's nice that you and your wife are beginning to get along so well," she said slyly. She looked uncomfortable in a pink lace Sunday dress but tried her best not to show it.

Pilot decided to divert attention from himself. "It looks like you're trying to get in your husband's good graces as well," he remarked. "I have to admit that I'm pleased. Is that makeup you're wearing?"

"Frances Lorraine and I have had some discussions about your motives for kindling your farce of romance," Marge said to Pilot to see if she could get a reaction.

Pilot sensed her intent. "It seems you and my wife have become quite chummy here lately. Do I have reason to be concerned? I get the idea that the two of you are planning something."

"Let's just say I'm giving Frances Lorraine the support she needs," Marge said and then added quickly, "You know, Pilot, she's not stupid." She glanced over at Oliver. "You're not fooling many people."

"Thanks for your advice," Pilot said. He left her to rejoin his wife.

"What do you think of Dennis?" Shaun asked Carmen as they found a private space in the yard.

Carmen gave Shaun a look of disbelief. "You are incredible."

"What do you mean?" Shaun replied, bracing for a confrontation. They were experienced at giving each other signs that arguments were close at hand.

"How dare you throw him in my face!" Carmen bellowed in a whisper.

"What are you talking about?" Shaun said, exasperated. "Can't this wait until later?"

"In Boston, you built up this man to be someone fantastic. He's all you talked about when you came home from here. I come here and the man hardly knows that I exist. So you certainly don't say much to him about me. Next, you hardly knew I existed when *you* took me over to introduce me. Finally, you were so goo-goo eyed when you were talking to him that your jaw nearly hit the floor when he started paying attention to that other man," Carmen complained.

"I can't believe you're doing this," Shaun said under his breath.

"Well, usually it's me that looks at other guys," Carmen said. "I look and that's the end of it. You never look at anyone except me. So, when you finally do look, I know that this man has really captured your attention."

"If that were true, then you would finally know how it feels when I don't have your attention," Shaun growled. " . . . If that was true. Dennis is as old as Uncle Julian, so don't be silly."

"I know what I see. It's written all over your face," Carmen said.

"Carmen, maybe you should go back to Boston," Shaun said. "I came here hoping we could get a break. Things have been crazy back East. I don't need this from you."

Dennis and Jeffrey were a good distance away from Shaun and Carmen.

"When was the last time you went to church?" Jeffrey asked.

"Well . . . uh," Dennis hedged. "To be honest, I can't recall the last time."

"Does that mean you've never been to church?" Jeffrey asked with a twinkle in his eye.

"I think I went on a field trip in school once," Dennis replied hopefully.

"I see," Jeffrey said. He stifled a chuckle.

"Is it that obvious?" Dennis asked, furrowing his brow.

"Well, let's just say we'll have to educate you with some manners." Jeffrey smiled.

Dennis let the silence build for a moment. "I enjoyed the service," he said with a nod. "But I only came because I knew you would be here."

Jeffrey's face went rigid. "I think it's time for me to go."

Dennis scratched his head. "Did I blow it?"

Jeffrey softened and looked at Dennis in awe. "No." He shook his head slightly. "I'll see you next week?"

Dennis smiled. "Sure."

Pilot noticed that Frances Lorraine was standing close to a man it was rumored she had had an affair with a few months ago. She wasn't talking to him and wasn't even facing him. He figured that they were close enough to suit his purpose. He confronted the man face to face.

"I advise you to keep your hands off my wife," he said evenly, but loudly enough for those around to hear. There were gasps in the crowd as attention turned toward Pilot and the man.

"What?" the man replied.

"I said, stay away from my wife or I will hang you by your toenails from the highest tree," Pilot said, gritting his teeth. He stood like a giant over the mild-mannered man. The man's wife's eyes were the size of saucers.

Frances Lorraine moved to separate the two men. "Pilot, stop this right now!" she said with shrill command.

"I mean it, Frances Lorraine. If this man takes advantage of you one more time, things will become unpleasant for him," Pilot growled. The attention of the entire churchyard was on him. "That goes for any man that comes anywhere near my wife!"

"Oh, Pilot, how could you!" Frances Lorraine cried as she ran from the yard.

Adam came from behind Julian and grabbed his arm. Emily was standing next to him, staring in horror at her father. "What in the devil has gotten into your father?" Adam said. He was very upset.

Julian looked in Dennis's direction. He could swear he saw a look of approval come over his face as his gaze turned to Pilot. "I think it is a case of who in the devil has gotten into him," Julian replied.

"Whatever it is, please do something about it. I can't have this happening," Adam said. He started toward Pilot.

Julian reached out to stop him. "I'll handle this," he replied. As he started to move, Pilot stormed after Frances Lorraine.

## 6

"You've been avoiding me and so has Pilot," Julian accused Dennis Jensen as he was coming up the lane to the big house. He spent a lot of time at the Lamond plantation and his time at the big house was brief. Under Julian's supervision, the Lamond plantation was moving away from producing sugarcane. In recent years, planters were sustaining heavy losses due to foreign competition. When the Pilots came to Louisiana, the family promised the farm's people that they would always produce sugarcane as long as the property remained in their hands. Julian didn't have that constraint with the Lamond plantation, so he sought other businesses that were more profitable. While that farm still produced some sugarcane, its main emphasis had shifted to warehousing mechanical parts for farm equipment, airplanes, freight trains, factory machinery, and other industrial equipment. Since there wasn't a heavy draw on profits, Julian was able to invest the money in obtaining equipment parts and putting them on shelves when somebody would need to purchase them. The initial investment was expensive, but the markup on sales was tremendous. Jack and Julian created this niche because somebody generally needed a part right away and they could provide it immediately. However, if potential customers ordered from the factory or another distributor, they could wait weeks or months for the part. Business was flourishing on the Lamond plantation.

"That's because we knew you were looking for us and we didn't want to hear what you had to say," Dennis sneered.

"Well, now that I have you . . ." Julian began.

Dennis interrupted, "Julian, the only reason that you're going to lecture me is because others have put you up to it. I'm helping a friend that's in a difficult situation. You and the others may consider my ideas immoral, but all you have to do is look at yourselves and I don't come out so bad. They don't have the guts to approach Pilot or my-

self, because they have their own issues. However, you still hold yourself to do the right thing and people take advantage of you. I know
Jack is upset, but look at him. He has a black girlfriend which is still
taboo in this part of the country. Despite what you do not say about
Adam, his closet is bursting at the hinges just waiting for him to come
out. I won't say anything about Emily, because I know she's a sensitive subject with you. What about Frances Lorraine and her scandals?
Personally, I don't think Shaun and Marge care too much about sav-
ing face. This family is filled with controversy and I will not be used as
a scapegoat for causing problems."

Julian was speechless, because he knew Dennis was right on all
counts.

"Tell your boyfriend to forget about the Pilots' problems. Things
will work out," Dennis advised with a softer tone.

Julian gave him a pleading look. "Can the two of you at least keep
your antics away from church? Please? As a favor to me?"

Dennis grinned. "Tell Adam that our scenes at church are done.
That's all I can promise. That doesn't mean I will keep from picking
on some of the members of his flock."

"I suppose this is the best deal I'm going to get," Julian said.


*A few weeks later.*

When Dennis arrived at Pilot's suite, he could hear Frances Lorraine
whimpering in her rooms. As he entered the parlor, he saw Marge
close the door to the distressed lady's rooms, leaving Pilot and Dennis
with some privacy.

"What's the matter with her?" Dennis asked.

"She's not very happy with me these days," Pilot replied slyly. "I'm
keeping close watch on her."

"What exactly are you doing?" Dennis asked.

"I'm spending all my energy on being the affectionate husband,"
Pilot said, crinkling his nose. "I think she'd rather it come from somebody else."

"How does Oliver feel about your blossoming romance with your wife right under his nose?" Dennis said glibly. He regretted the remark as soon as he said it.

Pilot turned solemn. "I doubt sometimes he realizes what's going on. I explain things to him and the reasoning. It seems he understands at times and other times he looks less coherent."

"How can you tell?" Dennis asked gently.

"There are times when tears stream down his face for no reason. Then there are other situations when he seems unresponsive," Pilot replied. "It's hard to tell now how the disease is progressing and what effect it's having on his mind."

"Our plans seem to be moving along," Dennis commented, changing the subject.

"Yes," Pilot agreed. "I think I can leave her alone for a few months. I doubt she'll be misbehaving for a while." After a pause he added, "Will you need to head back East for a while? We won't need to scheme again for a while."

"There's not too much waiting for me back there. I've caught up with my billing. I still have some work to do with the background work you've assigned to me. It appears to be more in-depth than we first thought." Then he hedged, "There're a couple of other things that I have my mind set on that need my attention."

"Are their names Jeffrey Martin?" Pilot asked coolly.

"Is it that obvious?" Dennis flushed.

"I caught on, but others are probably too wrapped up in themselves to notice, except for Shaun," Pilot replied.

"Shaun?" Dennis said with his brow furrowed.

"With my position, I'm required to be perceptive of my surroundings. I trained Shaun to be the same way. Besides, I think he has a crush on you," Pilot said.

"Great." Dennis frowned.

"Don't worry. I'm sure it's harmless," Pilot replied. "In some ways you're a lot like his partner with a few years of maturity."

"How?" Dennis laughed. "I've never been accused of being mature."

"Remember, they're young and going through growing pains. They think a lot of each other, but times could get tough," Pilot explained. "He looks at you as a social hero with a special charisma. That little Carmen is the same way and Shaun has a strong admiration for that. That boy wants to make a big difference in this world. It's his passion."

"So what do I do? I have no intention of being a sugar daddy." Dennis frowned. "Of course, it would be him taking care of me."

"It'll work itself out," Pilot said. "Stay as long as you like. You know you're welcome."

"At some point I'll have to return East," Dennis sighed. "Maybe it's time now. Some of the background checks can be done easier from there."

"What about Jeffrey Martin?" Pilot asked.

"There's nothing there to be lost," Dennis replied sadly. "That relationship got to be a dead duck in the water before it got started. I meet him at church each Sunday and we sit together. We don't converse much after the service, because it is his day of rest. He is too busy at other times to see me."

"At least make a point of saying good-bye to him," Pilot said with concern. "Despite what you may think, I believe it would hurt his feelings if you left without saying a word."

"I'll keep that in mind," Dennis replied.


Dennis was nervous. He had made several attempts to locate Jeffrey at home, but the physician always seemed to be absent. Finally, he sensed Jeffrey was home. His new white sedan sat in the driveway by the country house. As much as the doctor seemed to be away from home, Dennis was amazed to see that the flowers and shrubbery were manicured. The yard was practically overgrown; in good taste, of course.

He waited a few seconds after he had rapped his knuckles on the door. It seemed like he stood there for an eternity until Jeffrey came to the door.

"It is good to see you," Jeffrey said in a voice not much above a whisper, as he let Dennis inside.

Dennis thought he might be imagining things, but could sense the man was almost cordial. Could it be he was finally warming up to him?

"I know you are busy, so I'll try not to take much of your time." Dennis stood while Jeffrey took a seat.

"Please sit," Jeffrey said, offering a couch adjacent to the one where he was sitting. "If you have a few minutes, I'll get us some iced tea. You like yours sweet, right?"

"Yes," Dennis answered, "with lemon if you have it."

"Of course," Jeffrey replied pleasantly as he left for the kitchen. When he returned, he set the tray in front of them and started to pour tea into a glass.

"Thank you for sitting with me in church these past several weeks. I appreciate your company," Jeffrey said.

*Appreciate?* Dennis thought. *What a strange choice of words.* "I enjoyed being next to you. You've been good company," he lied. He was always tied in knots when he was with Jeffrey. He was afraid of saying or doing the wrong thing. He had sensed that the doctor was skittish and easily frightened. Dennis knew he would have to be patient if anything were to develop between the two men. He wasn't even sure Jeffrey had inclinations toward men.

Jeffrey was pleased with Dennis's reply. "I was going to invite you to supper when I saw you next. I have one or two friends that I would like you to meet. Are you available next Saturday night?"

Dennis slumped forward in his seat. If he were an overly emotional man, he would have burst into tears of frustration. He couldn't look at Jeffrey just now. He tried to say, "I would have loved to, but I am going back East for a while." Nothing came out when he opened his mouth. He had been waiting for such an invitation for weeks, or some hint of interest from Jeffrey. Now it was too late. He had already made his travel arrangements and a full schedule of appointments was waiting for him in Washington. Most of the work was for Pilot, but desperate law firms had been calling him to give them his talent for resolving hopeless cases.

Distressed by his silence, Jeffrey said quickly, "I understand if you have to check your appointments. You don't have to reply just yet. There's still time."

"No, no, it's not that," Dennis mumbled. His throat was dry so he took a big gulp of the refreshing tea. He placed the glass back on its coaster. "You have to know I've waited a long time for such an invitation. I hoped and hoped. I'm just surprised that it happened now."

"I don't understand," Jeffrey said with concern. He could sense that Dennis was upset.

Dennis rubbed his forehead and looked toward Jeffrey. "I'm leaving to go back East. It will be for some months." He shrugged and then jumped up to leave. "I don't know when I'll be back. I'm sorry, but I really have to go."

Jeffrey stood as Dennis hurried past him. Before Dennis was out of reach, he paused and grabbed Jeffrey's hand on impulse. He gave it a squeeze and then headed out the door.

# — 7 —

*A few months later.*

Shaun stepped into Pilot's office in the big house. The big man was on the telephone and thumbing over his notes. Over the years, Pilot had become used to Shaun slipping past him to get to his work as the patriarch's assistant.

For the past several years, Shaun had tried to keep abreast of the farm's activities. This was difficult to do from Boston. However, his first love was the farm. For Shaun, this would always be home. He wanted to be sure that the Pilot plantation remained secure.

Still, it was hard for Shaun to break away from Boston to get to Louisiana. He found himself going for months without returning to his southern home. At this point, he knew that he would have to travel south more frequently.

Pilot placed the phone on its cradle and glanced up into his adoptive grandson's face. Shaun was leaning with his backside against the front of the big man's desk, his arms folded together across his ribs. He sported his favorite black jeans with a blue cashmere turtleneck. Pilot was wearing the accepted farm outfit of a cotton white button shirt and tan trousers. "I have the feeling you have something on your mind," Pilot guessed.

"The farm looks terrible, Grandpapa," Shaun said.

Pilot clenched his jaw tight. "We've been over this."

"We need to find a solution," Shaun said quietly.

Pilot nodded. "I'm listening."

"I'm taking the semester off this spring. I plan to stay here to sort things out."

Pilot pushed his chair away from the desk, resting the palm of his hand on its edge. He turned directly to face Shaun. "You only have a couple of semesters left. I won't have you quitting school. Besides, you have your business back East that needs your attention. Also, you need to stay in that Boston house a couple more years to comply with your great-grandmother's will."

"That's all been taken care of properly. Carmen is running Smith Power with the trustees. He is fully capable. I will travel to Boston from time to time to fulfill any requirements," Shaun replied. He glided to a nearby stuffed chair and sat down at eye level to his grandfather. "You need help. You have too much on your plate."

"What do you propose to do?" Pilot said tersely.

"I plan to do some of the things that you have been unable to accomplish for whatever reason," Shaun replied directly. Neither man believed in mincing words.

"So you want to push me out to pasture and take over things," Pilot said, getting upset. "What makes you think the farm people will respond to you without my backing up your decisions?"

"The farm people have always respected me. They realize they need someone to lead them. In spite of my age and alternative lifestyle, they know I'm capable of doing what is necessary to make this farm work. They know things are not right around here. Someone needs to take charge before you start getting a lot of trouble from them," Shaun said.

"Shaun, I'm not ready to retire," Pilot exclaimed, regaining his composure.

"Grandpapa, you have too many problems. You have a selfish wife. In addition to that, you have a sick friend that needs your care. He responds only to you. You accepted the responsibility of taking care of him. It would be cruel of you to neglect him," Shaun said.

"The way you say cruel," Pilot growled. "Am I really that bad?"

"Some of your decisions of late do not put you in the best light. You embarrass your wife every chance you get. Dennis has been a poor influence on you."

"We better not talk about Dennis," Pilot warned.

Shaun kept silent for a moment before he resumed the debate. "Think about what's best for the farm, Grandpapa. Think about Frances Lorraine and Oliver. You are older now and can't do all the things you once did. You need to set your priorities and relinquish some of your responsibilities."

Pilot thought for a few moments. Calm started to come over him. Then relief could be seen on his face. He nodded slowly. "I know you are capable, Shaun. You've trained for years to run this farm. I don't know if you are doing what's best for your situation, but I honestly don't have the energy to worry about it." He frowned, then looked directly in Shaun's face. "I need to get Frances Lorraine out of here. I need to take care of Oliver. The farm is yours to run. What are your plans?"

"First to see why you have so much broken fencing and peeling paint," Shaun said with disgust.

"That's easy enough," Pilot said, bristling. "You just need to tell somebody to take care of it and it will be done next week."

"Next, there are too many farm people," Shaun said, shaking his head. "We can't afford to take care of all of them and there are not enough jobs to go around. They've built too many cottages along the old quarters road and now there is talk of construction up the cattle road."

"Well, since you've brought up the subject of the farm people, Mr. Sugarcane-Planter-Pilot, your first problem as chief operating officer is to find a way for all of them to start paying Social Security taxes," Pilot said with an amused expression.

Many migrant workers on plantations in Louisiana and southern Florida are illegal immigrants. Their labor is critical to the success of these plantations, so the government tolerates their presence. Every few years, the government offers amnesty to these folks to become U.S. citizens, so they can be taxed.

"What do you mean?" Shaun said. "I thought you had an exemption."

"No more, my friend," Pilot said, picking up a letter from his desk. "Planters are losing influence with politicians. Our special favors are coming to an end."

"That's ridiculous!" Shaun exclaimed. "If all of the farm people are required to file tax returns, they would get money back from the government, because they would fall under the poverty line. They will qualify for welfare."

"They also want to tax the food and shelter we provide for them," Pilot added.

"First of all, they grow their own food and build their own houses. It just happens to be on our land. That can't be taxed," Shaun replied angrily.

"Tell it to Uncle Sam," Pilot said. "I agree with you."

"I will," Shaun replied. "This just makes things harder for us. The farm people will have more money to spend, lessening the incentive for them to leave."

"Leave?" Pilot said with disbelief. "We will *not* make them leave."

"Of course not," Shaun replied. "I want them to choose to leave themselves. First, education will be absolutely required of all children. They will have to have a first- through twelfth-grade education. They will not be allowed to work or have their own cottage until they graduate from high school. We will pay for those who want to go college."

Pilot shook his head. "We already do those things. They know I'll pay their college tuition."

"We're going to have to enforce the education requirements. From day one, we are going to expect children in first grade to tell us what they want to do when they grow up, and it will not be working in sugarcane fields," Shaun promised. "This is all possible, Grandpapa. We just have to be organized in our approach and stand by our decisions."

"Explain," Pilot said patiently.

"There will be no more building of cottages. If families grow, then they will have to crowd into their existing homes. We will not tear down barns on the cattle road to build new cottages. If push really comes to shove, we will give housing allowances to live in town. They can commute every day."

"They aren't going to want to do that," Pilot mumbled.

"Exactly!" Shaun exclaimed. "They will be forced to look at other alternatives. There will also be no more growing fields. They will have to be more careful to conserve their food."

"Shaun, I don't know if they'll go for all of this," Pilot said skeptically. "I think you might overestimate the concepts that children have of careers in first grade and underestimate how the farm people will accept these changes."

"How could they not go for it?" Shaun asked. "There is virtually no more room on the farm for houses and gardens. I cannot have them tearing down buildings and taking over pastures in order to expand."

"Do you think all of this will work?" Pilot asked.

Shaun collected his thoughts. "If this house had only two bedrooms and you couldn't move, would you have had four children?"

"No, I suppose not," Pilot agreed.

"Also, you gave all your children a fine education. Jack and Emily are the only two who have stayed near the farm. The other two have left to go into the world to do great things," Shaun said.

"I think my two oldest boys left the farm because it wasn't big enough for their daddy and them. I don't know how much education had to do with it," Pilot said with a snort. "However, I do like the sound of your reasoning better."

Shaun let the remark pass. "Next, I need to travel to the islands to see if I can find a strain of sugarcane that is resistant to this fungus that is killing our sugarcane."

"I see they did teach you something in school," Pilot mused. "Can you do the field work yourself?"

"I can organize it," Shaun replied. "It might take a while."

"Okay, boy," Pilot said rising from his desk. "You run this place now. I pass the torch. Now you are the man Pilot."

"Julian?" A voice said on the other end of the telephone extension.

Julian was alone in the family room where the console television sat surrounded by a couple of overstuffed sofas and reclining chairs. His heels were resting on a circular rug while he sat sprawled on one of the olive green sofas. Most of the furniture had chintz slipcovers to protect it from the farm dirt. When the phone rang, he didn't expect it to be his only brother on the other end.

"Albert?" Julian replied, puzzled. Julian and his younger brother had never seen eye to eye. Albert was a year younger than Julian but had been much bigger when they were growing up. Albert used to bully him, making his life miserable. Julian remembered the other kids at boarding school calling his brother names for being obese. Albert sought to gain popularity by taunting his older brother. Julian was never one for violence, so he absorbed Albert's ridicule. Later when Albert discovered that Julian was homosexual, he belittled his brother's life "choice" by constantly haranguing him. Julian dealt with Albert's homophobic outbursts by avoiding him.

"Julian?" Albert replied with some hesitation. "It's Elizabeth. She's had a very bad stroke. The doctors don't know if she will live through it."

Julian was at a loss for words. He hadn't spoken with Elizabeth in a number of years. However, he had never thought of the world without her. At a young age, she had divorced their father and sent the two of them to boarding school from first grade through twelfth. She prided herself on sending them to the best schools and colleges that money could buy. With her personal responsibilities pushed aside, she became a great success selling stocks and bonds. After Julian graduated from college, Elizabeth and he conducted business together in Washington, DC. They had spoken almost daily during that part of his life. When he came to Louisiana, their lives no longer coincided.

"When did this happen?" Julian asked in a hoarse voice.

"Last night," Albert replied. Neither of them spoke for a moment. Then, as if Albert wanted to hurry the conversation, he quickly began to speak once more. "Julian, I'm rather busy at the present time. Being that you were closer to her than I, it makes more sense that you should go to Washington to see her."

Julian sighed. "I don't see why it has to be me, Albert. You know how I hate going back to that place."

"Julian, please," Albert begged. "I promise I'll do something when things let up a little. By the way . . . how is my son?"

"He no longer is your son. Remember?" Julian replied. He regretted the remark. Julian normally thought about what he was going to say before he said it. *It must be the stress of the moment,* he thought. "I'm sorry, Albert. I know it's not the time to talk about Shaun. It's just a sore subject. I guess I'll get on a plane, but it probably won't be until tomorrow. What hospital is she in right now?"

"Sibley," Albert replied. "Give me a call when you know something."

Julian set the receiver in its place. After a few moments, he picked up the phone again to make travel arrangements. When he had finished, Shaun came into the room.

"You don't look particularly happy," Shaun observed.

"I just got a call from Albert." Julian was careful not to say "your father" because the two had severed ties ten years before when Shaun was fifteen years old. Shaun had no choice in the matter. His father disowned him and his spineless mother stood by her husband. When Shaun was seventeen, Julian had adopted him as his son, but Shaun continued to call him Uncle Julian, which suited both of them.

Shaun frowned. "What did he want? To cause trouble?"

"No. Elizabeth had a bad stroke. I'm going to Washington first thing tomorrow," Julian replied.

Shaun always thought it was strange that Uncle Julian called his mother by her given name. He said that she didn't want to be reminded that she was a mother. Pilot disagreed when Shaun asked him about it years ago. He said that she preferred that everybody call her Elizabeth. When Albert referred to her as "Mommy," Shaun detected malice in the word. Pilot refused to call her Elizabeth but preferred Mrs. Steele. Elizabeth Steele was the name she had given herself to sharpen her image. When she was married to Uncle Julian's father, she was Emma Smith. In addition, she also used the title "Mrs." instead of "Miss" or "Ms." Shaun had long ago deduced that she was a complicated woman.

"Would you like for me to go with you?" Shaun asked.

Julian paused before answering. "Yeah, that would be nice."


Julian and his nephew put their bags in the condominium that he had given Shaun a few years before in Crystal City, Virginia. It was a high-rise building just across the Potomac River from Washington, DC. This was the place where Julian had lived with Dennis in the years preceding his departure for Louisiana. It had a panoramic view of the city, including the U.S. Capitol building, along with the Lincoln, Jefferson, and Washington monuments. It had been several years since Julian had set foot in the apartment, but he did not feel the nostalgia that he had felt on his last couple of visits. The place was now Shaun's to use as he saw fit. Shaun and Carmen would come and stay in the place from time to time for long weekends. He didn't want to sell it, because one never knew when it could come in handy.

When they had settled in and showered, they made arrangements to go to the hospital. They had a late afternoon appointment with the doctor. Despite the jetlag, they were able to tumble into the taxi to make the ride.

Her name was Dr. Andrews. She was a slender woman in a pair of flats with a white hospital coat. She met them at the nurses' station.

"Doctor, we're from out of town and we have no idea what kind of condition Elizabeth is in. Can you fill us in?" Julian asked. Shaun stood by while his uncle did the talking.

"Mrs. Steele was brought in a couple of days ago unconscious," Dr. Andrews explained. "Her housekeeper found her in bed when she failed to rise in the morning. The woman called nine-one-one and she was brought here. Honestly, we didn't think she would live through the day, but she's made remarkable progress. She has regained consciousness, but her entire left side from head to foot is paralyzed. Her right side is not much better, but it may improve."

"May we see her?" Julian asked.

"Yes." The doctor hesitated. "Just be aware that she is going to look a lot different from how you remember her. Come on. I'll take you to her."

Julian and Shaun followed the doctor to the intensive care unit where Elizabeth lay. She was asleep and breathing with the aid of a respirator.

Shaun grabbed his uncle's arm to hold him steady. Sensing he was fine, he released his grip. "Are you okay?"

Julian took a deep breath and nodded. "I'm okay. I just didn't expect this; she doesn't look like herself at all. She looks so sick."

Shaun pursed his lips and nodded to the doctor. "Why don't we step outside to talk?" Dr. Andrews suggested. "The nurse needs to check on her." A black woman holding a chart gave them a look of encouragement as they passed.

"Is she going to live?" Julian blurted as soon as they were through the door.

"Let's go and sit in my office for a few minutes. There are some decisions you are going to have to make," Dr. Andrews said. The three went into a small office with a desk and a couple of chairs. Various awards and certificates hung on the walls above a few bookcases.

"When is she going to get better?" Shaun asked. "Will she be able to go home anytime soon?"

Dr. Andrews looked straight into the young man's face, trying to conjure up her best bedside manner. "Your grandmother is a very sick woman. She is very fortunate to be alive. We were surprised she regained consciousness. She seems to be stabilizing nicely and we expect that she will be able to breathe on her own in the next few days if she continues to improve. Her progress will start to slow and it will most likely seem that she is not getting any better, but we just don't know." She looked at Julian. "We still don't know if she is going to make it. She could have another stroke or any number of things could happen in the next few days. But let's look at the bright side. Let's bet she will continue to improve. What you need to decide is how you are going to care for her."

Julian worked to keep his jaw from dropping. First of all, the concept of anybody taking care of Elizabeth seemed absurd. The woman took independence to an extreme. Next, he didn't know the first thing to do. "Doctor, I live halfway across the country from here. I can't possibly care for her here. I have a brother who lives in St. Louis and I know he won't be willing to do much. Are you sure she isn't going to make a full recovery sometime soon?" Julian asked with a frown.

Dr. Andrews chose her words carefully. "I don't think your mother is ever going to be the same again, Mr. Smith. She is going to need full-time care. It would be most advisable to get some convalescent care for her. I'll leave you two to discuss the matter," she said, getting to her feet. "Feel free to use my office as long as you like." She left the room.

The two men were both disturbed. Shaun looked at his uncle. "What are you going to do?"

Julian stared at the floor in thought and then spoke, shaking his head. "Elizabeth's worst nightmare. When she is ready, she will come to Louisiana to live on the Pilot plantation until she is able to tell us where to place her."

"You're not serious," Shaun gasped.

"What else am I going to do, Shaun?" Julian said, spreading his hands. "I'm swamped with work at the Lamond place and I have other responsibilities. I can't go back and forth from the farm to Washington for very long. She's just going to have to come home with me. Albert certainly isn't going to do anything."

"I understand," Shaun said in disbelief. "I just find it hard to imagine Grandmother coming to Louisiana."

"Grandmother?" Julian said, giving Shaun a puzzled look.

Shaun shrugged, "I don't feel comfortable calling her Elizabeth. She'll get used to it."

When the time came, Shaun had a private jet fly Elizabeth to Louisiana. Carmen volunteered to make the trip with her. Both Shaun and Julian were grateful to him. When she arrived at the big house, she was moved to a room on the same wing and floor where Oliver and Marge were staying. The wing was made into a convalescent center equipped with a staff of full-time nurses—at Elizabeth's expense, of course. She would have the best care and medical equipment to make her comfortable.

"This house is filling up," Pilot said, watching several tanks of oxygen being taken up the stairs. Shaun came through the doorway with his hand on Carmen's shoulder.

"I hope it will fill up more," Shaun remarked as he glanced toward Carmen. "I'd like to have a pool put in out back. Carmen likes to swim laps for exercise. Besides, I think we'd all enjoy it."

"That's really not necessary," Carmen said slightly embarrassed. "Your grandpapa may not want a pool with his house."

Pilot held up a hand. "Don't mind me. Your friend here runs this place now. He can do whatever he wants."

"I'm trying to make it so Carmen will want to spend more time here," Shaun explained, folding his arms around his boyfriend from behind. "I miss him horribly when I'm here and he's in Boston."

Carmen hedged. "You know our work keeps me busy in Boston. One of us has to be there." Carmen didn't like Louisiana, but he knew it hurt Shaun's feelings whenever he mentioned it.

"We'll work something out," Shaun said, releasing him from his grasp.

"You should make more use of that jet of yours," Carmen replied. "Why don't you build an airstrip out there instead of a pool?"

Shaun thought for a moment. "Maybe I'll build both. I think you may be on to something."

Carmen rolled his eyes. "I was only kidding, but go ahead and knock yourself out. It's your money. I've been trying to get you to spend some of it."

Julian came down the steps to the big kitchen where Pilot, Shaun, and Carmen were conversing. "Elizabeth seems to be settled in . . . we really don't have to tell her where she is, do we?"

Pilot commented, "Eventually, she's going to figure it out if Emily and the children start to float in and out of her room."

Julian brightened. "It would be great if we could get people to visit with her."

"We'll see," Pilot replied skeptically.

Adam came through the doorway. "How did the move go? I got here as soon as I could."

"Okay," Julian replied less than enthusiastically. "Are you ready to meet my mother?"

# – 9 –

"Is this Shaun Smith?" A voice asked through the phone extension that Shaun was holding. He was sitting at his desk in the office of the big house. He was the main tenant in Pilot's study, since he had taken over much of the day-to-day operations of the farm. Pilot kept a writing desk in his rooms on the top floor of the west wing. The cumbersome computer seemed to be in the way of the few sheets of paper scattered across the solid oak desk. The office decoration lacked a woman's touch. Pilot's tastes were simple and this room reflected his aversion to fashion. The walls were light green with a few dated prints of prize livestock hanging on them. The worn leather couch, with a pair of matching chairs, sat on beige shag carpeting just behind the desk, which was against the wall to the left of the doorway. On the far wall were three sets of windows. Through them, spacious cornfields extended as far as the eye could see.

"This is Shaun Smith speaking," he replied.

"Am I to understand that you are running the show at the Pilot plantation?" the man asked.

"For the most part," Shaun replied. "How can I help you?"

"I think we should meet in private to discuss an important matter concerning Elizabeth Steele," the man said.

Shaun sighed. "Unless you want to come out to the farm, I can't get away from here for a few days. I've got sugarcane stalks due to arrive from the islands any day and I have to be here when they come."

"I think you can find some time to see me," the man replied. His voice carried a light tone of sarcasm.

"Look, I don't even know who you are. If it's important enough, you will wait. I hate to sound rude, but I'm on a tight schedule at the moment. I'm due in Boston at the end of the week," Shaun said impatiently.

"Let's just say my name is Calvin," the man said. "I have some information concerning Elizabeth Steele and her son Julian that would interest you. I don't think you will want it to fall into the wrong hands."

His uncle's name got Shaun's attention. "What are you talking about?" he growled.

"We can discuss that when we meet," Calvin replied. "I will be in touch in the next day or two." The receiver went dead. Shaun returned the handset to its cradle. He shook his head. *What could this man possibly want? What gives him the nerve to tell me when we are to meet?* He went back to his work.

*A few hours later.*

"May I speak to Shaun Smith?" A voice asked.

"Speaking," Shaun grumbled. Calvin's call earlier that morning had not sat well with him.

"I think we should meet to discuss a matter concerning Elizabeth Steele. As I understand it, you are the one handling her affairs," the voice said.

"Actually, my uncle is the one you probably want to talk to about Mrs. Steele's affairs. You can reach him at the Lamond plantation," Shaun replied. "Do you need the number?"

"No . . . er . . . I believe I will deal directly with you. I understand you own the checkbook for the place . . . that is, the *big* checkbook," the voice continued. "We need to come to some sort of settlement."

"Who are you?" Shaun shouted. He gritted his teeth, getting to his feet.

"Let's just say my name is Bob," the man replied.

"Are you sure you're not Calvin? Didn't we speak this morning?" Shaun asked. "I told you. I don't have time for this nonsense."

"No. This is the first time we've talked. I think you will find it necessary to make time," Bob replied.

Shaun sighed. "All right. When do you want to meet? I leave for Boston at the end of the week and I can't be delayed."

"I think we can begin our business over the phone," Bob said in a controlled voice. "Mrs. Steele paid an informant from Price Communications a few years ago for some highly sensitive information regarding the submission of our tax returns. She held this information hostage until we gave her a tip as to when a merger was to take place. She forced us to make an announcement that the merger was off, sending our stock price plummeting. She bought up the undervalued shares. When the merger was announced, the price rebounded and she made a handsome profit. Needless to say, we had some unhappy stockholders and our reputation suffered. I have proof that she extorted money from us and I plan to sue her for millions unless we can come to some agreement. Can we do business or do I go to the feds?"

"I will need to consider it," Shaun said. "Will you turn over whatever you have upon payment? How much do you want?

"You'll get most of it. I want three million," Bob replied.

"Three million! You've got to be crazy!" Shaun exclaimed. "I don't know who you are."

"I will get back to you later this week. I have your phone numbers in Boston. I advise you to check your sources regarding Mrs. Steele's past activities with Price Communications. I believe you will find everything in order," Bob said. The receiver went dead and Shaun hung up.

Shaun logged onto Pilot's computer which was one of the first of its kind, and used the elder man's secret password to get into his classified profiles on personal and business contacts. When he got to the file index, he typed in "Elizabeth Steele." A flashing message came up that read "File sealed." Next, he typed in "Julian Smith." The same message flashed on the screen. Exasperated, Shaun decided that he needed to pay his grandpapa a visit.

He was up to something, but Shaun didn't have time to concern himself with it.

"I haven't seen Frances Lorraine. Where is she?" Shaun asked as he pulled up a chair next to the giant of a man in the nursery.

"She left as soon as she was able to get out of bed," Pilot replied. "She said she would be back in a few weeks and not to look for her."

"Are you still having her followed?" Shaun asked.

"Of course," Pilot replied. His voice was sturdy and full of conviction. "If she continues to behave herself like she has in the last nine months or so, she might just make a good wife. I should have been keeping her under my thumb since the day we were married. It would have saved us both a lot of embarrassment." Pilot sensed that Shaun had something on his mind.

Anxious to unload his dilemmas concerning his grandmother, Shaun began to speak. "Grandpapa, I need to get into some of the files in the computer. You have them sealed and I can't seem to access them."

"I see," Pilot replied. He was apprehensive about giving anybody the codes. He thought for a few moments. "Shaun, the sealed files concern family members. I don't even know what's in them. I had Dennis update the files and put them in the computer. I don't like to invade the family's privacy unless it's necessary."

Shaun pursed his lips. "Grandpapa, I agree with you one hundred percent. I respect privacy as much as possible. But this is *really* necessary."

"It's that Steele woman, isn't it?" Pilot guessed. "She hasn't been here very long, but the wolves have already come for her, haven't they?"

"Yeah," Shaun confessed. "I got a couple of disturbing calls today. Then I stopped answering the phones, but they continued to ring the rest of the afternoon. There were more calls than normal. I think they had to do with her."

Pilot nodded. "I guess all the people she irritated over the years are coming to get her while she's sick."

"Why now?" Shaun asked. "All of these people couldn't have been blackmailing her before her stroke. Why are they surfacing now?"

"She had something on them to keep them in their places. Now since she can't talk, they are free to play with her until she can speak again." Pilot grinned. "It seems that our Mrs. Steele didn't think of everything. You sure have your hands full, young Shaun. Good luck getting her out of this mess."

Shaun wasn't concerned about Elizabeth losing her millions for her unscrupulous conduct. He was more concerned about the call from Calvin involving his Uncle Julian. He had a sick feeling in his stomach. He wasn't ready to talk to Pilot about it until he had more information.

*A few days later.*

"We have to hurry up. I have a plane to catch," Shaun said to Calvin, trying to push through their meeting. He had dreaded getting together with this man and he wanted it to be over as soon as possible. They met at Lou's Restaurant in town.

"We're not going anywhere anytime soon, so you might as well order some coffee and sit tight," Calvin said as they slipped into a booth.

Shaun had been briefed by Elizabeth's dossier. The folder hadn't been updated in a few years, but it contained enough information to make this meeting with Calvin interesting. "Let's get this over with." Shaun was hostile. "What is it you want?"

"I assume you're updated with the situation with Mrs. Steele and her son Julian," Calvin said with a self-satisfied air.

"Calvin," Shaun started, "if you want anything from me, you're going to have to work for it. We're not going to *assume* anything. Also, I am not going to give you any information. If you intend to sell me anything, you are going to have to let me know exactly what I'm buying."

"Fine," Calvin replied. "I was just trying to save some time. You did say you were in a hurry."

"It's too late for that," Shaun sneered. "I have a boyfriend in Boston who is going to be very disappointed that I didn't make that plane. That was the only thing that mattered to me. I have plenty of time. I just don't intend to waste too much of it on you. Now what is it that you have?"

"All right," Calvin began, "I have proof that Mrs. Steele's ex-husband, Bernard Smith, your grandfather, is not Julian Smith's natural father. It seems your uncle is a product of a brutal rape that happened just before that failed marriage. It seems Julian . . ."

"It's Mr. Smith to you," Shaun growled.

"It seems Mr. Smith has no knowledge of these facts. He believes that Bernard Smith is his actual father. Mrs. Steele was able to falsify records and even fool her husband to believe that Mr. Smith was in fact his blood-related son."

"How are you able to prove this?" Shaun said in feigned disbelief. He had read it in Elizabeth's file, but he was determined to give nothing away.

"I have eye-witness testimonials. I am assured that if Mr. Smith were to further investigate the matter, he would uncover the full truth," Calvin replied.

"Then you have no solid proof," Shaun laughed. "All you have is hearsay."

"I have names of individuals. However, I don't think they are too anxious to talk. I wanted to give you the first opportunity to buy these names. I assume that you will want to make sure they are silenced for good. If you do not buy these names, I have someone else who would love to have them."

"Well, maybe I need to have a talk with my Uncle Julian. He was not particularly close to either of his parents. As a matter of fact, he would probably lose little sleep to learn that one of them didn't belong to him," Shaun said, clearly bluffing.

"As you may have guessed, Mr. Smith, there is more," Calvin said with satisfaction in his voice. "I am banking on Mr. Smith's frail mental capacity. I know he spent a long time in a sanitarium a few years back. This may be the thing to cart him back to the loony bin. The fact that his father was a sociopath rapist might not sit too well with him. It may be enough to push him over the edge."

"Maybe I'll take that chance. My uncle has a very sound mind these days. He no longer has those stresses that caused his past sickness," Shaun said defensively. He knew he would be buying those names, but he was jockeying for a lower price and hoping the man would relinquish any other strings.

"There's more," Calvin said, playing his final card. "In a few short years, Mrs. Steele stands to gain a great deal of money when you satisfy a residency requirement stipulated in your great-grandmother's will. You will have lived in her mansion in Boston seven years, allowing Mrs. Steele and yourself to collect millions of dollars from her estate. I'm aware that it is stipulated in her will that the firstborn, which is falsely Mr. Julian Smith, should inherit the money and Mrs. Steele her portion. If the true paternity of Mr. Smith comes to light, then you and Mrs. Steele are out of that money. Worse yet, your father, Albert Smith, whom you despise more than anything, will receive the millions once he moves into *your* house and lives there for seven years. That should be enough to seal this deal. I believe you'll stop at nothing to prevent your father from ruining you."

"You don't know me at all, Calvin, but it's my Uncle Julian that is foremost on my mind," Shaun hissed. "What is your price for those names?"


Shaun arrived back at the big house after his business transaction with Calvin had been completed. He was not in a pleasant mood.

"You seem a bit grumpy," Julian remarked as Shaun walked into the big house from the back door leading to the kitchen. He furrowed his brow. "I thought you were headed back to Boston for the next week or so."

"I got delayed." Shaun frowned. "I missed my plane and I miss my boyfriend. It hasn't been a good day."

"Well, there are a lot of phone messages for you. You sure are getting a lot of calls," Julian said. "Are you on the verge of a few hot deals?"

"No, not really," Shaun answered vaguely. "I'm sure they have to do with the sugarcane stalks from the islands that are going into the ground. I had some preliminary tests done to see if these strains are resistant to the blights that are devastating this parish. Are you interested in experimenting with any of these canes? They might help you over at the Lamond place." He was trying to steer the conversation away from himself.

"No," Julian answered. "I'll leave the experimenting to you. We will not be producing much sugarcane until the price of the yield goes back up . . . if it ever does go back up. We're concentrating on our other businesses."

"That may be smart," Shaun agreed. He paused a moment before asking, "Is Grandmother awake? I thought I'd pay her a visit."

Julian looked surprised. "I'm sure she'd love a visit. It's been hard for me to get anybody to stop by her room. Emily and Pilot refuse to visit her. She doesn't like children, so I don't let them near her. That has left Adam and me. We're both busy, so she doesn't get a lot of attention."

Shaun nodded and went to her room. When he got there, he excused the nurse, encouraging her to take a break. He wanted some time alone with his grandmother.

As he approached the bed, he could sense that she was awake. Her right eye was blinking normally, while her left seemed sunken into her skull. Her auburn hair was spread across her pillow down to her shoulders. He could tell the nurse had tried to comb it, but it still looked a mess. Gray roots had begun to show where the new growth had not been tinted. His grandmother looked like an old woman. Her skin was a pasty pale white. He could not help but look at her in an angry stare.

"I gather you used to enjoy confrontation and a good fight, Grandmother," Shaun growled. "Well, I am angry and I think you and I need to have a little talk. You've really made a big mess. You have plenty of incentive to get well. The sharks are out to get you while you lie peacefully in your bed. There is not an hour that goes by that I don't get a phone call from somebody trying to extort money from me, by revealing some of your despicable past behaviors. Frankly, I don't care if you lose all your money. I don't even care if they take away my inheritance in the process. These criminals think that I care enough about you to protect you from your past crimes of blackmail." Shaun gritted his teeth. "One thing I won't stand for is letting you take your son down with you. I am being blackmailed to keep Uncle Julian's true parentage a secret. I paid this man Calvin off, but I fear he may be back for more. I can only hold the other blackmailers off for so long before they start to launch an all-out raid on your reputation and money. You need to get better. I don't know how you managed to keep this Calvin at bay. You need to talk again and get on the phone to stop this person from ruining Uncle Julian. If you have any heart at all, fight to get well to protect your son from the awful truth."

There didn't seem to be the slightest reaction from Elizabeth. She remained motionless in her bed. Shaun left without excusing himself.

*A few weeks later.*

"Dennis, you've got to get over here. I need you," Shaun pleaded over the phone in the study of the big house.

"What's going on?" Dennis replied.

"It's Uncle Julian," Shaun explained. "Do you know the truth of his parentage?"

Dennis hesitated before answering. "Yes, Shaun, I do, but I'm still doing a lot of digging on it. Why do you ask?"

"It's Elizabeth," Shaun answered. "Since she's been here, I've been inundated with calls trying to extort money from me. I can't hold them off any longer. You've got to find out what she had on those people to keep them quiet. The biggest problem is this guy Calvin. I gave him some money a few weeks ago to shut him up from telling Uncle Julian the truth. He gave me some names of the people who know the truth, but now he says he has some more for sale for me to buy. What should I do?"

Dennis sighed. "Pay him off again. I'll jump on the plane and get there as soon as I can."

"Thanks, Dennis. I'm really counting on you," Shaun said.

# – 10 –

After Shaun got off the phone with Dennis, he decided to go outside for some air. When he reached the kitchen, he ran into Julian at the bottom of the steps. Julian had a grim look on his face and Shaun sensed fear.

"I was just coming to look for you," Julian said. He was ill at ease.

"What's up?" Shaun asked with concern. He felt the need to move past his uncle into the next room.

Julian made a feeble attempt to reach out for him, but all he could catch was air. "Shaun. It's Albert. He's here. I'm assuming he came to see Elizabeth."

Shaun turned toward his uncle, seething with anger. "Where is he? I don't want him in this house," he said in a low, hoarse voice.

Julian grimaced. He didn't know what to expect from Shaun. His nephew had a short fuse when provoked. During his adolescence, Julian worked with him to keep his destructive behavior in check. His outbursts wreaked havoc in all their lives. Shaun had been doing better keeping his temper under control. However, Julian understood his nephew, and the young man could be pushed only so far before his old tendencies resurfaced. "He's out in the driveway. I sent Adam to delay him from coming in before I had a chance to talk with him. I think they should be in here in a few minutes."

Abruptly, Shaun left the room. "Shaun . . ." Julian cried. But Shaun was not going to listen.

In a few moments, Adam came through the kitchen door with Albert in tow. Albert looked like he was expecting a warm greeting from his brother, but this was not the case. "Albert, you shouldn't have come here," Julian said with a frown.

"Julian, you know I had to come and see my mother," Albert snapped. Before Albert could move a step further into the kitchen,

82

Shaun entered from the opposite end of the room. He was carrying one of Pilot's rifles.

Shaun pointed the gun at his father and cocked it. "You have fifteen minutes to grab your bags and hitch a ride back into town. I believe it was fifteen minutes you gave me when you threw me out of your house ten years ago," Shaun snarled.

The men gasped. "Shaun, please put the gun down," Julian said nervously. He didn't move toward his nephew, because he sensed the young man's nerves were at peak pitch. He realized that Shaun hated his father enough to kill him. "Shaun, please. Let's talk about this."

"Please, Shaun," Adam pleaded.

"Enough!" Shaun growled. "Albert, you heard what I said," he said in a calm voice, then barked, "Move! Get out of this house and don't you dare ever come back!"

Pilot had heard the shouting from the other end of the house. He had figured out the situation by the time he arrived in the kitchen. "Albert, I suggest you do as the boy says," he said in a low, calm voice. "You can stay in the hotel in town. Your brother will contact you when the time is appropriate. For now, I believe my grandson means business."

Shock nearly paralyzed Albert. He began to speak, but Shaun moved his trigger finger. Without further delay, Albert turned to leave. He walked out of the house, to the end of the lane where the farm road met the main road.

"Shaun . . ." Julian started.

"Uncle Julian," Shaun replied, setting the butt of the rifle to the floor. His face was brimming with anger. He was taking deep breaths. "I don't want to talk about it right now." He handed the rifle to Pilot and left the room.

Julian spread his arms and let them fall, clapping his thighs. "I really don't know what to do."

"I'll talk to him," Adam said, taking charge rather than offering. "See about getting your brother into town before Shaun changes his mind and puts some bullets in that man." He glanced over to the gun Pilot was holding.

Julian hesitated. He suspected Shaun's ill feelings toward the minister. With no better idea of what to do, he agreed. He nodded and exited through the back door.

When he reached Albert, he was fuming. "Albert, this was really a stupid thing to do."

"Fine," Albert replied in an angry tone, "but my fifteen minutes are hastening to an end. I suggest you do something to get me out of here before you have to clean my dead carcass off your side lawn."

Julian let out a sigh. "Okay, get into the car and I'll take you to town."

The family had bought a brand new station wagon with plenty of fancy features, like electric windows and air-conditioning. It was blue with wood-grain running along the sides and rear of the car. Chrome outlined the wood-grained finish. It had a nice radio—which meant nothing since so few stations reached the farm. Julian liked to drive it, since it floated like a magic carpet. However, Julian wasn't thinking about a luxurious drive to town.

"Albert, you could have given us some warning that you were coming."

"If I did that, I know I would have been told not to bother making the trip," Albert replied. The car bounded down the main road. Dust was scattered in front of them, but Julian was accustomed to the screen, so he had little trouble navigating.

"Why did you come? I thought that you could care less for Elizabeth," Julian asked.

Albert sighed, then answered with impatience. "I wanted to see my son. What kind of man . . . if you can call him that, he has become."

"It's comments like that one that would make you less than endearing to him," Julian replied angrily. "Albert, you were a despicable father. It would have been best if you stayed away from Shaun."

"I know I gave up my rights to him many years ago, but I want to make amends," Albert said with a sad expression. "I know there has to be some good character in him, and I would like to get to know my son a little better. Julian, I am trying. Can't you see?"

"Albert, trust me," Julian answered with an edge to his voice. "It's too late. Go home and forget about it. For once, think about Shaun.

He's a happy young man except when it has anything to do with you. Can't you just let it go?"

Albert ran the palms of his hands along his face from forehead to chin and frowned. "Will he see his sister? Maybe that would be a start. Maybe she could start to bridge the gulf between him and me."

Julian thought for a few moments before answering. "I'll see what I can do. But it will have to be a while after he's calmed down. If he believes the overture is coming from you, he'll refuse. However, he might like to see his sister. I know she's a few years younger than him. They never had the chance to be close."

"Anything you can do, Julian," Albert replied with a forlorn look. "By the way, how is Mother?"


Shaun bounded up the steps to his room. It wasn't the chamber where Carmen and he stayed, but his boyhood room. He felt comfort there. It carried good memories of living in the big house from the time he arrived on Pilot's farm at the age of fifteen. Before his move to Louisiana, good memories were hard to come by. Albert and he had never gotten along from the day he was born. He respected his mother less. Albert had beaten Shaun countless times and the boy retaliated by making his father angry. Shaun smiled. *Even as a little boy I was smarter than him. He would have beaten me anyway if I hadn't made him so mad. At least I was able to get some satisfaction,* he thought. Shaun had always been proud of his sexuality. He used it as a weapon by reminding Albert that he was a gay little boy. Albert had punished his effeminate son's behavior and had tried to mold Shaun into an image that suited him. However, Shaun reacted in the opposite way, living openly as a less than masculine boy with other interests than most of the other males in school. He studied hard. He had been more comfortable in the company of little girls than other boys. He had accepted that he was different. When the girls would giggle and point out boys that they thought were cute, Shaun had either agreed or disagreed. The little boys made fun of Shaun at times, but he was smarter than they were. He was a good matchmaker and never hesitated to help others with their homework to get good grades. The children's parents were ecstatic over the help Shaun gave his fellow students. Children have their own language and adults often were not as effective with their tutoring. Shaun made parents happy with their kids, which made kids happier with Shaun. Despite Shaun's prowess at school, Albert had always been less than happy with him.

Adam popped his head in the door of Shaun's room. "Can I come in?"

Shaun frowned. "Sure."

Adam came in and sat on one of the parallel twin beds. Shaun sat across from him. "It had to be hard to see your father after so many years."

"He's not my father!" Shaun growled. "Uncle Julian adopted me a long time ago."

"Lucky for your Uncle Julian," Adam replied, trying to incite a smile from the young man. Instead Shaun let out a tiny snort.

Shaun started getting agitated, though he tried to be polite. He respected Adam. The minister had always been there for him when troubles occupied his mind. He would be thrilled to know this man had hooked up with his uncle, but he couldn't understand why the two kept it a secret from him. He knew both men well. The secrecy was coming from Adam. "I have a feeling that you have something to say about what I did downstairs."

Adam nodded. "Your demonstration was effective. I might have done the same thing in your shoes. I'm proud of you for leaving the bullets out of the shotgun."

Shaun chuckled, but he didn't want to talk about Albert just yet. "Why have you taken my Uncle Julian away from me?"

Adam creased his brow and tilted his head. "Shaun, your uncle, you, and I have always been best friends. This is still true. Has this been the reason that you and I haven't had much contact of late? I've noticed. I guess I figured you would say something if it were bothering you or it would work itself out. Tell me what's going on."

Shaun squirmed. Adam had always ministered to other people. People didn't know the man's deepest thoughts. He felt embarrassed for prying into the preacher's personal life.

"If we are so close, I think I have the right to know the extent of the relationship between you and Uncle Julian." Shaun flushed. Adam was a married man. That is, married to a woman. A nice woman.

"Is that what's been bothering you?" Adam asked, smiling. "Julian is special to me, Shaun, as are you. But your uncle and I have a different bond. We're the same age. I don't get many opportunities to share myself with other people. I have needs just like everyone else. Your uncle provides them for me. I make no secret of it."

Shaun felt frustrated. He wasn't getting his point across. How do you ask a preacher if he is having sex with your uncle? "I'm protective of my uncle, as you very well know. I have to keep him safe. I'll stop at nothing to do this. But I have to know what concerns him. My uncle and I never have secrets from each other, except when it comes to you. I know how he feels about Aunt Emily. When I ask him about the relationship he has with you, he says he can't talk about you. I know that it's you that's keeping him silent. That may be fine if he wants to keep that posture with other people but not with me." Shaun paused a moment. "Adam, are you and Uncle Julian romantically involved? Why all the secrecy?"

Adam sidestepped the question. He had a look of concern on his face. "Shaun, is Julian in some sort of trouble? Is he in danger? Is he sick?"

"Uncle Julian is fine," Shaun replied, avoiding the issue. He wasn't going to tell Adam that he was being blackmailed.

"Why are you being so protective? You almost seem obsessed," Adam said. He knew Shaun was hiding something and he was worried.

"Adam, you know if something were really wrong with Uncle Julian I would tell you. However, there are some things I'm not ready to talk about yet. I still have to work them through my mind." Shaun cast his gaze to the floor. "I'm afraid there will be a time when you and I are going to talk about it in more detail, but I still have a few things to work out."

Adam nodded. After a pause he looked into Shaun's face. "Shaun, like you, I'm not ready to talk about some things. I have to balance certain things in my life and I'm learning more how to do that each

day. I'm asking you to be patient with me. Just know that I do love
your Uncle Julian. I wouldn't do anything to cause him harm."

Shaun frowned. The man had a point. He couldn't be honest with
Adam about his uncle's problems. Perhaps Adam had valid reasons
for keeping quiet. Shaun was feeling hypocritical. However, it still
bothered him that he couldn't be involved in a special part of Uncle
Julian's life. The issue would have to lie for now. At least he felt better
for getting things out in the open with Adam. He wasn't satisfied, but
Adam did say he loved Uncle Julian. Was that enough of a confession? No, he wanted to know more of the everyday things. That
would have to wait.

"Okay," Shaun said, nodding. "Whatever it is you have with Uncle
Julian, please make sure he's happy."

Adam let out a big grin. "You bet." Adam moved to steer the subject back to Albert. "Shaun, tell me about how you feel about Albert
right now."

"I hate him!" Shaun growled. "I can't stand to be in the same room
as him. How's that for an answer?"

Adam felt for his young friend. He wanted to tell Shaun that a con-
suming hate for anyone was detrimental, but he guessed it would
push the wiry man away from him.

"He did some awful things to you, Shaun," Adam agreed. "I can
understand you feeling the way you do."

"He didn't beat you!" Shaun retorted. "Have you ever been humiliated by having someone who is supposed to be protecting you loathe
you beyond contempt?"

Adam didn't respond.

Shaun felt bad. "I'm sorry, Adam. You didn't deserve that. I'm still
feeling a bit raw right now. I could easily kill the man and have few regrets. Perhaps it's not a good time for you to be here."

"I'm not complaining," Adam said. "I'm just listening. Say what
you need to say."

Shaun frowned again. "Adam, I know you well enough to know
where this conversation is going to lead. After I blow some steam and
come to some sort of sense, you are going to say I need to forgive him.

I can't! He tortured me! Only if I manage to forget what he did to me can I begin to forgive."

Adam knew better than to argue with him. Instead he just nodded.

"Adam, I can't stand the sight of him. How am I supposed to forgive him?" Shaun asked.

"I have a feeling he came here to see you and not just his mother," Adam replied gently.

"I find that hard to believe," Shaun snorted. "The man regrets planting the seed that formed me. If I fell off the face of this earth, it will be one less faggot that he wouldn't have to kill."

"Maybe," Adam agreed. "Did you ever consider the possibility that he may regret the things he's done to you? What would you do if he sought forgiveness?"

Shaun felt troubled by the question. No, he hadn't considered it. He didn't want Albert to seek forgiveness. It was easier to hate him. "Adam, it hurts to think about him. How am I supposed to stay in the same room with him and not remember what he's done to me? It's too late. I know he can't hurt me anymore." He looked into Adam's face. "But he's still the same man. He hurts with words as well as with fists."

"If you decide to forgive him, that doesn't mean you have to have a relationship with him. Why would you want to subject yourself to one so cruel? It would be up to you to give him a chance that he clearly doesn't deserve. You would be justified and perhaps wise to have nothing more to do with him. Forgiveness means just letting go of the hate."

Shaun was feeling depressed. His anger over Albert's visit had cooled. He didn't want to think about it anymore. He missed Carmen.

"I think I want to be alone right now, Adam. I want to call my boyfriend in a bit. Do you mind?" Shaun said, getting to his feet.

Adam followed suit. He knew that Shaun had had enough for one day. He gave the young man a hug and left the room.

"It's good to have you back in town," Pilot said, getting up from his chair.

Dennis nodded, admiring the patriarch's surroundings. "So, these are your new digs," he commented. "Very tasteful; a far cry from your old office. Why the change?"

"Well, Shaun took over my old office, since he's been helping out with things on the farm," Pilot explained. "The idea was that I would spend more time in my living quarters. I have my writing desk with a telephone up there, but I miss having a den to clutter. The decorator cleared out one of these old parlors and set it up for me. Everyone hates these stuffy old parlors but Frances Lorraine, so I doubt it will be missed."

Pilot's new office was bigger than the one Shaun was using. The walls were painted blue and lined with oak bookshelves. A large matching desk bumped up against the wall by the window. Plantation shutters covered the single window on the far wall. There was a cream-colored overstuffed couch flanked on each side with matching wing chairs grouped around a coffee table. The furniture sat on a blue area rug a few shades darker than the walls. The floors between the edges of the rug and walls were dark stained wood. "The room is extravagant for my tastes, but my wife should approve when she comes back from her extended leave."

"How is the little lady? Have you heard from her?" Dennis asked, sitting in one of the wing chairs.

Pilot followed suit and sat down on the couch. The housekeeper brought a tray of sweet tea and set it on the low table. Then, she left the room, closing the door behind her. "No. I haven't heard from her, but I've been advised of her recent activities." Pilot sighed. "It seems she is back to her old ways."

"Are you having her followed?" Dennis asked, swirling the ice in his glass of iced tea.

"Of course," Pilot exclaimed. "However, she's outfoxed me. I can't humiliate her if she's nowhere to be seen. She's staying away from home."

"She can't stay away forever," Dennis mused.

"The word is she's been seen with another state senator. He's found her irresistible. His wife died a few years ago, so naturally he's enthralled with Frances Lorraine. Come. It's time to check on Oliver."

The two gentlemen climbed the steps to the second floor of the mansion and walked across to the west side where Oliver and Elizabeth were housed. Marge had her rooms in the guest suites on the floor above those. They entered Oliver's room. He was seated in his usual chair, neatly groomed, with his hair tied loosely behind his head. He wore a blue velvet suit, which was the style of the time. He looked handsome. The soft classical music that he used to find soothing was playing in the background. Pilot longed to hear him play the piano or one of the fine stringed instruments that his slender fingers used to pick. He remembered the time they shopped together and found an old harpsichord in a private museum. Pilot was thrilled when he was able to convince Oliver to let him buy his friend that precious gift. Pilot claimed that it would be he who would reap most of the benefits by having a talented musician play for him. Pilot treasured those memories.

"How has he been?" Dennis asked as he patted the sick man on the shoulder. He looked into Oliver's dark brown eyes for any sign of recognition. If there was any sparkle of understanding, Dennis failed to see it.

Pilot knelt in front of Oliver, placing his hands on the man's lap. "He's looking more beautiful every day, wouldn't you say?" Pilot replied, looking at his unblemished face.

Dennis nodded and answered, "Yeah, I believe so." He sat in a nearby chair. "Are we going to talk about Frances Lorraine?"

"I suppose," Pilot replied, his light mood dispersing. He rose from his kneeling position with some effort.

"It looks like you've put on a couple of pounds. Are you getting around okay?" Dennis teased. Pilot usually carried 300 pounds easily, looking rather fit. It took a good twenty more pounds for anyone to notice a slight change in girth.

"With Shaun taking more of my daily responsibilities, I don't get to walk around the farm. I guess I need to do something about that. I don't need to carry extra weight at this stage of my life. I'm big enough as it is." Pilot paused. "You slimmed down nicely the last time you were here. It looks like you've porked up."

Dennis frowned. "Yeah, I need to start running again while I'm here. Billy's continued to run while I've been gone. Now he's too fast for me and is running with Julian, or 'Matt,' as he calls him. Billy says he's going to get New Billy to run with me. I should be able to keep up with a nine-year-old. Why does everyone run around here? Aren't there other things to do to keep in shape?"

"We don't have too many gymnasiums around here, so the folks have to make do with what they have. And that's not very much, my friend," Pilot mused.

"Do you still need to divorce Frances Lorraine?" Dennis asked, changing the subject. He was careful to choose his words when the issue of divorce came up.

"If we were Catholic, I would call it an annulment," Pilot countered. "I should never have married her from the beginning. I guess with Louisa dying and Oliver getting so sick at the time, I wasn't in the right frame of mind. I don't believe in divorce. Never have. But I have to do what's best to preserve this family. She poses too much of a threat to us. Evidently, she is back to her old tricks."

"And a few new ones," Dennis replied. He regretted being flippant. "What about this senator?"

"He favors bringing gambling to Louisiana. Not good for sugarcane; at least for the sugarcane farmers. The gossip is making me a laughingstock with the other planters. I have no more clout with them. However, my grandson is gaining status. Shaun has managed to find a few strains of sugarcane that are resistant to the blight that's been killing our sugarcane for the past several years. He's been willing to help the other planters. Maybe there's hope for us yet," Pilot said as he leaned back into his chair.

"I think it's time to lay the final piece of the puzzle," Dennis said with a smirk. "We need to catch her in bed with the senator and take pictures and sell them to the tabloids . . . anonymously of course."

Pilot gasped. "How are we going to do that? And how is that going to help us? I'm humiliated enough without having my wife's naked body smeared all over the press."

"Well, maybe enough of the state's judges will see the pictures in grocery store checkout lines and feel sorry for you. You never know. I'm sure judges have their circles of gossip just like the rest of us," Dennis surmised. He paused. "We need a plan. I'm sure your people can find out when the senator and Frances Lorraine will snuggle next. We'll just be there to take pictures quietly without them knowing it."

"Can't we just hire someone?" Pilot complained. "At my age, I may have trouble climbing ladders and peeking into bedrooms with a camera through windows."

"I'll do the peeking. Besides, you need to throw another jealous rage on the senator's doorstep to attract their attention, thus keeping it away from me," Dennis said, formulating a plan. "If we hire someone, the pictures will just wind up in the wrong hands."

"Whatever you say," Pilot said with a deflated look. "I'm not looking forward to this."

"Come on," Dennis said. "It's almost over. You've been the faithful husband. You've caused enough public scenes to show how hurt you've been by her cheating ways. After this, I'm sure she'll agree to a nice reasonable divorce settlement without taking your family and you to the cleaners."

"I sure hope you're right," Pilot said. He wanted to believe his friend, but he wasn't convinced. What choice did he have? He could not devise a better plan on his own. He didn't have a good feeling inside, but the thought of Frances Lorraine made him feel worse.

Marge was standing outside of Oliver's door listening to the two men talk. She had come from seeing Elizabeth and had left when Julian came to spend some time with his mother. She was ecstatic with what she heard. She was inventing a plan of her own. She went to phone Frances Lorraine.


When Dennis was through visiting Oliver and Pilot, he left the two men alone. He stopped to see Elizabeth next door and found Julian propped up beside her with a photo album.

"Hey," Dennis said as he walked to the foot of the walnut four-poster bed. The foot posts had been removed, so the nurses could have easier access to Elizabeth. Dennis noticed that it was a hospital bed camouflaged in wood. *Clever,* he thought.

Julian's faced lighted up when he saw Dennis. "Hey. It's good to see you. You've gained back your weight."

Dennis frowned. "That's a nice way to greet someone after you haven't seen them in a few months."

Julian laughed. He was proud of himself for coming up with the jibe. "I just said what I thought you would've said if we were in opposite shoes."

Dennis laughed. "Am I that predictable?"

"Come here," Julian beckoned. "I want to show you what I looked like as a little boy. Shaun found this old scrapbook in the attic of the Boston house."

Dennis felt a touch of warmth inside. He had seen plenty of pictures of Julian's family in the years he had known this man. Julian loved photographs. He had albums full of photos of the children and others that he cherished. He went to the head of the bed to humor the blond-haired man. He sat on the other side, leaving Elizabeth between them. "I never thought I'd see the day when we would be in this position."

Julian laughed. "I agree. She has very little to say about it, so I guess it's possible."

"How is she?" Dennis asked. "I mean, is she getting better?"

"Some," Julian chirped. "She's focusing more with her good eye. She's moving her fingers and toes on her good side. Her arms and legs are better as well. The therapist is working with her paralyzed side, but she is in noticeable pain when that side is being worked. It tires her. She sleeps the rest of the day after the workout. They're going to try to help her sit up in a day or two."

"Can she talk at all? Will she ever be able to speak again?" Dennis asked, trying to suppress any kind of hope. He didn't want to make Julian suspicious.

Julian noticed the interest in his mother, but was happy to converse. "She groans at times," he said, looking into her face. "Talking will be a ways off. Nobody really knows how much she'll recover. A lot depends on Elizabeth and how much she wants to get better."

"You seem to be spending a lot of time with her," Dennis said. He was surprised at the amount of attention that Julian was giving her.

"Well, we can't argue when she's like this," Julian said, rolling his eyes. "She's staying still long enough for me to hold a one-way conversation with her. She never cared too much for photos, but I figure she has little else to do. I had an antenna tower put up outside, so I could get some radio stations to catch the financial programs she likes so much. Billy comes by to read to her. Since he likes to read, I figured he could read out loud to her, so that both could enjoy themselves."

"You're being good to her, Julian. I hope she appreciates it," Dennis said. He was moved by his friend's new-found affection for his mother.

"It's kind of nice having a mother around," Julian quipped. "I'm forcing her to get to know the family better. I've started bringing the children in to see her. They get bored with their visits. I'm sure that she gets just as bored." He paused. "It's nice that she has to do what I say for once."

"You know she might make you pay for that remark some day."

Julian changed the subject. "Oh, I almost forgot to tell you. Emily and I took Jesse, Jay, and William to school in Switzerland for the spring term. We ran into Candace in Paris! She promised to keep an eye out for the boys. They still remember her. You know how fond the children and she were of each other before she left Louisiana. Emily was so moved to see her that the two had few words to say to each other our entire visit. We shared some meals together."

"Eh . . . I didn't think Candace and you were all that close when she lived here," Dennis said with discomfort. "I don't know if it's such a good idea to get involved with her again, since she was never nice to you."

"Funny. That's what Emily said," Julian replied. "But she's changed, Dennis. She was so nice and kind to me. She seemed to have a list of compliments for me. You never can have too many friends. Especially since the boys will be so far from home."

Dennis was not happy about Julian's friendship with Candace. Pilot and he were the only ones who knew that Candace killed Robert Lamond several years ago in a mad rage. Originally, she had framed Julian for the murder. Pilot, Emily, and he worked hard to expose her for the killing. In the end, Pilot and Dennis made a deal with Candace to stage the scene as an accidental suicide. Then Candace agreed to leave the States and never return.

Candace was the former governor's wife and a close friend of the Pilot family. Robert found out that she was having a secret affair with Billy and blackmailed her. Fearing the consequences of a young black male taking advantage of a vulnerable older white woman, she covered up the murder by shifting the blame to Julian. He was seen with Lamond just before he was killed. He was the perfect suspect.

Robert was obsessed with Julian. He used Candace's affair with Billy against her, so that she would spy on Julian. Robert was causing the Pilots a lot of pain. Candace loved the Pilots, while she could have cared less about Julian. She was torn between her allegiances. The stress of keeping Billy safe was too much for her. She snapped and in a rage she shot Robert in the chest at close range.

Robert and Julian had made their peace just before he was killed, so she was going to be relieved of her plight. She didn't know of her release, so she pulled the trigger. Robert and Julian were able to unravel their feelings for each other. For various reasons, the two men had suppressed their passion for each other. Until the very end. On the night of the murder, Robert and Julian faced the fact that they were madly in love with each other. Julian felt some responsibility for the man's death and was grieved that their relationship ended when it was just getting started. Now it seemed Candace was back in their lives.

"Be careful of her, Julian," Dennis advised. He expressed a few more pleasantries then left the room.

On the steps of the big kitchen, Shaun was sitting and watching the late afternoon sky. It was an hour until sunset and the western sky was blushing with golden streaks. Dennis took a place next to him. "How are things?" Dennis asked.

Shaun was in a less than favorable mood. "So-so," he responded.

Dennis smiled, looking at the young man's profile. "You wanna tell me about it?"

Shaun frowned. "I just had a telephone conversation with my boyfriend."

"I would think that would have made you happy," Dennis commented. There was caring in his voice.

"It did," Shaun confirmed. "We have issues, but it's no big deal. We can work through them, but it's just so hard to do so far away. He doesn't like it here, so we have to wait and work through our squabbles when I return East."

"Distance makes things tough," Dennis agreed.

"I wish he'd grow up," Shaun fumed. "Why can't he come out here sometimes? I wish he could be more like you. When I needed you, you came."

Dennis crinkled up his nose. "You know, I'm not the best role model. You better save that for your uncle. What are some of your issues?"

"Well," Shaun hedged, "we are both dominant in the bedroom, if you know what I mean. I've learned or acquired a liking for him being inside me, but I still would like to be the aggressive one at times."

"Can't you switch off?" Dennis asked with a confused look.

"He won't do it. He says it hurts him," Shaun replied. "It's not a big enough deal to break us up, but I feel like I'm always the one that has to compromise."

"What does he say when you tell him how you feel?" Dennis asked.

"He says he feels like he is the one who has to compromise," Shaun answered. "He believes I put the farm ahead of our relationship and that it's my first love. He says we are not together enough to work out our sexual problems."

"At least you both know how the other feels," Dennis said, trying to comfort him.

"Like I said, we can work it out. It's just so hard to do far away. I will be in Boston the whole summer finishing up school. We'll have a lot of time together then," Shaun replied with hope.

"That time should be really good for you guys," Dennis said with encouragement.

Shaun looked into his friend's face and said, "We both are looking forward to it. He's a great guy. He's doing the lion's share of the work for Smith Power. The business is as much his as it is mine."

The two men paused for a few moments until Shaun spoke again. "Dennis, what am I going to do about my grandmother? We have all these civil suits against her demanding money."

Dennis made a temple with his hands, resting his elbows on his knees. "I've given it some thought. Julian says that Elizabeth is improving. Tell those stinking hyenas that Elizabeth has taken a turn for the better and is very anxious to talk to them. Express her impatience to meet with them. That should be enough to make them squirm for a while. It sounds like they're counting on the assumption that she will never get better. Let's give them something else to think about."

"They act like they know what's going on in this house," Shaun objected.

"Shaun, you're going to have to do background checks on all the people that come through the big house. It could be a nurse or housekeeper."

"Or it could be that Marge woman," Shaun said with a snort. "I don't trust her."

"Could very well be," Dennis agreed. "Shaun, you have the resources you need. I suggest you use them all."

Julian came through the kitchen door with Dr. Jeffrey Martin.

# – 12 –

Dennis looked down at the ground. It was unusual for the tall man with brown wavy locks to be speechless. He could not force a word to his mouth. He was aware that he was being rude not to acknowledge the slender handsome doctor. With the force of a giant crane, he lifted his head toward his former husband and failed love interest. Julian had that perpetual look of happiness on his face that he wore these days. Jeffrey had a look of light surprise on his round face as he turned to confront Dennis. His short dark cropped brown hair dusted the top of his head. Without looking, Dennis knew the man was adorable. Jeffrey was aware that his mouth hung open and made a conscious effort to close it. Rather than stare at the ground as Dennis had done, he simply stared in awe at the man with the big chest and narrow hips. His eyes bore through the wire-rimmed glasses and settled onto this man's face. Shaun sensed the discomfort of the situation between the two men and made a hasty exit. Julian lingered as Jeffrey departed.

"Jeffrey," Dennis called after him. Still, he could not bring himself to gaze upon his face. Jeffrey couldn't bring himself to reply, so he nodded in Dennis's direction and proceeded to tote his carrying case to his car. Dennis didn't let his gaze trail after him. However, he was aware of the car door as it slammed shut. In a short time, he heard the engine scream down the farm road.

"Do you want to talk about it?" Julian asked as he lowered his body to a sitting position on the steps.

"Not really," Dennis replied as he rocked back and forth with one foot perched on the middle step with the other resting on the ground next to the bottom step.

"You know, I'm usually the last one to figure things out, but I know you well enough to know that the young doctor has hurt you," Julian surmised.

Dennis shrugged.

Julian knew Dennis well. The broad-shouldered man was often more vulnerable to people than he revealed. The flamboyant lawyer cared for the welfare of people, and was often hurt by disappointments. Dennis tended to steamroll over his problems by forcing his emotions to propel him toward the next case rather than think too much about the one lost. However, with personal issues, this was sometimes difficult to do. "Tell me what happened, Dennis. It will make you feel better," Julian said with a gentle tone.

Dennis frowned. "Nothing. That's the problem. When I left last fall, I was sure that there was little chance with Jeffrey. But on the day I was leaving, he was friendly for a change. It makes me crazy to think about it. I don't know what draws me to him, but I don't like it. I had decided he was self-centered and I was tired of his stand-offish personality. I guess he . . . decides when he'll be nice to me. I just don't get it. Why did it have to be when I was set to leave?"

"He must have some caring traits if he's a children's doctor," Julian replied. "Children take a lot of patience to work with. Maybe he's asking for someone to have patience with him. You know, Dennis, with all your high-energy escapades, you still can be a patient man. You have waited a long time for him to come to you to just give up on him."

"I wish I knew what he wants from me." Dennis sighed. "I was convinced it was little, because I was the one who made all the overtures. That last day, he invited me to a social call. I guess I was hoping for something more intimate. Julian, I waited for weeks and months for him. I abided by his wishes when I wanted more from him."

"Can you ask him about these things? Can you tell him about your feelings?" Julian asked.

"In some ways I think that I know him so well without saying any words. I sensed that from the very beginning. They were just feelings without words. I just knew. I believed that if I just waited, he would open up to me. I was looking forward to that day when the ice would crack," Dennis explained. "When I open up to him, he clams up like I frighten him. I'm tired of dealing with him. If things were meant to be, I wouldn't have to try so hard. I'm through trying with him. But he still affects me. Eventually, I'll get over it."

"That's too bad," Julian replied in a somber tone. "You both are such nice guys. But don't count the doctor out. He's a smart man though inexperienced. Don't rule anything out, Dennis. Try to take it as it goes."

"I wish I could say that I felt better." Dennis frowned.

"You will," Julian said, getting to his feet. "I have to say good-bye to my crazy nephew. He's leaving for the summer."

"I'll be sorry to see him go," Dennis replied.

"So will I," Julian said.

Dennis settled down on the back stoop to sulk some more. He had moved because he didn't want to run into anyone else. He thought about going to the old quarters road to the little cottage next to Billy's family to get some privacy. As he got up, Pilot was showing a man out the back door of the big house. He hadn't seen the man come into the house, so he figured he must be a stranger who had entered through the front door.

"I'm sorry for being in the way," Dennis said as he moved from the walkway.

"It's okay," the man replied with a smile and a glint of shyness in his topaz-colored eyes. His teeth were white as pearls in a perfect set and his butterscotch hair was curled tightly to his head. Some brushed the top of his eyebrows. He was dressed neatly in what looked like his best clothes for a special occasion, with pressed tan cotton trousers and a white cotton button-down shirt. Dennis could see that someone had attempted to press and starch the shirt. It didn't reflect poorly on the man, but one could see that he didn't dress up too often. The man was hot! He had a deep and beautiful tan, with rippled muscles defining his body. His shirt clung to his torso for one to see all the tight curves of his body. *I didn't think that there were any gyms nearby,* Dennis thought. *How is he able to maintain a body like that?* The young man held his hand out to Dennis to shake. Dennis felt the urge to suck in his gut to hide the little belly he had acquired over the winter months. He figured that it was hopeless. This man was at least fourteen years his junior. Besides, this was Straightsville, USA. He wasn't going to get any loving in this part of the country. He took the hand in his, and the young man squeezed it in a slow firm shake. "My name is Simon," the young man said in a baritone voice.

If Pilot noticed the chemistry between the two men, he didn't let on. Instead, he decided to make formal introductions.

"Dennis Jensen, this is Simon Potter," Pilot said. "If you'll excuse me, I'll let the two of you get better acquainted, while I get back inside. I'm sure I'll be hearing from you soon, Simon."

Dennis let his hand fall to his side as he stood face to face with this striking young stud. Dennis stood a couple of inches taller and was broader in the shoulders. His own waist was beginning to fill out where this man was trim with the slenderness of youth. Although he had well-developed muscles, the man was by no means bulky. Dennis could see that this man was used to hard work! His hands were heavily calloused like Julian's used to be when he worked in the fields after he first arrived on the plantation many years ago. Yet his abdominal muscles were ripped. He could see them through the threads of the cotton shirt. Dennis was embarrassed as he felt a slight stirring in his loins. *I thought that this only happened to young men. It must have been a long time since I was close to anybody,* he thought. Dennis believed that he would choke if he should utter any words. Still, he was able to get out a few syllables. "I'm pleased to meet you."

Simon continued to grin. "The pleasure is mine. You wanna walk me to my truck?"

"Sure," Dennis replied, still dumbfounded. The two men walked side by side toward a rusted-out pickup truck.

"So are you a part of this farm here or are you just staying on for a while?" Simon asked with ease.

"I'm here for a while anyway," Dennis replied. He was nervous. "Do you always have a grin on your face?" he remarked.

"No. Not usually," Simon replied with a laugh while his grin increased. "Only when I have reason." He opened the driver's side door of his truck. The door complained with a creak. "I need to get some lube for that."

"What brings you out here?" Dennis inquired.

"I came to beg the man Pilot for a loan until after the sugarcane grind, so my farm won't close down," Simon said.

"You're a farmer?" Dennis asked with his brow furrowed. Most of the planters with such responsibility were older than this man. There weren't any new farmers coming into the parish.

"Yep," Simon replied, climbing into his truck. He closed the door and continued through the open window, "Feel free to come by sometime. I'd be glad for the company. Pilot might be obliged if you did it to see about his investment."

"Sure," Dennis replied. He couldn't think what else to say.

Simon waved to the tall man. He nodded good-bye as he started to back out from the drive onto the farm road.

"Wait!" Dennis exclaimed. Simon stopped the truck and stuck his head out the window. "When is a good time for me to come?"

"Well, maybe later this afternoon. The day is shot for too much more work. And I'm already cleaned up and dressed for visitors. Come on over anytime," Simon replied. He continued to back out of the driveway.

Dennis watched the truck go down the farm road. *Could this be a date! Gee. It's been so long since I've had one. When was the last time I had a date? With Jeffrey? Were they really dates with Jeffrey?* He didn't want to think about Jeffrey just then. He thought about going into the big house to shower and shave. He wasn't going to wait too long. However, on a last-minute impulse, he thought about fetching New Billy to go for a run. He needed to lose five pounds in a couple of hours.

Jack was angry. He came into the big house and marched up to Pilot's rooms. He was going to see his daddy right now and he wasn't going to wait. Marge was right behind him, although he wasn't aware of it.

Jack slipped into Pilot's rooms while Marge slipped into Frances Lorraine's unoccupied rooms next door. She was going to listen in on this conversation and she wasn't going to miss a word.

"Daddy, I need to talk to you," Jack said before Pilot could set the receiver down on its cradle. The younger man was a smaller version of his daddy but was by no means a small man. He was brawny with flowing red hair. He didn't keep the style of the other men on the farm, who kept theirs closely cropped to their scalps.

"Sit down, son," Pilot said, trying to soothe his youngest son. He could tell the man was upset.

Jack quieted as he sat in a high-backed chair next to the writing desk where Pilot was sitting. "Now what has you in such a state?" Pilot asked.

"I want to divorce Marge," Jack said in an even tone. "You know that I tried for years to make that marriage work before I made other arrangements. She lives here and I live over at the old Lamond plantation. We've barely spoken in months, if not years."

"Son," Pilot started. He knew he had to be delicate in choosing his words. "You know I sympathize with your situation. You've made tremendous sacrifices through the years to keep your part of the family intact. You know what the family's position is on the subject of divorce. There is no divorce! It's been that way in this family since the beginning when Travis came to the region. Tradition will not allow us to change it now. Besides, you seem happy with your current arrangement. Why change it? Marge is part of this family and always will be."

"What about Frances Lorraine?" Jack said, glaring at his father. "I know about your plan to divorce her. Now, Daddy, I know about traditions and I have stood by them. I can't say I have such strong beliefs in them as you do, but I respect the ones who set them long ago. However, as leader of this family, if you break with tradition and divorce Frances Lorraine, I'm going to divorce Marge and marry Lisa!"

"Lisa!" Pilot hollered. The two men were on their feet. He made every effort to control his voice. "You can't marry a black woman! It will never fly in this parish. Tradition or not, people will never accept a joining of mixed races. It will never be! Think about it, son. You may even have to worry about your safety. People in these parts will never put up with this nonsense!"

"Well, it's not nonsense to me!" Jack exclaimed as he started to leave. "You won't be able to exclude me from the family. I'm sure I have enough votes with my brothers, Emily, and Julian to keep you from disinheriting me." Jack paused to regain his composure. "Now Daddy, the choice is yours. The tradition can stay as it always has been, or if you choose to divorce Frances Lorraine, you can expect another severing of ties between Marge and me."

Pilot buried his face in his hands as Jack left the room. Meanwhile, next door Marge had a sly smile on her face as she hastened toward her rooms.

When Dennis arrived on Simon's farm, he couldn't find the man. There weren't any people around. The farm was much smaller than Pilot's. The house was a modest clapboard structure painted white. The two barns on the farm were in good repair. A few shrubs were planted along the perimeter of the house. In the pasture in front of the house, a few cattle and goats were grazing in the late afternoon sun. In back of the house, a large vegetable garden thrived with a great variety of kitchen favorites. Behind the barns were rows of corn as far as he could see. Where was the sugarcane? Perhaps Simon was in some other field. He wondered if he should leave but figured the drive was too long to go and then come back later. He went to the other side of the house where he had seen some lawn furniture. He considered sitting on a chaise lounge to wait for his new friend. Approaching the lawn furniture, he caught a glimpse of a body doing some pull-ups on a bar supported by two posts planted in the ground. He guessed it was Simon working out under the shade of a tall old tree. Dennis had yet to turn the corner, so he was sure Simon hadn't seen him. He could see the taut body glistening with sweat as Simon was straining to get the last few repetitions completed. He was wearing a pair of jumper shorts with the elastic waistband from his cotton briefs showing above the waistband. His hips were so narrow that the shorts didn't have much to grip to hold around his waist. He wasn't wearing a shirt, so Dennis could see that the heat and workout were conspiring to make this handsome man's skin perspire. The contours in his legs tightened as his arms contracted to pull through each repetition. He wore white socks and a pair of worn tennis shoes. Dennis could see the sweat stream down his breastbone and trickle past his belly button into his shorts. He didn't move. Instead, he stood and watched.

When Simon was through with the pull-ups, he turned his palms to grip the bar in the opposite direction to do a set of chin-ups. After a couple sets, he hit the ground next to a discarded jump rope and did several sets of push-ups. Dennis noticed his muscles were not overly big, but they were ripped . . . and strong.

It seemed that Simon was finished with his exercises or at least was taking a break. He remained seated on the ground with his legs stretched out in front of him, almost facing the direction where Dennis was concealed. He was examining his hands as he rubbed them together. Dennis decided that this was the time to make an appearance.

As Dennis rounded the corner, Simon met his gaze. With a look of recognition he said, "I was wondering who was watching me."

"You could tell?" Dennis asked. He blushed. He squatted in front of Simon so the man wouldn't have to crane his neck to speak.

"No," Simon replied. He whispered, but his baritone voice made a rich and vibrant sound. "Can you tell when someone is watching you?"

"I guess so," Dennis answered with awe. "But it's usually when I'm working on the job. I get paranoid; afraid of getting caught."

Simon shrugged. "I thought it was kind of hot." Then a slow grin escaped him. "More so since I caught you watching me. I haven't performed a workout in front of an audience for a long time." Then he shook his head. "I could feel your eyes covering my body. It was like having sensual hands on every inch of my skin."

"You knew it was me," Dennis asked. He was trying to suppress his enthusiasm.

"No, not really," Simon replied. His eyes flashed with laughter as he sensed Dennis's disappointment. "Come. Let's get a drink of water. I'm thirsty." He bounded from the ground and headed for the house. Dennis could not help but follow.

As they entered the house through the door on the back porch into the kitchen, Dennis could see that a bachelor lived here. There were dishes in the sink and the kitchen table was cluttered. The appliances and kitchen furniture dated back a few years. The dark hardwood floors were distressed, with the polish worn away. The walls had been painted the same pale green as Pilot's old study that Shaun now occupied. Simon threw his sweaty towel on top of the white enamel kitchen table. He offered Dennis a seat on one of the green vinyl chairs with wire backs and went to the sink to search for a couple of clean glasses. Dennis swept the chair clean with his hand before sitting on it. Simon cleared the sink of dishes, dumping them into a nearby bucket. He squirted some dish soap in his palms as he washed a couple of glasses. Then he pulled a pitcher of water from the icebox and poured them both a drink. He set a glass in front of Dennis while taking a gulp of his own.

"Feel free to hang around while I go and change," Simon said, feeling the relief of his thirst. "Unless you want to keep me company while I clean up."

"Sure," Dennis replied. He followed Simon through the house, enjoying the view. He took his time examining Simon from the crown of his head down to his socks and sneakers. The curls of his dark butterscotch hair were pressed to his head from the heat he created during his workout. His back was bare and glistened with sweat. Dennis could see the perspiration bead down the middle of his back. His white workout shorts with the elastic band around his waist draped loosely over his firm buttocks. Dennis held his eyes there longer. Then his gaze continued to fall. Simon's fuzzy legs were chiseled like the rest of his body down to his white bunched-up socks. Dennis felt the pull in his trousers start to move.

He noticed the other rooms of the house were orderly but had a musty smell that gave him the sense that they were not used. When they reached the bedroom, the bed was made and the room had an aura of tidiness, except for a couple of used glasses on the nightstands and a pile of clothes tossed on a nearby chair. The bed stood between two windows along the far wall. The nightstands sat underneath the window sills. The décor was dated. Pale rose-colored cotton material draped the windows with sheer netting covering them. The drapes were bound with tiebacks. The bedroom faced south, which allowed some afternoon sunlight to shine through the windows. Enough light filtered through the sheers to keep someone from sleeping during the day. Dennis dismissed that thought, since Simon most likely rose before first light. The bed was covered with a cream-colored spread thin and worn with use. The same was the case for the tan carpet covering the dark hardwood floors. The dresser stood against the rose-colored wall, painted a shade lighter than the drapes. Dennis noticed a television set and sound system against the wall to the left of the windows. At that corner of the room, a door opened onto an outside balcony. To his right was a pair of straight-backed chairs with clothes thrown across them. Another door opened into the bathroom.

"Did you decorate the place yourself?" Dennis asked.

Simon frowned. He knew the room was far from impressive. "The house has changed little since my parents left," he said, falling into a chair. He motioned for Dennis to have a seat on the bed. "It's enough for me to keep it the same as it was without making many changes. As you can see, I don't have any help to keep the place up." His voice was deep but quiet. Dennis noticed his face showed little expression except when he smiled. Simon appeared to be a serious man who kept his thoughts to himself. However, if prompted, he was easy with his speech.

"Where are they now?" Dennis asked, sitting on the edge of the bed with his hands resting between his thighs.

Simon folded his hands across his belly with his legs stretched out in front of his chair. "They moved to St. Louis. My sister went with them. The farm became too much for Daddy. It wasn't making much money anymore. The Dominican migrant workers' wages had been getting high. It was a lot of work for little pay. They are older now, so they sold most of the land . . . to the Pilots and left the rest for me."

"Why didn't you go with them?" Dennis asked. "You are a young guy to be saddled with the burden of running a farm by yourself."

Simon sighed like a man beyond his years. "I'm a farmer, Dennis. That's what I am. That was what my daddy was before he took the money. Nowadays, he sits on his front porch twiddling with his thumbs with nothing to do. I know it worries Mama to death having him under foot all the time. I need to work. Working the land is what I know."

Dennis nodded.

"What about your folks?" Simon asked.

Dennis looked at his friend, lost in thought. He couldn't imagine being young and stuck on a farm in the middle of Louisiana. He didn't know how old this man was, but he had to be somewhere in his mid-twenties. "My parents live back east in Washington. I see them often . . . at least when I'm home. I've been lucky to have great parents. My mom and dad have always been supportive of the way I've lived my life. I wish everybody could have parents like mine. But like yours, they're getting older. Dad will retire in a couple of years. They travel a lot. I suppose they will do more of it once he stops working."

Dennis caught a look of awe on Simon's face for a moment. "How old are you, Simon?"

"Twenty-five," Simon answered. After a moment he gave a slight grin. "I suppose you're older than me."

"Yes," Dennis answered without revealing more information. He flushed with embarrassment. He didn't make a habit of being attracted to younger guys. He didn't feel drawn to Simon as he did to Jeffrey. Rather he felt pulled to the younger man. It didn't help matters that Simon had a hot body. Dennis decided that the attraction was pure lust and that he wouldn't push himself on Simon. However, something was pulling at him. He sensed a need coming from Simon. He wasn't sure if this need was sexual. Maybe the guy was seeking conversation. He did live here all alone. Maybe he should just leave. What business did he have with such a young guy? He was embarrassed to be attracted to someone who was seventeen years his junior.

Before Dennis could say another word, Simon stood up and moved past the foot of the bed. "I need to get cleaned up. I'll put on some music while I shower." He went to the sound system on the far wall and put a record on a turntable. After a moment, a melody of light jazz began to play. He turned around and gave Dennis a winsome smile as he walked through the door to the bathroom. Since Dennis was facing the doorway, he couldn't help but watch. With little fanfare, Simon drew water from the faucet of the shower and dropped his shorts to his ankles before stepping out of them. He bent over to pick them up and then tossed them into a nearby hamper. With the grace of a lynx, he stepped into the shower, letting the curtain drop behind him.

Dennis felt a chill that sent a shudder down his spine. He sat dumbfounded on the bed. He started to feel nervous. He felt he must look stupid, being a spectator for this man's private showing. But Simon hadn't seemed modest. Normally, Dennis was used to seeing naked men in locker rooms for the different sports he played. At those times, there may have been quick inspections to make sure that everyone else had the same parts that he did. This time he couldn't help but feel aroused.

Simon was quick with his shower. Dennis heard him turn off the faucet and draw the shower curtain to the side. He couldn't see him at this point but he could hear every movement. He imagined the movements as he heard them. The pictures in his mind were powerful. He felt the nervous anticipation of seeing this young man's entire body in the flesh. Simon stepped on the bath mat in full view. He had tan skin except for the white area around his buttocks and the nest of brown pubic hair below his navel. He dried himself with deliberate motions, taking his time with deliberate gestures. Dennis's mouth started to water. He swallowed as he continued to watch. Simon reached for a light-colored terrycloth towel. He clasped it in both hands and started moving it across his skin. He started by toweling his shaggy, curly hair. Dennis was surprised at its length, because most of the curl had fallen since his hair was wet. After he toweled it off, some of the curl returned, shortening its length. He felt Dennis's eyes flash through his body, but he said nothing.

The light over the washbasin reflected the water on Simon's skin, creating a sheen that glistened over its surface. The beads of water took on a bluish tint on his tan skin. Dennis gazed softly upon this muscled Adonis as he continued drying himself. He toweled the contours of his muscles, starting at his shoulders, moving over his pectorals, sinking down to his hard abdominal muscles. Surrounded in a nest of gold pubic hair, his penis lengthened to its natural position as it began to warm. Simon bent at his knees facing Dennis as he moved the towel over his chiseled thighs and calves. Even the man's feet were sexy.

When Simon was through drying himself, he wrapped his towel around his waist, tucking it in at the crest of his pubic area. He glided soundlessly into the room and stood in front of Dennis. "Are you comfortable?" he asked. "Can I get you anything?"

Dennis shook his head, not able to speak.

Simon raised a hand to his ear, trying to remove a tickle he was feeling. "Um, Dennis? Can I ask you something?"

Dennis shot a nervous glance at Simon's face. Seeing a gentle expression, he nodded.

Simon started in a shy voice, "When you were growing up, were you different from the other boys?"

Dennis nodded solemnly. "Yes." He let his gaze fall away from Simon.

"Dennis?"

Dennis nodded to prompt the young man to continue.

"Um . . . you know when you first came here today and I knew you were watching me? I thought it might have been you. . . . It was okay."

Dennis nodded.

"Dennis?"

Dennis looked at the young man's face to give him the attention he desired.

"Um . . . you know when you were watching me dry off just now?" he asked, licking his lips.

Dennis continued to watch his face.

"I . . . I didn't mind," Simon said.

Dennis held his palm out toward Simon. Simon took his hand. Dennis felt the tickle of rough calluses on his own soft hand. He gave it a gentle squeeze as he stood up in front of Simon. The handsome man let Dennis pull him close. Both men started to breathe shallowly as Dennis placed his hands just below Simon's lateral muscles. Feeling the hard flesh, a pang of desire welled up inside of him. He looked into Simon's big brown eyes with genuine awe before touching his mouth to Simon's tender lips. A tingle of electricity went though his body. As the two men pressed close, Simon's towel dropped to the floor. Simon pushed Dennis against the edge of the bed. Dennis had no choice but to fall backward onto the bedspread. Simon was on top of him as the cushion of the mattress absorbed the fall. Simon knew that only men could enjoy such rough play. Dennis let his hands roam over Simon's contoured back. He could feel each hard ridge of muscle. He let his hands slide over the hot man's hard flesh, covering his buttocks. They had more give than the rest of his flesh. They were smooth, without the downy fuzz that covered Simon's legs and forearms.

Simon let a raspy moan escape at Dennis's strong touch. He started to move his pelvis back and forth against Dennis's midsection. Without warning, he ripped the buttons off Dennis's shirt in a desperate effort to remove it. He buried his face in the wiry hair on Dennis's chest and teased it with his teeth. He moved his lips from the breastbone down the furry trail to the small orifice that was his belly button. He felt the quiver in the big man's stomach as he nuzzled him. He loved the soft flesh of Dennis's stomach. He continued to run his lips through the fuzzy patches. He unbuckled Dennis's belt, then stood up beside the bed to pull off the trousers. He could feel his own erection press against his belly. He removed the shoes and socks. Blood rushed through his veins as he saw what he wanted. He climbed on top of Dennis and pinned him in a vulnerable position. He could see by the look in his eyes that his cock needed relief. He straddled the big man's cock and let it glide along the area between his balls and anal orifice. He felt his penis give a jolt when Dennis's manhood rubbed the sensitive area between his bottom cheeks. He bent over to kiss Dennis full on the mouth. Now he was in the mood for roughhousing. He pinned the big man's arms back over his head. He challenged the larger man to take control, but Dennis let him continue. Simon grazed his lips along Dennis's neck and listened as a groan escaped from his lover's lips. Dennis turned his head away and flexed his neck muscles in slight protest. Simon nuzzled his armpits to catch his musky scent. He could no longer hold back his desire. He moved his lips down to Dennis's cock and took his hardness into his mouth. Dennis groaned in ecstasy, arching his back.

Satisfied enough saliva covered Dennis's member, Simon straddled him. He reached behind him with his hand and roughly plunged Dennis's cock inside his bottom. He slowly started to rock so the penis moved roughly in and out of him. He rode Dennis the way he rode one of his horses through an open meadow. He grunted as each thrust hit that sensitive area between his cheeks. He rode that threshold where pain and pleasure kept crossing the line. The bed complained below them while the headboard slammed against the wall. He could feel Dennis give a slight extra thrust and then a gasp escaped. As his lover convulsed inside him, he touched his cock with his hand to draw the foreskin back and he let his own essence squirt in a trail to Dennis's chin. He could feel his insides relax as the convulsions at the base of his folds slowed. When they stopped, he slumped forward to graze his lips over Dennis's mouth. Gingerly, he pulled himself up so Dennis's spent member could leave his body. Although he was in good shape, he moved stiffly to Dennis's side and collapsed next to him. He refrained from speaking until his breath returned to normal.

Dennis spoke first. "I don't think I've ever felt something like that before."

Simon shook his head slowly. "No. I couldn't get enough. We'll have to do it again." He paused for another breath. "But not tonight. I have to get some sleep. It's getting late."

Dennis looked at the clock on the nightstand.

Simon guessed what he was thinking. "Remember, I'm a working man. I have to get up early," he replied, snuggling closer to Dennis. "You're welcome to stay if you want."

"I'd love to," Dennis replied, "but I have to get the truck back to the farm. They'll need it in the morning."

"Do you want to do it again tomorrow?" Simon asked, resting his hand over Dennis's heart.

"Well, it's Sunday tomorrow," Dennis stammered. "Will you be at church?"

Simon shifted his weight to his back. "I don't go to church. I have a respect for God, but not for religion."

"I don't make it a habit of going either," Dennis conceded, "unless I'm on this side of the country. It's kind of expected on the farm to go."

Simon nodded absently. "You don't have to screw me tomorrow, but it would be nice," he teased, running his hand over Dennis's furry chest.

"Tomorrow sounds good," Dennis replied. A feeling began to stir in his loins. He changed the subject to deflect his desire. "Do you work on Sundays?"

Simon gave a yawn before replying. "I have to get up to milk the cow and feed the animals. There's little time to rest on a farm. On the seventh day God did rest, but he still had to take time to feed the animals and milk the cow. Somehow, I don't think they would have done without that day."

As Dennis rose from the bed to get dressed, Simon eased into sleep. When he finished pulling on his clothes, he went to Simon's side of the bed. He bent over and kissed his cheek before he started to leave. Simon opened his eyes. "I'll show you out," he said, sitting up.

Dennis touched his chest and pushed him back toward the mattress. "No need," he said. "You go to sleep. You need your rest if you're going to be ready for me tomorrow."

Without resisting, Simon lay back down, turning over on his stomach, then reached to hug his pillow. After a moment, he drifted off to slumber. Dennis tiptoed through the door.

## 13

"You're up late," Dennis commented as he bounded up the front steps to the porch of the big house. Emily was seated in one of the rocking chairs. It was a pleasant spring night, cool enough for a light sweater. The weather wouldn't be turning hot for another couple of weeks. The crickets were chirping and there wasn't a cloud in the sky. Dennis decided to visit with her for a few minutes. He knew there had to be a lot going on in the big house that was difficult to accept, but she never uttered a word of discontent. One might assume she was an easy pushover, because she never voiced her disapproval. However, she was a strong and powerful woman. She had a way of making people listen to her. She was charming.

"It's Saturday night. It's a night for howling at the moon and causing mischief," she replied with a sparkle in her eye. "I haven't found any trouble, but it's not midnight yet. The moon is bright enough to make things promising."

As Dennis sat down in a rocker next to her, she asked, "So where have you been tonight to come back with the buttons ripped off your shirt?" Ordinarily she wouldn't have made such a comment to anyone, but Dennis was different. She knew she could get away with it and not cause him embarrassment.

"Well, uh . . ." Dennis started to stammer. He didn't have his quick wit functioning tonight. Emily and he liked to banter at times. Knowing he faltered, he frowned without giving a reply.

Emily wouldn't let him go. "Did you and Jeffrey make up?"

A sense of surprise came over him. What would make her ask such a thing? Julian must have said something to her. They had a strange relationship. They were close in an odd sort of way, more like siblings than husband and wife. They kept separate bedrooms, but he could hear them talking and giggling late into the night sometimes before one or the other would pad into his or her room. On more than one occasion he would pass by one of their rooms, and they would be lying side by side with their arms folded around each other with the door open. "No," he replied. He saw no point in hiding what he had been up to tonight. Julian would tell her anyway when he found out what happened. He couldn't keep things from Julian very long. They knew each other too well.

Emily sensed that the subject was a delicate one, so she didn't press him. She kept silent, prompting him to continue.

"This was done by someone else," he replied, pulling the shirt from the front of his body, exposing the tears and missing buttons. "Simon. Do you know him?"

"He's that young farmer to the south of here, isn't he?" Emily replied, trying to place the man. "He keeps to himself. Nobody knows much about him. He stopped coming to the Baptist church years ago, even before Julian and I started going to Adam's church. He was only a boy at that time, but I think his parents continued to go there until they left the parish."

Dennis flushed at the mention of Simon's age. "I guess that's him," he replied with resignation in his voice.

"You don't sound too happy about it," Emily replied with surprise. "Do you want some tea? It's cool out here."

"That would be nice," Dennis agreed.

"I'll go make some," she offered. "Maybe you want to go for a sweater or at least get a clean shirt," she teased.

Dennis gave her a wary glance. "It is cool out here. If someone else comes around, I don't want to have to explain this shirt again."

"Good," Emily replied with a grin, rising from her chair. She was pleased. "I'll enjoy your company while I sit out here."

When they returned to the porch, both were relaxed. Emily enjoyed Dennis's company. They had become friends several years ago when the two of them, along with Pilot, uncovered the murder of Robert Lamond. Robert had been a childhood sweetheart of hers and a close friend of the family. She had almost married him, before settling on Julian to be her husband. She didn't know the final details of the man's death, but Dennis had concluded that it was an accident and would give no more information. She knew that Candace, who was the governor's wife at the time, was involved in Dennis's investigation, because she had helped with uncovering the facts surrounding her mentor's implication. She had to turn her head and look the other way like every good Southern woman who couldn't be bothered with such affairs. Emily had had to turn her head a lot these past few years and she was getting tired of it. At least with Dennis, she could get the truths that she wanted. Maybe it was time for her to take on issues instead of leaving them to others. She was tired of being hurt because of the actions of others that had little to do with her. She had refused to involve herself with other people's problems, because she didn't want to be caught in the middle.

They sat back down in their rockers and she poured the tea. "What's up with Daddy and that rascal wife of his?" she asked.

Dennis raised his brow. He was surprised with her sudden interest. "I didn't think that sort of thing interested you."

"Daddy is getting older. It's time I started keeping a watchful eye on him. I believe the time is coming when Julian and I will head this family. We both know my husband has no interest in that responsibility, as he has his hands full with other things. Shaun is young and even though he wants to be here to see to things, he has his ties in Boston. That leaves my brothers and me. Since I am the only one who lives on the farm and the only one of the siblings that gets along with Daddy, the farm has fallen into my lap."

"You don't seem pleased," Dennis commented. He sipped the tea. "This is good."

"Thank you," she answered. "I'm tired, Dennis. I'm tired of being a woman. It's a thankless job. I work hard to do the work that women have always done on this farm. I see that the farm people are fed. I make sure the vegetables are taken from the gardens and canned so we all will have plenty to eat all year around. I am the leader of the farm women and have been for some time. In turn, I am supposed to be protected and revered by the men on this farm."

"I know you have a great deal of respect here on the farm," Dennis said, wrinkling his forehead with concern. "I think you're the most revered of all men and women around here. You underestimate how powerful your influence is."

"Well, I need to start using it if this is the case," Emily said. Her mood was grim. "I have the sense that this family is coming apart. I can no longer look the other way just because I'm a woman. The men aren't doing their job."

"What are the problems?" Dennis asked. "What can I do to help?"

Emily looked over at him. "Dennis, I am glad you're here. I really am. I think we have been unfair to involve you with so much of our dirty linen. We have a lot of it. I'm afraid you are going to end up hurt by the Pilots. For your own emotional sake, I advise you to go on home. Feel free to visit anytime, but just as a guest. You have no reason to have to fight our battles. I know it isn't just a job for you here. Your feelings for the family are growing deeper and I suspect we are just going to cause you great pain."

Dennis frowned and a very sad look came over his face. "Emily, I don't know how much of a home I have to go back to in Washington. My friends are all getting sick. Some of them are dying."

Emily could see he was very upset and she was concerned. "What is it, Dennis? How can it be just your friends? Are other people back East getting ill?"

"Gay men," Dennis answered. "It started on the West Coast and New York. Now it's worked its way down to Washington."

"Does Julian know?" she asked. "Some of them must have been people he knew."

"I haven't told him yet," Dennis answered. "It's been on the news the last few years. I know he must have some idea. But you know Julian doesn't like to face things that are unpleasant. He feels it doesn't concern him, so he keeps it from his mind. It will eat at him, then one of these days he'll ask about it."

"I'm sorry, Dennis," Emily said as she started to rock lightly. "Are you okay? Is it something you could catch?"

Dennis shook his head. "No. I don't think so. I feel pretty good."

Emily decided to change the subject. "You never said what you thought of this Potter boy. What's got you agitated?"

"You said it. Boy," Dennis frowned. "I feel like a dirty old man."

Emily paused in thought for a few moments. "He has a lot of responsibility for one so young. Kind of like our Shaun."

Dennis scratched his head. "Maybe that's it. He's the same age as Shaun." He paused, then fidgeted. "You know, I think Shaun has a little crush on me. I always thought it was kind of cute. I think of myself as his uncle. Sort of like Julian is. So, I feel I should think of Simon the same way, but I don't. If only he didn't look so young. He looks like he just started shaving."

Emily paused another few moments. "He's not Shaun and you're not his uncle. He's an adult fully able to make his own decisions. If you take away Simon's choices and make his decisions, then you would be treating him like a child." She continued her train of thought. "Maybe you should stay, Dennis. I think everyone around here, including me, sees you as invincible. I think that's what Shaun finds attractive about you. But you're a man; a man who needs to find his way. Maybe some time away from the East will do you good. I just hope we don't destroy you in the process."

"Which brings us back to the point," Dennis said, guiding the conversation. "What can I do to help you? I'm going to stay for a while as long as I'm welcome. If my past comes to play the same refrain, I'm sure I'll wear it thin." He waited for a moment, then looked toward her face. "By the way, are you here by yourself?"

"It seems everybody's out, so I'm with Louis and Candy." Emily sighed, gazing into the night.

"That hardly seems fair," Dennis countered. "Why aren't you out and about? It's Saturday night."

"I'm just getting over a fever that's been bugging me from time to time," Emily answered. "It goes away quickly. I wanted to get some rest."

"Maybe you should go to the doctor," Dennis said.

Emily snorted before replying. "I think it's more like hot flashes, dear. You know; the change of life."

"You're young for that, aren't you?" Dennis said with surprise. He sat back in his rocker to give it some thought.

Emily did not seem concerned. She stretched out her legs and discarded her shoes. "It's different for every woman. It'll be a relief when it's done." She returned to the previous subject. "We need to do something with Frances Lorraine, Marge, Jack, and Shaun. The momentum toward disaster is building. Maybe you could push it to a head before it blows out of control. I'll be the one to help pick up the pieces."

"Shaun?" Dennis said with interest.

"Yes," Emily replied. She moved her arms from her lap to the arms of her chair and continued a steady easy rock. "When he's here, he seems stressed. I thought some of it may have to do with the separation from Carmen, but now I think there is more to it. I have a feeling it has something to do with Julian."

"Julian," Dennis exclaimed, trying to conceal the surprise in his voice. "What does he have to do with it?" *She's a smart lady,* he thought.

"I get the sense that Shaun is worried about him, but then I know how protective they are about each other," Emily said, thinking out loud. "I guess it has to do with the fact that when Shaun first came here, they felt the need to stick together. They're close. I feel that Julian has let Shaun grow up and let him fly from the nest. I don't think that Shaun has done the same. He keeps a close eye on Julian."

Dennis didn't feel at liberty to discuss with Emily that Shaun was being blackmailed to keep Julian's parentage secret. Indeed, the responsibility rested on the young man's shoulders. Like he did with Pilot, he could advise the two. This role was stressful enough. "Maybe it has to do with Adam," Dennis suggested. He felt he was walking on a tightrope. Like Shaun, he didn't know the boundaries or the type of relationship that Julian, Adam, and she had with each other. "Julian and Adam are chummy, and I get the idea that Shaun feels left out at times."

Emily mulled the suggestion over. "Perhaps," she said. Then her mind went back to the original subject. "I'm not sure I approve of Daddy's methods for dealing with that woman. I'll be frank. I more than suspect your influence. Do you really think that dirty tricks are going to get rid of her?"

"I don't know if I'd call them dirty tricks," Dennis said. "But I do admit we're using unorthodox methods. Do you have any suggestions? She will try to strip your family of everything if your daddy decides to divorce her."

"Why do they have to divorce? Why can't she just go away somewhere like Candace did?" Emily asked. "I see a plan unfolding that is devious. Those plans often come out different than hoped."

"I don't know what else to do. Pilot is stubborn and refuses to budge an inch, and she's uncooperative," Dennis answered. "My instincts tell me to do nothing and let things play out no matter how bad they turn out. Pilot wants to win and he's willing to play dirty. He thinks that she started this filthy feud."

Emily took a breath as if she had just locked onto a thought. "Don't underestimate her, Dennis, no matter what you and Daddy do. Underneath those big curls lies a clever woman. To win, you are going to have to find out what she really wants and then make her pay for it."

"What do you mean?" Dennis asked with a confused look. He stopped rocking.

Emily relaxed and then chuckled. "I don't know. I was thinking out loud. I'm sure you'll figure things out." She paused. "Do you want to go for a walk before turning in for the night?"

"Sure," Dennis replied, rising from his chair. "That would be dandy."

## 14

"I thought we'd have a few words before church this morning," Dennis said to Pilot in the kitchen early Sunday morning. Pilot, Emily, and he were the only ones up yet, since the others had been out late. "Maybe we could have some coffee in your study?"

"This is Sunday," Pilot complained. "We don't discuss business."

"Well, this is personal," Dennis countered. "I have a mandate from your daughter. You don't want to cross her, do you? She lets you get away with enough as it is."

"My my," Pilot said, taken aback. "She must have taken you by the ear and given you something to think about."

"Not really," Dennis replied. He filled the carafe full of coffee so he could take it with them to the office on the far corner of the big house. "She has a good deal of charm about her. You could get ten lashes with a wet noodle and not even know it. She gets her point across."

Pilot thought for a moment before rising from the table. "Agreed."

When the two men reached Pilot's posh office, they closed the door behind them and settled into the positions that each had become accustomed to taking with their numerous meetings. Dennis relaxed into an easy chair that didn't go with the rest of the fine décor in the office, and Pilot took his place behind his desk. Each man elected to hold his coffee mug in his hands instead of setting it on the desk or coffee table.

"Let's have the latest update on your wife's comings and goings," Dennis prodded. The subject was not pleasant for Pilot and Dennis knew it. Just the same, he figured that their charade had lasted long enough. Emily was right. It was time for a resolution.

"Nothing has changed much from the last time we talked. She is involved with that ranking state senator," Pilot replied.

"Is she shacking up with him?" Dennis asked.

"My sources tell me she keeps a residence at a hotel but spends a great deal of time at his place. I get the hotel bills, so that information checks out," Pilot explained.

"Any hope that she will be coming home soon?" Dennis asked, taking a slurp of his coffee. It had gotten cool enough to drink.

"I keep after her about coming home, but she seems in no hurry. There are too many incentives to stay away. She is content to spend my money and to keep company with the senator. Do you think I should throw another jealousy scene?" Pilot asked with dread. He wasn't sure those episodes were working to rattle Frances Lorraine.

"Not now," Dennis said, stroking his chin. He was staring into space. "I think we ought to keep the pressure off for a while. Let's let her get comfortable and worry-free. I'm banking she'll tire of the hotel room and move in with the senator. When that happens, we'll make our move. We have to be patient. We have to score on our next hit." He paused a few more moments. "I do think we could help her along with moving from the hotel. You can have your people encourage the cleaning people to make two or three extra stops in her room each day. When she complains, have all the service stopped. Have room service come extra early one morning when she's been out late at night and have her waked up before she is ready to rise. I bet instead of switching hotels, she moves in with the senator. If she moves to another hotel, we'll do the same. Pay those people well and they'll do what you want."

"This latest plan sounds like it will take some time. I may be broke by then if she keeps up her latest spending habits," Pilot mused.

"We have to be patient if we plan to win," Dennis said.


*Later that morning after church.*

Julian, Emily, and the children along with Dennis ventured out onto the church lawn after the service. The children were left to play with the other kids. It would be the only chance for them to play that day, since it was the Sabbath. Adam's rules for church behavior were more relaxed than those of the Southern Baptists, but Pilot's habits were hard to break. When they got back to the farm, it would be a time of rest and quiet. The adults took advantage of the time after church to talk with their friends on a beautiful day. It was cool for the time of year, even though it was late spring.

Dennis couldn't help but catch Jeffrey's eye. The handsome doctor stood staring straight at him from the edge of the church lawn leading to the cemetery. Before he could look away, Jeffrey started toward him.

Jeffrey wanted to shout but managed to keep his voice in check. He knew Dennis would hear him. "Dennis, don't go," he pleaded.

Dennis had turned his back, but froze at the sultry sound of the man's Southern drawl. Jeffrey's accent was not as pronounced as Simon's. Educators at the highest levels try to iron those drawn-out vowels from their students' speech. However, a charming remnant still remained in the sound of Jeffrey's soft and gentle voice. No wonder children found the man comforting. Who could be afraid of someone who spoke with such soothing tones?

Dennis turned to look at the man who stood the same height as he did, but whose body was lithe and slender. The navy blue suit and gold wire-rimmed glasses gave him an air of sophistication. *He is so different from Simon,* he thought. Dennis tried to look comfortable in this situation though he knew he failed. At least he hoped he looked indifferent. As Jeffrey approached, Dennis held out his hand for Jeffrey to shake. "Jeffrey," Dennis greeted him, trying to force a smile.

Jeffrey took his hand, surprised by the formality of this meeting. Jeffrey wasn't interested in exchanging pleasantries. "Dennis, I thought we might get together to iron out our misunderstandings." Before the broad-shouldered man could refuse, he continued. "Are you free this afternoon? I could fix us lunch at my place."

A look of hurt flashed through Dennis's eyes before he could restrain the emotion. He thought briefly. "Do you really care about our misunderstandings or do you want to talk out of a sense of obligation?"

Jeffrey pursed his lips. "I don't know why you are angry with me. And yes, I do care . . . very much. Please say you'll come."

Dennis let out a sigh. "I already have plans for this afternoon. Can we do it some other time? When are you free next?"

Jeffrey thought for a moment. "I have plenty of time Thursday afternoon. Can you come for an early supper?"

Dennis took a moment before nodding. "Okay, I'll come. See you Thursday."

As Dennis moved to depart, Jeffrey called after him, "Oh, Dennis." Dennis turned around to face him. "I look forward to it . . . to Thursday." Dennis gave him a half-smile and continued on his way.

When Dennis arrived home with the rest of the family, they could see Simon leaning against his pickup truck in the lane leading up to the big house. He was waiting. Dennis was embarrassed because of the attention that was directed at him. The faded jeans Simon was wearing hung loose at his waist. He wore a matching denim jacket since it was a cool morning.

Pilot approached the two men as they were about to greet one another.

"I know you don't go to church on Sundays, young man, but we don't discuss business on the Sabbath on this farm. I will let you know of my decision for you buying back your farm in the next day or two."

"That will be just fine, Mr. Pilot," Simon replied. "It's Dennis I've come to fetch."

"I'm going to spend the day with Simon," Dennis said.

Pilot seemed disinterested. "Okay, well, get on with you two boys. I guess I'll see you at supper?" He looked toward Dennis.

Dennis gave the patriarch a frown.

"Well, I guess I'll just see you later," Pilot replied, then walked toward the big house.

"Are you ready?" Simon asked Dennis.

"Yeah. Come on. Let's go," Dennis replied as he climbed into the passenger side. Simon could tell he was uncomfortable, but the young man didn't say anything. The fact that Simon was young still wasn't sitting right with him. Now it seemed that everyone else knew what he was up to with the attractive farmer. Simon didn't seem to care that he was being seen with an older man. Dennis figured this was something that he was going to have to get past. He believed that he should be proud to have a hunk like Simon sitting next to him. He smiled to himself, then placed his hand on Simon's knee.

Simon returned the gesture with a grin of his own as Dennis removed his hand. "Feel better?"

"Yeah," Dennis said, breathing a sigh of relief. "It was just weird that everybody knows my business . . . which is okay. I just need to get over it." He looked over at his friend. "You know, they have all guessed that we're bedfellows. Does it bother you being seen with an old man like me?"

"No," Simon replied. He could care less what anyone thought.

"I guess I'm not too old to learn something," Dennis mused.

Simon turned his head, giving Dennis a knowing look. "You weren't too old in bed yesterday." They didn't speak much the rest of the way to Simon's farm.

Simon put the truck in park when they arrived on the farm. He scooted closer to Dennis. He reached over with his left hand to Dennis's far cheek and moved his face toward his own. He brushed his lips against Dennis's mouth and then gave him a long kiss. "Come on. Let's go," Simon said, bounding out of the truck. He waited for Dennis to get down from the passenger side. When Dennis fell in step with him, Simon reached out his hand and waited for Dennis to take hold of it.

"We're not wasting much time," Dennis said as they made their way up the walk.

"What's the point?" Simon replied. "We have business waiting." He led Dennis up the stairs to his bedroom.

When they reached the chamber, Simon wasted no time. He began to shed his clothing. After they were both stripped, things slowed down. There wasn't a rush like the previous night. They were standing next to the bed by the chairs that now held their discarded clothing. Simon moved close to Dennis and brought his hand to embrace the back of his lover's neck. He pulled his face to his own and gave him a long, powerful kiss. Next, he brought his body closer to Dennis, so that their nipples touched. Dennis led them to the bed and gently pressed his friend onto the bedspread. Now Simon took charge. He straddled Dennis's body as he had done the night before. He rose to his knees and put some spit on Dennis's cock.

Dennis could feel the tight grip around the head of his penis as Simon spread his cheeks and let Dennis ease inside of him. His eager partner sat hard on his cock and he felt the grip move down the shaft of his penis. He closed his eyes and imagined his cock fitted into a tight cocoon wrapped with moist heat sliding back and forth inside this beautiful man. He felt the man's muscles contract with every gyration. It seemed Simon's insides were pulling him further and deeper inside like some powerful vacuum. His powerful bottom muscles never fully relaxed with each stroke. The strength of the pulling motion increased with every buck. Dennis was unable to hold back any longer. He gritted his teeth and spent his load.

As Simon felt Dennis's hot semen surge inside him, he sat hard, then touched his own cock around the tender base of its head. He moaned as white gism spit from his cock onto the fuzzy patch of skin surrounding Dennis's navel. Once Simon was sated, Dennis could feel his muscles relax inside as the contractions started to subside. As the strength left Dennis's cock, Simon lay down beside his lover. He moved close and let his arm drape over the man's expansive chest. He kissed the mound of chest that was nearest to him and spoke for the first time.

"That was the best sport," Simon said. "You were great."

"I didn't do anything except lie on my back," Dennis protested.

"Well, it helps that you have a big hard cock," Simon explained.

Dennis felt self-conscious. "It's not so big."

"It's in proportion to the rest of your body," Simon replied. "You're a big boy."

"Does it feel better the bigger it is?" Dennis asked.

Simon thought before answering. "Different. Maybe not better. I think I like the challenge." He nestled deeper into the hair on Dennis's chest and squeezed his man tighter.

"You didn't seem challenged to me," Dennis responded. "In fact, you didn't seem to have any trouble at all," he said as he reached and squeezed the closest butt cheek.

Simon giggled as he pushed Dennis's hand away. "I think I'm pretty good with my bottom."

Dennis glanced between Simon's thighs. "Your cock is much bigger than mine. Don't you like putting it to use?"

"Not really," Simon replied, contemplating the thought. "Too bad it all goes to waste."

"You don't like to . . . ?" Dennis asked, pumping his hips.

"No," Simon said, shaking his head with his cheek still resting against Dennis's breast. "My skills are best in one area. I choose to do it there and forget the rest."

Dennis thought this over. "I can see your point. You're good at what you do."

Simon continued to play with the fuzz on Dennis's chest. "I need to milk the cow and feed the animals. Do you want to come?"

"Sure," Dennis replied, stroking his head. "I never did get that tour you promised. You do want me to give a good report to Pilot, don't you?"

"Do you think my grades in bed will help?" Simon said as he bounded from the bed. He started to dress.

"You're sure of yourself," Dennis commented, propping himself up on his elbow, his hand cradling his head.

"Not in many things," Simon said. "But I know I'm good with my bottom."

Dennis got up and swung his feet over the side of the bed, sitting up. He frowned. "I should have changed before we left. I guess I was anxious to leave and wanted to hurry to get out from the farm."

"So was I," Simon said with a big grin. However, his motives for wanting to get Dennis off the Pilot farm were different.

Dennis let the comment pass. "Do you have any clothes I can wear? Some *big* clothes?"

Simon pulled on his jeans and thought for a moment. "You can wear my overalls. They are adjustable at the straps and I wear them big." Then he shook his head. "No. They'd still be too small. You're too broad in the chest. I'll see what I can do." He continued to dress and Dennis continued to watch.

Simon got an idea. "Here," he said, throwing Dennis his sweaty running shorts. "Those have an elastic waistband and you can wear one of my T-shirts. I don't have any shoes to fit you."

"I can go without shoes. You don't have any clean shorts?" Dennis said, sniffing the shorts. Then he decided he didn't mind the musky odor. "These'll be fine."

Simon snorted as he watched him sniff the shorts. He threw a clean T-shirt his way. After they finished dressing and drank some water, they headed toward the barn. Simon took Dennis's hand as they walked down the lane from the little frame house. He liked feeling close to Dennis.

"You don't mind if someone sees us like this?" Dennis asked, holding up their joined hands.

"I don't care if you don't," Simon replied without much expression. "I don't think there's anyone around this part of the farm at this time of day, especially on a Sunday. The migrants are resting in their quarters. Besides, this is my farm. I can do what I want."

"You're different than the rest of the people around here," Dennis said. "You seem comfortable with yourself and the way you are. It's refreshing. I miss that about home sometimes, but then again, people know I'm gay. I make no pretenses about it. All the other gay people around here, except for Shaun of course, seem to hide that part of themselves. Even Julian."

"Julian?" Simon asked with a confused look.

Dennis grinned. "You must know about Julian. He was my lover back East years ago. That's what brought me to Louisiana. I followed him here and became close with the Pilots. That's why I come back. I do special projects for Pilot. More as a favor than anything."

Simon opened the barn door and ushered Dennis into the shaded interior. Simon took a pail of wash water and bathed the cow's udder. Then he grabbed the clean bucket he brought from the kitchen and began to set up underneath the cow. She fidgeted, as she was ready to be milked. The young man spoke to the cow to soothe her. "I heard stories about Julian when I was a kid. Everyone did. Then they said he reformed. I gave up hope after that."

"No. He's not reformed," Dennis replied. He didn't know whether to mention Adam's name or not. He didn't see the harm, except that Simon didn't press the issue further.

"Julian's hot," Simon stated as he started working at the cow's udder.

Dennis was amazed at how quickly Simon's hands moved in a steady rhythm. Surely a machine couldn't extract milk much faster. "He's an old guy like me," Dennis exclaimed in disbelief.

"You have to get over being old," Simon replied in a firm voice while he concentrated on his task.

Dennis tried not to feel insulted by being called old. He caught the truth behind Simon's remark. "Well, I guess I'm not that old," he said as he pulled up a bale of hay to sit on near Simon.

Simon didn't reply.

"Why are you attracted to me?" Dennis asked. He felt that he might as well talk about what was bothering him. "A guy with your looks could do much better than me . . . someone younger than me."

"I don't know," Simon replied. He rose from his stool and strained the milk into a five-gallon container to transport it. "We'll take this over to the migrants. I still have some from this morning." He rinsed the bucket out, then gave the cow some fresh water and hay. "I'll be right back. I'm going to put this in the back of the truck," he said, taking the container of milk with him.

Dennis was feeling vulnerable and angry with himself for being so insecure. It was plain that the guy liked him. He wondered if he behaved like a sex star with all his partners. Maybe he couldn't be selective. There couldn't be many choices for him, since he was so isolated here at this farm. Was Simon desperate for male companionship? Could it have been any man that could satisfy his needs? By the time Simon returned, he was despondent.

The two men walked to the other end of the barn. Simon fed and watered the hogs, chickens, and other animals. He noticed Dennis's somber mood. Then he recalled their last conversation. "You know, I don't like boys. I like you. I don't know why I do. I just do." He didn't know what else to say.

"There must be other guys . . . what are they like?" Dennis asked, staring at the ground.

Simon thought for a minute. "Well, I don't get many chances with other guys. When I was a kid, I played with other boys, as boys will do. Later, I just asked some of the boys without girlfriends to come to the farm. Other times, I would notice an older man looking my way. . . . That's about it."

"I see you're not shy," Dennis said, starting to relax. The situation Simon had been in didn't sound attractive, but the man seemed to have taken care of himself. He didn't detect a sense of desperation or starvation for companionship.

"Well, I hit on you pretty good yesterday," Simon smirked. "I thought you were hot."

"Maybe we can work out together some time," Dennis said. "I'd feel better if I did something to take care of myself. I lift weights at home, but didn't see much opportunity for that here. I see you get by with other things. Maybe you can show me."

Simon nodded in agreement. "That would be cool." *It would also be a good excuse to get him over to the farm,* he thought. "Can you stay the night?"

"Sure." Dennis nodded. He was pleased. "How will I get back in the morning? I know you start early here."

"I'll get you into town, so you can catch a truck going to the Pilots'. It will be early," Simon replied.

"Okay," Dennis agreed. He followed after Simon, completing the rest of the chores. They fell into a playful mood with laughing and good-natured teasing.

# – 15 –

*A couple of days later.*

Pilot and Dennis settled into chairs in Pilot's office.

"All it took was a couple of days of overzealous housekeeping and Frances Lorraine checked out of the hotel. She's staying with the senator as his guest until she can make other arrangements," Pilot stated with a satisfied look on his face. "Good job on your part."

"It's not done yet," Dennis warned him. "We've just begun."

"What next?" Pilot asked.

"All we have to do now is get photographs of her with the senator living in their love nest. It would be best if we could get them copulating, but we'll see what we can do. Maybe we'll create a late-night episode to shock them. Then we'll get the photographs to the tabloids, embarrassing both of them, and then Frances Lorraine will be so humiliated that she'll want to give you an agreeable divorce settlement."

"Do you really think this will work?" Pilot asked. "For some reason, I don't feel overly confident."

"Maybe it won't, but we have to start somewhere. It will be one step in the process. We'll just continue to hound her until she gives us what we want."

"When do we move on this?" Pilot asked.

"Tonight," Dennis said.

"So soon?" Pilot replied with surprise.

"Yes," Dennis said with impatience. "Let's get going with this."

The senator's red brick house didn't fit in well with the other houses in the district, an affluent neighborhood in Baton Rouge. It was a colonial that sat at the crest of a knoll with a driveway leading up to it. It was easy to tell the senator wasn't born in Louisiana, but from somewhere up North where houses such as these were commonplace.

"Is this against the law?" Pilot asked as they approached the front porch, with tall white columns supporting the roof.

"No . . . so far," Dennis replied. "We're not trespassing yet. We've just come to call on your wife. What we're about to do may be considered unwelcome."

"Well, it's late," Pilot said. "Do you think they're sleeping?"

"It's two in the morning, so I would guess," Dennis replied. "Where do you think they're sleeping?"

"Let's have a look around," Pilot answered. They started to walk around the yard, examining its perimeter. "My guess is, it's that window over there," Pilot said in a whisper as he pointed. "It's on the second floor and the window is open. It's cool tonight, so air conditioning is not needed. The night is perfect to open a window for fresh air."

"We have to find a way for me take their picture while they're in bed," Dennis said, thinking of a plan. "How am I supposed to get up there?" He looked at the tree standing next to the house. He didn't relish the thought of climbing it to peer inside the bedroom.

"Look over there by the house," Pilot exclaimed, moving underneath the window. "There's a ladder. You can use that."

"I don't know," Dennis said. "What if it falls? It would wake them up. Then we'll be caught and sitting in jail. We'll be the laughingstock of the newspapers."

"It's either that or climb the tree," Pilot said encouragingly. "I'd do it, but my back . . ."

"Don't worry about it," Dennis interrupted. "I'll use the ladder."

The two men positioned the ladder against the house. It was tall enough to rest under the window.

"It appears God may be on our side yet," Pilot whispered.

"We'll see," Dennis grumbled. "I'm the one going up the ladder." He looked from the bottom of the ladder to where the end was set below the window. For some reason, it seemed a long way up. "I guess we should get started. Just please hold the ladder so it doesn't fall. I don't want to break any bones. Do you know what you're supposed to do?"

"Yes. After you get up there, I'm supposed to go to the front door and pound on it demanding to see my wife. They will wake up and be so distracted by my racket that they won't notice you taking pictures."

"Maybe they won't have clothes on. Maybe they'll turn on a light, so I can get a better shot of them sitting up in bed together," Dennis said hopefully. "Okay, here it goes." He started up the ladder. "Hold it steady!" Dennis whispered. He was halfway up and making a lot of noise with each step, as the metal ladder vibrated against the brick side of the house.

Inside the room, a woman's voice asked, "What's that?"

"Huh?" A man's voice answered as he struggled to stay in deep slumber.

"I thought I heard a noise," the woman replied, now wide awake.

Outside, Dennis froze in his position. He was uncomfortable, since the pitch of the ladder had him extended forward, causing him to keep his back in an exaggerated arch. Pilot had left to go to the front door. Somehow, he had to try to get the rest of the way up before Pilot started banging on the door. However, if Frances Lorraine decided to look out the window, their scheme would fail.

"Go on back to sleep. It's probably a cat chasing a squirrel," the man replied. He didn't want to get up out of bed. He was exhausted. The couple had gone through one bottle of champagne too many in celebrating their cohabitation. "Come on back to bed."

"Okay," the woman replied. She lay down and moved closer to the man. She couldn't sleep. She was agitated that something was amiss.

Dennis could feel the ladder shifting. It started to slide sideways to the right. He tried to hold it steady, but all he could do was make more noise. The ladder picked up momentum and sent him crashing to the ground along with it. He couldn't contain a shriek as he hit the ground.

"Now you had to have heard that!" the woman exclaimed, sitting upright in bed.

"Okay, Frances Lorraine. We'll see what it is," the man replied, wiping the sleep from his eyes. He sat up in the bed. His side was closest to the window. He stood and stepped toward it.

They heard a sharp crack coming from downstairs. "Oh my gosh! What's that?" Frances Lorraine asked, moving to the man's side. "I think someone is trying to break into the mansion. They tried the window and now they're trying somewhere downstairs. Do you have a gun?"

"Yes. It's in the drawer of the table next to your side of the bed. Go get it for me," the man ordered.

She fetched him the pistol. "Don't be afraid to shoot," Frances Lorraine said. "I think this person means business." She paused. "Maybe you should check outside the window. What if this person comes back?"

They heard the crack downstairs again. "It's the front door!" the man exclaimed. "He's trying to break in down there. Hurry, we have to stop him before he gets inside. He may be armed."

The crack sounded again. "Frances Lorraine? I know you're in there. Come to the door this instant!"

"Oh no! It's my husband!" Frances Lorraine shrieked. "If you won't use that pistol, I will." She grabbed the gun from him and headed down the steps.

Dennis moved each of his limbs slowly. He was sure that he had broken something. He had to move quickly, but his body couldn't get past the shock. It was like wading through quicksand to get to his feet. He needed to get out of the way before the people upstairs could see him. He pushed that thought aside. He needed to hurry to the front of the house to stop Pilot and get away from this place posthaste. Once he got to his feet, he hurried to the front of the house. When he got to the front steps, there was a surprise waiting for him.

"You're going to face him looking like that?" the senator asked, following Frances Lorraine.

"I'll tell him that I'm your temporary guest until I get resettled," Frances Lorraine replied, huffing and puffing as she scurried through the entrance foyer of the house.

"I think he'll find that hard to believe with that pink see-through negligee I bought you. It isn't covering a trace of your body," the senator said. He was anxious. He had heard of Pilot's gruesome rages, but Frances Lorraine had convinced him that the stories were hearsay and held no merit. She could be convincing. He started to worry about his chances for reelection if Pilot had gotten wind of their affair. He again wondered how he could have been so stupid. "Maybe we should wait, Frances Lorraine," he begged.

"Not a chance!" Frances Lorraine shouted. "This nonsense is going to end once and for all." She grabbed the knob and swung the door open. She was ready for a showdown with her husband and nothing was going to stop her.

When the door opened, a steady flow of flashbulbs went off. Frances Lorraine was so startled that she backed into the senator and threw her arms around him. More bulbs went off.

"Senator, would you care to comment about your ongoing affair with Mrs. Pilot?" a woman asked.

"How long have you been sleeping with Mrs. Pilot?" another asked. "Is she a permanent bedmate?"

Frances Lorraine began to sob. Desperately the senator tore her arms from around his neck and thrust her out toward the mob of reporters. He closed the door, letting it hit her rump. The reporters swarmed around her.

"Let's get out of here!" Dennis shouted to Pilot over the chaos in front of them. They were a few yards behind the reporters and it would be moments before they turned their attention toward Pilot, the beleaguered husband.

"I'm right behind you," Pilot said.

Dennis couldn't decide if he should bring wine or flowers to Jeffrey's house for supper. He thought wine might be safer. Flowers could have a greater significance than he wanted. This was to be a platonic social visit. Jeffrey had some issues he wanted to discuss to clear the air. The doctor didn't seem the type who wanted to keep enemies around, so Dennis chose to make peace. Perhaps they could be friends. Dennis had some misgivings about having any contact with Jeffrey. He had shunned Dennis once too often. Jeffrey had teased him; strung him along to think there could be a chance that the two of them could be close. No, the wine was a better idea.

It was hard to come across a bottle of wine as many parishes in Louisiana are dry. Julian suggested a neighbor might have a bottle, so

Dennis was lucky to find one. He wondered if Jeffrey liked wine. Did it get in the way of his religion?

He knocked on the wooden door with the leaded glass window. It was the cloudy variety that prevented anyone from seeing inside the house.

Jeffrey opened the door. "Hi, right on time. Come on in." He ushered Dennis over the threshold.

Dennis was feeling nervous. Since he had gotten to know Jeffrey better, he could tell he was nervous as well, but he still did a good job hiding it. He came through the door into the living room with the matching sofas. He turned around, still clutching the bottle of wine. "Do you like wine?" he asked, holding it in front of him.

"With supper," Jeffrey replied, taking the bottle. "But I'll open it now if you'd like a glass."

Dennis thought a glass might calm his nerves, but he declined just the same. He wanted to keep a clear mind. "No, I'll wait, thank you. Water will be fine for now."

"I'll open it to let it breathe for a while," Jeffrey said, taking the bottle into the kitchen. He walked under the archway and through the large dining room to the kitchen. Dennis moved toward the fireplace. Light cotton curtains covered the windows. Dennis guessed the archway on the far wall led to the bedrooms and washroom. It was a small house, all on one floor, with the feel of a cottage or gatehouse. It was cozy but plenty big for a man living alone.

Jeffrey came back with a goblet of water and another clear one half filled with wine. "I thought I'd start with a glass," Jeffrey said, sitting on the same couch as Dennis.

He must be nervous, Dennis thought. He attempted to get up to move to the adjacent couch but Jeffrey placed a hand on his shoulder to stop him. Dennis relented and sat back down.

"I'd like us to be comfortable together," Jeffrey said, taking a sip of wine.

"Okay," Dennis replied, taking a gulp from his glass.

"Tell me what you've been doing," Jeffrey said with a look of interest.

"Helping Pilot with his work and a few personal items of his," Dennis answered.

Dealing with Frances Lorraine, Jeffrey guessed. It was known throughout the parish that she didn't spend much time on the Pilot plantation.

"And you?" Dennis asked in return. "You look well."

"Good," Jeffrey said, nodding in agreement. After a pause he said, "I've missed you."

Exasperated, Dennis fell back into the sofa. "Why are you doing this?"

Jeffrey pursed his lips. "I'm trying to figure out what I did wrong. Why are you so angry with me? I was hurt when you took off from here before you left to go back East."

"You were?" Dennis asked with surprise.

"Yes."

"I didn't think that you were warming up to me at the time," Dennis replied, staring into his hands resting on his lap.

"I don't have a lot of experience with close friendships . . . especially those from the heart," Jeffrey confessed. "That is where you've been coming from . . . isn't it?"

Dennis nodded. "Yes. I sensed that I needed to be patient. Then weeks and months went by and you still seemed . . . indifferent. When you invited me to meet your friends, I thought you wanted me to be one of your pals." He admitted, "I didn't want that. I wanted more. I thought you had discarded me."

"No, that's not what I was doing," Jeffrey said.

Dennis was awed by his friend. He seemed to be an emotional guy, but one had to know him to detect the signs. It was obvious that he had become adept at hiding his true feelings. Maybe it had to do with his upbringing or the fact that he was a doctor.

"Tell me what was going on with you at the time," Dennis said.

Jeffrey sighed. He'd come this far. He thought that he might as well be honest about what he was feeling. It wasn't easy. It was new for him. He had spent his life keeping his thoughts to himself. "I'm not experienced. I live here in this house alone. I tend to my patients. I go to church on Sundays. Sometimes on Saturday nights, a group of four gentlemen get together for supper, cards, and drinks."

If Jeffrey were prone to blushing, he would be red. Dennis caught the subtleties that he had missed in the earlier months of their relationship—the minute pauses in speech, the slight pivot of his head, among other things.

Jeffrey looked away from Dennis and toward the far corner of the ceiling. "Of course, I don't know what my preferences are. . . . I have my dreams and fantasies, but that's it. I've never been close to a man."

Dennis was awed but not surprised. What kept this man afraid? "What about when you were a boy? Didn't you ever experiment with the other kids?"

"No," Jeffrey replied, shaking his head and swallowing his emotion. His voice sounded controlled, but he was feeling anything but composed. "I was square as a kid . . . a real nerd. Nobody would share something like that with me. If they would, I doubt I would have been brave enough to do something like that. I would have been afraid of getting caught. I wouldn't have wanted to disappoint my parents."

"Women?" Dennis asked. He found it hard to believe that somebody in his middle thirties had never been in love before or had sexual relations.

"No," Jeffrey answered. "Not even close."

"Well, we have that in common," Dennis remarked with a grin.

"Really?" Jeffrey was curious. He figured that every other man had been with at least one woman.

"How do you know then?" Jeffrey asked. "You haven't even tried. Maybe you would like women."

Dennis shook his head with a frown. "I was confident of what I liked at an early age. I didn't have the pressures to conform like other people had. I have great parents. They've always encouraged me to be the person that I was born to be."

"My parents were great people too," Jeffrey mused. "I never gave them the chance to fully understand me; perhaps because they were so old when I was born. I don't think they had planned to have children. I just happened to come along in their later years. I'm sure they were surprised to be fine parents. I couldn't have asked for better ones. My daddy was in his fifties when I was born. My mama was only a few years behind. That's why I became a doctor. I wanted to be able to take care of them when they became old. But they couldn't wait that long. I lost them while I was in college. I turned my attention toward children, because I believed they were so good to me as a child. They were good role models."

"I believe supper is about ready. Besides, I need a break," Jeffrey said, rising to his feet. He put his hands behind his neck to stretch. Some of the tension in his body had been released. "Are you still mad at me?" he asked in his normal voice and expression. Nothing betrayed the vulnerability he was feeling.

Dennis guessed as much. Standing, he touched his friend's cheek with the fingertips of one hand. "No, I'm not still mad at you. I never was; just confused. I understand better now."

Jeffrey was a good cook. He had gone to a lot of trouble to prepare a first-class meal. "It's just dinner," he said, deflecting Dennis's praise. There were baked carrots in a sweet sauce, corn pudding, a creamed spinach casserole, and crawfish on a bed of small-kernel rice covered with a special tangy sauce. Jeffrey had even cranked his own ice cream for dessert.

"You are talented, Doctor Martin," Dennis said with a flirting look. He liked the doctor. They had a pleasant and easy conversation during supper. They talked about each other's college years. Dennis tried to leave out as much about Julian as possible. He didn't think it would be good to talk about a former love when courting another man. When Julian's name did come up, Jeffrey was interested in what he had to say. Beyond that, Jeffrey was polite enough not to press.

Jeffrey had kept to himself during college and got excellent grades. As he had stated earlier, his ambition had always been to come back to this parish to be a country doctor. His parents had sold their big farm years ago and retired on the present smaller one and lived in the little house Jeffrey now occupied. A few acres satisfied Jeffrey's need for the privacy. Other than the mowers coming to cut the fields, only patients would occasionally come to see him.

The two men cleared the table. Jeffrey washed the dishes while Dennis dried. They chattered about Jeffrey's patients, and Dennis shared his jogging exploits, first with Billy, then New Billy. When they were finished, they faced each other in the kitchen with an awkward silence. Jeffrey dried his hands with a towel while Dennis stood leaning against a countertop opposite him. He steadied himself on his feet then he moved toward Jeffrey. "Can I give you a hug?"

"Okay," Jeffrey whispered.

The doctor looked composed, but as soon as Dennis embraced him, he could feel the tension ringing through the man's wiry body. It was hard, and so was something else that was growing, brushing the side of his thigh. Jeffrey wanted to pull away, but Dennis wouldn't let him. Instead he rubbed his back with the palms of his hands in a soothing motion. The muscles in his back were small but firm. No extra flesh on this man. "Relax," he coaxed Jeffrey. "Let yourself go." Dennis felt some of the tension ease as Jeffrey's breathing deepened. After a few minutes Dennis released him and gave him a kiss on the cheek. He led him to the couch and they sat down together.

"You'll have to teach me," Jeffrey stated between breaths. His voice was gruff.

Dennis reached forward and planted a kiss on his puckered lips. He could almost feel Jeffrey's nerves rattling. "Here," he instructed. "Sit on the floor between my knees." He pushed away the cocktail table to make room.

After Jeffrey complied, Dennis started massaging his shoulders. After some of the muscles relaxed, he ran his hands over Jeffrey's small pectoral muscles. They were firm. He touched the hard nipples through his buttoned-down shirt and undershirt. "It's okay," he said soothingly. But Jeffrey couldn't relax. Dennis figured out that it wasn't fear that had the man wound up but desire. Fear was giving way to lust. He guided Jeffrey back onto the sofa next to him. He brushed his lips over his mouth and Jeffrey gasped. Dennis moved his hand over the bulge that was pushing up Jeffrey's loose dark slacks. The touch elicited a sharp groan and the man's legs went rigid. Dennis ran his tongue along the side of his neck. "I've waited a long time for this," he said.

Jeffrey couldn't move or return any of the gestures. When he did, he felt clumsy. He tried to do what Dennis had said and that was to relax. Whenever he thought he was close to accomplishing that, a jolt surged through him.

After moving his hand over the stiffness in Jeffrey's pants, Dennis deliberately unfastened the big buckle of Jeffrey's belt. Next, he undid the buttons of his shirt and ran his hands beneath the undershirt to fondle the hard nipples. Jeffrey continued to breathe in short, shallow gasps. Dennis reached underneath the cotton briefs and took hold of his stiffened cock. Dennis couldn't recall ever holding such an erect penis. It stood straight at attention and cleaved to Jeffrey's belly. He stroked up and down, drawing short groans from Jeffrey. With a final groan, a stream of white gism spun over the T-shirt covering his chest.

When his breathing returned to normal, Jeffrey was surprised at how relaxed he was. He noticed that his pants were down at his ankles and his genitals were exposed. His penis was still hard, but did not have the throbbing ache that it had earlier. He started to pull on his pants and then stopped. He turned toward Dennis. "I haven't done anything for you."

"We'll take care of that," Dennis replied. Without fanfare, he undid his pants and dropped them below his knees. Next, he undid the buttons of his white cotton shirt.

"I . . . I don't know what to do," Jeffrey stammered.

Dennis took Jeffrey's hand and started to guide it over his own body. His hands were lean and fine like the rest of his body. Dennis lifted the hand and examined it. The complexion was dark, a light coffee color like the rest of his body. He replaced the hand on his chest. He moved it down the fuzzy trail leading to his navel. There he slowed the pace until it reached the arching member that was pressed against his belly. He moved Jeffrey's hand to clasp the shaft of his penis and started moving it up and down at a gentle pace. Dennis let out a groan of relief. He could feel Jeffrey start to guide his hand himself, so he let his hand fall to his side. He closed his eyes to enjoy the sensations that he was feeling. After a short time, he reached for Jeffrey's lips to kiss them. Jeffrey stopped his massage, unsure what to do.

"Keep going," Dennis instructed between breaths. When Jeffrey resumed the movement, Dennis started grazing his lips with his own. As the tension started to mount, Jeffrey instinctively increased the sliding motion until Dennis spent his semen on the front of his belly. Both men lay back on the couch to enjoy the afterglow.

After a short time Jeffrey asked, "Was it okay?"

Dennis turned to him and replied, "I should say so! You can see the evidence." He pointed to the puddle covering his stomach.

"Will you stay the night?" Jeffrey asked with softness in his eyes.

"Well . . . I have the truck outside . . . they're going to need it in the morning," Dennis explained with disappointment.

Jeffrey had a quick response. "I can follow you to the farm. Then I'll tote you back here and bring you to the Pilots in the morning. . . . It will have to be early. . . ."

"Don't worry, I'm used to early these days," Dennis mused. Then he pushed thoughts of Simon from his mind.

They spent the night cuddling and kissing, talking about intimate things, getting to know each other as new lovers. They didn't get much sleep.

## 16

When Jeffrey and Dennis pulled up the lane to the big house, they held a long kiss before saying good-bye. As Dennis trudged toward the big house, he could see Julian sitting on the back porch reading a newspaper and drinking a mug of coffee. He looked up as he saw Dennis approach.

"This is getting to be a regular habit for you," he commented.

"I'm glad you're so interested in my whereabouts," Dennis grumbled. He was beginning to slip into a foul mood as the weight of the world settled onto his shoulders.

"Uh oh," Julian said with a feigned guarded look. "I know that look. We will have to talk about this, but it will have to wait. Frances Lorraine arrived home last night and the big house has been like a tornado ever since. You've missed the excitement. Pilot wants to see you in his office as soon as possible. However, I suggest you go and clean up first."

Dennis shook his head and moved past Julian to enter the big house.

When Dennis entered Pilot's office, the big man stood to address him. For the first time Dennis could remember, the patriarch had not been on the telephone. "We'll have to skip all the pleasantries and get right to the point. Frances Lorraine is home and she's making all sorts of threats."

As if on cue, Frances Lorraine waltzed through the door and let it slam behind her. "And I assure you that they aren't idle threats," she said in a guttural voice as she glared at the two men. She was dressed to the nines as usual, with her dark walnut tresses covering her shoulders. Her long yellow silk dress revealed her most voluptuous assets. She exuded feminine sexuality, which was lost on the two men. She knew this and it only infuriated her more.

Before she could speak further, Marge knocked, then came through the door. "Frances Lorraine, you have a call on the house line. The man said it was urgent."

Frances Lorraine gave a long sigh and smoothed her dress as if to regroup. She gave the two men a half smile and said, "If you two will excuse me for a few moments, I'll be right back." She started to lose some of her regained composure. "I'm not finished with either of you, so you better be here when I return." She stormed through the door and left the three speechless for a few moments.

Dennis gave Pilot a wary look. "Well, at least we were able to get her dander up. Now maybe she'll be willing to leave and give you a reasonable settlement."

"Yes, the plan, as unorthodox as it turned out to be, seems to have accomplished our task. My contacts tell me that picture of her in tears on the senator's doorstep will be plastered all over the tabloids in a special edition. It was a stroke of genius to get the press there, but you really should have told me your plan."

Dennis furrowed his brow. "My idea! I thought it was you who arranged that."

"No . . . I . . .," Pilot started to retort.

"I'd appreciate it if you would talk as if I was here," Marge interrupted. "It was my idea. I arranged for the reporters to be there at the right time."

The two men stared at her in disbelief. "You!" they cried in unison. "Why?" Pilot asked with a puzzled look. "You're supposed to be her friend."

"I've been your spy," Marge confessed. "I've been the one supplying your informants with all of their information."

Dennis had so many questions that he started to blurt them out all at once. "Why have you been acting on your own without consulting first with us? What's your motive to bring her down? You could have really messed things up!"

Marge's face was impassive. At that moment, she reminded Dennis of Elizabeth Steele. "First, if you two knew my plan, you would have found a way to blow my cover. If I was able to track all of your conversations and comings and goings, surely someone else could too. You were far from elusive. There are spies in this house. You must be aware of that."

"Fine," Pilot replied, restraining his emotions. With a gesture he held Dennis at bay. "What stake do you have in bringing Frances Lorraine down?"

"It's simple," Marge replied. "I want to protect the family's interests. I want you to divorce Frances Lorraine, so Jack can divorce me. If she carries away an extravagant settlement, it will mean less for me."

"But if you and Jack divorce, you lose all your voting rights," Pilot remarked. "It defeats your purpose of splitting with him."

"I'm sure we can come to some agreement." Marge remained steadfast. "What I want is simple. I want half of what Jack has. If I ever remarry, I'll relinquish everything to the family. I don't plan to remarry, so that part should be simple. If by some chance I do, it will only be to improve my situation. You see, the family's well-being is in my interests." She moved to a nearby armchair and sat on the edge. "Now," she said, crossing her arms. "Can we work together?"

"I don't see why not," Pilot said, relinquishing his skepticism. "You have proven to be resourceful."

Frances Lorraine breezed through the doorway into Pilot's office. Her face was flushed and a wisp of hair had fallen into her eyes. She removed it from her sight. "Now, where were we?" she asked, looking at Pilot. Once again, her emotions started to rise. She gritted her teeth. "Now you will talk to me! I've had enough of your attempts to dodge me. Now that your boy is here, we can discuss our settlement. I find it a pity that you need him here to back you up, but it's just as well." She gestured toward Dennis. "I have an earful to give him."

Pilot, Dennis, and Frances Lorraine remained standing, while Marge sat away from their line of fire, perched on the end of the armchair. "Now," Frances Lorraine said, gathering momentum. "My offer still stands. I want half of the Pilot holdings. This includes full voting shares equal to yours. I won't accept anything less."

"Forget it," Pilot replied. He felt he held the upper hand. "You've done nothing to help the family business for years. You have only sought to undermine everything we have set out to accomplish. It's almost as if you wished to sabotage our efforts. I wanted to avoid a full-length scandal and I think that's what you've been holding over my head. The family will just have to weather the storm. I'm going to divorce you with what I think is a fair settlement. It will be much more than you deserve."

"Everything you have said may be the truth, but that's not the point," Frances Lorraine countered. "You have been a miserable husband and I've earned every penny I've taken from you." She looked over to Dennis then back to Pilot. "It seems the two of you have been pals for a long time. Robert Lamond was a friend of this family for many years until a screw or two came loose. It's my opinion, as the first lady of this family, that he was treated shabbily. I believe some recourse is needed. You two covered up the murder years ago and I will have no trouble proving it. You will do as I say or I will expose you both and you will rot in prison for the rest of your lives."

Dennis remained silent with difficulty. It was one thing to defend other people's actions and remain indifferent, but it was another thing when it came to oneself. However, Pilot was well versed in these situations. Dennis admired the way he could carry himself, when he must be seething inside. He would let Pilot handle this.

"This is absurd!" Pilot exclaimed with a condescending gesture. "I'm afraid you're grasping at straws, Frances Lorraine. What is this proof?"

"Well, it's Candace herself, darling," she replied, fluttering her eyelids. She was beginning to enjoy making her husband squirm. "She can't wait to come home. She's broke and homesick. I told her I'd make it possible if she cooperated."

"She doesn't have a thing," Pilot bristled. "Lamond's death was an accident. It's on public record."

"Well, I believe Candace," Frances Lorraine pouted, then smiled. "From what I understand, she left in a hurry. Anyone in a rush like that had to be sloppy in covering her tracks. Besides, I heard she was lousy with details. I'm sure she left some footprints along the way. I'm going to investigate." Then she turned to Dennis. "When I get what I need, dear, I'll expect those pictures of Candance and Billy that you have."

The two men kept silent. She had them in a corner. Frances Lorraine moved to leave the office. When she got to the door to open it, she turned and faced Pilot once more. "I'm warning you," she said in a low, guttural voice. "You leave me alone. You have pushed me too far and I intend to make you pay for it. I'm going to make your life even more miserable until I get what I want from you." Then she turned to Marge. "At least I have one friend in this house. Let's go, Marge, and leave the men to plan more plots."

Marge left with Frances Lorraine.

"We've made a mess," Pilot said, falling into his chair. "All of our plans have backfired. Thanks for the help." Pilot ran his hands over his face.

"There were always risks," Dennis retorted. "You were aware of them."

Pilot didn't reply.

There was a knock at the door. "Sir, the governor is here to see you," the maid advised.

"Have him wait in the parlor. I'll be with him shortly. Make sure he's comfortable," Pilot requested. His tone was gentle. No matter what mood he was in or what crisis on the table, he was always respectful to the staff.

When the maid left, Pilot frowned. "The last thing I need is to deal with that sleaze-bucket this morning."

Dennis was thinking. "What's the problem with him?"

"He was governor a few years ago," Pilot explained. "He's Candace's husband. Have you ever met him?"

"No," Dennis answered. "Was he part of our cover-up of the Lamond murder?"

"I don't know," Pilot replied. "It happened so quickly like we instructed Candace to do. She took care of the details."

"What does he want with you?" Dennis asked, sliding into his usual chair.

"He wants to be elected to the United States Senate. He wants my help. He has had so many scandals and shady deals. He doesn't have a chance of winning. I don't know why I waste my time with him."

"I have an idea," Dennis said, with a familiar flicker in his eye. "Why don't you push the governor to win the election? In return, tell him to start spending time with your wife. If he somehow wins the election, maybe Frances Lorraine will dump the family altogether to join him. She won't be able to resist his important parties."

"There's no way he'll win if he's got her by his side," Pilot said with a snort. "She's got just as much baggage as he does. Remember, we just got her plastered all over the tabloids. Besides, once he gets a little attention from her, he'll ditch her when it comes close to election time."

"Well, *she* won't believe that she's a liability. She will think of herself as an asset," Dennis said with growing excitement.

Pilot gave it some thought. "Once she gets her hooks into him, he will be an easy target for blackmail to get what she wants." He paused. "It's a long shot, but it's worth a try. She's already out to destroy us. What else do we have to lose?"


Pilot greeted the former governor in the parlor. "Good morning, Governor. It's good of you to join me this morning. Did the housekeeper get you some coffee? Would you care for something sweet to go with it?"

"No, no," the governor said, smiling. He started to sweat on top of his bald head. He was an older man with a comb over. An expensive suited covered his pear-shaped body. He stood a full head shorter than Pilot.

"Come on, Governor, let's sit down," Pilot said, ushering his caller to the uncomfortable yellow sofa and circle of chairs. "How are things?" He helped himself to a cup of coffee.

"Well, as you know, I'm thinking of making a run for the Senate," the governor said, getting to the point. "I'd like to have your backing."

"Well, Governor, you know that you all but deserted the other sugarcane farmers and me during your last term in office. Unfortunately, your interests turned to casino gambling."

"Yes," the governor agreed. He had been expecting this line of conversation. "I'd like to see it as an oversight rather than desertion. I believed that the casinos would bring our state a lot of easy tax revenue. It's too bad we only managed to get them on the riverboats. It's sad to say that all my resources were . . . temporarily . . . allotted to securing gambling for the state."

Pilot had grown to hate this crooked man. The sugarcane industry had been declining for many years. Instead of helping, his administration levied heavier taxes. He was sure that kickbacks from the gambling people were involved in order for the governor to push for it so hard. "I understand," Pilot said, starting to gather his own agenda. "Things happen to divert our attention. Had you another term in office, I'm sure you would have made amends with us."

The governor nodded with relief. "Thank you for understanding my position."

"Of course," Pilot replied with false sincerity. "But you know, it's going to take a lot of work and arm twisting to get the planters of the parish to back you. I'm sure to have to call in many favors."

"I appreciate anything you can do for me," the governor said happily. Then he added with a serious tone, "But I think it may be a good idea for you to keep a lower profile. You know, make phone calls; no public appearances on my behalf." He sighed. "I want you to know I empathize with your soiled . . . reputation of late. The media can be so cruel. . . . Remember, all the dirt comes out in the wash. Everyone will forget your troubles and think of you as the great man you are. But just the same . . . try to keep your assistance under wraps, if you know what I mean."

Pilot had had enough of this creep. He rose to his feet to end the meeting. He held out his hand for the governor to shake. When the governor took has hand, Pilot looked the man straight in the eye. "By the way, I was wondering if you could do me a small favor."

The smile started to fade from the governor's face. He knew that Pilot's help wouldn't come for free, and when someone said small they always meant big. He offered, "I'll see what I can do."

"It's really nothing," Pilot started. "Really a little thing . . . my wife, Frances Lorraine . . . you know her well?"

"Well . . . not that well," the governor replied, with beads of sweat starting to appear on his head. He was aware of Pilot's jealous rages. He had to admit that Frances Lorraine was a beautiful woman and he had more than once coveted her for his own bed.

"Well . . . I'm sure that it would make her overjoyed if you took her to supper one night . . . soon. She has always been impressed with you," Pilot said in his broadest attempt to flatter.

"Uh . . . I don't know . . ." the governor started before Pilot interrupted.

"I don't know how you could say no," Pilot said, clapping the shorter man on the back. He tried to use his height advantage to intimidate the man. "Whatever happens, you have my blessing."

"I hope I don't sound crass, but you have not been too pleased with men giving attention to your wife," the governor replied hoarsely. "Every man in the state knows to stay away from your wife!"

Pilot bristled. "Oh that. They're lacking in taste and didn't give her the reverence she deserves. You see, I'm a busy man . . . I know everyone is busy, but Frances Lorraine requires a great deal of care. You know, a man of my age has enough trouble getting out of bed in the morning, much less dealing with a vibrant woman. No, I'd rather Frances Lorraine make friends with people I trust . . . people like you. Besides, it's only one little supper. What harm could come of it?"

"I guess one small meal won't hurt," the governor concurred.

"She'll be traveling to Baton Rouge in the next day or so. I'll forward what hotel she'll be staying in once she gets into town. Once she's settled, you can call on her and show her a big night on the town. She'll love it."

## 17

Dennis came out on the front porch of the big house to clear his head of the past few days' activities. As he stood in front of the steps he felt a shiver inside. Looking into the distance, he held his hands in a prayerlike position against his face, thinking of his life the past few days. *Simon, Jeffrey, Pilot, Frances Lorraine . . .*

Julian saw Dennis exit the big house and hastened after him. He opened the screen door and stepped onto the porch. "Dennis, come. Let's sit down."

"Not now, Julian," Dennis pleaded. "I'm really not in the mood to talk."

"Why not just get it over with?" Julian asked. "You know you're going to be miserable until you do."

Dennis nodded and went to a nearby rocker. He sat on its edge with his elbows resting on his knees. Julian sat in the chair next to him. "You've been busy," Julian said, prompting Dennis to start talking.

"Yeah," Dennis mused. He was having trouble getting started.

"So tell me about last night. Did you and Jeffrey make up?"

"Big time," Dennis replied. "It was wonderful. He opened up to me for the first time. He shared all his fears and hopes with me. I don't think he's ever done that with anybody before last night."

"That has to make you happy, doesn't it?" Julian asked. He was looking at Dennis and reading all his cues.

Dennis's attention was elsewhere. He stared off into space, trying to collect his thoughts. After he was able to pull one in, he met Julian's gaze. "Yeah. Things are more complicated than that."

Julian nodded.

Dennis took a deep breath and turned his head toward the noon sun. "I am so weighed down, Julian. I have Pilot's problems to contend with along with some of Shaun's. Now I have a personal life after taking the last several years off. I don't know what to do about Jeffrey and Simon."

"Simon?" Julian replied. "Is he still in the picture?"

"Big time," Dennis answered with a frown. "I have issues surrounding both of them and I don't know what to do. Which one should I choose?"

"Didn't you just start seeing both of them? Why do you have to choose now?" Julian asked. "I mean, you and Jeffrey were casual before last night. At best that was several months ago."

"That's true," Dennis grumbled. "I feel like a slut."

The answer seemed simple to Julian. "Dennis, you just started dating the two of them. It's too early for commitments. For all you know, they could be seeing other people. Whether you tell each of them about the other is your business, not theirs. Do what is comfortable for you."

"Maybe some time to sort out my feelings for both of them would be good before choosing or informing them about each other," Dennis replied, less than convinced. "I just have this nagging feeling that both of them aren't going to like it that I'm less than exclusive with them . . . especially Jeffrey. Simon may be more understanding."

"What are some of your misgivings? What do you like about each of them?" Julian asked, trying to help his former lover. He was also curious.

"Simon is great," Dennis said with pride. "It's so much fun to be with him. He's easy to entertain and it doesn't take a lot to make him happy; definitely low maintenance. He lives a simple life and doesn't ask for much. He's absolutely gorgeous and I could swear that he's a former sex star. He's hot. I've never had sex as intense as it is with him. I don't know if that will last, but I think it will always be good." The jubilant look left his face. "But Julian, I feel like a child molester. He looks so young . . . younger than Shaun. That bothers me."

"Do you think of him as a child?" Julian challenged him.

"No," Dennis replied. "He's all man. Strong as can be. He likes older men. He even thinks you're hot."

"Even?" Julian snickered. "Is that so hard to believe?"

He got Dennis to chuckle and smile. "You know what I mean."

Julian nodded with a look of amusement.

"He also thinks I'm hot," Dennis said with disbelief. "I don't feel hot like I did a few years ago. I used to turn all the heads. Now I only turn a few."

"We all get older, Dennis," Julian replied. "Looks only last a few years. There have to be other things about yourself that give you confidence."

"It's easy for you to say," Dennis laughed. "You're still hot."

"And so are you," Julian shot back. "You just don't understand how you are. If Simon thinks older men are hot, then there must be something you have that younger guys don't have. Did you think of that?"

"No." Dennis shook his head. "I guess not. Simon says I worry too much about being old," Dennis conceded.

"Did he say it like that?" Julian asked, unable to contain his laughter.

"Well . . . yeah, but he didn't mean it in a bad way," Dennis replied in a soft voice.

Julian was doubled over with laughter.

"It's not funny. You're not helping!"

"I'm sorry," Julian replied, regaining his composure. "So you're working on the age thing. That's good. And you're working on not thinking you're a slut. That's also good. What about Jeffrey?"

"Jeffrey needs me . . . I mean really needs me," Dennis replied.

"And you are naturally drawn to people who need rescuing," Julian commented.

"I like helping him," Dennis retorted.

Julian nodded.

"I think he's fallen for me," Dennis said with pride. "It's what I've wanted for a long time. I worked so hard for it. Now I have it. I want to appreciate it."

"You've won the prize," Julian added.

"Yes," Dennis agreed. "I want to enjoy it for a while and see where it goes."

"What's so complicated about that?" Julian asked.

Dennis frowned. "What happens if he gets scared again and shuts me out? I don't want to go through that again. It hurt so much the last time when he rebuffed my overtures."

"That's why you don't put all your eggs in one basket," Julian said. "Date around. It's too soon to be sandbagged with one man." He paused. "But you may have to choose at some point. Keep that in mind."

"You know," Dennis started, "I went years without any love interests and now two pop up at the same time. Isn't it strange how things work out sometimes?"

Julian nodded. He knew about things happening all at once.

*Boston.*

"I got a letter from my sister," Shaun said, peering through his silver-framed glasses while sitting at his writing desk in the library of his Boston mansion. This is where Carmen and he spent most of their time doing schoolwork or business.

"You never mention your sister," Carmen said, coming from behind Shaun. He wrapped his slender arms around his boyfriend. "I forgot you had one. What's her name?"

"Leah," Shaun replied. He took the letter opener from his middle drawer and began to slice the letter open. "When I left St. Louis, she was a little girl. I guess she's grown now or at least getting close." He turned toward Carmen. "You know, I was never close to her. We had a wide age difference. I didn't pay much attention to her. I guess I was just trying to survive. I wonder what it was like for her to grow up with Mom and Papa."

"Maybe you could invite her for a visit," Carmen suggested. "It's a few weeks till the end of summer. She should have time."

"Let's see what's in the letter," Shaun said, turning back toward the desk. He pulled the letter from its envelope.

Dear Brother:

I know we don't know each other, but I must see you. I know it's probably out of the question for you to come to St. Louis, so

I'd like to invite myself to Boston. I understand you have a
friend, so maybe you and he could talk about me visiting. I realize that you most likely don't want to call the house, so please
write to me. Send me a schedule when it will be convenient for
me to come.

Affectionately,
Leah

Shaun reread the letter, then laid it on his desk. He mulled it over until Carmen broke the silence. "What are you going to do?" He moved
behind Shaun to tenderly massage his lover's shoulders, then leaned
forward and planted an affectionate kiss under his ear.

Shaun pursed his lips. "I'll send her a plane ticket, I guess. Is next
week okay with you?"

Shaun sent Carmen to the airport to fetch Leah. When she arrived
at the Boston mansion, some of the help took her two suitcases to the
room where she would be staying. With this accomplished, she was
shown to the library where Shaun was waiting. Carmen made himself
scarce, so brother and sister could have a chance to get acquainted.

Shaun thought it would be silly to embrace his sister, since they
hardly knew each other. Instead, he elected to be formal. "Hi, Leah.
I'm your brother, Shaun," he said, extending his hand.

Leah, like Shaun, was slender and cut from the same mold except
for her small perky breasts. Her hair was styled in braids pinned
neatly behind her head. It was the same dark shade that Elizabeth
pulled back into a bun behind her head. She reminded him of their
grandmother. As they stood together, he noticed she was a couple of
inches shorter than he was. She wore a light cream cashmere dress
with matching pumps and hose. Gold earrings adorned her ears.
Matching bracelets hung from her wrists and rings circled her fingers.
Even her manicure was immaculate, with an off-red polish. To be polite, Shaun smiled warmly to greet her and met her eyes. Her makeup
was exquisite, with her lips matching her nail polish.

"Shaun, you're just like I remember you," Leah said, grasping Shaun's hand.

*This does not look like a little girl,* Shaun thought. *In fact, she looks rather grown up!* A girl of Leah's sixteen years might come across as silly trying to look like a woman before her time. Not Leah. She was dazzling, with an air of extreme sophistication. "You're not at all like I remember you," Shaun retorted. "I can't believe you're so glamorous. Does Albert let you dress like that?"

Leah smiled and laughed. "Papa lets me do anything I want. He always has."

"Come, let me get you something to drink," Shaun said, beckoning his sister to sit on a small cream-colored couch that was a few shades darker than her dress. "What would you like?"

"A glass of white wine would be nice," Leah replied.

He hesitated. He wondered if he should serve her alcohol. He dismissed the thought. He was not her keeper. She could have what she wanted. "Sure. Coming right up." Shaun sent to the pantry for a glass of wine and seltzer water for himself.

They chit-chatted about Leah's airplane flight to Boston until the drinks came. After a couple of sips, Shaun gave her a lead for conversation. "So Leah, tell me about yourself."

Without missing a beat she remarked, "For starters, I'm a lesbian."

"Well, that cuts right to the point," Shaun said with a snort. He was surprised.

"I see no point in wasting time," Leah retorted.

"You don't look like a lesbian."

"It's true. I pass."

"I'm surprised you know this so young," Shaun said. He was proud of his sister. "Especially for a woman."

"I'm more like you than you realize," Leah responded. "We look alike—except I'm prettier—and we've known about ourselves all of our lives." Then she remarked, "Have you always been so black and white? You seem to categorize people in neat little columns. There are many shades of lesbian like there are many differences between every woman. That's what makes us so interesting." She took another sip of her wine.

"I've been accused of that more than once," Shaun agreed. "Maybe sometime I'll change."

"What does your boyfriend think?" She laughed.

"He's the same way," he quipped, matching her grin. "Except he has his ideas and I have mine. It makes for an interesting relationship."

"I'll enjoy getting to know you both," Leah said, draining her glass. She set it on the table.

"What does Papa make of your nature?" Shaun asked. "I doubt he's pleased."

"I'm not foolish enough to tell him," Leah replied, crossing one leg over the other. "I've never had a girlfriend, so there's not much reason for him to suspect anything. The fact I haven't had any boyfriends hasn't displeased him. I'm sure he'd rather I wait for that."

"So you're not out."

"I'm out to myself," Leah replied with an edge. "That's what's important for me now. The rest will come later. I'm not foolish enough to come out to Papa and Mother at this stage. They adore me. I've had the perfect childhood."

"He never beat you?" Shaun asked with a look of shock.

"Neither of our parents ever laid a hand on me," Leah said. "They were members of the PTA and I was a Brownie when I was seven years old. We were the perfect family."

"I guess things got a lot better after I left." Shaun frowned.

"Things got better for you too," Leah pointed out.

"Yes. If Albert ever did anything good for me, it was sending me to Uncle Julian," Shaun agreed.

"I look forward to meeting him," Leah said sincerely. She fidgeted for a second with her nail polish before looking at Shaun. The gesture seemed rehearsed. She regained her focus. "Shaun, one of the reasons I am here is to ask a favor of you."

"Yes," Shaun replied with ease. He was warming to his sister. He guessed at some point it would be hard to refuse her anything.

"I hope at some time you will make up with Papa," Leah said in a controlled voice. She wanted to keep from blurting her request.

Shaun started to feel uncomfortable. He stood up from the adjacent couch and walked across the room to the fireplace. He stared at the spines of some books filling the bookcases on each side of the mantle. He couldn't face her. "That's not possible," Shaun said in a gruff voice. "We've severed our ties. I'm no longer his son and he's no longer my papa."

"Shaun, he wants to make amends," Leah pleaded.

"Leah," Shaun replied in a higher voice, "he disowned me. Can you imagine as a teenager what it was like to have your parents give you away for adoption? I didn't know Uncle Julian when I went to him. He was a stranger. I was brave, because my anger pushed me. Other than that, I was devastated. I knew he had always hated me, but there was always a glimmer of hope that he didn't until he sent me away."

"You didn't make things easy for him, Shaun."

"I wasn't supposed to. I was a child. A child who needed unconditional love," Shaun said, staring at the floor. He didn't like reliving his old pain. "Look, can we talk about something else? You just got here. Let's not start off on the wrong foot."

"Okay," Leah relented. "Just think about it, Shaun. It may be good for both of you to work out your differences."

Shaun nodded. "I will, Leah. But for now the answer is no."

"I have another request for you, Shaun," Leah said, changing the subject. "When I finish with school, I want to work for you and Carmen."

"You just come out with all of it," Shaun said with amazement. "But I don't see any reason why not. You are my sister. I think our great-grandmother would have liked you coming aboard."

"I know I hit you with this all at once, Shaun," Leah conceded. "I wanted to get it all out of the way, so we could enjoy the rest of my visit. I look forward to getting better acquainted with you and Carmen."

## 18

*Summer's end.*

Shaun walked along the farm road approaching the big house. He was coming back from looking over the farm to see the state of things since he was last home.

Soon Carmen would be arriving from Boston. They had their difficulties, but even with the shortest of separations Shaun was always excited about their reunions.

Shaun saw Julian sitting on the top step of the front porch next to Adam. He was pleased with his uncle. For some time, he sensed a relaxation about him that he guessed had to do with Adam. He wanted to be a bigger part of their lives, but was resigned to the fact that this wasn't going to happen for a while. He hoped that he would regain a close friendship with his uncle, so they could share each other's secrets.

Something inside Shaun told him to wait. He watched as Adam rose and gave his uncle's shoulder an affectionate squeeze as he left Uncle Julian to go home.

A short moment later, he saw Aunt Emily come and sit beside Uncle Julian. They exchanged a few words, and that familiar stressed look came across his face. His jaw tensed and remained fixed. After a few minutes, she rose from her seat and gave Uncle Julian a similar squeeze to his shoulder.

Shaun hastened to the front porch. Uncle Julian didn't spend as much time on the cans by the fence as he used to, but Shaun figured that was where he would be headed.

He sat next to his uncle on the porch as if trying not to disturb him. "How are things?" he asked.

"Good," Julian said, nodding. He turned toward Shaun. "It looks like you're going to have another cousin."

"What?" Shaun replied. He couldn't believe it. "How is that possible?"

Julian snorted. "You got me. Things like that happen."

"Er . . . how do you think Adam will feel about this?"

Julian let out a sigh and pursed his lips. "Adam will be fine. There's no need for concern."

"You know, you can still leave whenever you want," Shaun said. "Things are different around here now. You'd get to see the kid whenever you wanted."

"I know," Julian said with a forlorn look. "I guess I've been feeling that way for a while. I could go anytime, seeing that the three oldest children have opted for boarding school. The other two are not far behind. You know very well I can't go. I've been happier these past few years than I have ever been in my life. I have everything here that I could possibly want. I guess for the first time I felt I could do anything I wanted to do."

"It bothers you that the children are leaving at such a young age. I know it hurts you," Shaun said.

"Oh, they love their mama and daddy, but I understand their desire to get off the farm. It's easy to get cabin fever, especially since there is a big beautiful world out there to see. They needed to go. It's just the time I had with them has gone by so quickly. I didn't expect them to leave the nest so soon."

"You can still go," Shaun said again.

"No, I can't," Julian said. "I love my life here. Besides, I know for some reason inside that this child will be special."

"How did this happen, Uncle Julian?" Shaun pressed. "I didn't think you and Aunt Emily were that close anymore."

"Your Aunt Emily has been going through a rough time, Shaun," Julian explained, relaxing into his seat. "It's true we're more like siblings than husband and wife. But we are familiar with each other. Sometimes we need each other and we fall into old habits. Sometimes years go by," he mused. "We thought she was going through the change of life . . . obviously not. She hasn't been regular in her monthly cycles for some time now. Months go by."

"Isn't she young for that? She's just forty-two . . . not much younger than you." Shaun was puzzled.

"I don't know about those things, Shaun. I just go by what she says. She gets a fever from time to time, then she gets better for a while," Julian explained. "On top of that, it's been really hard on her to have the children leave. We were in Europe. She was ill and we were both upset at saying good-bye to the boys for summer camp before school started. I guess that brought us together. We were able to give each other some comfort."

Shaun had a thought. "It could be the same illness that made her mother sick. Maybe you should have her check with the doctor. Change of life or not, a visit wouldn't be a bad idea."

"You could be right," Julian said resignedly. His spirits were low. The poor baby. Neither of his parents were excited that he was going to be born. "I'll talk to her about the doctor."

Shaun got up to leave. "Don't wait too long. And don't brood too long."

"I won't," Julian replied, then added, "Billy and I are supposed to run in a few minutes. After that, I think we'll have supper with his folks."

After Shaun had left, Julian sat for a few more minutes.

## 19

"We need to meet," the voice said at the other end of the extension.

"No we don't," Shaun retorted. He was sitting at his desk in his office in the big house. "We've concluded our business. You've tried my patience to its limit. There's no more money!"

The man sighed. "Must we go through this every time? We'll meet at the same place. Tomorrow at eight."

"You forget things wind up early in these parts," Shaun growled. "It will have to be four o'clock."

"Very well then," the voice replied. "Don't be late."

Shaun slammed the phone on its receiver as Julian walked into his office.

"Having a bad day?" Julian asked.

"No, no," Shaun replied, gaining control of his anger.

"Do you want to tell me about it? You seem upset." Julian took a seat at the edge of Shaun's desk. He looked into his nephew's face.

Shaun averted his gaze, then took a deep breath before finding his composure. He smiled at his uncle. "It's nothing I can't handle," he replied. "You know farm business. You go through the same things."

"That I know," Julian agreed. He moved over to the sofa the color of lime peels and dropped into it. "I just wanted to tell you that your aunt is doing well. It is as you guessed. She has an infection like the one her mother had that took her life. It seems to be a resilient strain."

"Is she going to be okay?" Shaun asked. He moved into an easy chair opposite his uncle.

Julian nodded. "The doctor said we caught it early and he said the baby will be fine. The downside is that your aunt has to stay off her feet for the next five or six months. She's not too happy about that."

"It sure is better than the alternative," Shaun muttered.

"She's drained and I'm sure the pregnancy won't help in getting her strength back," Julian said earnestly. "Maybe you could spend some time with her?"

"Sure." Shaun nodded. "I'll make sure I find time for her every day."

"How's Carmen?" Julian asked, changing the subject.

Shaun frowned. "We're not doing so hot right now. He hates it here. We did so well together this summer. I thought we had turned the corner."

Julian rose from his sitting position and laid a paternal hand on his nephew's shoulder. "Maybe you ought to think about spending more time in Boston and less here on the farm," he said. "Your life there is more important than the one here. You're old enough now to jump the nest. You and I will always be close at heart if not by distance."

Shaun hung his head between his knees, then turned to face his uncle. "It's not that simple, Uncle Julian. There are things here that need my attention. Grandpapa is tied up so much with his personal life. You are stretched to your limits with your work and life here. I can't just leave when I'm needed."

Julian sighed. "I know how it is to feel loyal to this family. Still, you have options and choices. You need to take care of yourself, Shaun."

"I will, Uncle Julian, I will," Shaun replied.


"You're late, Calvin," Shaun growled.

Calvin slid into the booth on his side of the table in Lou's Diner, the pair's regular meeting place. The table was the same one as always and the waitress knew better than to disturb the two men. Neither was there to eat or drink. However, Shaun would leave a generous tip. "I'm here to do you a favor."

"Nonsense," Shaun said, gritting his teeth. "Listen here, you moron. I'm the one calling the shots now." He leaned forward and said in a deep, forceful, but hushed voice. "Mrs. Steele wasn't happy with your recent activity regarding her son's interests. She says . . ."

"What do you mean, she says?" Calvin said, turning a shade paler. "I know for a fact she is still incapacitated."

"Well," Shaun said, starting to toy with his fork. He sensed the man's unease. "You can see for yourself. She's dying to converse with you face to face. Naturally, I wanted to spare her the ordeal of meeting with scum like you, since she's still in a fragile state, but you leave me no choice. Come to think of it, she will rather enjoy eating you alive. Maybe it will aid in her recovery," Shaun mused. "Yes. I think it will. When can we arrange the meeting?"

Calvin was white in the face by this time. "My source has been telling me that she is . . ."

"Now, Calvin," Shaun said in a condescending tone, "you know the people you are paying to spy for you are just telling you what you want to hear. That way, you will continue to pump money to them. They're playing you like a harp, you fool! All you had to do was keep the money you extorted from us and stay away. But no, your greed wouldn't let you. Now it will be your complete demise."

"Please tell me that Mrs. Steele isn't well," Calvin pleaded. "If she is, then it's too late."

"Too late?" Shaun asked with a puzzled look. "What are you talking about?"

"That's why I called this meeting. I needed to warn you. I was hoping that this would be my way out of the matter," Calvin said.

"What are you blubbering about?" Shaun asked. The confidence he had gained was beginning to fade.

"I was forced to sell this information to another party. This person was my source that was telling me that Mrs. Steele was still indeed ill. I was willing to give you back some of the money so that you would keep Mrs. Steele at bay and quiet. I know it was a feeble attempt, but I had to do something. If Mrs. Steele is talking, then it's too late for me . . . I'm afraid it's too late for all of us. I'm sure the buyer is planning to use the purchased information to devastate your uncle."

"Well, it's never too late," Shaun quipped with false security. "Who is this buyer?'

Calvin took a gulp of air. "Frances Lorraine Pilot."

"What do you mean you have to leave for a while?" Jeffrey bellowed.

He was walking along the country road with Dennis after church one Sunday. The air still held humidity despite getting into the fall. A breeze would hit from time to time to relieve the perspiration underneath their Sunday outfits.

Dennis frowned. He guessed that Jeffrey wasn't going to be happy about his departure, but he hadn't guessed how bad his boyfriend's reaction was going to be. His other boyfriend was much easier to placate. Simon's only words were that he would be good and randy upon Dennis's return. "It will only be a few months. I have to help out a friend. He needs me in a bad way. He'll be locked up in jail with a lot of bad men if I don't help him. I'll be back before you know it."

Jeffrey had already been irritated with Dennis before this conversation. Their time was Saturday afternoons and nights. He liked to have Sundays to himself after church. After all, it was the Sabbath. "You always have to come to someone's rescue, Dennis. Why do you feel the need to do it?" He continued without waiting for an answer, "What about the Pilots? Don't they still need you? I thought you were working for them."

Dennis figured that Jeffrey was irritated about giving up his Sunday afternoon. He wanted to break the news to Simon first, because he guessed that his farmer friend would accept the news with grace. Simon believed that his friend had important business and needed to be away at times. "I've finished all my work for the man Pilot," Dennis retorted. "We are waiting to see the next move Frances Lorraine makes. It appears she's teamed up with the former governor for the moment, so I haven't had much to do."

"Dennis, you can't go gallivanting back East when you get bored, when you have a life here," Jeffrey argued.

"Jeffrey, all I'm doing is helping a dear friend. He begged me for help. I couldn't refuse him," Dennis pleaded.

Jeffrey didn't say anything for a few minutes, as he was lost in thought. Dennis walked by his side, hoping the situation would be over soon. He had hoped for a few moments of discomfort over the news and then a nice afternoon spent at Jeffrey's house.

"I guess this is it then," Jeffrey said with conviction.

Dennis could now see that Jeffrey had worked himself into a bout of internal hysteria. He was hard to reason with when he was in this state. "Jeffrey, please don't . . ." Dennis begged.

Jeffrey shook his head, trying to suppress tears. "You won't be coming back! I know it!"

Dennis tried putting his arm around Jeffrey to console him, but nothing could accomplish that.

"How could you leave for months and just expect me to be waiting for you upon your return . . . if you even decide to come back? How dare you take me for granted like that! I'm not just some toy you can take out from under the bed when you feel like playing with it! I am a man with feelings and needs that happens to be in a relationship with you. You're not being fair to me," Jeffrey said.

Dennis was thankful that they were far enough down the country road away from the church not to be within earshot of others. "Well, why don't you come with me then?" Dennis offered. "At least for some of the time. I don't think it's fair that I should have to give up my life back East for the sake of this relationship. Why should I be the one who has to make that sacrifice and stay here?"

"You know I can't leave my practice here," Jeffrey retorted, amazed. "There would be no other competent doctor to take over for me. The children in this parish need me."

"Well, my friend needs me," Dennis argued. He was able to remain calm throughout the debate. If he were as passionate as Jeffrey, the argument would have spun out of control.

"Fine. You go. I trust that you know I won't be waiting if you decide to come back!" With that, Jeffrey stormed off toward his car. Dennis frowned. At least he wouldn't have to decide which boyfriend to keep.

## 20

*A few months later.*

It was late January, a month before the sugarcane stalks were to go into the ground for the spring planting. Shaun was sitting on the stoop of the front porch of the big house. He had gone to Boston soon after the Christmas holidays and had only now returned to Louisiana. It was difficult to get Carmen to come to the delta region; however, he had agreed to spend the holiday season with Shaun and his family this past year. But, it was impossible to get Carmen to make another trip with him.

Maybe because Carmen wasn't with him, Shaun felt a continuing rift between Uncle Julian and himself. *Could I be just imagining it?* Shaun wondered. *Maybe it's because Uncle Julian has a boyfriend that he has less time for me. If I only knew for certain that Adam and he were involved.*

At that moment, Julian came bounding out the front door. When he saw Shaun, he settled on the top step next to him. "Here you are. I've been looking for you," Julian said with a broad grin.

Shaun nodded to his uncle, acknowledging his presence. It felt good that Uncle Julian had sought him out.

"I know you just got here and all, but Adam and I have decided to take a trip. We're leaving in a few days and will be gone for a couple of weeks. The time seems right, as Adam has a break in his schedule and Emily is not due for another month. We'll all be busy when the baby comes," Julian said.

"Where will you be going?" Shaun asked.

"We're going on a riverboat cruise," Julian replied. "We'll be making stops along the way to visit towns for a couple days at a time."

"Are you sure it's okay to leave Aunt Emily at a time like this?" Shaun asked. "I mean, she was sick and now her time is near."

Julian fidgeted for a moment before answering. "Actually, she asked to come with us. She's up and about now and strong as a four-year-old filly. So it will be the three of us."

"Won't that be awkward?" Shaun asked. "How can you bring your wife?"

"Well, she wants to come," Julian said. "I don't see why she shouldn't if she feels up to it. It will be her last chance for peace and quiet for a while."

"Well, why can't I come?" Shaun countered. "If she's not in the way, I shouldn't be either."

Julian stroked his chin for a moment before replying. He nodded a couple of times. "Sure. Why not?" He rose to his feet to go back inside the house. "We leave Saturday."


"Are you sure you should be going?" Shaun asked Emily as they walked from the big house to the lane where the station wagon was sitting. Shaun thought Emily looked weary, and he felt concerned for her.

"Yes." She nodded as she handed Shaun her bag. "I'm tired of being tied up in that house. I've been in bed for the last six months. Now the doctor's declared me fit, so I want to get out. I don't intend on venturing out with you boys. I'll just stay on the boat and enjoy the water."

When the foursome arrived at the dock where the riverboat was berthed, they parked the car in the designated lot. Julian asked Shaun to fetch a cart to ferry their belongings to the boat, then asked whether Emily could make it to the boat okay.

"I didn't come for you to worry over me. This is Adam's and your vacation. I'm just along for the ride. If I need anything, I'll get Shaun to tend to me," Emily said.

Julian chuckled. "Okay, now you're on your own."

Emily smiled in approval.

As they approached the boat, they were able to see what they would be cruising aboard for the next several days. The boat glistened white from bow to stern with three decks. Each deck was outlined by a white-painted railing. On top of the boat above the upper deck, the pilot house framed a majestic pair of smokestacks emitting trails of languid steam into the still air. At the stern of the watercraft the wooden paddlewheels churned, loafing until they were powered up to propel the craft upstream against the current.

They got their cabin assignments and were welcomed onboard. Shaun had a key to his cabin, where he would be quartered alone. Emily had her own cabin, while Adam and Julian shared quarters.

By the time all were settled, the afternoon had worn on toward tea-time. After a couple glasses of iced tea, the foursome had supper together, then retired to their cabins. They were used to going to bed early.

With the differences in time zones between Louisiana and the East Coast, coupled with the differences in Boston bedtimes, Shaun slept later than the rest.

"Where are Uncle Julian and Adam?" Shaun asked as he met Emily out on the promenade deck the next morning.

"The two of them got up early and went exploring off the boat for a couple of days. They'll catch up on the river," Emily answered.

"How could they do that?"

"Oh, they'll be all right," Emily assured him. "They're big boys."

Shaun sat down next to her. The waitress inquired what he would like for breakfast. After Shaun gave his order he finished his thoughts. "I wanted the chance to spend some time with him . . . with Uncle Julian, I mean. I feel like I've lost him. I've felt this way for a long time."

"Now, Shaun, you know that's not true," Emily disagreed. Other women might have patted his hand next to hers, but Emily was not one to offer affection. Julian was the same way.

"It must be more difficult for you," Shaun said, offering a lead. He had never held back what he thought. "I mean being together with those two guys. How come you wanted to take this trip?"

"I told you. I was tired of being nailed to that house and farm. I've always wanted to take a riverboat cruise. Julian and I were supposed to take one on our honeymoon, but a terrible flood forced us to cancel our plans," Emily said.

"But he's taking it with someone else instead," Shaun blurted out. "Doesn't it make you uncomfortable to be with him when he wants to be with someone else?"

"No," Emily replied. "Julian and I have taken plenty of trips together. Now he wants to go with his best friend. They want to spend some time alone together."

"I think they may be more than just best friends," Shaun snorted. "How can you just look the other way?"

Emily was starting to get irritated. "Shaun, I don't think it's questions about my feelings that are distressing you. So if we're to continue this conversation, I suggest you get to the point and tell me what's bothering you."

Shaun's food came. After picking at it for a few moments, he answered, "I just don't want to hurt your feelings."

Emily took a taste of her coffee and stared out onto the water. The riverboat was making a slow churn up the river. It would be stopping at port shortly for those passengers who wanted to go ashore. "Your Uncle Julian and I are more like siblings than husband and wife. There is little that one does without the other knowing about it."

"How do you explain that?" Shaun asked, pointing to Emily's swollen tummy.

"Some things are personal, Shaun," Emily replied. "I'm not used to someone asking such questions."

"You told me to tell you what's been bothering me so much," Shaun retorted. "I'm doing my best. It's hard to say it all in one sentence."

"Yes, I did tell you that," Emily sighed. "I know it seems that nobody wants this baby, but Julian will one day. I know my husband. The circumstances of its conception . . . let's just say I don't expect them to happen again. It was just one of those things. Does that answer all of your questions?"

"What about Uncle Julian and Adam? Do you know if they are romantically involved? If they are, why doesn't it seem to bother you?" Shaun asked. There, he had said what was bothering him.

"Yes, Shaun, I do know," Emily replied. "But I can only tell you what your Uncle Julian has told you. I know he doesn't mean to keep things from you if that's what he's doing. Just know if he's private about some things in his life, he has very good reasons. Don't be too hard on him. I know he thinks the world of you."

"The three of you seem to have some weird triangle," Shaun replied in frustration. "Somehow it seems you get the worst end of the deal."

"I'm not complaining," Emily said. "It may not seem like it, but I get everything I need."

"Well, I don't," Shaun said with defeat. He pushed away most of his breakfast. "I want my uncle back."

"Come on," Emily said, finally resting her hand on top of his. "Let's enjoy this cruise together. It's you and me for the rest of this trip."

*A short time later.*

Emily gave birth to a healthy baby boy. He was seven pounds eight ounces, with two sets of five toes and five fingers. She insisted on naming him Julian after his daddy. Julian was not pleased at having a namesake, but realized it was important to Emily. He had a difficult time calling the infant by his own name, so he referred to the baby as "Number Six," since he was their sixth child. It wasn't long before the others in the household referred to the baby as "Six," so the name stuck.

Emily decided that they were going to use different methods to raise this baby than they did with the others for a number of reasons. With the first three children, responsibilities were either split or were shared by both parents. That meant that there wasn't one true primary caregiver. Both parents were not happy that the three oldest boys elected to leave home at such an early age. Emily and Julian wondered why the children would want to escape their care when most other children would be homesick. Emily decided to expend most of her energy caring for Louis and Candy, while Julian would be responsible for Six. Emily would still have plenty of time for Six and Julian would be there for Louis and Candy.

Emily was still given to her fever sickness and needed extra sleep. This would not have been possible if she had to wake up in the middle of the night for feedings and wet diapers. Therefore, it was Julian's task to give around-the-clock attention. It took about a minute for Julian to be glad that he had a new son after he was born. Julian was a busy man, so he was forced to take Six along on his various errands.

Adam and Julian were curled side by side in a double bed inside a rustic cottage on Adam's farm. Six was sound asleep in a cradle on the side porch. The tiny cabin sat on top of a hill overlooking an expanse of woods. This place was made for Adam to have a quiet space where he would not be disturbed. Since Adam was the head pastor at his church, people were always stopping by to see him at the main house. Most of the time, the saints would bring food items or other things that they made as gifts for their beloved leader. Other times, folks who were heavy laden with all sorts of trials would pay visits. The only people who knew of his secret retreat were his wife Nancy, Julian, and perhaps a couple of others. Nancy had instructions not to interrupt him when he was in his place of solitude.

The cabin was an unpainted wooden structure consisting of one big room. A double bed was set against one of the board-on-board walls. A door to a bathroom opened at one end. The entire opposite wall was a screened window from the waist up. From this viewpoint a dense stand of timber could be seen overlooking a hill. The cabin had the feeling of resting in a nest surrounded by nature. Screened windows continued to wrap around the sides of the structure, which were complimented with matching screened porches. One of the porches made a good place for babies to sleep in their bassinets.

Julian propped himself on one elbow and started to run a finger along Adam's chest. Adam's eyes were closed, but he made a move to bat Julian's caressing fingers away. "It tickles," he murmured.

Julian pulled his hand away in time to escape the blow. After Adam had settled his hand at his side once more, Julian began tracing the contours of Adam's smooth white chest.

"Come on, Julian, I'm trying to rest," Adam complained, catching Julian's wrist. He shoved Julian's hand away and turned on his side away from Julian.

"I'm just giving you a little lovin'," Julian explained with a grin. He began to massage Adam's chest from behind.

"Yeah, I feel your lovin' right up against my backside," Adam snorted.

Julian nibbled on his earlobe, then kissed just behind it. "Come on and give me just a little lovin' before you go off to sleep."

Adam flipped onto his back again, pushing Julian away. His eyes were wide open. "Julian, I can't believe you. Is there ever a time when you don't want sex?"

Julian laughed. "You don't give yourself enough credit. It's because you're by my side that I always want some lovin'."

"Julian, the wind could blow under the sheets and you would be ready," Adam said. He pulled Julian close. "These times with you are the only moments I have to relax."

"Well, it's not like you have to do anything," Julian replied. "Just lie there and relax. I'll do the rest." He climbed between Adam's legs and pulled the minister's ankles over his own shoulders. "See. It's easy. You lie there and relax, then I'll do the work," he said, gyrating his hips.

Adam broke out laughing. "It's amazing after nine years you still find me so desirable."

Julian fell back beside him. Adam was awake. Mission accomplished. "I do," Julian admitted. "Today more than the first time."

Adam paused a moment before speaking. "You seem happy, Julian."

"I am," Julian responded with wonder. "Why do you say that?"

"Well, you weren't so happy Six was on the way. Now that he's here, you seem to have taken to him," Adam explained.

Julian rested his head on Adam's shoulder. "It's true," he agreed. "I guess I had to get used to the idea of having another child. It's been a long time. I thought that Emily and I were through producing babies years ago. I assure you there won't be any more."

Adam smirked. "We're venturing on dangerous ground, you know."

"I know," Julian agreed. "The deal is, we live in the closet as lovers so it won't interfere in your church activities."

"I think I've done okay over the years not questioning the relationship you have with Emily and your family," Adam said, more to himself than to Julian.

"You have, but the deal goes for Nancy as well as Emily," Julian added.

"Come on," Adam snorted. "You know it's been many years since Nancy and I have been together. I don't think I could ever do it again."

"You know, we don't have to talk about this," Julian advised him. "We never have before and we have it worked out okay."

"Maybe we should talk about some things," Adam said. "I know that you and Shaun are having some difficulties. I think it's because of me."

Julian brushed the comment aside. "That's not what you want to talk about. Maybe we should talk about Emily and me."

Adam turned to look Julian in the face. "You've never wanted to before. As a matter of fact, you have always preferred we didn't."

Julian thought for a moment. "I know, but now Six is here. I know there have been questions in your mind. Maybe about my commitment to you?"

"Maybe," Adam replied.

"Ask," Julian commanded.

"Okay," Adam said slowly. "It's like I said, Nancy and I haven't been close since before you and I met. Since you're involved with a man, involved with me, how do you do it? I assume you and Emily have remained close through the years."

Julian didn't like talking about this subject. He loved Adam, but he felt his relationship with Emily was private. Still, it seemed their arrangement was going to have to change. The "no questions about Emily" policy was going to have to change. The "nobody in the church knowing" policy was going to have to change. Shaun was hurting because of their deception.

"Emily and I . . ." Julian began, "Emily and I are close friends, Adam. We've been through many trials together, as have you and me. It's not like we have this passionate relationship. We never have. It's been one of comfort . . . like friends. Of course she knows of the relationship you and I have, you know that. I could never have kept that from her. It's like I have my friends and she has hers, then we have the family together."

"But what about Six? There must be something. I know I sound jealous. I hate it that we're talking about this. It's the deal. I have to accept it," Adam said.

Julian could feel the tension between them now. He could understand why Adam would be concerned, but he didn't know how to convince him not to worry. "Adam, Emily and I are like kids together. Playmates. We tell each other secrets. We laugh. That's about it. Six came along when we were both upset about the boys going off to school. We tried to give each other some comfort. I guess I believed it was a one-time thing. I think she felt the same way. It's just that the one-time thing brought us Six. Also, it was within our deal. If it wasn't, things would have worked out differently."

"I guess I knew this arrangement wasn't the best, but it was practical," Adam conceded. "I guess I wasn't feeling special to you." He shrugged. "I'm glad all this happened. I like Six. I think he's a neat baby."

"I told you all you had to do was lie there and I would make you feel special," Julian said with a grim attempt to regain the humor.

Adam rolled on top of Julian. "I'll show you the one who'll just lie there."

## 21

Julian arrived back at the farm late that afternoon, after spending most of the day with Adam. It was the first quality time the two had spent together since Six was born. A walk in the woods, listening to good music, some tasty food, and of course the time to come together was all a man could ask when spending the day with his mate. Julian felt good that they had made some headway in clearing up some of the ambiguity in their relationship. Not talking about things seemed to have worked for years, but now it was better to get things out in the open. One of the things he wanted to do was talk to Shaun.

As Julian drove up the lane, he could see that there was a great deal of commotion on the front porch. A limousine was parked out front with a driver and Billy was unloading several suitcases. It could only mean one thing. Frances Lorraine had returned home after a nine-month absence.

"Hey, what's happening?" Julian called out to Billy as he carried Six up the walk to the big house.

Billy shrugged. "Just the Missus coming home." That was all Billy said as he moved the heavy luggage up on the porch.

Julian went to help with his free hand.

"Get on up from here," Billy exclaimed. "I got it covered."

"How is it you're up this way?" Julian asked, putting down the suitcase.

"Missus saw me jogging alongside the road on her way up here. The car slowed down and she lowered the window to speak with me, asked me to ride in the car. I did like she wanted and got in the car," Billy explained.

Julian was astonished. "Why would she do that? Are you friendly with her? I didn't know she ever paid you any mind."

Billy fidgeted for a moment. "I don't know about any of that. She asked a lot of questions about you; about how you were." He paused a moment before he asked, "Are you in some kind of trouble again?"

Julian laughed. "I sure hope not! What put that idea in your head?"

"Just a feeling," Billy answered. Then he proceeded with his work.

Sensing that the conversation had ended, Julian said good-bye. "Tell your mama that I'll bring Six down for a visit real soon."

Billy nodded acknowledgment, and Julian went inside the big house through the front door. Julian expected if Frances Lorraine was back in the big house, home would be exciting. He snuck through the hallway to his office. He tucked Six in his bassinet and turned to his desk. On top was a large package. He unraveled the knotted twine that held it together.


Shaun arrived from the other side of the farm to see Billy hauling the heavy luggage into the big house. "What's the fuss?" he asked Billy as he came out through the screened door.

"Missus is home," Billy replied.

Shaun started to feel nervous. "Have you seen Julian around?"

"Yeah," Billy answered. "He went inside a short time ago. He had Number Six with him."

"Thanks," Shaun replied as he brushed past him to go inside the big house.

Shaun walked through the house to check on Uncle Julian. Instead, he ran into Pilot in the front room. "I see your wife is back," Shaun said with a frown.

"You sound almost as happy as I am," Pilot replied. Both men remained standing as if the conversation wasn't going to last long.

"I was kind of hoping she was gone for good," Shaun replied. "Why's she back? Is the governor giving up on her?"

"I don't know," Pilot said, stroking his chin in thought. "But I'm sure we'll find out soon enough."

Pilot began to move toward his office. "W-wait a minute," Shaun said.

"Yes?" Pilot said as he turned back to face Shaun. He could tell by the sound of the young man's voice that something was bothering him.

"I have something to tell you. I was hoping that Frances Lorraine wouldn't be coming back, so I wouldn't have to alarm anybody."

"Yes," Pilot said, drawing out his adopted grandson. He had the feeling he wasn't going to like what Shaun had to say.

"I found out a little while ago that Frances Lorraine has access to information about Uncle Julian's parentage," Shaun said. "What do you suppose she means to do with this information?"

"She *what!*" Pilot exclaimed in a harsh whisper. "Why are you just now telling me? She means to make trouble, that's what."

"I figured as much," Shaun replied with a defeated look. "I thought of telling Uncle Julian, but I couldn't think of any way to soften the blow. I hoped telling him would never be necessary. The only way to know would be if she actually were to tell him."

"Shaun, maybe we could have done something sooner to stop her. I just hope it's not too late," Pilot said worriedly. "We have to think of a way to placate her."

Frances Lorraine walked into the room. "The only way to placate me is to give me what I want." She sported a pink spring dress that accentuated each curve of her body. Her hair was done in her usual stylish fashion.

"And what may that be?" Pilot asked. All three remained standing. "By the way, welcome home. I hope your stay is short."

Frances Lorraine displayed a sly smile. "Maybe, maybe not," she said as she sauntered across the room. The eyes of the two men followed her. Finally, she looked up at both of them. "I want a quick divorce, plus half of everything that belongs to the farm."

"That's ridiculous!" Pilot exclaimed. "I don't even own half the farm. All the children have shares. You know that."

"I don't underestimate your prowess," Frances Lorraine remarked. "I can't help it that you were foolish enough to give away the farm. You will just have to get it back. You can give me all of yours for starters." She went to sit on an arm of a sofa.

"Frances Lorraine, it's just not possible," Pilot said, shaking his head. "Even if I could, I still don't like the idea of divorce. I know my antics of the past couple of years are hardly laudable but neither are yours. You would be just as guilty in divorce court as I would be."

"Then you leave me no choice," Frances Lorraine said, getting to her feet. "I will make your lives miserable, especially one of yours, until you acquiesce. Don't think of causing me any harm, because I have several watchdogs."

"What do you mean?" Shaun snarled. "Who are your targets?"

Frances Lorraine laughed as she replied, "Well, it's your uncle, dear. He's the logical one. I'm going to make sure he's locked away back at the mental institution with the key lost."

"Why him?" Shaun sneered as he edged closer to her. Pilot held out an arm to block him.

"Because, dear," Frances Lorraine purred, "it seems he is and always has been the center of everyone in this house. Everybody wants to be sure poor Julian is alive and well. He receives more attention than anybody here. His well-being affects all of our lives. So, I'm going to hit this family where it's most vulnerable. And that's Julian."

"I'm sure we can work something out," Shaun said, taking a placating tack.

"It's too late!" Frances Lorraine growled. "The ball has already started to roll. The first phase has begun. I want you to know that I mean business. Give me what I want and be done with me!"

Shaun left the front room to find Julian. He went to his uncle's office and didn't bother to knock but barged in unannounced. He saw Julian set down some unfolded papers and photographs. Julian lowered himself to his desk chair with a blank look on his face.

*Oh no,* Shaun thought. *This can't be happening.* Shaun knelt before his uncle. "Uncle Julian, please tell me you're okay," he pleaded.

Julian looked right through Shaun before looking away.

"Say something!" Shaun begged in earnest. He grabbed Julian's arms and shook them.

Julian turned to look at his nephew. "It's my fault," he mumbled. "Everything is all my fault."

*A few days later.*

"Why is she still here?" Shaun hissed. Pilot and he were sitting on the back porch with their legs dangling over the edge.

"We're supposed to be reasoning with her, remember," Pilot reminded his grandson.

"As long as she doesn't go anywhere near Uncle Julian," Shaun replied.

"We're following him closely. The staff has specific orders to prevent her from seeing him," Pilot said.

"Did you find out what Frances Lorraine has been up to these last several months?" Shaun asked. "I know she's been hanging with the governor, but did you get anything specific? She seems to want to settle your marriage in a hurry."

"She wants to make a run for the state senate and she's been soliciting the former governor's support," Pilot explained.

"How can that be?" Shaun asked in amazement. He brushed the hair away from his eyes. "Her name has been dragged through the mud as a fornicator and a deranged woman. How does she expect to get elected to office without making a complete fool of herself?"

Pilot snorted. "Frances Lorraine has a different way of looking at things. Don't underestimate her. She's been able to foster her image by portraying herself as a battered spouse. It was the cruel advances made by her enraged husband (that's me) that drove her to seek safety in the arms of another man."

"Weren't there several?" Shaun asked with a confused look.

"Well, yes, but her press releases don't indicate those; only the ones the press was able to verify on their own. She claims the other accusations were spread by her sick husband," Pilot explained. "Anyway, as a result of claiming to be a victim of abuse, she's garnered a great deal of support from women. And we know that she is more than capable of winning support from most men."

"But is that really enough?" Shaun asked.

"Well, there was an incident when she saved a child from drowning," Pilot commented. "She was speaking before a women's group on a pier, when a child fell into the water. Without a thought, Frances Lorraine extended her sun umbrella to the lad and he grabbed onto it.

She was called a hero and is now lauded as an active proponent for child safety." Pilot scratched his head and added, "She's gotten some good press."

As Pilot talked with Shaun on the porch, Dennis hopped out of a pickup truck that had stopped at the corner of the farm road and the lane leading up to the big house. In the South, folks that come to call go to the back door. One can always tell a stranger is calling when the front doorbell rings. Dennis had a suitcase in one hand and a large bag thrown over his shoulder. By the time he reached the back porch, Shaun could see that he was dressed in a gray suit and a tie loosened around a white-collar shirt. He was sweating in the Louisiana heat.

"I got here as soon as I could," Dennis said as he reached the porch. He set his baggage in front of Pilot and Shaun.

"No need to rush," Pilot said. "The man isn't dying."

"How is he?" Dennis asked, removing his tie.

"He blames himself," Shaun replied.

"Shaun has been monitoring his uncle day and night," Pilot said. "I was able to convince him to come out for some air." He turned to face Shaun. "You know, you don't have to stay camped out by his door. He's going to be okay."

"I just want to be there if he needs anything," Shaun said defensively. "I owe him a lot." He fidgeted. "I should have told him sooner."

Dennis tried to refrain from sounding impatient. "Well, tell me about him, Shaun."

"It's like the message I left for you," Shaun began. "Frances Lorraine got hold of the information about how Uncle Julian was conceived and that his father was a serial rapist. She gave it to Uncle Julian."

"For what purpose?" Dennis asked.

Shaun then replayed the conversation Pilot and he had had with Frances Lorraine.

"This has gotten way out of hand," Dennis said, getting upset. "She has to be stopped."

"I think she's only begun," Pilot said. "She's a cunning woman. I have the feeling she's got a lot of tricks up her sleeve."

"Well, we need to keep Julian out of it," Dennis stated.

"We can't protect him forever," Pilot replied. "We can't keep him locked up."

"What else does she have?" Dennis asked with a bewildered look. Despite wearing a suit, he sat down in the grass facing the two men.

"We don't know," Pilot replied. "We just know she intends to send Julian back to the mental hospital. I got the sense she has more ammunition to use."

"Can't you give her what she wants?" Dennis exclaimed. "I know it may be expensive, but it's because of your family's trouble that Julian is caught in the middle. You may just have to bite the bullet."

"I can try, but it will take months, maybe years," Pilot replied, "Frances Lorraine wants her way right now. A lot of circumstances are involved. I would bow to her wishes and give her a divorce. As soon as I do that, Jack will divorce Marge and marry that black girl Lisa and folks will no longer be able to look the other way. In this parish, I don't think they could ever be safe. Interracial relationships just aren't tolerated. Next, all my children own the farm by shares. Even though I still own the most, I own well under fifty percent. She wants fifty percent of the farm. We've had storms and disease the last few years, so cash is low. I can't buy back all the shares I need. If I borrow the money from the bank, it will jeopardize the future of the farm people and I can't do that."

"Well, we've tortured Frances Lorraine and that hasn't worked," Dennis said. "I guess we'll just have to fight battle for battle."

"Maybe she'll have an accident," Shaun muttered.

Pilot glared at the young man.

"Just a thought," Shaun said with a frown. "Wishful thinking."

"It wasn't that long ago I saw you restrained from using my rifle," Pilot retorted.

Shaun began to protest when Dennis interrupted. "So what is Julian doing now?"

"He's locked himself in his room and won't come out. He's been in there for days. He won't even come out for meals or see anyone except Emily. He has Six with him and that's it. He'll speak with the house staff from time to time and he'll speak to Aunt Emily," Shaun explained.

"What did Emily say?" Dennis asked.

"She says that he has only said a few words regarding Six's care," Shaun replied.

"Is that it?" Dennis asked.

"He told me when he first found out that everything was all his fault," Shaun said. "He has it twisted that he's the reason that Elizabeth is a cold, calculating, miserable woman; that if he wasn't born that she would have turned out better or at least differently."

"But that's not true," Dennis said with disbelief. "He's something good that came of an awful situation."

Shaun shrugged.

"I'm going to see him," Dennis said, standing up.

"You can try, but nobody else has been able to get in there to see him," Shaun replied.

Dennis went to put his things in his room and catch a shower. He dressed, then went to Julian's room. He had moved his quarters some time before to the other side of the house to be near Elizabeth. Dennis had also moved near Shaun's room. He tried the doorknob. It was locked. He knocked and said, "Julian?"

When Julian didn't answer, he knocked again. "Julian? Come on and open the door. We need to talk. We've known each other the longest. We can get through this."

Dennis heard a click in the doorknob. He waited a few moments to see if Julian would open the door. When he didn't, Dennis tried the door once again and it opened. He entered the room, which was dominated by three large windows spaced evenly apart on the far wall, framed in dark blue drapes and covered by white sheers. A four-poster bed and a set of nightstands bordered the wall to the right. The floor was covered with lush blue carpeting.

Julian was sitting in a chair near the windows, facing away from Dennis. Six lay in a cradle close to the bed. As Dennis approached, Julian asked in a gruff voice, "Who knew?"

Dennis didn't say anything for the moment. He hadn't expected this question. He didn't know what to expect. He had never seen Julian being weak. The whole time they were together as partners, Julian never showed it when he felt vulnerable or lacking courage. He had heard stories of the man's past difficulties. "Eh . . . what did you say?"

"Who knew about all of this?" Julian said with greater force. He still faced away from Dennis.

"Is that really so important?" Dennis responded. "The fact is that now you know. We have to figure out what to do about it."

"So, you did know," Julian accused him. He stood up and faced Dennis for the first time.

Dennis nodded.

"Why didn't you tell me!" Julian hissed, keeping his voice low for the sake of the slumbering baby.

Dennis pursed his lips. "Julian, you know I was hired by your family to secure a variety of information. It was not my place to tell secrets. I was hired to do a job and confidence was part of the deal. It was the others' decision to tell or, in this case, not to tell."

Julian nodded. "Well, I am a part of this family and I have just as much of a right to know this information as anyone else. I want to . . . I demand to know who else knew about my conception."

Dennis thought for a moment. If he worked for the family, then he worked for Julian too. "Pilot and Shaun were the only ones who knew, except of course Elizabeth."

A defeated look came over Julian's face. "Shaun?" He edged away from Dennis and went back to his chair.

"Julian?" Dennis got no response. He gave the handsome man an affectionate squeeze on his shoulder. Then he left the room, knowing he would get no more out of him that day.


"What did he say?" Shaun asked as Dennis slipped out to the front porch. Dennis was hoping to make a clean getaway to go see Jeffrey. He figured that visit would be quick, so he would go get a warm welcome from Simon. But, seeing that he wasn't going anywhere anytime soon, he fell into a chair. Pilot poured him a glass of cold lemonade.

He took a large gulp before answering. "The man is not happy. He wanted to know who knew about the rapist and Elizabeth."

"What did you say?" Shaun asked.

"I told him the truth. I said that Pilot and you were the only ones to know."

"I imagine he was not too happy to hear that," Pilot mused.

"Why did you tell him?" Shaun asked.

"Because he had a right to know," Dennis replied forcefully. "It's his business. Obviously deceiving him hasn't benefited him. I work for him just as I work for you and Pilot. I was paid by the family, so I guess I work for all of you unless I'm otherwise informed."

"Those files were meant to be confidential," Pilot said evenly.

"Well, the cat was let out of the bag and I wasn't the one who did it. He would have figured out who knew about it," Dennis said.

"That's true," Shaun agreed. "But why tell him now when he's in such a state?"

"Have you tried keeping things from your uncle when he's angry?" Dennis asked.

"Good point." Shaun frowned. He got up to go inside. "I guess I better go look in on him."

A minute later, Shaun knocked on Julian's white-painted wood door. When he got no response, he tried the brass doorknob. He was surprised when it turned. He slipped into the room. "Uncle Julian?" he called softly.

From his chair Julian mumbled, "I guess I should have fastened the lock."

"I've been worried about you," Shaun said as he approached his uncle.

Julian turned to face him. Shaun saw hurt mixed with anger in his eyes. Had he been crying?

"You knew," Julian accused him in a low voice. He was seething with anger.

Shaun nodded.

"I can't believe you deceived me," Julian continued. Shaun thought he could see the hurt in his uncle's eyes turn to hate.

"That wasn't my intention . . ." Shaun started.

"I kept you here as my own son," Julian said with growing anger. "More than that, you were special in a way the other children could never be. How dare you betray me, to find out the truth from that awful woman!"

"I was trying to protect you, Uncle Julian, honest," Shaun said. He was trying hard not to burst into tears. "I didn't want you to go back to that hospital."

"Well, you see that I'm not going anywhere," Julian said through gritted teeth. "Get out of here! And don't come back!"

Shaun was stunned.

"Go on!" Julian said. He turned away from Shaun.

## 22

Dennis left the front porch after Shaun ascended to the big house. Pilot was gracious about not detaining him. Dennis wanted to see Jeffrey; he missed him. He didn't have much hope of the doctor taking him back. Dennis realized that he had been gone much longer than expected. He was on a poor streak with ruining Frances Lorraine, but his luck back East had been much better. Being in Louisiana had given him a new prospective on his career and he had returned to Washington with fresh ideas. He was in court for the first time in many years and had done well on a case. There were promises of more high-profile cases.

Dennis approached the door to Jeffrey's house. He paused before knocking. If he were a praying man, he would have made some petition to God. He figured he'd give it a shot anyway. He asked for strength. Isn't that what people usually did?

"Hi," Dennis greeted Jeffrey as he opened the door.

Jeffrey didn't utter a word. He left the door open and turned back into the house. Dennis followed and cursed himself for not paying more attention in church. Surely people prayed for things other than items on their Christmas lists. Given the chance, he would listen to Jeffrey more closely when he talked about such things.

"I see you're still mad," Dennis observed, taking a seat on the couch. He was hoping that Jeffrey would follow suit, but the slender man remained standing, leaning on a wing chair.

"I don't see the point of being angry," Jeffrey replied. "You've made your choice. You've been gone almost six months. Did you expect me to wait around for you?"

"I missed you," Dennis said.

Jeffrey didn't reply.

"Jeffrey, you have to realize, I haven't been ready to make a commitment . . . a full commitment to us," Dennis started to explain. He felt the need to be honest; at least partly honest. "You are forcing me to make a decision to live here in Louisiana with you or alone in Washington. It's a tough choice and I can't make it yet. Washington is my home. Many of my friends have died, but there are still a few hanging on and they need me. When I do make a decision, or if you give me the opportunity to make a choice, I will commit to a life here or in Washington. Can't we continue to just date a while? I know at some point I'll have to make a choice. I just can't do it now."

Jeffrey nodded like a little boy who had just been scolded. "I realize the sacrifice you would have to make. I wish I could be more understanding." Jeffrey looked Dennis in the eye, then looked away. "I love you."

"I know you do," Dennis replied feeling guilty. "Please just try and hang with me. We've come this far."

"I don't think I can," Jeffrey replied. "You've hurt me, Dennis."

"Can you at least think about what I've said?" Dennis asked, getting to his feet. He wanted to take the dark-haired man in his arms to take away the pain.

Jeffrey paused a moment before nodding. He flinched when Dennis sought to touch his arm. Dennis let his arm fall to his side.

Another thought came to Dennis's mind. "Do you think you can stop over and see Julian? He's very sick."

"I'm not that kind of doctor," Jeffrey mumbled.

"I know," Dennis answered. "His health is okay . . . at least I think it is. He's had some emotional problems in the past. I'm worried about him. It would sure mean a lot to me if you could help."

Jeffrey nodded. "I'll see what I can do. I'll think about it. I'm not promising anything. Tell me what's going on with him."

Dennis explained the events leading to Julian's crisis.


Dennis drove up the lane to Simon's farm. He hadn't notified the young stud that he was back in Louisiana, just as he hadn't told Jeffrey. He slowed the pickup to a crawl as he saw Simon by the house. The bib of his overalls was hanging below his shirtless body, while the back straps dangled over his rump. Dennis could see the hose spraying water over his entire body, as Simon wetted his hair and drank some water. He wondered how he could have stayed away from this hot man all these months. He must have been a fool.

"Those overalls must be hot to wear," Dennis commented as he got out of the truck and slammed the door. Even this early in the spring, the humidity was heavy and the temperature was warm. Dennis thought cotton trousers would be more suitable.

Simon turned and looked at Dennis, with no more surprise than if he had just seen him yesterday. "Yeah, they are," Simon agreed. "You want to help me take them off?"

Dennis raced to grab him. With the hose still running, both were soon soaked. But neither man cared. They were just happy to see each other. Dennis gave Simon a long, deep kiss. All at once, he was happy.

"Do you remember what I said I'd do to you when you came back?" Simon said in a throaty voice.

Dennis nodded.

"Then let's go." Simon took the man by the hand and led him to the house.

# – 23 –

"Shaun?" a voice called on the other end of the phone line.

"Yes, Leah it's me," Shaun answered. He was sitting in his office pouting after his visit with Uncle Julian. He was tired of the whole ordeal.

"Is this a good time to talk?" Leah asked.

"Not really, Leah, I've had a bad week," Shaun replied. He had an idea what she wanted.

"This won't take long, Shaun, but I have to ask you to be patient," Leah started. Her voice was calm, with a hint of emotion. Shaun couldn't tell if it was genuine. "Papa wants to see you."

"Absolutely not," Shaun retorted. "Not now, not ever." He paused. "Leah, this really isn't a good time right now. Uncle Julian . . . he's not doing real well. I'm tied up with him and don't have time for Albert at the moment."

"I'm afraid this is urgent, Shaun," Leah said with a slight edge in her voice. "You know, since Uncle Julian wasn't the firstborn of Grandpapa Bernard, it was Papa that should have gotten the estate; not you or Uncle Julian."

Shaun fumed. "Tell Albert he can have all of it. I don't care. I'm not going to discuss it with him. How did he hear about it so soon?"

"Papa said that someone named Frank L. Pilot telephoned him and spilled the information. Next, the documentation to substantiate the claims was sent to Papa special delivery."

"That's Frances Lorraine Pilot," Shaun growled.

"Sorry, I didn't know," Leah replied.

"I wasn't snapping at you, Leah. I apologize," Shaun said. "I'm under a great deal of pressure now. Uncle Julian hasn't taken the news well."

"Why? Is he that broken up about not being Grandpapa Bernard's son?" Leah asked. "I thought you told me that Uncle Julian wasn't all that fond of his parents."

Shaun explained the entire situation to her.

"That's awful," Leah commented.

"You see, that's why I can't deal with Albert right now."

"Shaun, Papa said that he will let you keep the inheritance if you'd only see him," Leah said. "He wants your forgiveness."

"Leah, the last time I saw Albert, I came close to killing him," Shaun replied. "I don't want to go to jail as a result of the next time I see him."

"Shaun, think of all the good you and Carmen have done with the money since it was given to you. Think of all the people who would lose out if you shucked this responsibility to your family," Leah explained. "Papa doesn't want to live in Boston for ten years. He feels important in St. Louis."

"Leah, why is this such a big deal to you?" Shaun asked.

"I want to come and work with Carmen and you. Remember? I can't promote my agenda with Papa running things. It would be a disaster," Leah explained. "Besides, I care what happens to you."

"I'll think about it, Leah," Shaun said resignedly. "But I want to wait until Carmen gets here in a couple of weeks. I don't want to go through it without him."


Shaun went back to the porch where Pilot was sitting with Adam. "He won't see me," Adam was explaining to Pilot when Shaun came out the door. He remained standing. Pilot was still sitting on the top steps.

"What did he say?" Pilot asked, turning to face Shaun.

"Plenty," was all Shaun said. He didn't want to explain the situation with Adam present. Adam wasn't one of his favorite people at the moment.

"Aren't you going to tell us?" Adam asked. Shaun knew that Adam was worried, but his training to remain calm covered his true emotions.

"He's upset," Shaun said. "I don't want to talk about it right now."

Adam let his emotion show. "Shaun, you and Dennis are the only people he's let see him now. Surely you can say something."

Pilot took his time getting up from his sitting position. Shaun noticed it took more effort than usual for the man to rise. *He's getting older,* he thought.

"I have some things to tend to in the house," Pilot said as he hurried through the screen door. He didn't want to be part of this conversation.

"Adam, I don't need this right now," Shaun replied with effort. "I am so tired." A tear ran down his cheek. "I've been so worried about him. I can't sleep at night. I walk by his room all day and night to be there when he finally decides he needs somebody. On top of that, my papa wants to come see me and may want to take my business away from me. How much is one man supposed to take?"

"Not much if he tries to go it alone," Adam replied. Adam extended a hand to beckon the young man to sit beside him on the edge of the porch. He waited for the tears to stop.

"Now tell me what's going on," Adam said. "I want to help."

"Well, I don't want to talk about Uncle Julian right now," Shaun said. "Just know I screwed up big time. He'll tell you all about it when he's ready. I think he'll be fine."

Adam nodded.

Shaun continued, "Papa wants to come and see me. The thought makes me want to vomit."

"Why does he want to come?" Adam asked. He knew Shaun would keep talking once he got started.

"My sister says he wants to ask my forgiveness for all the rotten things he did to me," Shaun replied. "I can't just forgive and forget, can I?"

"No, you can't," Adam agreed.

"So you don't think I should see him?" Shaun asked. He thought all ministers were big on forgiveness.

"That's your decision, Shaun," Adam replied. "I can understand if you don't see him."

"I can't do it," Shaun said, shaking his head. "Not now."

"You don't have to." Adam gave his knee a comforting pat.

"I thought you were going to say that I should forgive him," Shaun said with relief.

"What is it about forgiving him that concerns you?"

Shaun was thinking hard, looking straight ahead with his hands clasped between his knees. "I can't just start visiting him. I don't want to go to St. Louis on holidays and I don't want him to come here or Boston. He's still the same person. I don't want anything to do with him."

"Just because you forgive someone doesn't mean you have to have a relationship with them," Adam offered.

"It doesn't?"

"Not at all. Why would you? He did terrible things to you. You still might not feel safe with him. Like you said, he is the same awful person . . . even if he is remorseful. Why give him the chance to humiliate you again if the possibility exists?"

"I thought I was supposed to forgive and forget," Shaun said. "I just can't."

"You can forgive and still have nothing to do with the man," Adam advised. "If that's what you think is best for you. And having known you for many years, I would have to agree that it would be the best idea."

"How could I forgive him and then have nothing to do with him?" Shaun asked.

"Albert would ask you to forgive him for his transgressions against you. Then you would tell him he is forgiven. Even if you don't feel it in your heart, you could say it. The desire to do so should free you from some of the torment. Meaning, you could then tell yourself that you were moving forward in your life with a bright future in sight. That way, you would let go of the baggage of the past. I believe God would bless you all the more for doing something like that, because Albert would feel relieved to move on with his future," Adam explained.

"What if he expects me to pretend nothing happened and wants me to visit him?"

"I would tell him that the two of you need to take things one step at a time," Adam answered. "Say you're not at that point at the present time." Adam thought for a moment before continuing. "Shaun, I wouldn't plan on that happening if that is what you're afraid of. The man hasn't changed. He must know you have a partner living in Boston. I would be surprised if he now embraces your open homosexuality, when he was against it when you were growing up."

"That's a relief," Shaun said. "You've giving me a lot to think about, Adam. Thanks."

Adam grinned, then nodded. Helping Shaun distracted him from worrying about Julian.

Shaun sensed that the conversation was about to change. He tried to think of something to make the pastor feel better. "Adam, Uncle Julian doesn't want to see anyone now, so don't take it personally. I wish I could say I was lucky I got to see him. All I got was an earful of anger. I think that's part of the reason he doesn't want people to visit. He's hurt, so he lashes out. It's not like Uncle Julian to do that and he knows it." Shaun frowned, then nodded. "I think we should give him the time he needs. I know I'm not going to see him until he calls for me. I suggest the same for you."

Adam rose from his sitting position. "But he is speaking? Emily described him as depressed, functioning just enough to help look after Six."

"Six sleeps a lot like new babies do," Shaun explained. "Uncle Julian is confused. He thinks he's the one that made Grandma Elizabeth so mean. He won't listen to reason."

"That's absurd!" Adam said. "All he ever has tried to do is help that woman."

"Did you know her when she was well?" Shaun asked, rising to stand with Adam.

"Not very well," Adam said. "She seemed pleasant enough. Except I remember a distinct lack of warmth. Her smile seemed forced and insincere. Julian never did talk about her much."

"No, he didn't," Shaun agreed. After a pause he added, "I'll tell Uncle Julian you will call him if I'm given the chance."

Adam sighed. "I'll be back tomorrow morning. Please call me, Shaun, the minute he snaps out of this thing. I'm really worried. The longer this thing goes on, I'm afraid the worse it will be. He could slip into a deeper depression. You know, when I met your uncle, he had just come out of the hospital."

Shaun nodded. "You've never talked about it much."

"Well, he was preoccupied at the time. Things were not good for him when he returned home from upstate," Adam explained.

"Was he really better?"

"He seemed okay," Adam said. "He tired easily. We were just getting to know each other. When things started to settle down after the Lamond murder was resolved, he sank into despair for a while. He was upset about the death of Robert Lamond and it took a good while before he would open up about what he was feeling. Also, he felt guilty about hurting your Aunt Emily's feelings."

"I remember the part about Aunt Emily. We talked about that a lot. We didn't talk so much about Robert Lamond. All I know is their affair was brief before he died. And they had made peace with each other," Shaun said.

"They didn't have time to sort through all their feelings before the man died. I think that left Julian with a feeling of unfinished business," Adam said. "Anyway, he had Billy's family to lean on back then. He is close with them, and he still holds Billy close to his heart. Now he's all alone and that concerns me."

"I'll talk to Grandpapa Pilot to see if we could get his old doctor here," Shaun suggested.

"That's a very good idea, Shaun," Adam said, giving the young man a cuff on the shoulder. "Let me know when he's coming. I want to be here."


Chuck Rawlings and his buddy Mitch Stevens lived together on Chuck's farm. He inherited the place when his father passed away just a few short months ago. The farm gave Chuck a reason to come back to Louisiana from Alabama where he worked as a trash man.

Chuck and Mitch remained friends through the years since high school, because they had a lot in common. Both were maimed for life after teaching Shaun Smith the difference between men and women. Neither would be able to father children or perform husband duties. *It was just for fun,* Chuck thought, *Shaun Smith got exactly what he wanted. Twice.* But Smith had to go and spoil things for the two men. Chuck knew Smith played a dirty trick and was responsible for their subsequent kidnapping. When they awoke from the ordeal, they knew their lives would never be the same.

The years of bitterness and anger caught up with Chuck. He wanted to get even with Smith. Stevens would help him. He had always followed close behind Chuck and he did what he was told. Heck, Mitch was a virgin before he did Smith. Smith was going to pay. Chuck was biding his time. He would wait for the perfect opportunity.

# – 24 –

"Julian, it's Jeffrey Martin," Jeffrey said. He was outside the door of Julian's bedroom. "Can I come in?"

After a few moments, Julian unlocked the door and let the doctor inside. "Is something wrong with the children?" Julian asked. Jeffrey could tell the man was tired. He looked like he wasn't sleeping well. He had circles under his eyes and it seemed like he hadn't had a shower in a couple of days.

"No, they're fine," Jeffrey said, taking a seat opposite Julian's chair. He dropped his black medical bag next to his chair. "I came to see you."

Julian was puzzled. "But you are a children's doctor. Why would you want to see me?"

"I understand you've been feeling down of late. What's going on?"

"I'm sure you know all about it," Julian said, bristling. He got up and paced around the room. He stopped by the bed and folded his arms across his chest. "I don't want to talk about it."

"Okay," Jeffrey agreed, nodding his head. "Does anything hurt?"

"I'm in pain but it's not physical," Julian said. "I wish everyone would quit worrying and leave me alone!" The baby stirred. Julian went over to rock the cradle until he went back to sleep.

"Well, how about an exam?" Jeffrey suggested. "Just to make sure everything else is okay. You don't look so good."

"I'm fine," Julian said. "I didn't think you were that kind of a doctor."

"I specialize in pediatrics, but I'm still qualified to do routine exams . . . just to make sure everything is working as it should," Jeffrey said. "I think, if anything, it will put the others at ease to be sure there is nothing physically wrong with you."

Julian thought for a moment before agreeing. "All right."

"Good," Jeffrey said, getting to his feet. "How about getting yourself cleaned up? I'll be here with the baby."

Julian looked at him with concern.

Jeffrey smiled. "Remember, babies are my business. I think little Six will be in good hands."

This brought a faint smile to Julian's face. He went into the bathroom to clean up.


"How is he?" Shaun asked from the steps of the front porch as Dr. Martin came through the door after seeing Julian. Pilot, Dennis, and Emily were with him when the tall, slender man let the screen door close. They were all standing, because they sensed the doctor wouldn't be staying long.

"He's fine," Jeffrey replied. "He checked out okay. I drew some blood, so we'll have that looked at by tomorrow." His face became more sober. "My main objective was to watch his behavior and to ask him a few questions: Was he sleeping? Eating? He won't talk about what's bothering him. He's irritable. I did manage to get him to clean himself up. He's becoming more depressed as the days pass, from what you and he tell me. He needs to snap out of it. Who holds the most influence over him?"

Everyone looked at Emily. She shook her head. "I've never been able to make Julian do other than what he wants to do. He'll talk when he's ready to talk."

"Will he talk to Adam?" Jeffrey asked.

"He won't see Adam," Shaun replied.

"His old doctor from the hospital is retired, but maybe he'll pay a visit to Julian," Pilot suggested.

"That may be a good idea," Jeffrey agreed.


Dennis escorted Jeffrey to his car. "Thank you for coming, Jeffrey," he said. "I knew you would be able to help."

Jeffrey turned to Dennis. "It was my pleasure. I like Julian. I hope he will be okay."

"What do you mean?" Dennis asked. "He is going to get better, isn't he?"

"I don't know." Jeffrey shrugged. "He's already had one depressive episode in his life. The chance that he'll have others is good."

"What can we do?"

"I'm afraid it's up to Julian," Jeffrey replied. "He's the one who has to do it."

Dennis nodded.

"Dennis, I was wondering if you'd be free to stop by my place Tuesday evening," Jeffrey said.

That was several days away, Dennis was thinking.

"I know it's not our usual Saturday night date . . . at least not our old one. But Tuesday would be good for me," Jeffrey explained.

Dennis nodded. "Okay."

Jeffrey opened the car door. Before getting inside, he reached out and let his palm touch Dennis's cheek. Then he got in the car, closed the door, and backed out of the drive.


*A few days later.*

"Julian, it's been a long time," Dr. Hopkins said as Julian let his old friend into his room.

Julian nodded. He spoke little now.

He sat before Dr. Hopkins and stared into the older man's face. Dr. Hopkins was in his sixties, on the heavy side of the scale. He had a salt-and-pepper beard and matching fringe around his head. He wore heavy wire-rimmed glasses.

"You're not wearing your white coat," Julian said. His voice was hoarse.

"No," Dr. Hopkins said. "I'm just here to visit a friend."

Julian nodded and stared down at his feet.

"Why don't you freshen up? It will make us both feel more comfortable. Can we leave the baby with his mother for a while?" Dr. Hopkins asked.

Emily had been reluctant to take Six away from Julian. The baby seemed to be the only thing that interested her husband. She noticed his diapers were changed and that he was clean and fed. She kept a regular eye on both of them. As long as she said little, Julian tolerated her presence.

Julian nodded as he went to shower. Dr. Hopkins called Emily from the front room to fetch Six.

With a shower and a fresh set of clothes, Dr. Hopkins noticed that Julian seemed more alert and less preoccupied. "Now, doesn't that make you feel better?"

Julian nodded.

"What seems to be the trouble?" Dr. Hopkins asked.

"I don't want to talk about it," Julian said. He rose from his chair and paced across the room.

Dr. Hopkins remained calm. "Now Julian, we've been through this before. We both know where it got you."

Julian turned to the doctor. His eyes were red from lack of sleep and full of pain. He bit his knuckles. "It's my fault! I'm the one who caused it all!"

"What did you cause, Julian?" Dr. Hopkins asked.

"I caused her to be . . . to be a bad person . . . a bad mother. I caused her to have her stroke. I'm the reason she's bedridden. I'm the one who made her ruin those people's lives and take all their money. I caused her to blackmail, cajole, kill, and murder," Julian said.

"Tell me how you did it, Julian," Dr. Hopkins said.

Julian came and sat on the edge of his chair.

"That man raped my mother," Julian said. He cried for several minutes.

"Yes, he did," Dr. Hopkins agreed after Julian gathered himself.

"He's my father," Julian replied, his tears reduced to dry heaves.

Dr. Hopkins nodded.

"I never thought I'd see the day when I wished with all my might that Bernard Smith was really my papa," Julian chuckled hysterically. "It's funny how things work out."

"Why is this all your fault?" Dr. Hopkins asked.

"Because I'm living proof of what happened to her. That's why she sent me away to school. That's why I hardly saw her growing up. She couldn't stand the sight of me," Julian said. "The more she saw me, the more wicked she became."

"She could have given you away at any point, Julian, but she decided to keep you," Dr. Hopkins said. "Did you think of that?"

Julian didn't say anything. He felt confused. However, he felt a sense of relief. Maybe he would be able to sleep that night. Things would make better sense with a good night's sleep.

"I think we've had enough for now," Dr. Hopkins said, getting to his feet. "Do you feel better?"

Julian stood to join him and nodded. Dr. Hopkins raised his eyebrows.

"Yes, I feel better," Julian said. This scene had been rehearsed many times. A verbal response was expected.

"You know what you need to do?" Dr. Hopkins asked, going to the door.

"Yes," Julian answered.

"I'll be around if you need me," Dr. Hopkins assured him.

"I'll be fine, but thanks for coming," Julian said. He closed the door.


Downstairs in the front room, Emily, Pilot, Shaun, Adam, and, to their dismay, Frances Lorraine were waiting for the doctor to return.

"How is he?" Adam said, getting to his feet with the others as Dr. Hopkins entered the room.

"Fine for now," Dr. Hopkins answered.

"For now?" Shaun asked.

"Is he going to make it?" Frances Lorraine asked. With the exception of the doctor, every other face in the room wore a sneer.

"That is up to Julian," the doctor said.


Soon after the doctor left, Shaun turned toward Frances Lorraine. "What is she still doing in this house?" he growled.

"She still is a member of this family," Pilot stated. The conviction in his voice was less than firm. He had resigned himself to a confrontation and he didn't know how he was going to avert it. He wanted her out as much as the others did. Still, he knew he couldn't throw her out and risk the legal ramifications.

"Not anymore," Emily said. She turned to Frances Lorraine. "I want you out of this house. You are no longer welcome here. You can either remove your things from your rooms or I will have them packed up for you tomorrow."

"And if I refuse?" Frances Lorraine replied with amusement. "After all, I did marry into this family. This house is as much mine as it is yours."

"Emily, please!" Pilot exclaimed.

"You leave me no choice," Emily said. "This house belongs to the farm. According to the bylaws of our business, the governing family is sovereign. Daddy relinquished his duties to Shaun, Julian, and myself. Since Shaun spends a good deal of time back East, that leaves Julian and me as heads of the family, and this house is ours for the time being."

"I didn't agree to give up control!" Frances Lorraine growled, her temper beginning to show.

Emily kept cool. "No, but you've been away for months at a time. You have neglected your responsibilities, thus forfeiting, with your husband, any claim to this house and its governing family. I want you out!"

"Emily, there has to be something we can do," Pilot pleaded one last time. He knew she had the power to overrule him. He knew his daughter well enough to know that she wouldn't back down.

"Daddy, I have been patient," Emily said. "Some time ago, I prompted you and Dennis to come to some kind of resolution. You have failed to do so. I speak for my husband and myself. Now get out!"

"I don't see your husband saying anything of the kind," Frances Lorraine cooed with a smirk.

"Do what she says," Julian said in a low voice, coming into the room.

"Uncle Julian, what are you doing down here?" Shaun asked, concerned. The last thing he wanted was for his uncle to face more emotional trauma.

"I came to see what all the shouting was about," Julian replied, taking a seat in an easy chair. "You all have waked the baby. I won't be able to settle him until you quiet down."

"Your wife has thrown me out with nowhere to go," Frances Lorraine said with a whimper in her voice. She dabbed her eye with a blue silk handkerchief that matched her satin dress.

"You can go to the Lamond house," Julian replied wearily.

"What! I don't want her there with me," Jack shouted, coming into the room. The baby wailed loudly upstairs.

Julian rose from his chair and looked toward Jack. "You are welcome to stay here. As my wife has stated, Frances Lorraine is not. That is my house . . . at least for now. I won't have this family torn apart. Are you with me?"

Jack looked at the floor. He didn't like the solution, but for the family's sake would agree to it. He nodded. "Look lady, if I have any trouble from you, you are out on your duff."

"I won't live in a house with a Negro woman. She'll have to go," said Frances Lorraine.

"Look, woman . . ." Jack started.

"Jack, maybe you should have Lisa stay with her people for the next couple of days until we can figure something out," Pilot advised him.

"Daddy . . ." Jack started to protest.

"Look, son," Pilot retorted, "we can't have a scandal along with everything else." He looked toward Frances Lorraine. "At least not another one if it can be avoided."

Frances Lorraine let an evil smirk escape as she dried her eyes with her handkerchief. The family was in turmoil and she loved it.

"I can't stay in this house with her here," Jack exclaimed, pointing toward Marge.

"Why? I don't care if you're here as long as your mistress doesn't come along," Marge snapped.

"Marge, would you mind staying with Frances Lorraine at the Lamond house for a while?" Emily requested. "At least I know that the two of you are on friendly terms."

"Why, I think that's a wonderful idea," Shaun chimed in. "Surely you wouldn't mind, Marge."

Pilot gave Shaun a warning look, although he agreed. "If you wouldn't mind, young lady." Pilot felt relieved that he would have a spy in the Lamond house. One thing that was good about having Frances Lorraine in the big house was that he could keep an eye on her.

"I know at least one of them that would love the idea," Shaun snickered.

"That's enough, young man," Julian ordered.

Shaun frowned.

"I guess the terms are favorable," Frances Lorraine said, relenting, and then added with a scowl, "as if I have a choice." She started for the stairway. "Come dear." She beckoned Marge. "I need some help packing before my belongings are strewn across the front lawn."

"As my young nephew suspected, I'd be delighted to join you," Marge replied, following close behind the dispossessed mistress.

As Frances Lorraine reached the first step, she turned to face Emily. "You may have expelled me from this house, but you haven't heard the last from me. I am still free to come and go from this place." She looked toward Julian. "Our business has not been concluded, son-in-law." Before anyone could respond, she whisked herself up the stairwell.

Julian followed her up the stairwell to tend to the crying baby, when there was a knock at the front door. It was unusual for someone to call at that entrance, so he paused to see who it was. Jack went to answer it.

Within moments, he came in with Bernard, Julian's father . . . at least the one he had always thought was his father. Julian looked up the steps toward his room.

"I'll go," Emily said as she brushed past him, giving his arm a reassuring squeeze.

"Oh, Julian!" Bernard cried as he started toward his son.

"Papa, please," Julian pleaded. "I'm really not up to this."

Apparently, the others were not up to it either, as they retreated from the room. As if on cue, Bernard shifted from emotional distress to a cool and business-like demeanor.

"All right, where is Elizabeth? We need some answers," Bernard said.

"She's hardly in a position to talk," Julian said. "Certainly you are familiar with her circumstances."

"I don't care. I want to see for myself. Take me to her!" Bernard ordered.

## 25

"I'm glad you could come," Jeffrey said to Dennis as he led the burly man over the threshold. "You look very nice."

Dennis sported a neat pair of beige slacks and coordinated sport jacket. Besides his traveling suit, these were the nicest clothes he had with him. People here seldom wore ties except to church. "You said to look my best, but I'm a far cry from the way you look."

Jeffrey smiled. He had on a summer tuxedo. "I don't get to wear it much," he said, smoothing the lapels. "I thought this time might be special."

"Are we in for a night of celebration?" Dennis asked. He stood face to face with Jeffrey, a few feet apart. The distance was awkward. Dennis wondered if he should give the slender man a hug. With a jerky motion, Jeffrey moved forward to embrace him. Both men were nervous.

Dennis glanced toward the back of the house. He was impressed and flattered that the dining room had been set with Jeffrey's best china and silver.

Jeffrey pulled away and nodded with slight anxiety. "I think it is," he replied. "I'm glad to have you back. I wanted to make a presentation to show you. I also wanted to say I'm sorry for being such a jerk. Deep down I knew you would come back. I also knew you had to go. I knew I would miss you terribly and I didn't know how to express it."

Dennis drew closer to him. Their motions were less awkward now. He smoothed his hand down Jeffrey's spine. He always had liked the feel of the small ridge. He pushed his fingers between the starched collar and the nape of his neck and massaged it. Dennis knew that this would relax him. Jeffrey sighed as he went limp and let himself lean on the big man. "Welcome home," he said.

"Thank you," Dennis replied. "I think I would have reacted the way you did if you had done the same to me. Except I know I would've taken you back. I wasn't sure that you would do it."

Jeffrey pulled away. He wanted assurances that the situation would never repeat itself, but he refrained. He wanted the evening to be a celebration. He looked toward the dining area. "I hope you like it."

Large vases of beautiful wildflowers were set around the room on various side tables. Jeffrey had brought out his finest silver and linen. The room was full of the scent of the flowers. The evening was cool, so the windows were left ajar to let in the refreshing breeze. Dennis could smell the rich scents coming from the dishes sitting on warmers on the side tables. There was a bottle of wine breathing on the table. Jeffrey seldom tasted alcohol, and even more seldom in his house.

"Where did you get all these beautiful flowers?" Dennis asked, visiting each arrangement.

"I drove to my aunt's house and went through her garden. I spent two hours picking the best ones," Jeffrey explained.

Dennis wrinkled his brow. "But she lives two hours away. That must have taken the better part of your morning, for these look so fresh."

Jeffrey nodded.

"Then you came back and prepared all of this," Dennis mused. "Wow! I'm impressed."

Jeffrey was pleased.

"I like your silver. I haven't seen it before," Dennis said, walking along the table. "It really shines."

"I stayed up late last night polishing it," Jeffrey admitted. "It belonged to both my grandmothers. Being the only grandchild, I was fortunate enough to claim it in my inheritance. It's been in the family for years."

Dennis lifted the cover of one of the serving dishes. "Wow! This meat smells terrific! I never knew you were such a good cook."

"It is a thick sirloin that I pounded relentlessly to make it tender. Then I left it to marinate for two days. It should be tender enough to cut easily with a fork. I will be disappointed if that's not the case. The sauce I reduced three times under a normal fire. It should be rich and flavorful."

Dennis tapped his tummy. "Well, I'm glad I brought my appetite. I think I'm going to enjoy every bite."

"I made a special rice custard for dessert. I think you'll like it. You've probably never had it before tonight. It's a Creole dish, made with heavy cream."

Dennis abandoned the thought of counting calories. His diet would have to take the night off. "Can the food wait a bit? Can we have a glass of that wine together?"

"It's red, I'm afraid," Jeffrey said, a little remorsefully. "I am only serving it because you serve red with meat. I'm not used to it. Will it be all right?" He brought two crystal glasses and the bottle into the living room.

"It will be fine," Dennis assured him. He beckoned Jeffrey to join him on the couch. He chuckled to himself about how many times they had made love on this piece of furniture, because they didn't want to take the time to go to the bedroom. "You'll get used to the taste after a few swallows and then you'll start to enjoy it. Then you will start to feel its warmth and will be pleased by it." Dennis knew that Jeffrey liked things to be explained in advance. Jeffrey needed a forecast and prognosis for most things in his life. Maybe that's why love was difficult for him. Love is unpredictable. Dennis guessed that the evening had a course to follow and was carefully planned. Unlike Jeffrey, Dennis found it intriguing to wonder where the evening would lead. He could see the wheels turning in his friend's mind.

They sat close together and had some wine. It went straight to Dennis's belly, where it lit a small fire. On an impulse, he reached for Jeffrey's lips and found them with his own. It was a gentle kiss that he let linger for a few moments. He reached inside Jeffrey's jacket and rubbed his large hand against the sharp-starched white shirt. Jeffrey guided Dennis on top of him, spreading his legs, letting Dennis nestle between them. After a long kiss, Jeffrey announced that it was suppertime. "Come on," he said, pushing Dennis away. "The food is ready. I want you to enjoy it before it's past its prime."

Dennis wanted to protest, but realized that Jeffrey had gone to great lengths to prepare this enormous meal, so he acquiesced and followed the wiry, tight body into the dining room. Jeffrey ate little himself as he served Dennis each course. They chatted about Dennis's adventures back East over the past several months. Jeffrey was fasci-

nated as Dennis recounted the steps of the court case that put him
back on top as one of the better litigators in Washington.

"I'm going to need to let this digest for a while," Dennis said, getting to his feet from the dining room table.

"I'll put on some music," Jeffrey replied. "You go into the living
room and relax while I get to the dishes."

"Why don't you let me help?" Dennis protested.

Jeffrey shook his head. "Go on now. Let me get to work. I'll join
you soon enough."

Dennis smiled to himself. When Jeffrey relaxed, some of the country boy came out in him. The proper dialect of an educated doctor
would take a break for a while. He went to the sofa and sat back,
propping his feet on the cocktail table. He decided to remove his shoes
and loosen his tie. Jeffrey did say to relax. As he lay back, he closed his
eyes and let the classical music enter his consciousness. He felt so
happy at this moment. He had the love of a handsome man who
wanted nothing more than to please him.

He must have drifted off to sleep, because it seemed only moments
later that Jeffrey joined him.

"Do you want dessert?" Jeffrey asked.

Dennis reached for his friend to join him. Jeffrey knelt by the
couch. "In a minute," Dennis replied. "I want to spend some time
with you first." A look of faint disappointment came over Jeffrey's
face. "Come on." Dennis smiled broadly, pulling Jeffrey close. "We'll
get to it later," he promised. He started to loosen the doctor's tie.

Jeffrey started to feel happy with the attention he was getting. He
giggled as he felt the tickle of Dennis's lips against the bottom of his
throat. It wasn't long before both men had their clothes off.

Then the spontaneity ended. Jeffrey pushed Dennis away and lay
on his back with his legs spread. He positioned Dennis between them
in the manner in which he wanted him. "I wish to engage in sodomy
tonight," he announced.

Dennis was astonished, as this would be a big step for them. "Ah . . .
that's fine," he replied. "But do we have to call it that?"

Jeffrey shrugged. "Well, okay, but what shall we call it then?"

Dennis snorted. "I don't know. How about intercourse or something? Or maybe we should just do it and call it nothing."

"Okay," Jeffrey agreed. "I'm ready. I prepared myself in advance, so everything should go smoothly. I have the oil handy, because I suspected we wouldn't make it to the bedroom."

"Jeffrey, this isn't a science experiment," Dennis chided him. "We are supposed to be making love." He could see disappointment in the man's face, as his eagerness seemed to subside. To recapture his enthusiasm, Dennis tickled his stomach. "Relax." He smiled. "This is supposed to be fun."

A wry grin came over Jeffrey's face. "Okay, I'll try. I've just never done this before and I want to do it right."

Dennis settled at Jeffrey's side. He resigned himself to the fact that this was not going to be impassioned, but a mission of detailed instruction, so he decided that they should talk about it first. That would be more Jeffrey's style and he would enjoy it more from an intellectual standpoint. "So," he started, running his finger along the fuzzy dark trail between the man's navel and sternum. "What brought this on? You've always shied away from anal sex. Why the interest now?" Before tonight, sex between them had been simple, but satisfying all the same. Jeffrey had religious hangups about sex between men. In the beginning, he reasoned that as long as they didn't become "one flesh" that God wouldn't mind if they kissed and masturbated each other. After several weeks, Jeffrey decided that oral sex might be okay with God, because it was something male couples could do, because it wasn't real intercourse. Dennis never questioned Jeffrey's reasoning too much because, of course, he never agreed with it. Therefore, he would only half-listen to Jeffrey's monologues. He figured that Jeffrey had his own way of dealing with matters. However, he was surprised with this latest revelation. He thought anal sex would be too much for them as a couple, and it would never be part of their repertoire.

Jeffrey fidgeted before answering. "I took your advice and went to talk with Adam about these things. As you said, he was helpful. I was surprised." Among their arguments, Jeffrey refused to listen to Dennis's claims that Adam and Julian were lovers. "He's a minister," Jeffrey would protest, "He wouldn't do such a thing. They are both married. One of them has six children, of which one is a newborn."

"I assure you," Dennis had answered, "Julian and I have been close through the years and he is not reformed, wife and children or not."

"Did he ever tell you that he was engaged in such a relationship with Adam? Did either say Adam demurred to such preferences?" Jeffrey had retorted. "I think it's as it seems. They are best friends. Adam is a man of God. Julian and his family have always gone to church every Sunday."

Dennis would tire of arguing about the subject. Perhaps Jeffrey had missed his calling and should have been a cross-examiner.

"What did Adam have to say?" Dennis asked, returning to the present.

"As you predicted, he was supportive of me," Jeffrey said. "I was straightforward about my feelings toward you and men in general. I feel less desperate now." He looked Dennis in the eyes. "Maybe that will help us get along better."

Dennis nodded in agreement.

"Like you, he got impatient with me when I got philosophical. He stressed that I needed to try to make things simple and less complicated," Jeffrey continued. "I brought up the subject of sodomy."

Dennis didn't know why he hated that word. Perhaps because the term implied that those engaging in it were doing something wrong. He kept his opinion to himself. "What did he say?"

Jeffrey grimaced. "He said that God was too busy trying to save souls to worry about people doing sodomy. He said that God could care less, as long we didn't bring harm to others. If we use sodomy to feel closer to God, then God will be happy. He then quoted the Bible: 'Those who are not against us are for us; the same standard applies to God.' "

"It sounds simple to me," Dennis replied. "I hope you listened to him. He's a wise man." Dennis wasn't sure he believed what he had just said, although he had a new respect for Adam. At least the man wasn't a total hypocrite. Dennis didn't like what he was doing to Julian by keeping him closeted. Maybe he had been too hard on Adam. Any church would be lucky to have Adam as its minister. An openly gay preacher would not sit too well with the people in the pews.

"It sounds so simple yet so complete," Jeffrey replied with a serious look. "I'm going to have to mull it over for a while to appreciate its full meaning, but I do think we can proceed. Do you want to do it?"

"You want to receive it first?" Dennis asked. People sometimes had their preferences, but he was surprised Jeffrey wanted to experiment this way first. "I think it's more difficult that way, although some find it enjoyable."

"I want to try it this way," Jeffrey replied. "What intrigues me the most is why a man would desire to have a penis in his anus. I have to admit, I do crave it, so there must be something to it."

Once again, Dennis climbed on top between Jeffrey's legs. "Now just tell me what to do," Jeffrey instructed him.

Dennis took his lover's legs over his shoulders and looked into his eyes. How could he love a man so full of odd quirks? This act would be a sequence of events and so would subsequent couplings. He had gotten to know Jeffrey and his complicated thought processes well. The man's desire would build as the chain of events progressed. The anticipation of a known response would leave him breathless. Dennis could predict the responses as Jeffrey experienced them. It delighted him to see his partner excited. Still, Dennis was more of the sensual sort and the sight of this beautiful man sent shivers through his body. He looked over his lover with his cream Creole coloring. His body had the light definition of one who took care of himself but was not concerned with big muscles. His pectorals were small but were defined and fuzz accented these small mounds of flesh. A trail of fine hair led into a dark forest. On a bed of curls lay the most beautiful cock he had ever seen. It had a perfect shape, not too big, not too small. It shared the same cream color as his skin as it lay half hard on his belly. It was the kind that stood up when he was aroused. His balls complemented his cock; not too big or too small. They seemed to hang the normal length. Dennis ran his hands along the soft flesh inside of Jeffrey's thighs and felt the downy fuzz of the tight curls covering them. The trail of fuzz picked up again from the base of his scrotum to the sensitive button where his cheeks began to part.

His own cock was at full arousal. It got hard, but it stood straight out and sometimes got in the way. However, in this position, it was going to be more practical. *Now I'm starting to get into this,* he thought. *I'm beginning to think like him.* He laughed to himself. Jeffrey smiled in response as he sensed that Dennis was enjoying himself.

"Now this is going to feel funny at first. I'm going to ease a finger inside you," Dennis explained.

"I'm ready," Jeffrey answered. "Go ahead."

Dennis spit into his hand and massaged it along the opening nestled between his cheeks. He slid his index finger inside and began to move it around in tiny circles. He noticed Jeffrey's wince and saw that his penis was losing its starch. "Relax. It will start to feel good in a minute."

"It feels . . . it feels like I have to go to the bathroom," Jeffrey declared.

*This is going to be a long night,* Dennis thought. "Just relax," he ordered. "That sensation will go away and start to feel good. I said it would feel funny at first. Remember all the preparation you did? Everything will be fine." He could feel Jeffrey begin to unwind.

"It's starting to not feel bad," Jeffrey said. "I think I'm going to like it."

"Good," Dennis replied. He added another finger without announcing it first.

"Ooooh!" Jeffrey complained. "What are you doing?"

"Take a deep breath. Just relax." Dennis moved his fingers in small circles. He could feel the moisture building inside and decided that Jeffrey was almost ready. He noticed that the man's cock had stiffened again. He wondered if he should slip in another finger.

He elevated Jeffrey's legs to give him a favorable position to enter. He applied more spit to the waiting cleft. As he was ready to penetrate, Jeffrey said, "Wait!"

"What's the matter?" Dennis said, perplexed, as he stopped.

Jeffrey pulled from under the sofa cushion a prophylactic. "You better put this on first. I read in one of my journals that people are using these to guard against that horrible disease that's going around."

"Do you really think this will help?" Dennis asked.

"Nobody knows for sure, but they think it might be spread from homosexuals engaging in sodomy." Jeffrey shrugged. "I figured it's better to be safe until we know more."

"Okay," Dennis agreed. He trusted Jeffrey's judgment on medical matters. He didn't want him to get sick if it could be prevented. With some difficulty, he slipped the thin-skin apparatus over his cock. He frowned. "I don't think spit is going to work with this thing."

"Here is some petroleum jelly." Jeffrey offered it from his stash. "That should help you slide in."

The prophylactic felt strange as Dennis spread the jelly over his cock. It hardened once again as he stroked it. Once again, he towered over Jeffrey with the man's legs raised over his shoulders. He wanted to place his hand on the couch for support but stopped, because he didn't want to stain it with the jelly on his hand. As if on cue, Jeffrey reached down and produced a towel. "Thanks," Dennis said as he wiped his hands. Now determined that there would be no more interruptions, he thrust his cock inside Jeffrey quicker than he wanted.

Jeffrey groaned. Dennis wasn't all the way in yet, perhaps three-quarters. "Relax. Take a couple of deep breaths."

Jeffrey complied and started to feel better. After a couple of repeated pushes, Dennis was inside. "Wow!" Jeffrey gasped. "That feels good!"

"Yes, it does," Dennis agreed, feeling happy. Now he felt he could relax. He spit in his hand and took Jeffrey's penis in his gentle fist. He stroked it, as he was familiar with how Jeffrey liked it, while he pushed his own cock in and out of his lover's bottom. He sensed when Jeffrey was ready to shoot, so he pushed deeper with more force to make the loaded gun go off. He eased out, pulled the shield off his cock, and brought himself to a quick orgasm across Jeffrey's belly.

"That was great!" Jeffrey exclaimed, unable to contain his excitement. "I really enjoyed that! Will I be sore later?"

"It was great," Dennis agreed as he moved to Jeffrey's side. "To answer your question, I don't know. Possibly."

"I don't care," Jeffrey exulted. "This was the best." Then he thought for a moment. "Why didn't you finish inside me? Didn't it feel good? Was I not firm enough?"

Dennis started to laugh. "It felt great. I could have finished in you, but sometimes your bottom starts to hurt you after you shoot. I wanted you to feel good. There will be other times."

"Okay," Jeffrey said, wrapping his arms around him. "I love you."

Dennis hugged Jeffrey close. "What about that fancy dessert of yours?"

## 26

"I have to go," Dennis said, placing the phone in its cradle.

"Why?" Jeffrey asked, pulling a robe around himself. "I was hoping you could stay the night."

"I will be back. I promise," Dennis said, pulling on his discarded clothes in a hurry.

"But it's late," Jeffrey protested. "Maybe we should call it a night."

Dennis stood, clothed, and kissed him full on the mouth. "I will be back. Nothing will ruin this night. I want to wake up with you in the morning."

Jeffrey smiled faintly, and then a worried look came over his face. "Is something wrong? Is there a problem at the big house?"

"It's Julian," Dennis replied. "His father has decided to pay a visit, and Pilot insists I be there to help officiate. I just want to make sure he's safe, and then I'll return. Go to sleep and I'll sneak in sometime in the night.

Jeffrey nodded. "I want Julian to be safe. I'm glad you're seeing to him."


Bernard spent twenty minutes pleading with Elizabeth to speak to him. She appeared to be awake and had her eyes fixed on him.

"Why doesn't she say something? She's had enough time to recover," Bernard said with impatience.

"It's true she hasn't been progressing as we would like, but I don't suppose she can help it," Julian replied, joining him. "Shouting at her will do little good."

"She doesn't look like she's had a stroke," Bernard growled. "Isn't one side supposed to droop?"

"She's received physical therapy every day. It's my guess that it's helped," Julian said. "She appears to have regained some reflexes.

We've sent for a specialist who is in great demand. Coming to a small parish in Louisiana hasn't been his greatest priority."

"Can't you pay him enough to make it worth his while? This is critical, Julian. We must get to the bottom of this mess. There's no question in my mind that you are my son by blood," Bernard exclaimed.

Julian wanted to share the same conviction, but his doubts were greater. He felt that when he had his thoughts sorted out that everything would make sense. "Believe it or not, some people are not motivated by money. He has commitments, which he intends to stand behind."

"We'll get to the bottom of this," Bernard growled. "Where is that boyfriend of yours? I want some answers from him. Isn't he the one digging for facts around here?"

Julian looked at Pilot, standing at the far end of the room. "I've sent for him. He'll be here," Pilot said. He detested Bernard's presence. He also detested Elizabeth's presence, but at least she was unable to talk. The couple had come to Louisiana for an extended stay years ago to see their son, and they more than wore out their welcome.

Dennis walked into the room. "I suggest we start talking," Bernard said, taking charge. "Where are these ridiculous facts about a serial rapist fathering Julian? I can vouch that I was there when Julian was conceived. I rushed clear across the world within days of his birth. I would know he's my son. He looks just like me."

Dennis failed to see the resemblance. He looked toward Pilot, who must have been thinking the same thing. Dennis also wondered, did he look like Elizabeth? "We know Elizabeth had a baby. I'm raising the question: are we sure it was Julian?"

"I can't take this," Julian said, as he made for the door. "I was too little to remember where I came from anyway. When you have some concrete facts, let me know."

After Julian left the room, Bernard scolded Dennis. "You could have been more sensitive. It's bad enough he has to question his paternity, but to suggest that the mother he adores is not blood related is in poor taste."

"We need to get all the facts straight," Dennis said. "We were bound to cover a number of issues that would upset him. It's better that he left the room until we can reach some common ground."

"Maybe we should go to my office to discuss this," Pilot suggested, eyeing Elizabeth.

"No, I want her to hear all of this, so when she wakes up, we won't have to repeat these ludicrous charges," Bernard overruled him.

"Uh . . . I'm not sure she understands," Dennis remarked. "I am inclined to think she would be talking by now if she did."

"Nonsense!" Bernard exclaimed. "That woman is going to talk someday. If I have to kidnap this specialist to get him here, I will."

"Let's move on this," Dennis said, changing the subject. He had a promise to keep and he didn't want to break it.

Shaun walked into the room. "Uncle Julian is upset. He walked right past me in the hall without saying a word. What's going on?"

All three men declined to comment. They knew of the difficulty uncle and nephew were having, and the discomfort involving their personal issues hung in the air.

"We're trying to get to the bottom of your uncle's true lineage, grandson," Pilot explained. "Perhaps another head will help."

Bernard compared the older man with the younger. The closeness between the two seemed unlikely, with their disparate personalities. "Fine. Let's get started." He looked at Dennis. "Since you are the expert with questions, I suggest you get started."

"Bernard, where were you when Julian was born?" Dennis inquired. Pilot settled in a chair, while Bernard paced the room, deep in thought. Shaun was leaning against a window frame, while Dennis stood with his arms crossed, one hand stroking his bristled chin.

"I was in an important summit in Luxembourg trying to work my way through some trade restrictions with my partners on the Continent," Bernard explained. "I got word that my wife had the baby, so naturally I had no choice but to take a three-day break in the talks. I went back to Washington, spent two evenings with my wife and son, and then headed back overseas."

"You only stayed a few hours with your new son?" Pilot remarked with distaste.

"It was the least I could do," Bernard said. "He was my firstborn . . . and he is still my firstborn. I don't care what any medical records or investigative reports say."

"In other words, you had no idea what was going on?" Dennis said.

"Everything seemed to be going as it should, except that Julian did seem to be early," Bernard replied.

"There has to be something you noticed. You deal with people all the time to find their strengths and weaknesses. Think, Bernard," Dennis admonished him.

"Well, I don't know the ways of women and their biological cycles. I've had no time or interest to learn about them. But I recall Elizabeth having some difficulty early in her pregnancy. I didn't pay a mind to it. I figured if the baby didn't make it, we'd just try again. Things with the next child went okay. After the first few weeks, things seemed to even out," Bernard explained.

"What else?" Pilot interjected. "Did Elizabeth gain weight, take time off from work, other things that women do during that time? The timing of her pregnancy is of the essence. In the reports, this was referenced time and again."

"Forget the reports," Bernard sneered. "There could be a million explanations for variations. Why don't we concentrate on the obvious faults of the lab results?"

"Bernard, I know these things are hard to accept, but you have to try to be objective," Dennis reproved him. "We have to reconstruct that year.

"The blood results may not say who Julian's father is, but it does say who is not. And it is not you. The pictures of the rapist heavily favor Julian. The timetable for the gestation coincides with Elizabeth's rape. Everything fits to verify the report's claims. And I hate to hurt your feelings, but Julian doesn't look anything like you. You're seeing what you want to see."

Before Bernard could object, Shaun spoke first. "But he does look like his Uncle Matt. I've seen pictures of Uncle Matt. From what Uncle Julian says, Great-grandmother Smith used to comment on this all the time."

"You see what the boy says!" Bernard exclaimed. "That seals it. The rapist is eliminated. It's obvious I'm my son's father."

"How well did Elizabeth know your brother Matt?" Pilot inquired.

"Oh, don't be ridiculous!" Bernard retorted. "Matt died before Julian was born. Don't even think about it."

"Any other *known* siblings?" Pilot pressed. "Granny Smith had your sperm frozen for future use. What would stop her from doing the same for Julian?"

"She only insisted that be done as a result of his death," Bernard explained. "She wanted to be sure there would be heirs. And no, there are no other siblings . . . known or not. I would know such things."

"I don't know how you succeed in business with your preconceived notions," Pilot replied.

Before Bernard could object, Shaun said, "What happened after Uncle Julian was born? We don't seem to have come up with anything odd before his birth. Does everything fit with the report after his birth?"

Dennis squinted thoughtfully. "You are right. There is very little if anything about events after his birth in the reports, except the original birth certificate was tampered with to show Julian was born nine months from the time that Elizabeth could safely claim that Bernard was Julian's father. How could you be so stupid, Bernard? Why didn't you ever question the facts?"

"Six months . . . nine months . . . What difference does it really make? I told you, I pay little attention to the ways of women other than to be there at the beginning. I have little time for the rest."

"How was Elizabeth's behavior toward the baby after he was brought home from the hospital?" Dennis inquired. "Anything odd?"

"Odd for most people or just Elizabeth?" Bernard quipped.

"Come on, Bernard!" Dennis exclaimed. "You're not helping. No more wisecracks at Elizabeth's expense."

Bernard sighed. "She was bored with being a mother within the first week, from what I was told . . . you see, I wasn't there a whole lot. I had a nurse stay with the two of them, and she reported back to me every so often. It didn't take long for Elizabeth to figure out who the snitch was. She had the woman deported to Central America for a trumped-up petty crime."

"That's odd." Dennis furrowed his brow. "That seems excessive, even for Elizabeth. Why not just fire her? It's not like her to come up with such an elaborate plan to dismiss an employee. Didn't you think it strange?"

"Well . . ." Bernard started. He stopped pacing and stared at the floor. "I didn't know the woman had been put out for some time. When I hadn't heard from her, I assumed everything was fine. After some time passed, I forgot about her." He looked up to face Dennis. "It was weeks before I saw my wife and son."

"That's a heck of a way to keep a marriage going," Pilot sneered.

"From what I understand, you are not one to talk about keeping a marriage together," Bernard retorted.

"I see it didn't take long for the gossip to spread," Shaun muttered.

"Enough!" Dennis exclaimed. "Let's get back to the matter at hand." He turned to the red-faced Bernard. "I want to hear more about the circumstances surrounding this foreign woman."

"She was Spanish-speaking," Bernard replied. "Elizabeth was fluent in Spanish. You have to hand it to her. She made the most of her humble beginnings to become so educated."

"All right," Dennis said, avoiding another tangent. "So, you and Elizabeth conversed with this woman in Spanish."

"No, Elizabeth did," Bernard corrected. "I had an intermediary. I had no time for such folks. I just wanted facts."

"Then you must have notes," Dennis surmised. "Do you keep things dated and numbered?" He knew the answer.

"Of course! You know with my dealings I have to have records for everything I say and do," Bernard concurred. He squinted at Dennis. "You know this. I get sued regularly and I must have my conversations detailed for my defense."

"Are you that crooked?" Pilot asked in disbelief. He made a mental note to check his latest brief on this pathetic man.

"I wouldn't call it crooked," Bernard bristled. "It's the normal way of doing business. Everybody has to interpret the politics of the situation. It's crucial for success."

"Okay," Dennis interrupted. "You have your notes. How can we get access to them?"

"I just happen to have them with me," Bernard said. "I suspected we would be going over this material."

"Do you mind if I look them over?" Dennis demanded more than asked.

"Well . . . uh . . . I don't know," Bernard hedged. "Well, okay. It was so long ago that I don't suppose any harm can be done."

"Good," Dennis said with emphasis, ending the meeting. "Get them to me, and then I have to be going."

"This is not how I envisioned spending the morning together," Jeffrey said as he turned over in bed to face Dennis. The lawyer was staring through his gold wire-rimmed glasses at Bernard's notes. "You did not get much sleep last night."

"I don't know what to make of this," Dennis said, ignoring the remark and setting the papers on the down comforter before him. "Why this erratic behavior concerning this Spanish nurse? This woman gets a huge pay raise and then is fired."

The obvious came to Jeffrey's mind. "Maybe the nurse was blackmailing Elizabeth until Elizabeth found a way to get rid of her for good." He picked up a piece of paper. "It says that Elizabeth had someone paid to clear out the nurse's belongings after she left. That means she must have left the country in a hurry with just the clothes on her back. Elizabeth wanted her out . . . fast."

"I suspected the same thing," Dennis concurred. "But what could she know? The baby had been born and was in the nursery. Things didn't seem strange until long after Elizabeth was home from the hospital. If the woman didn't speak English, she was unlikely to overhear conversations or read any notes that she found while she was cleaning. She had to have seen something."

Being a doctor, Jeffrey was naturally interested in medical records. He glanced at Julian's baby records until something caught his eye. "Dennis, this is odd."

"What?" Dennis said, reaching out to stroke his lover's head.

"The blood type. The blood type in these records indicates it's type O. This does not match what I received back from the lab from the sample I took from Julian the other day, which was type B," he reported. "This means Julian could have been sired by the rapist, because the rapist was type O or Bernard, because he is type AB. How can this be?"

"I think the real question is," Dennis replied, looking at Jeffrey, "who is Julian Smith?"

## 27

"Bernard, I want some answers," Dennis said. They were alone in Pilot's study the morning after their discussion. Dennis was tired. He had been up most of the night. Folks rose early in Louisiana, so he was not awarded the luxury of sleeping late. Jeffrey, in an attempt at romance, had served him an early breakfast in bed at 6:00 a.m. He had just managed to fall asleep. He insisted on cornering Bernard alone without interference from Shaun or Pilot. He believed that he could control the conversation better this way.

"I have nothing to hide." Bernard was in a foul mood because he had been prevented from making his morning phone calls.

"I'm not suggesting you do," Dennis lied. "Maybe you have just forgotten a few things."

"What do you want?" Bernard asked. He was getting bored with the ordeal. He had an afternoon flight out of Louisiana.

"Bernard, you're not leaving until I have some answers, so I suggest you be forthcoming," Dennis warned him.

Bernard had lost interest in the whole matter. Julian's latest blood type no longer ruled out the possibility that Bernard was Julian's father. Julian's father could be the rapist or Bernard. This was enough for Bernard. He had his heir. He could care less about the details. As soon as Julian was told of these facts, everything would be back to normal. As far as he was concerned, the father whom Julian idolized growing up was indeed his by blood. Why question the inconsistencies? Everything in life could be challenged. Why sweat it? "Can't you just let this go? We have what we need," Bernard complained.

"Don't you even want to know who Julian is? He obviously is not the baby that Elizabeth brought home from the hospital. There is a strong possibility that he's not even your son. Where did he come from?" Dennis asked.

"Julian and Elizabeth match up, as do Julian and me," Bernard said simply. "The hospital made a mistake with the blood samples. It happens all the time."

"Julian also matches up with the rapist," Dennis countered. "The only perfect hit was Elizabeth. We need to get that nurse here to ask questions. Can you pull some strings?"

"Well, it may be difficult . . ." Bernard replied.

"Not as difficult as I can be," Dennis challenged him. "Remember, Bernard, I know a lot about you that could make things unpleasant, not to mention dangerous, for you."

"I know similar things about you," Bernard replied.

"My dirty underwear has been aired enough times to start a laundromat. Despite my high-profile cases, I still can't get a good job. What more can you do to me?" Dennis retorted.

"You do have a point . . ." Bernard agreed. "I'll see what I can do."

"And find Elizabeth's sister while you're at it," Dennis ordered. "We need to question her."

"Why?" Bernard complained. "She wasn't even around at that point. I don't ever remember seeing her."

"There are so very few people around anymore that were in contact with Elizabeth back in those days," Dennis said. "We need to find those that were closest to her. We have to cover all the bases. She may know something."

"She may be dead for all we know," Bernard grumbled. "Wouldn't you think that we would have heard from her in all these years? Especially with her sister being sick. Also, Elizabeth is rich. When the two of them grew up, they didn't have two nickels to rub together. Don't you think the scent of money would have attracted her? If there was bad blood between the two, the perfect time for this lady to cash in is now when Elizabeth can't defend herself."

"You're absolutely right, Bernard," Dennis concurred impatiently. "There are so many questions. That's why we have to find her. We'll get Shaun to help you dig."

"Where is Uncle Julian?" Shaun asked Emily as the two stood in the children's room. Emily, who home schooled Louis and Candy, was getting ready to give them a quiz.

Emily sighed. "I don't know, Shaun. He left before the rest of us woke this morning. He didn't say where he was going. He just left a note. He was extremely upset last night . . . overwhelmed with the events of yesterday."

"What did the note say? He must have indicated where he was going," Shaun cried in disbelief.

Emily reached into the pocket of her blue dress. "Here's the note. You can see for yourself."

Shaun read the note: *Gone off for a while. Six is with me.*

"Aren't you worried? I don't think he's so stable," Shaun said.

"That's what Julian does when he can't cope, Shaun. He runs," Emily said, picking up the tests. She went to where the two children were sitting. Shaun assumed that she no longer wanted to discuss the matter. However, he was not going to be dissuaded.

"He has your son. Aren't you concerned?" Shaun asked.

"He's safe with Julian," Emily replied, defending herself. "The thing that's keeping him going is caring for Six. I'm surprised at you, Shaun. I would think your attitudes would be more progressive. Julian is the primary caregiver to Six. If a woman took her son off on a trip somewhere, nobody would think anything of it. Why shouldn't a capable man like your uncle be able to take Six along with him?"

"I know Uncle Julian is able to take care of my cousin," Shaun replied. "I am just worried about him. Your lack of concern unnerves me. Unless . . . you know where he is, don't you?"

Emily fidgeted a moment before answering. "I have a good idea," she said, returning to her desk.

"Well, where is he?" Shaun pressed.

Emily looked Shaun straight in the eye. "I said I had an idea. I didn't say I knew for sure. I can just tell you he's safe, Shaun. If he wanted anyone to find him, he would have said where he was going. We need to let him alone to deal with things on his own terms. He's a grown man."

"I just need to be sure he's okay," Shaun argued. "He's been through a lot. Frances Lorraine has threatened to further torment him. If she finds him with nobody to turn to for help, I don't want to think what he'll do. Also, Dennis and Grandpapa have indicated that there is going to be more turmoil for him as they are discovering more truths. I have to find him."

"I can't help you, Shaun," Emily replied.

Shaun understood that Emily would always stand by his uncle's wishes. She always had. He shared the same respect for her. He guessed that was why they had been able to stay together all these years despite their obvious complications. An idea popped into his head. "I bet Billy will help me," he said.

"Shaun, please," Emily pleaded. But it was too late. Shaun was out the door.


Billy was at the big kitchen when Shaun found him during the lunch hour. Shaun sat across from him at one of the long tables as Billy spooned food to his mouth, one bite at a time. Billy ate alone unless Uncle Julian joined him for lunch. "I wanted to know if you have any idea where my Uncle Julian is," Shaun said in an even voice. He tried to hide his desperation.

Billy took several bites before answering. Shaun figured that he was guessing where Uncle Julian might be. "I can't say," he replied.

"You must have an idea," Shaun prodded. He always got along well with Billy. He was smart despite lacking formal education. He read a great deal, which kept him current on national and international events. He didn't speak about what he read, but Shaun was convinced that the man had a lot going on in his head.

"I can't say," Billy repeated.

Shaun became frustrated. He believed the man knew where Uncle Julian was. He thought about ordering Billy to tell him, but wondered if Billy would even comply. He was loyal to his friend Matt. He also guessed that if Uncle Julian had told Billy where he was, he had given his friend special instructions to keep it to himself. Then something occurred to him. He wondered why he hadn't thought of it earlier. *The cottage on the quarters road. That's where Uncle Julian is.* "Thanks, Billy," Shaun said, getting up from the uncomfortable bench attached to the long table. He scurried off to the farm road.

"That was quick work," Pilot commented. He and Dennis were situated in his study.

"Yes," Dennis agreed. "I have to admit that Bernard is able to get people to do what needs to be done. His international connections are impressive."

"When will the nurse be here on the farm?" Pilot inquired.

"Bernard is having her jetted to the nearest airport and at the same time having Elizabeth moved to get the care she needs," Dennis answered.

"He had all this arranged before he left this afternoon?" Pilot asked in awe.

"Bernard likes to impress," Dennis said. "That's why he works so hard with people around the world. He wants to be a mover and a shaker. I guess to some degree he is."

"Elizabeth and he were perfect for each other," Pilot growled with disgust. "I don't understand why their marriage didn't work. It seems they both wanted the same things."

"They decided to be competitors instead of working together. You know how those egos are," Dennis answered.

"I guess," Pilot sighed. Then he asked, "Was this nurse agreeable to coming?"

"For the right price, anything is possible," Dennis quipped. "I didn't ask for details. All I know is she is coming for questioning and will stay as long as she is needed. You don't mind if she stays in the house, do you?"

"No, I want her to stay here. And I want a close eye on her," Pilot ordered. "I don't want Frances Lorraine to be able to get her hands on her."

"Agreed," Dennis answered. "I'll get Billy to get someone to keep her company. Why didn't you try to unload Frances Lorraine on Bernard? He would have found her irresistible. He could have found something impressive for her in his firm. He always has a glamorous woman on his arm. He takes good care of all of them."

"Because Frances Lorraine is obsessed with ruining me," Pilot growled once more. "She will stop at nothing. She's put everything else on hold."

"Well, keep it as a thought," Dennis advised.


Dennis went out to the front porch to get some air and a few minutes of relaxation. He continued to worry about Julian. Where was he? Emily didn't seem to be worried, so maybe he shouldn't. Perhaps it was better for Julian to be away for a while until things settled down.

Adam came through the single French door and joined him on the porch. The two men stood facing the field in front of the big house to the right of the farm road.

"Hey," Dennis greeted him.

"Hi," Adam replied.

"Thanks for your talk with Jeffrey," Dennis said with a touch of forced warmth. He was trying to like Adam. He felt he should admire the guy. Dennis knew that the preacher was making the best of an awkward career. He couldn't think of a better person than Adam to be the shepherd of all the folks that he had come to care about in Louisiana. He just didn't like the way it affected Julian, with secret meetings with his lover behind closed doors. He didn't want that for Julian. However, what else could Julian do? He was married to a woman with six children in a place that was uptight about the subject of homosexuals. In reality, the situation suited both of them.

Adam nodded to accept his thanks. It also concluded the short discussion. He was going to discuss matters of his sheep with others. To change the subject he asked, "Do you know where Julian is?"

"No," Dennis said, looking away. It was his turn to change the subject. He didn't want to get into a discussion about Julian with Adam. He knew that the minister would end up getting a piece of his mind.

However, Adam wasn't about to let it go. "Come on, Dennis," Adam cajoled him. He was trying not to sound as if he was pleading for information.

Dennis could see that despite the confident, calm, and pastoral concern that Adam consistently displayed, the man was frantic and about to break. Dennis was going to push until he got some honest answers from the minister.

Adam was gifted with a pastor's patience and willing to wait with compassion for answers to come to the people he counseled, but this situation was hitting too close to home for him. "You must know it has been difficult for me to wait. Julian won't see me. I don't know why. I'm worried about him. I don't live in this house. I don't have access to know what is going on with him. This family is proud and reluctant to let outsiders know what is going on in there . . . even reluctant to explain the complete truth to their pastor."

"Well, this is a family matter," Dennis said in a condescending tone meant to exclude Adam from that mix. "There are some things that friends will have to wait until later to understand . . . if of course the *family* decides to convey it at all."

"How do you fit in?" Adam asked with a trace of the frustration he was feeling. "Why do you consider yourself so privy to family matters?"

"Because I live in the big house," Dennis replied. "Also, I make no pretension as to what I am and what I mean to this family. As a result, they accept me according to my true nature."

Adam bit his lip. He could feel himself coming unglued. He had not been able to sleep since Julian started to reject him. He was feeling so alone. The only person he ever had confided in was Julian. Now he was gone. Now there was no one he could turn to for comfort, except this man who despised him. How he missed Julian! He turned to leave.

"Wait, Adam," Dennis called after him. Adam kept going. "Please! I was being unfair. I'm sorry."

Adam turned to face the big man. His eyes were red, but there were no tears. "I have to see him," he choked. "Just to make sure for myself he's okay."

Dennis nodded. "I'll find him, and then give him your message. I'll do what I can to make him see you."

"Why do you hate me so?" Adam asked with pain in his eyes. "What have I ever done to you?"

"It's not you," Dennis replied, finding some compassion. "I'm just protective of Julian . . . and Shaun . . . and this family. It's my nature."

"Believe me, I feel the same," Adam replied, pleading his case. "Yet I feel like the outsider you've painted me to be. You don't know me very well, yet you found an insecurity of mine. You must be good at what you do." Then he asked, "Why do you feel these people need protection from me? They are my sheep and I am their shepherd. Why would I cause them harm?"

Dennis knew this man was hurting, yet he felt this was not the time to spare him more burdens. "First, you have hurt Shaun. You of all people should know what Julian means to that kid. Yet with your secrets and the lie you live, you have driven a wedge between his uncle and him. They haven't been close in some time and now they are barely speaking to each other. Next, you have hurt me. I adore Julian and always have. He keeps an important . . . maybe the most important aspect of his life from me. Talk about feeling like an outsider. How do you think I feel? I want Julian to be happy, yet I don't know what's going on with somebody I consider to be my best friend. I miss him. And finally, there is Julian. You know how he gets. He can be melancholy at times. It's not good for him to be isolated from people who care about him. This place is full of mosquitoes and unbearably hot in the summer. He only stays here because he knows he needs to be around people who love him. Julian is no good alone, yet he is all by himself with you."

Adam bowed his head. "I don't know if I can possibly deal with all you've said right now. I just know I have to see Julian for my own sanity. You're right. I'm too dependent on him and I've made it so that he's probably the same way about me, yet he won't see me."

"You know, he pushed those kinds of feelings away when he came to Louisiana, because he had other issues plaguing him," Dennis reminded him. "Don't let him do it again. When you see him, promise that things will be different. Give him something he can hope for when he comes back to us."

"Everything I have done has been for the sake of the greater community of my church. It's true that some of those closest to me have had to make sacrifices," Adam defended himself. "I can't promise that I will make changes, but I will promise to think about what you've said. I'm sorry for hurting you. I can try to make restitution to Shaun. I'll have to talk with Julian about the rest. I just didn't know. He never complained about anything. I always thought things were fine between us."

"Hang in there," Dennis said, placing a hand on the minister's shoulder. "I'll get you to see Julian. I have to warn you, though. This whole thing is far from over. He's going to need us all."

"Uncle Julian?" Shaun called on the small porch of the cottage.

Julian opened the screened door to invite his nephew inside. However, his expression let it be known that he was less than thrilled with being disturbed.

Shaun sat down on the familiar chair that he had liked when he spent time in the cottage. Uncle and nephew had lived there together when Shaun first came to the farm. Julian and Emily were separated at the time for many months before the two moved into the big house to join the family. Julian sat on the edge of the kitchen table with his hands braced on its edge. The baby was sleeping in the back bedroom.

"I needed to know you were okay," Shaun said. "I was worried. How are you?"

"I'm fine," Julian replied. "Look, Shaun, I don't know if this is the best time . . ."

"Well, it's going to have to be," Shaun growled, getting to his feet. He had had enough of pent-up emotions and was determined to get a few things off his chest. "I'm sick and tired of being cast aside by you. I haven't slept a full night since all this has started. I have been so worried. I said I was sorry for not telling you the truth about your birth. But Uncle Julian, you have been less than honest with me the last few years. You have cut me off from a big part of your life. You started the rift between us and now we barely talk. I'm tired of taking the lion's share of the blame for it and I won't stand for it any longer. We're going to patch things up. And yes, this is the right time. You have to confront all the issues in your life, not just the unpleasant ones. You are going to have to talk about things. Pilot's wife has just begun to make things miserable for you. Dennis and Pilot are working right now to uncover more unpleasant things. In other words, things have just begun. You can't run and hide without telling those who care about you. It's not fair to us. Are you going to fight or are you just going to let life beat on you?"

Julian thought for a moment. "It's my turn to say I'm sorry, Shaun. I'm not really mad at you, but I do wish you had come to me before. Just be truthful with me from now on. Okay?"

Shaun nodded.

Julian looked away while he put his thoughts together. "Perhaps I have been selfish of late. This whole thing was a terrible shock to me. Can you imagine what's it like to know you were sired by a slimy criminal in hate who violated so many women? I am the product of that. I'm mixed up. Somehow, I feel guilty and dirty and I hate myself for who I am."

"But it's not your fault," Shaun blurted. "You're nothing like him."

"I know, Shaun," Julian concurred. "But it's the way I feel right now."

"Why does being away from your family help?" Shaun asked. "You need us. You need to talk about these things to help sort them out."

Julian rubbed his hands over his face. "There is too much going on at the big house right now. I need some peace. Besides, Shaun, they are my in-laws. It's not the same. Billy's family became my family when I came to this farm. I feel comfortable with them. They are going to help me through this . . . especially if things get worse. I'm going to need them."

Shaun could see his uncle's point. "I just wish you had told somebody. Remember, years ago you ran away when things got tough and the folks you left behind didn't find you for years. In the back of my mind, I'm afraid of that happening again. I would be beside myself, Uncle Julian."

"I promise you that I will never do that again," Julian replied. "I was young then and less mature than you are at the same age. I was about your age then. Also, I have responsibilities now that I didn't have back then. In addition, I despised the people I left behind. I'm fortunate now to have people that love me. That has been why I've stayed in this place. I can't see myself leaving."

"That makes me feel better," Shaun said, letting out a sigh of relief. "But what about you and me, Uncle Julian? We haven't talked like this in a long time."

Julian slumped. "You mean, Adam." Julian paused. "The reason I have never discussed Adam with you is because I thought it was an issue between you and him. I'm sorry for hurting you, Shaun. I just always thought the two of you would work it out. I will talk to him about it, though I can't promise when. I'm sure the three of us will reach a comfort level that can work to make you happy. Despite what you say and feel, Shaun, I have always felt close to you. I guess you felt differently. I'm sorry for not being more sensitive." He went over to Shaun and gave him a big long hug. After giving him the noisy sloppy kiss he always gave him, he let him go.

"Is it all right to tell the others where you are?" Shaun asked.

Julian nodded. "Ordinarily, I would have known better than to worry them. Tell them I'm sorry. But also, Shaun, tell them to be respectful of my privacy. I don't want a parade of visitors unless they have something they need to discuss with me."

Shaun nodded.

"I know you are busy enough as it is, but can you tend to my farm responsibilities for a while? Pilot is under enormous pressure and I fear he has let some things go," Julian said.

"I've been tending to those," Shaun assured him.

Julian cocked his head and asked, "When are you going to see that boyfriend of yours? You guys have gone too long without being together. Do you have a trip planned?"

"He's coming out here for a while," Shaun said. "I need him here with me despite his dislike of the place."

"Maybe he'll grow to like it," Julian said.

"Maybe," Shaun replied. "I'll drop by for a few minutes tomorrow, Uncle Julian, to see how you are."

Julian nodded, and Shaun headed out the door.

"Is she here yet?" Pilot asked over a cup of coffee while sitting at the kitchen table next to Emily.

"She'll be here any moment," Dennis replied as he descended to the bottom step.

Emily got up. "I'll get your breakfast. Coffee is fresh in the carafe on the table in front of Daddy."

"Thanks," Dennis replied with affection. "Have you heard from Julian?"

"No," Emily replied. "He's probably in the cottage on the quarters road if you need him. I'm sure he's settled in by now. I think Shaun has already been to see him. He's not speaking to me. He's still asleep, so I guess he is less worried and getting the rest he needs."

"You don't seem worried," Dennis commented. "You think he's all right? We were hard on him the other day."

"I know my husband . . . almost as well as you do," Emily replied. "He'll be okay as long as we don't *drive* him nuts."

"Poor choice of words," Pilot muttered.

"Have to keep the humor, Daddy," Emily chirped, setting a plate in front of Dennis. "Besides, Julian wouldn't mind."

There was a knock at the front door. "I think our guest has arrived," Pilot said.

The housekeeper came into the kitchen. "Mrs. Rodriguez is waiting in the front parlor." She paused for a moment. "She's brought a large amount of belongings with her. What do you want done with them?"

"I think she's going to milk this visit as long as she can. It can't be pleasant in her homeland," Emily mused. Then she asked, "Has Mrs. Steele's room been cleaned out and remade?"

"Yes ma'am," the housekeeper replied.

"Have her things brought up there. And please, if they are too heavy, get some help. I don't want you lifting things twice your weight," Emily ordered.

"Yes ma'am." The housekeeper left the room.

"Can you have some tea brought to the front room?" Dennis asked, looking at Emily. "I suggest we get started," he continued, shifting his gaze to Pilot.

"Aren't we going to give her time to get settled and freshened up?" Emily asked with concern.

"The sooner we get started the better," Dennis overruled her. "She will have plenty of time to freshen up later . . . especially if she plans to stay a while." He walked to the door, then turned back toward her. "By the way, have you brushed up on your Spanish?"

"Yes," Emily replied. "I'll be fine as long as she speaks slowly. It was my strongest of the three languages I studied in college." Emily had majored in foreign languages in college. She was fluent in German, French, and Spanish. She was glad to have the chance to speak some Spanish, as she needed the practice. The children were learning Spanish and French at the moment, so this should be helpful.

Among her belongings, Mrs. Rodriguez had brought with her several bunches of cut flowers. They were plentiful in South America and bought for mere pennies. She wanted her hosts to be pleased. She was in no hurry to return home.

Dennis, Pilot, and Mrs. Rodriguez exchanged a series of smiles and nods before Emily arrived in the room, bringing a pot of hot tea and cups. She greeted Mrs. Rodriguez in Spanish.

With Emily translating, Dennis said, "Let's get started." He decided against further pleasantries. He figured the woman knew why she was here.

Mrs. Rodriguez lost her smile and became uncomfortable. "Is Mrs. Steele here?"

"I assure you she is not," Dennis replied.

"And she is not well?" Mrs. Rodriguez asked with worry in her eyes.

"She's been sick for many years," Dennis exaggerated. "She'll never be able to harm you. She is a vegetable." Dennis hoped that Emily would be able to translate the term.

Mrs. Rodriguez relaxed into her seat, so everything seemed to be going smoothly. Dennis figured he would get the sequential details later in the conversation, but he had a pressing concern at hand. "The baby Mrs. Steele gave birth to at the hospital over forty years ago, was it the same baby she brought home days later? I understand you cared for her from the time of her unfortunate ordeal some months before. What can you tell us about the birth and events afterward?"

Mrs. Rodriguez took a deep breath. Before she could speak, Shaun entered the room and took a seat. He was dressed to meet Carmen at the airport late that afternoon. He helped himself to a doughnut.

Again, Mrs. Rodriguez took a breath. "Are you sure Mrs. Steele will not be able to get to me?"

"I have no doubt," Dennis replied.

"Okay," Mrs. Rodriguez replied. "I will tell you what I know. Which do you want me to answer first?"

"Who is this baby we call Mrs. Steele's son?" Dennis said.

"Mrs. Steele had a bad time with her baby when she carried him," she started. "She carried him six months before he was born. He had a head of black hair much like that of Mr. Smith. The baby was healthy and some days later we took him home to his nursery, where everything seemed fine. Mrs. Steele would ask after him but would otherwise pay little attention to him. She was studying day and night for her school. She said she always made perfect grades. This was important to her."

"So the baby was healthy and all was fine," Dennis prodded.

"Yes," Mrs. Rodriguez continued. "Mr. Smith soon came home to see the new baby. He was happy. He said the baby looked just like himself and could I see the resemblance? I said I could. He seemed happy enough, so the next morning he took another plane and I didn't see him for weeks . . . maybe months. Then one day it happened. Three months after we brought little Julian from the hospital, we found him dead in his crib. I was sure he was dead. He was stiff. I ran for Mrs. Steele and brought her to the nursery. She seemed calm and unconcerned. She said the baby was sick and needed some rest. She said she personally would take him to the doctor. I cried and cried. I was so upset. Mrs. Steele sent me to my room to get myself together. She said to take the next couple of days off to rest. When she returned to the house that evening, she said the baby would be in the hospital for a couple days, then he would return to us. She was right. Two days later, she brought the baby home and placed him in his crib. She smiled at me and said the baby had a small cold and was all better now. I couldn't believe my eyes. I know that baby was dead, yet here he was living and breathing in his crib. I picked him up and began to feed him. I know many babies look alike but I could tell that this was not the same baby. Mrs. Steele sensed my doubt. It wasn't long before I was accused of some crime and sent back to my country."

"Did you commit a crime?" Emily asked.

"No," Mrs. Rodriguez said. "When I went to the bank to cash my paycheck, the buzzer went off. The man in the uniform searched my purse and found a small pistol and a bag of white powder. I've seen the powder before in my country and I knew what it was. I knew it was bad to have it here in this country. I tried to run away, but I was put in handcuffs. I was back to my country within days. When I got back home, there was money waiting for me in an envelope with a warning never to speak about what happened in Mrs. Steele's house. I have felt much guilt for my part for more than forty years. I'm glad to make the confession now."

"Do you know where this second baby came from?" Dennis asked.

Mrs. Rodriguez began to doubt herself. "I don't know. Maybe there wasn't a second baby. Maybe I was confused. I've been over this in my mind a thousand times. But then I remember the baby was so stiff. Also, you can always tell when the spirit has left a body to be with God. This tiny body was just a shell."

"Where did this second baby come from?" Dennis asked.

"I don't know," Mrs. Rodriguez answered.

Dennis grilled her some more and then decided that all had had enough for a while.

"What next?" Pilot asked after Mrs. Rodriguez, Shaun, and Emily left the room.

"I need to talk to Julian," Dennis replied. "I need to talk to him now."

"Good luck," Pilot said. "He hasn't been cooperative so far."

"Well, that's going to have to change," Dennis said.


"Hey," Dennis said as he greeted Julian. He didn't bother knocking. He just trudged through the door as if he'd done it every day. The late morning sun was getting closer to noon.

"Hey," Julian replied.

"How are you?" Dennis asked.

Julian gave a couple of short nods. "Good, all things considered. I'm spending some time with Billy's family and I think it's doing me a world of good. I explained things to Jeannette and Billy last night. Somehow telling them made things not seem as bad." He paused. "I get the feeling that you didn't come by to see how I was doing." He offered refreshment, which Dennis accepted.

"Not entirely, but I would like to visit," Dennis admitted. "I have a few things on my mind that might take you from your troubles for a few minutes. But I don't have too long. I'm driving to the airport to fetch Carmen with Shaun. We won't be back until tomorrow." The two men sat near each other in the living area in front of the turned-off TV set.

"With all you have going on, why are you going with him?" Julian inquired.

"Because he asked me." Dennis shrugged. "I like spending time with him, much the way you do."

Julian smiled. He was pleased. After a pause, a twinkle came to his eye. "So, how are things on the man front? Boys got you in a stitch?"

Dennis frowned. "You must be feeling better. You've started to make fun of me again."

"I can't help myself," he replied with a grin. "You're such an easy target. What's up?"

"I think I have to choose between the two of them now." Dennis frowned again. "I think I missed the boat on this one. I'm too late making a choice. One of them is going to be hurt. The other may not forgive me. I could lose them both."

"Which one are you going to pick . . . providing you still have a choice?" Julian asked. "Why do you feel at this moment you have to choose? Have things changed? Seems like things were working out well."

"I think Simon is okay. He's so easygoing," Dennis answered. "However, Jeffrey is a different card. Things have gotten more intense with him. He tells me he loves me."

"What do you say?" Julian asked.

"Nothing." Dennis shrugged. "I tell him I'm not in a position to make commitments, since I really live back East. He seems to accept this answer to a point, until I suggest that I have to go back for a time. Then he gets upset with me."

"So, where are you with this?" Julian asked again. "Have you made up your mind?"

"No," Dennis said, bowing his head. He looked up at Julian. "I wish I could put the two of them together and make one person. Not because I want to change either one of them. I just want both of them."

"What's your plan?" Julian said.

Dennis sighed. "I'm going to level with both of them. Maybe one will reject me and the other will forgive me. Then I won't have to choose. It will be easy."

Julian made a face. "That doesn't sound like a good plan. I suspect you can guess what the results would be."

"Kind of," Dennis admitted. "Simon doesn't seem as bothered by the things that make Jeffrey angry. He may be able to look past it while Jeffrey may not."

"Don't underestimate either one of them," Julian warned. "Jeffrey has proven unpredictable and Simon is not as capable of expressing his feelings. He still has them."

"You haven't been much help," Dennis growled. "You were supposed to tell me what to do."

"I guess I learned from Adam," Julian chuckled. "He always says people have to find their own answers. He just tries to guide them in the right direction."

Dennis mused for a moment. "The man is dying to see you. He has a funeral today. I think he has the day free tomorrow. You may want to consider seeing him. He's upset."

Julian nodded. "Tell him to come on down. I'll be waiting for him."

Dennis nodded. He felt a wave of discomfort come over him, as he now needed to reveal the unpleasant news. "You said you wanted us to start being honest with you. I have some updates that will not make you happy. Do you want me to wait until I have more concrete answers?"

Julian got up and paced the room. He turned to Dennis biting his fist. He nodded. "Go ahead."

Dennis explained the interview with Mrs. Rodriguez and the suspicions Pilot, Shaun, and he were feeling. "What do you think? Are you too upset to talk? I would really like to get your input, since it affects you."

Julian regained his seat. He shook his head. He was calm. "I don't know, Dennis. I'm starting to feel those overwhelming feelings again. I'll have to sort through it." He paused. "Don't worry. I'm not going to slip into myself again. I've accepted the idea that my parents may not be my parents. It's just that the whole serial rape thing still unnerves me. I haven't finished dealing with those issues."

"You know," Dennis warned him, "you may never know who your real parents are. Despite what Bernard thinks, if Elizabeth somehow regains the ability to communicate, she will vehemently deny the death of the first baby. She will never admit to not being your mother."

"Somehow I don't think it's her love for me that would inspire her to reject any notion that someone else is my mother," Julian said.

Dennis agreed. "She would lose all Shaun's money if it's found that she's a fraud. She has plenty of incentives to get well. She needs to stand competent to claim her share of the trust. I think we can figure that she will fight to recover."

"I feel guilty now, because I don't care if she recovers. I don't care if we don't find the truth. I don't want any of them as parents!" Julian said angrily. Then he added more gently, "My family is here with Billy and his family. They are the ones in my heart. They took me in when they didn't have to many years ago. My pedigree made no difference to them and neither did the color of my skin. That is the unconditional love that I had sought all my life. Then one day, it was set in my lap. I've always appreciated Old Bill and his folks. They are the best."

Dennis nodded. After the moment had passed, he asked, "Do you know anything about Elizabeth's sister?"

"No," Julian replied, shaking his head. "I don't even know her name. Why?"

"We need to find her. I suspect she was around at the time of your birth. She may have some answers. Were Elizabeth and her sister close? What did Elizabeth ever say about her?"

"I know nothing about her," Julian said, trying hard to come up with a memory. "I didn't even know she had a sister until my Grandmother Smith mentioned it shortly before she died. When I questioned Elizabeth about it, she flatly refused to discuss it. I wasn't interested in family history at the time, so I forgot about it." He turned to Dennis. "How are you going to find her?"

"I put Shaun on it," Dennis replied. "That's what he's working on this afternoon. Also, he is working to obtain your original birth certificate." Then he smiled. "I need to get your footprint at some point."

"Why?" Julian asked, furrowing his brow. "I have them both in the big house. Why go to the trouble?"

"To be sure yours matches with the ones on official record," Dennis explained. "The print from the birth certificate we have is missing, but maybe it will show up at some point. If you were a replacement baby, maybe it will help find out where you came from if Elizabeth's baby really did die."

"Why not believe the woman?" Julian asked.

"Because she's a liar," Dennis said. "Her family in South America has no scruples. They are a nasty lot. She's milking this visit for all it's worth. She's in no hurry to go home. She says it may take her a few days to remember everything. I hope there are some threads of truth in what she tells us. Maybe we can get some leads." He stood up and gave Julian a hug. "I need to be going. I'm glad you're feeling better. I'll tell Adam to see you tomorrow here at the cottage."

"Thanks for everything, Dennis," Julian said. "You've been good to me through the years."

Dennis nodded, then exited through the door.

## 29

"Hi," the young woman said as Julian opened the door. Her hair with rich tones of light brown was tied up in braids along the sides of her head, then secured in a tight bun in back. Her skin was a creamy color except for her face, which was accented with makeup. The loose jewelry she wore on her wrists looked expensive. Her white cashmere dress gave her an angelic appearance. Her gestures and expressions unnerved Julian.

"Uh . . . hi," he replied as he fumbled for words. After a minor pause, he invited her into the cottage. "Come in."

"Is everything okay?" she asked.

"Yes," Julian said with a sheepish grin. "You remind me of someone I know."

"Perhaps it's my grandmother. Papa says I remind him of her," the woman replied. "My name is Leah, Uncle Julian. I'm Shaun's younger sister."

"Leah?" Julian said with disbelief. "You're supposed to be a teenage girl. You seem to be on the petite side, but you look so grown-up. Have a seat. What can I get you?"

Shaun had told her the farm was dry, so she resisted her thirst for white wine. Was it too early in the day? "I'll have whatever you're having."

"My friend next door . . . she brings sweet tea each day. Will that be okay?" Julian asked, going into the kitchen.

"Yes," Leah said. "You're just as Shaun described you, Uncle Julian. You know he's crazy about you. He can talk about both Carmen and you for hours if I let him."

"I'm sorry for staring at you so," Julian apologized. "It's just that you are the spitting image of Elizabeth . . . at least when she was younger . . . how odd. I feel as though I'm talking to her in some way.

The way you move and the way you speak is uncanny. So like her. Shaun should have warned me."

"I don't think he ever heard her talk," Leah replied. "Besides, she's sick and people don't look the same when they're ill."

"True," Julian agreed. "You also have her knack for reproving me in a subtle way like she does . . . did. She was a charmer when she wanted to be." After a pause he stated, "You have to be all of sixteen. How do you happen to be so grown up?"

"It must be my upbringing. Papa doted on me so," she replied, picking up on some of Julian's dialect.

Julian noticed her every move. Just like her grandmother. Everything she did was reasoned and calculated. Her movements and speech were purposeful. "If you're anything like Shaun says, I'm sure you are a delightful young lady."

Leah guessed what he was thinking. "I hope you judge me by my own merits and not of those of my grandmother."

Julian took a sip of his iced tea as he joined her in the living area. She held hers without tasting it. He no longer felt the need to put up a polite front. He figured she knew . . . or guessed what he was like. Should he just treat her as if she was Elizabeth? His mother was dangerous if one did not keep one's guard up. "I'm sure you came to see me with some other purpose than to introduce yourself," he said.

Leah was amused. "I see with your present . . . illness you don't miss a beat."

She decided she was going to like her uncle. She would have to try not to be hard on him.

"If you're anything like your grandmother, I'm not up to it," Julian stated. "Are you a nice girl or do you play games?"

"I play games," Leah replied. "But I'm not vicious. I'll be gentle."

"Why are you here?" Julian said, trying to get to the point.

Leah paused for effect. "I'm hoping my brother and my papa will come to some sort of reconciliation."

"I want no part of it," Julian said. "It's none of my business . . . or yours for that matter."

"You know my brother," Leah reminded her uncle. "Things eat at him until they are resolved. He still has issues concerning Papa."

"He hates Albert," Julian said. "It's deep seated . . . and probably rightly so. It will be just digging up old hurts."

Leah got to her feet to go. She had accomplished what she set out do. The seed had been planted. "Just try to keep an open mind, Uncle Julian. I have grown fond of my brother. Despite what you both think of my papa, I believe he's a good man. Our family has been through a lot of pain through the generations. At some point, we have to start to fix it."

"It's something else for me to think about," Julian sighed. "It will be a while before I can sort through your request. I have issues of my own to contend with right now. I'm trying to pull out of a depression these days. Your matters will have to wait. If I'm rude, I'm sorry, but that's one of the reasons I've taken refuge here. I can't deal with the politics of being nice at the moment."

"I'll leave you with your thoughts," Leah said, clasping her hands. She started for the door. "I hope we can be friends, Uncle Julian. We need to get our family together."

Julian accompanied her to the door as she continued to speak. "I'll be staying at the big house for a while. I've come to visit Shaun and Carmen for a spell. I believe he's arriving midafternoon."

Carmen was irritable on the drive back to the farm. It was bad enough to come to this part of the country, which he utterly despised, but to have that big hunk Dennis with his boyfriend on the long drive to the farm was the icing on the cake. They hate gays out here. Shaun and he were working so hard in Boston to end the antigay rhetoric. To come to the heart of it made him sick. If the hate for gays wasn't bad enough, he knew what people must have been saying behind his back when they saw him. He looked different from the rest of these people due to his Native American heritage. What these people had forgotten was that his people were here first. No, they probably think of Native Americans as the conquered people. "Just give them a chance," Shaun would say. "There are some good apples in the bunch." Fine, that could be true, but the fact that Dennis was driving down the road chatting with Shaun made things miserable.

When they got into the station wagon, Carmen asked Shaun in a harsh whisper, "Why did you bring him? You know how I feel about him."

"We're not going to fight already," Shaun replied. He took Carmen's hand. "You just got here."

Carmen pulled his hand away and sulked the entire way to the farm. He wanted to be alone with Shaun. These long stretches of time apart were hard on him. Sometimes he wondered how much Shaun cared about their relationship.

## 30

"What are you doing here?" Julian growled. He let the screened door slam without inviting his guest inside and retreated into the bowels of the little house.

The screen door opened and Frances Lorraine pushed inside. "I warned you that you hadn't seen the last of me," she crooned, smoothing her dress. She carried a small purse under her arm. She sauntered closer to where Julian was standing in the kitchen. She had to remind herself that seduction wouldn't work with this man.

"What do you want?" Julian said with anger in his voice. He leaned against the kitchen counter and looked the determined woman in the eyes with contempt.

"I have something with me that I felt you might find interesting," she replied, tapping her purse. She moved in front of him. Julian brushed past her and moved to the living area.

"If you think I'm going to just lie down and let you destroy me," Julian said, turning to her, "you have another thing coming."

"I feel it's my duty to help you no matter what you think," Frances Lorraine said, following him out of the kitchen. "It's not my fault that your family thinks you're too weak to handle messy truths. I would think you would thank me for being honest."

Julian sighed. He was tiring of the visit. "Get on with your business and let me be . . . and yes, I do want to know the truth about things, no matter how awful. I just wish it didn't come from you."

Frances Lorraine took a medium-sized envelope from her purse and slapped it down on the table in front of the sofa. "I think you will find the contents interesting," she purred. She flashed an evil grin and then whisked herself through the door. Before she was out of earshot, she warned, "I will be back, Julian. The fun is just beginning."

After she had gone, Julian picked up the envelope. *No more lies,* he thought. If the contents were unpleasant, he would have to deal with them. For some reason, this woman wanted to hurt him. What could she do that was worse than she had already done? He tore open the tan envelope and removed its contents. It was a single sheet that seemed to be a photograph. He paled as he examined it. He took it to the sink and let it drop. From a drawer, he extracted a book of matches. He removed one to strike it. Before he held the match, he studied it once more. It was a man who looked like himself in a prison uniform. At the bottom of the picture was a black box with some writing on it. Julian didn't care to read it, because he had an idea who the man was. He turned the offensive photograph face down and burned it.

Dennis removed Carmen's suitcase from the trunk of the Ford wagon. The smaller man seized it from him and stormed toward the big house. He labored to drag it up the lawn. Shaun and Dennis stood and watched him huffing and puffing as he pulled the baggage across the front porch.

Shaun shook his head as he started for the house. Dennis trailed behind. "I don't see why he gets like this."

Shaun reached the porch and collapsed on the top step. Dennis sat down next to him. "He'll be all right. Just let him get settled."

Shaun placed a hand on Dennis's thigh and looked Dennis in the face with puppy-dog admiration. "I just wish he could be more like you. He's just being a big baby. Sometimes I wish it were you and me together. I know you're older and don't see me that way. I just wish sometimes."

Dennis was aware of the young man's attraction to him. Shaun had a crush on him. He suspected that Carmen knew as much and had reason to feel threatened. On impulse, he turned Shaun's face toward his own and planted a kiss on his lips. It wasn't a quick peck such as friends or relatives give each other, but revealed passion.

Carmen started to unpack his things, arranging his belongings in the drawers of the chest. He smoothed the mussed garments. He began to feel guilty. Maybe he had overreacted. Of course Shaun loved him and not Dennis. If the two of them were having an affair, would they be stupid enough to be together in front of him? Certainly not! They would do everything to hide their relationship from him. No, he knew he was overreacting. He was glad to see Shaun. He had missed him so much. One of the things they were going to talk about this trip was how they could spend more time together. Shaun always had to stay in Louisiana longer than he had planned. Carmen now accepted the fact that this would always be the case. Instead of arguing with Shaun about spending more time in Boston, he figured it would make peace to make the present situation work. He stopped what he was doing to go find his boyfriend to see if he could patch things up.

When he reached the doorway to the porch he could hear voices. It was Shaun and Dennis murmuring. They were giggling about something. He glanced through only to see Dennis in a passionate embrace with his lover.

Carmen was aghast. *How could he do this? He must have brought me here to humiliate me. What have I ever done to him except to love him?* He held his tears and rushed back to his bedroom.


When they broke free, Dennis examined Shaun's face, while Shaun stared at his knees.

"Wow! That's not what I expected," Shaun gasped.

"Was it that good?" Dennis replied.

"Well . . ." Shaun started. He met Dennis's gaze. "I felt like I was kissing Uncle Julian." He looked at his knees again. "I thought it would be different."

"I'm crushed," Dennis smirked. "I guess I'll have to practice my pucker."

"It's not that," Shaun replied with a giggle as he blushed. "It's just you're not Carmen."

"He senses your attraction, you know," Dennis said. "That's why he acts the way he does. He's not stupid."

Shaun frowned. "He's the one with the straying eye. I just know it will never lead to anything. I trust him." He took another long breath.

"On the other hand, I never have a straying eye." He looked at Dennis. "Until I met you. I guess he thought that if I had the chance to go with you, I would. He may have been right."

"But you don't want me," Dennis replied with a big grin. Again he was amused. "For some reason, you see me as a mature and responsible Carmen." With mock amazement he added, "No one has ever accused me of being mature or responsible before you."

Shaun thought for a moment. "You are both passionate about your causes. I find that attractive. I know you think you've slipped some in your looks, but you haven't. Both you and Uncle Julian are maturing well. I hope I'm as lucky. Carmen will be like you guys, except he will always be beautiful in my eyes . . . no matter what."

"So, this means I lose out," Dennis sighed. He tried to keep from laughing.

Shaun reached to give the broad-shouldered man a hug. As he embraced him he replied, "Every guy needs a hero. I'm lucky to have two of them in Uncle Julian and you."

Dennis broke from him and looked at him squarely. "Are you sure you don't want another kiss? You know, just to be sure."

Shaun blushed. "You never are going to let me live this down, are you?" He shook his head. "I don't need any more convincing." He got up and reached for the screened door. "I'm going to check on him."


Shaun entered the bedroom, where Carmen was stuffing his suitcase. "What are you doing?"

"I'm leaving," Carmen growled.

"But you just got here," Shaun complained.

"I don't want to be in your way any longer," Carmen replied, slamming the suitcase shut. "I'll leave you to your lover."

Horrified, Shaun guessed what Carmen had seen. "That wasn't what you think, Carmen. He means nothing to me. Dennis was just trying to prove a point."

"It didn't look like nothing to me," Carmen said, dragging the bag through the door with both arms.

Shaun couldn't fight the impulse to help him. Carmen looked so pathetic struggling with the luggage. "Don't touch me!" the slender man hissed. "My attorney will be in touch."

"You can have everything," Shaun replied. "Without you, it all means nothing."

"Fine, then you can stay in Louisiana with your old man lover," Carmen shouted as he moved down the steps.

"I'll get Billy to drive you where you want to go." Shaun sighed. He acquiesced because he knew that Carmen was stubborn and would find a way to get off the farm. At least with Billy, he knew that Carmen would be safe. Also, Carmen liked Billy, who was one of the few people on the plantation Carmen could relate to. Both were well-versed in world events.

Dennis joined Shaun as they watched the station wagon lumber down the farm road. Despite further protests from Shaun and Dennis, Carmen was intent on getting back to Boston that night.

"He'll be fine," Dennis said soothingly. "He just got a shock and it hit a sore spot. He'll calm down."

"I sure hope so," Shaun replied. "He was really angry."

"Come on," Dennis said, beckoning Shaun into the house. "There are some messages waiting for us and we have to go through the mail. It will get your mind off things."

"Okay." Shaun frowned.


"Uncle Julian's birth certificate is here . . . at least the second one," Shaun said as he sifted through the mail.

"What do you mean?" Dennis asked. "The second one?"

"We assumed that Grandmother Elizabeth found a way to doctor Uncle Julian's birth certificate to make it look like he was born nine months after she was married, thus eliminating the possibility that the rapist was his biological father. With the evidence we have here, I believe what we have are two babies. One was born to Elizabeth, i.e., Emma Jones, nine months after the rape and six months after her wedding date. The next baby was born ten months after the wedding date to an Elizabeth Jones, stating Grandpapa Bernard was the biological father."

"It's interesting Elizabeth used the name Jones both times," Dennis commented while looking over some other material in his hands. "We know she never used the surname Smith, but why would she put Jones on the certificate when she had changed her name to Steele? It just doesn't make sense to put Elizabeth Jones on the birth certificate."

Shaun had a hunch. "What was Grandmother Elizabeth's sister's name?"

Dennis put down what he was examining and pawed through some of the phone messages and mail. A look of surprise came over his face. "Elizabeth Jones," he replied. "She disappeared almost forty-five years ago and hasn't been heard from since. There have been a number of inquiries as to her whereabouts through the years without success."

"Wow!" Shaun exclaimed. "Do you think this woman could be Uncle Julian's mother?"

"Could be," Dennis mused. "Elizabeth knew at the onset of her marriage that she was having a difficult pregnancy. She couldn't be sure that if the pregnancy failed that she could get pregnant again, because there was so much damage done in the rape. So, she solicited the help of her sister to pull off a backup plan in case the first pregnancy failed. If Elizabeth couldn't produce an heir, she would have been a worthless player and tossed out on her ear with a modest divorce settlement. No, she had to do something."

"So, she had to get help," Shaun said following the train of thought. "How could Grandpapa Bernard have sired another baby on another woman without knowing about it?"

"The frozen semen samples," they both replied in unison.

Chuck and Mitch watched as the Pilot's station wagon parked next to the drugstore in town. They saw a small, wiry man exit the automobile from the passenger side and slam its door. "Who is that in Pilot's wagon?" Mitch asked with mild interest. They were sitting outside the lumberyard next to the drugstore waiting for their pickup to be loaded. The drugstore was within earshot, so he spoke under his breath. "He sure sticks out like a sore thumb in these parts."

Chuck nodded as he watched.

Billy got out of the driver's side. "The last bus has left. You better stay at the hotel and leave in the morning."

"There is no way I'm staying in this town one night," Carmen shot back. "What about the next town?"

Billy shook his head. "I think it might be a little late."

Carmen pounded the roof of the car with his fist and shouted, "I'm going to kill Dennis Jensen. He should have stayed away from my Shaun!" He didn't care where he was. He was leaving anyway. "Come on. Let's try the next town. I'm going to catch that bus."


Simon heard every word Carmen said. He was parked near the dime store. He wouldn't have thought that Shaun Smith was Dennis's type, but then again Dennis was a man and was inclined to take advantage of what was available. Simon stood clear of those nasty boys, Chuck and Mitch. They had tormented the little queers in school. Shaun Smith was the only one who would stand up to those bullies. More often than not, he would get his face bashed in as a result. Simon had a pretty face and had no desire to have it scarred. He could've taken on those boys and whipped them good, but why take the risks? Nobody bothered him in his school days. He used to play baseball and basketball with the school teams until his daddy decided he was needed on the farm full time. Luckily, his mother had talked his daddy into letting him finish high school.

Maybe guys in school used to whisper about him and his ways. He passed as normal, but he didn't pay any attention to girls like the other guys did. Simon didn't care for women. He found them boring. He used to coax one of the boys to the farm who wasn't seeing a girl at the time for some relief. Most of the time he could give a suck job, but there were occasions when he got what he liked most. These few encounters were one-timers, so Simon didn't get action as often as most of the straight boys. Yes, these girls with religion gave it up as often as the girls who didn't have it. At least that's what the guys in the locker room said.

Simon was concerned with the boy who was so upset with Dennis. He had to be stopped before he could cause any harm to the man who had come into his life and satisfied his deepest urges. After he saw that Chuck and Mitch had left, he crept from the shadows and leaped into his truck. Dennis was in trouble. He knew what he had to do.

Chuck and Mitch jounced down the dirt road not far behind Billy and Carmen. "What are we doing?" Mitch asked. Most of the time, he didn't ask questions. He just followed Chuck. However, this time he knew something was up.

"We are going to have a little fun with this little queer that belongs to Shaun Smith," Chuck replied with an evil grin. "We can get Smith where it hurts most. Yes, this evening that little critter won't be hurting as much as Smith's guts."

Mitch started to protest. He knew what happened the last time they crossed Smith. That pesky freak was too smart for them. But when Chuck had that nasty look in his eye, there was no stopping him.

## 31

Shaun strolled out to the front porch after one of the staff told him Dennis wanted to see him there. He was feeling a sense of relief. He felt closer to Dennis now because Dennis had helped him resolve some of the conflicts inside him. Despite what Dennis had said, he was a more mature influence. He was like Carmen in many ways, so that Shaun was sure the big man would give good counsel. Hopefully, Carmen would settle down and talk to clear up the misunderstanding. At least that was what Dennis said would happen.

"What's up?" Shaun asked, giving Dennis an affectionate clap on the shoulder. "Did you find out anything more about the mysterious sister?"

"Sit down, Shaun," Dennis said, beckoning. The two men sat on the edge of the porch. "I'm afraid I have some terrible news."

"What is it?" Shaun asked. Was something wrong with Uncle Julian? He seemed to be doing better. He had heard that Frances Lorraine had been around to see him. What kind of trouble was she causing now?

"It's Carmen. There has been an accident," Dennis replied.

Shaun bolted to his feet. "What happened? Tell me!" Shaun shouted. "Tell me he's okay."

"Well, Shaun." Dennis swallowed. "The sheriff just left after giving me the news. The car that Billy was driving went off the road and caught fire. Carmen was thrown from the car. There's not a lot of hope." After another pause he added, "Billy was killed. He was trapped in the station wagon and unable to escape from the fire."

Shaun started for the lane. "Where is a truck when you need it? Come on! We've got to get to him. Where is he?"

Dennis got up to follow. "He's in the doctor's office in town. They're getting a truck ready to transfer him to the parish hospital."

"They can't care for him there!" Shaun exclaimed. "That place is archaic."

"That's the best we can do right now," Dennis replied. The lawyer in him started to take over. "Shaun . . . uh . . . who is responsible for him? Do we need to contact his folks? Decisions have to be made."

"Come on!" Shaun pleaded. "We can deal with that later."

"Before we go, we need to make some phone calls. Instructions need to be given," Dennis said. He stood firm.

"We've taken care of all that," Shaun said. "We have every legal document necessary for each of us to be in charge of the other's interests. We are as married as the legal system will allow."

"Okay," Dennis replied with relief. "I'll make the calls. You need to go get the paperwork. Then we can go."


Shaun rushed inside the big house and Dennis started to follow him. As he turned, he noticed a big car pulling up the farm road. He waited to see who was arriving. As the doors of the white limousine flew open, Frances Lorraine, wearing a flowing blue dress and white petticoats, stepped from the car. With a touch more grace, an older woman followed her. She looked a few years older than the last time Dennis had laid eyes on her, but then, we all do . . . except for Frances Lorraine.

Dennis sauntered over to greet them. At once he said to Frances Lorraine, "Leave us." He gave the siren a glare that indicated that he wouldn't take no as an answer.

With a light curtsy, she waltzed up the walk to the big house. Nobody would protest her presence, since everybody would be going to the hospital. She would order a glass of iced tea on the front porch and watch every last one of them leave down the farm road.

"Candace, I wish I couldn't say I'm surprised to see you," Dennis greeted her. "I thought we had an agreement."

"I think it's moot at this point," Candace said. "The man I was protecting is dead. You have no hold on me."

"I see it didn't take long for you to hear the news of his murder," Dennis commented, "unless you had something to do with it."

"From what I understand, it was a terrible accident," Candace replied with grace. "He was distracted by that hysterical twit he was chauffeuring. He took his eyes off the road, then hit a pothole and was pitched off the road."

"You seem to know a lot about what happened in such a short time . . . maybe too coincidental," Dennis said.

"I have my sources, same as you," Candace said. "I can assure you that I had nothing to do with this one. I did have a great deal of affection for the man. We were in love many years ago, before you made me leave. How can you think I'd hurt him?"

"You've killed before," Dennis reminded her.

"Yes," Candace agreed. "And the world is a better place having done so. You can't prove anything. It's my word against yours. Those tapes you recorded, as amateurish as they were, are worthless to you. Any fool could doctor them to make them say what they wanted. They're so raw people will believe some slingshot lawyer manipulated them while trying to clear his boyfriend of a terrible crime. I'm a politician's wife. Everyone knows there are those who wish to discredit us for their nefarious purposes."

"After all these years, it's convenient that you show up at the time of his death," Dennis said. "Do you think people will wonder why? What brought you here, besides a good motive to kill him?"

"What do you mean?" Candace bristled. "I was homesick."

"You were more than homesick," Dennis sneered. "I've been keeping tabs on you. You were distressed when you heard that Billy married and had children so soon after your departure when your affair with him ended. You haven't been able to forget him and you were enraged that he was able to move on with his life. I find it hard to believe you were homesick for this swampland."

"You're right," Candace said, "I was distraught by Billy's behavior. But I didn't kill him. I have alibis. I haven't been alone a single moment since I've been back in the States. I've been careful."

"Why did you come back?" Dennis asked.

"It's Pilot's latest wife," Candace replied. "She put it together somehow and was able to determine that I killed Robert Lamond and that you and Pilot blackmailed me into leaving the States. I have no loyalty to her. I know she's trying to steal my husband from me while squeezing Pilot though the wringer."

"Then why have you allied yourself with her?" Dennis asked.

"She is well connected . . . especially with men," Candace replied. "She promised that I had nothing to worry about in coming back to Louisiana. I was told I could trust her."

"She's using you," Dennis said. "What does she want from you?"

"She wants me to divorce my husband in exchange for my freedom. At the right price, I may grant her wish. I haven't gotten a raise in my stipend from my husband in years. I want to live a little better. But I wasn't planning to take my chances if Billy had lived. I was going to come here, grant the divorce, and take my money back to Europe. I don't miss Louisiana all that much."

"It's all plausible," Dennis replied. "I'm going to have to make your case airtight before I believe you. I smell a murder. I'm meeting with the sheriff at the site of the wreck after I take Shaun to town. I'm sorry, but I have to go. I have to deal with a hysterical twenty-six-year-old."


Frances Lorraine watched the last car descend the farm road as she emptied her glass of iced tea. Candace came through the door.

"Where have you been?" Frances Lorraine asked, rocking in her wicker chair on the front porch. Candace joined her in the other chair but declined a glass of tea. She was flustered after her talk with Dennis.

"I wanted to avoid Emily," Candace replied. "Our relationship has been strained in recent years."

"I thought you looked after their children while they were in Europe?" Frances Lorraine commented with disinterest. She had other things on her mind.

"That was at her husband's request," Candace replied. "We seem to get along well now. I am fond of the children as he is, of course. It somehow forged a bond."

Frances Lorraine rose from her chair, having paid little attention to Candace's reply. "I need you to stay out of trouble while I go pay a visit to someone. I hope you can manage that."

Candace sighed. She was tiring of this woman. "I will have some tea. I hope you won't keep me too long in this country. Despite what anybody thinks, I am grieved by the latest news. Let's sign the papers giving you what you want, so I can take my money and leave."

"I need you here for a few days," Frances Lorraine responded. "There is someone I want you to see, but he's not up to it yet. I'll find something to keep you occupied. Do you still have a yearning for dark flesh?"

"Just go on and do what you need to do," Candace replied. "I'll be fine."


Shaun was pacing the waiting room of the small hospital. Pilot, Emily, Jack, and the others had come to join him while they waited to see if Carmen would live. It was late in the evening now and there was still no word. Finally, the doctor came from the tiny intensive care unit.

"Mr. Smith?" the tall, thin doctor in his mid-forties inquired. He glanced behind Shaun, looking for an older man that fit the description of a parent.

"That's me," Shaun replied, standing closer in front of the doctor. He pushed his irritation aside. "I'm responsible for him, as the paperwork indicates."

"Are you sure?" the doctor pressed. "You don't look like a family member. What relation are you to him?"

"Look, I don't have time for this," Shaun growled. "I am his *special friend* if you get my drift. Please get on with this. How is he?"

The doctor was dismayed, but he decided to proceed. He suspected the real people that were concerned with this patient were somewhere in this room. He decided to address all of them. "Mr. Smith . . . that is, Carmen Smith is resting. I'm afraid the prognosis is not good. He's sustained multiple factures, particularly in his skull, and is suffering from internal bleeding. We are running out of blood."

"Can you use my blood?" Shaun asked.

"We would have to type it . . . uh . . . unfortunately we can't allow just anybody to contribute anymore. You know . . . the blood crisis of the day."

"If I type, you can use my blood," Leah replied. There were a few grumbles from the others.

"Where are Uncle Julian and Dennis?" Shaun hissed. "They'll help."

"I'll help," Pilot said, glaring at the others. "I'm sure the others will." Then he added, "Your uncle will be around at some point, but you have to remember he's dealing with trauma of his own. Billy and he were the best of pals . . . kind of like family. He has to be taking it hard about now."


The sheriff decided that he was giving the orders. He instructed Dennis to meet him at his office. He wanted to wrap things up, so things could be peaceful. The last thing he wanted was for some pervert lawyer to be stirring things up. The sheriff remembered Jensen from the Lamond murder years ago. The man had a way of sticking his nose in where it didn't belong. Rumor had it that he had something to do with the abrupt dismissal of the murder charges against Pilot's son-in-law. He could have cared less if the man went to prison being that he was queer or at least had been. But it cast a shadow over his office. He was responsible for charging the man with murder and then it was overturned by a trumped-up accident. He guessed that things had worked out for the best. The Smith man seemed to have turned things around and was a respected man in the community. He did father six children.

The sheriff did some inquiries like he was trained to do. He found that the little squirt had threatened in public the very man that was trying to help him. Queers. They turned on each other, but stuck together just the same.

Dennis walked into the sheriff's office and sat comfortably in a chair in front of his desk as if they conversed like this each day. "So, what do you have?" Dennis said.

The sheriff knew that it would do no good to blow off this smart man, who could run circles around him. He had heard that for whatever reason, Pilot was fond of him, so he decided to cooperate. This way, the man would leave his office sooner.

"I know you've been to the site, so I'm going to be truthful with you," the sheriff started. "I suspect the wagon was run off the road by surprise. The tire marks don't indicate braking. But a couple sets of other fresh tire marks were made about the same time. In my opinion, it wasn't an accident."

"I agree," Dennis replied. "I appreciate your candidness."

"I did the prelims and I suspect you will do the same," the sheriff said. "I would say get out of my way, but you happen to be hooked up with an influential man in this community. I will permit you to carry on the investigation on your own. If anyone asks, you're assisting me. Just try to make this quick. The minute folks hear there are queers involved I'll never hear the end of it, so hurry it up."

Dennis figured that it was the most he could get. "Who have you questioned?"

"I happened to be at the dime store when I heard a few things. Your boy came in and caused quite a stir with his loud mouth. He was planning to kill you. Sounded like he had an elaborate plan with guns and all. But you can't believe all you hear. I bet the boy never laid a hand on a pistol. Anyhow, it seems that the boys with no balls started after him when he left town. The next step will be to ask them a few questions. Keep in mind that they hate queers more than most folks. People here don't pay too much mind to queers, but these two seem to watch out for them."

Dennis got up to leave. "I'll go pay them a visit."

"I wouldn't go onto their property. They're apt to shoot first and ask questions later. They'll claim you're trespassing. You won't live to refute the charge," the sheriff warned. "They're most likely at the road house on the other side of the parish. You can catch them there. You're a brawny sort. You should be fine there."

The hour was getting late. Dennis figured that he could make one more stop before the night grew too late to question anybody. He floored the pickup down the lonely dark road on the long drive to the other side of the parish.

There were several cars in the parking lot surrounding the weathered shack that housed a redneck country saloon. As he stepped from the truck, he could hear music blasting from the jukebox. When he walked in the door, his eyes adjusted to the dim light coming from a few uncovered bulbs. He could see a couple of pool tables in the back with overhead tube lamps lighting the green felt surfaces. To the right, a long bar stretched from one end of the front room to the other. One side of the bar featured a line of rough-looking men. There were no women. Dennis guessed it would be dangerous for them here. On the other side of the bar, a middle-aged man with a white apron tied around his belly was serving drinks.

Dennis had memorized the description that the sheriff had given of the two men that he came to find. He believed he saw them nursing a couple of fingers of whiskey at the middle of the bar. They were perched on stools. Dennis noted an empty stool next to the pair. Before ordering drinks, he studied the two men. He sidled up next to them. "Are you Chuck and Mitch?"

Chuck turned his head. "What do you want?" he mumbled in a hostile voice. He turned back to his friend. Dennis motioned for the bartender. The man came to wait on him. "A fifth of whatever they're drinking."

The bartender raised his eyebrows, then set a short glass in front of Dennis and started to put the bottle next to it. Dennis stopped him and directed it between the two goons. This got him the attention of Chuck and Mitch.

"Well, I guess you can't be too bad," Chuck replied. "I'm Chuck and this here is Mitch. Who are you?"

Because Dennis figured that they would recognize his name, he lied. "Brad. Brad Davis. I'm helping out the sheriff. Thought you could give me some assistance." He tried his best to copy their drawl, but figured he was doing a poor job. The two didn't seem to notice. They were probably soaked with whiskey.

"Like a deputy of sorts?" Mitch asked.

"Something like that," Dennis answered.

Chuck started to pour them each a drink. When he went to fill Dennis's glass, he placed his hand over it, to indicate he didn't want any. "You know, on the job and all."

"If we're going to talk, you're going to have to drink with us," Chuck said.

Dennis removed his hand and nodded. Chuck poured him a finger. He motioned for Dennis and Mitch to take a drink. "Here's to honest answers," he said, raising his glass. The three men proceeded to throw back their heads and down their drinks. Dennis didn't care too much for whiskey but drank it to meet the grubby men's challenge.

"What can we help you with?" Chuck asked.

"I understand you were at the dime store this afternoon," Dennis said.

"Yeah, what of it?" Chuck said, refilling their glasses. Dennis took a small taste of the booze. He had no intention of downing another shot, but he wanted to make it look like he was drinking with them.

"Not too much, just wondering what you saw," Dennis said, taking another sip.

"Nothing unusual," Chuck replied. "Just this little queer ranting on about this guy Jensen and how he was going to kill him for messing with his man." He looked at Mitch and the two men started to laugh out loud.

"I understand you didn't like his friend. That you had a run-in with him a few years back." Dennis quickly added, "That you got the best of him."

Chuck got an angry glint in his eye. "No, we don't care for him. Everyone knows that. I suppose everyone knows we want to get him one of these days."

"Well, the little man got into a bad accident soon after you saw him leave. He's lying in a hospital bed fighting for his life right this minute," Dennis said, refilling all of their glasses.

"What are you saying?" Chuck growled.

"Nothing." Dennis shrugged. He was starting to feel the effects of the whiskey. "Shortly after he left you, you were seen following him along the same road. I was just wondering if you saw anything. You know . . . that can help with the investigation."

"What investigation? I thought you said it was an accident," Mitch piped up. Chuck turned to glare at him to shut him up.

"Well, there are some of us . . . at the sheriff's department of course that think somebody pulled a dirty trick . . . to help the accident along," Dennis explained. "'Know anything about it?" He took another gulp of whiskey, then lifted the bottle and motioned for the two men to have their glasses filled.

Chuck was starting to slur his words. "That's true. We started after him and the black boy down the road . . . probably headed for no good. Then we noticed a beat-up piece of junk pickup following us for a good little while. We thought the road was getting crowded so we thought about getting off it and going about our business. We couldn't do anything if someone was going to be seeing us. So, we figured we'd go about it another time. A few miles out of town, we turned off and headed back to my place."

"Do you have any idea who could have been in that pickup truck behind you? Did it continue to follow after you turned off?" Dennis asked, trying to concentrate. The liquor was beginning to cloud his mind. He decided that he wouldn't have any more. The two other men were drunk and wouldn't notice him no longer drinking with them.

Chuck went to pour himself another round. He handed the bottle to Mitch and he did the same. "Yeah, he kept on going after him," he answered.

"Do you know who it was?" Dennis pressed.

"Yeah, it was that pretty farmer from the other side of town. You know, the one that doesn't say much and keeps to himself. Only see him every few weeks in town. I suspect he don't get out much. Heck of a baseball player though. He should've kept playing. Could've been a star or something. It was something always peculiar about him, but nobody bothered him in school. I suppose because he was so good in sports; not to mention he was strong as an ox. Probably could've taken on the three bigger guys in school and beaten 'em."

"You mean Simon Potter?" Dennis said with surprise.

As drunk as Chuck was, he still realized that he had hit upon something. "Yeah, Potter. That's him," Chuck replied.

Dennis berated himself for letting the two men know that he recognized Simon's name. Then he passed it off. They were so drunk that they probably wouldn't remember this conversation. "Gentlemen," Dennis said, getting to his feet, "thanks for your time."

– 32 –

It was late when Dennis arrived at the hospital. He guessed it
would mean the world to Shaun if he stopped in. He suspected Shaun
would be there all night hoping for Carmen to wake from his coma.
He was surprised to see the family there keeping him company in the
waiting room. It was late and the folks were not used to being up at
this hour. All would have chores to do in a few hours. The only ones
absent were Emily and Julian.

"How is he?" Dennis asked Shaun as he came into the waiting
room.

"Not good," Shaun replied, staring at the floor. "Where have you
been?"

"I've been doing some investigating on your partner's behalf,"
Dennis answered.

"Is that why you smell like you swallowed a still and have smoke all
in your clothes?" Shaun shot back. His nerves were raw.

"Sometimes investigations take you into undesirable places," Dennis explained. "I'm making progress."

"What are you talking about?" Shaun asked.

"Shaun, the sheriff and I suspect that Carmen and Billy didn't go
off the road by themselves. We think they may have had some help."

Shaun began to pace back and forth. "We have to catch them!" he
exclaimed. "We need to go." He grabbed his coat and gritted his
teeth. "Whoever did this is going to pay." He looked at Dennis. "Did
you find out who did it? Who are they?"

"Calm down," Dennis said, grabbing him by the shoulders. "I will
have some answers soon. You concentrate on taking care of your boyfriend. Let me do the rest."

Shaun nodded a few times, regaining his composure. "Okay. But
when you find them, they will wish that they had been the ones in
that car."

269

Dennis started for the door. He wanted to leave. Pilot stopped him at the exit. He made a face as if a stench was in the air. "Son, you have liquor on your breath. We all are upset. I understand you taking the death of your friend hard, but alcohol isn't the answer."

"Relax, it isn't what you think," Dennis assured him. "Remember, your savior aligned himself with prostitutes at one time to fulfill his purpose."

"I'm glad church is teaching you something, but there is such a thing as restraint and holding to your resolve. I can't condone such an action."

"Well, I didn't have the time Jesus had," Dennis claimed. "I had to act fast. I think I'll be able to wrap things up shortly."

There was a disturbance in the stairwell outside the exit. "Get your hands off me! I'm here to see my son!"

"But sir, visiting hours are over," a nurse explained. "We cannot possibly let any more people inside the waiting room . . . please, sir, you're waking the patients!"

"Daddy!" Leah exclaimed. "I'm glad you could come."

"Great!" Shaun sneered. "Why now of all times?" He started to walk away. "See if you can get rid of him, Dennis."

"Albert, what are you doing here?" Dennis asked angrily.

Albert brushed at his nose. "My, my, I guess we know where you have been. Couldn't you have picked a better time to party? Surely the men could wait."

Dennis was impatient. "If you have to stay, please go to the other end of the room . . . away from Shaun. Don't go near him." He glared. "He's fit to kill."

Dennis made to leave once more. Before he took a step, Adam walked through the door. "I came as soon as I heard. How is everything?"

"Ask Shaun," Dennis sneered. "If you're going to ask about my breath . . . yes, I have been to the bar."

Adam shook his head distractedly. "No . . . how is Shaun holding up? Maybe I can help."

Shaun waited until Adam came close. "What can I do?" Adam asked.

Fierce resentment caused Shaun to lash out. He was tired and not about to restrain his temper. "You can give me back my Uncle Julian! I need him now."

Adam pressed his lips together. Dennis interrupted before he could say anything. "Maybe you should go." Then he turned to Shaun. "Adam is just trying to help." Shaun turned away and went to sit on the other side of the room.

"Have you been to see Julian?" Dennis asked the minister.

"No. Not yet. I just got back from my trip," Adam explained. "I suppose I'll go tomorrow . . . that is, if he'll see me now." He shook his head again. "More trauma for him. Maybe I should start thinking of his feelings instead of indulging in self-pity. He'll come to me when he's ready. I guess that will be some time from now."

"Go to him tomorrow," Dennis said firmly. "You need to, for your sake as well as his . . . just do it and stop feeling sorry for yourself."

Adam nodded. "I'm going to wait here for a while. Maybe the family would like me to stay even if Shaun doesn't." Adam went to sit down.


Emily came back to the big house from the hospital to tend to her two children. When she arrived, she found Simon sitting on the steps of the back porch.

"He's been sitting like that for hours," Candace explained. "He says he's waiting for Dennis. He wouldn't say any more; 'yes ma'am' and 'no ma'am'—after a while, not even that. I just went inside and let him alone."

"Okay," Emily answered, dismissing her former mentor curtly. "I'll see to him."

"Simon, is there something I can help you with?" Emily asked, holding open the screen door from inside. "Would you like to wait inside where it is more comfortable? Candace says you've been out here for some time."

Simon continued to look toward the farm road as he answered, "No, thank you, Missus. I'll stay here." He didn't say any more. Simon wasn't comfortable and just hoped she would go away. As if on cue, Emily went back inside. At least she didn't stay and chatter like that other woman did. He continued to look toward the farm road.

After a while, the pickup truck carrying Dennis rolled up the farm road to the lane in front of the big house. Simon was at the side of the truck before Dennis could open the door.

"I guess you have something to tell me?" Dennis asked through the open truck window.

Simon nodded.

"Well, let me get out," he said. Simon stepped back as Dennis got out of the truck. "I need something to drink. You can come inside with me."

Simon moved ahead a few steps and retrieved a glass of iced tea from the porch. "The lady who talks too much gave it to me. I didn't drink it. You can have it," Simon offered. "It's better to talk out here."

The two men eased to the steps of the back porch and sat side by side. They were silent for a few moments. "Well, why don't you start from the beginning?" Dennis prodded. He knew this man of few words might have difficulty telling a story of any length.

Simon nodded. Dennis moved closer to him, so their thighs touched.

"I was at the dime store this afternoon tending to an errand," Simon said, beginning his story. "This little man with that black man named Billy came to the drug store next to the livery. Those two bad boys Shaun tangled with a few years ago were there. I've always tried to stay away from them as they are mean and make trouble. The little man yelled out that he was going to kill you for messing around with Shaun. I figured you could hold your own against him, but wanted to follow him just the same until they got out of town. Those two nasty boys took up the same notion and traveled close behind them for a few miles. After a while, they took another road, but I kept after Billy and the little man." Simon continued to gaze forward as if he was watching the scene play before him. "This car came from the other way toward the wagon carrying the two of them. The car must have hit a patch in the road and went to the center, hitting the side of Billy's car. This made Billy's wagon go into a ditch and tumble over. The car kept going."

Simon's speech started to quicken. Dennis figured that this was his way of getting upset, or being moved at least. Remarkably enough, Simon kept going without a break. "I pulled up to see what I could do. I pulled the little man from the car and set him to the side. The car started to catch fire. I couldn't get to the black man called Billy, because the car was wedged on its side in the ditch. I think he was knocked out because he didn't call for help. I was going to try and set the car back up, so I could get him out, but the fire got too strong. I couldn't save him. I pulled the little man further from the fire." He paused a moment. "That's what happened."

"What did you do then?" Dennis asked.

"I kind of figured I'd get you before I did anything else. The little man seemed safe enough, so I went home, cleaned up, then came here and waited for you," Simon explained.

Dennis thought Simon probably didn't do all the right things, but how often does one come across the scene of an accident? Despite the man's calm exterior, he must be torn up inside at what he had witnessed. He nodded. Yes, probably a nice hot shower was a good way to calm himself and clear his head while he tried to think of the next thing to do. He put his arm around the strong man's shoulders. He was as sexy as always with a loose blue muscle shirt covering his torso. "I'm proud of you. It couldn't have been easy. It's possible you saved a life. The little man's name is Carmen. And no, I didn't mess around with his boyfriend. It was a misunderstanding."

Simon didn't say anything as he leaned into Dennis's embrace.

A few questions came to Dennis's weary mind. "Can you describe the car, Simon?"

Simon nodded once as he straightened back up. "It was a white four-door car. Like one of those that people pay by the day to drive."

Dennis couldn't understand how Simon knew it was a rental car, but then again, Simon noticed details that other people overlooked . . . or just missed. "Did you happen to get the license plate number?"

Simon stared out into the field across the farm road. After a few moments he nodded. "Yeah. It was a Louisiana plate." He gave the number to Dennis, who wrote it down. He wanted to put in a call to have it traced.

"Can you stay here tonight?" Dennis asked, getting to his feet.

Simon stayed put and gave Dennis a bewildered look.

"I mean we can go down to Julian's cabin and stay there. I want to check on him anyway," Dennis explained. After getting a less than enthusiastic response he added, "Come on. The cow can wait a couple more hours. You're too tired to make the drive home. I don't want you in a ditch. And I'm too tired to drive you."

Simon hemmed. "She's not going to be too happy with me, but I guess it will be okay."

"I'll be right back," Dennis advised. "I need to make a quick phone call and grab some clothes."

*The next day.*

It was early. Julian rose before the sun, mostly because he found sleep elusive. He heard some other sounds from other rooms in the cottage. He thought he recognized Dennis's voice and that of another. By the time he had pulled on his clothes, they had left. He went through the motions to make some coffee, but could stand to drink only a cup. It was muddy and full of grounds. He figured even with the sadness, Jeannette would have made some and would welcome him at such an early hour. He doubted she got much sleep.

He was feeling so much pain at the moment. It had kept him tossing and turning through the night. Where did the pain belong? Was it because he didn't know who his parents were or was it where it belonged, with Billy? He didn't know. Now it was even worse with so little sleep.

There was a sound on the front porch. Once again, he recognized the footsteps. He wanted to get up and slam the door and lock it . . . if only it had a lock. It was too late. She was in his living area.

"Good morning, Julian," she greeted him in a chipper voice.

"Get out," he said.

"Now, that's not very nice," Frances Lorraine purred.

"Spit out your ugly gossip then get out," said Julian.

"You don't seem too concerned with what I have to say to you," she cried with feigned hurt feelings.

Julian slouched back on the sofa. "You can't possibly make me feel worse than I feel at this moment. Now spread your poison then leave."

"I'm sorry to hear about dear Billy," she said with forced sincerity. When she saw that his attention was waning, she decided to come out with her latest. "I don't suppose you heard that Candace is back."

"That's nice. Give her my regards," Julian said. "I hate to sound trite but, as nice as she is, I'm not up for visitors."

Frances Lorraine sauntered behind the sofa facing the back of Julian's head. "I don't think you are going to be happy with her at all once you hear what I have to tell you."

"What gives, Frances Lorraine?" Julian said, growing impatient. "Hurry it up. I've got things to do. I need to be getting next door."

"Didn't you wonder why she disappeared after Robert Lamond's death?" Frances Lorraine asked, relishing the moment. "Your big daddy and big boyfriend cut a deal with her. You see, she is the one who killed your lover, Robert Lamond. She's been roaming scot-free all these years . . . caring for your children. What's worse is Emily knows about it. Everyone knows about it except you, you weak boy! They don't think you could stand the truth."

"Nonsense," Julian said. "Everyone knows he died as a result of an accident." He started to rise to his feet. "Now if you don't mind, I really . . ."

"I have proof," she said, going for the door. She opened it and beckoned in the next visitor. "Come in, Candace."

A hurt look came over Julian's face as he realized that what Frances Lorraine had been telling him had been true. "Julian, I wanted to tell you myself," Candace started to explain. "It was an accident. You have to believe me. I came here with this woman today to apologize myself. I hope you'll be able to forgive me some day."

Anger flushed Julian's face. "I almost went to prison because of you! I would have been executed by the state or knifed by the inmates!" He stood and went to Candace. "Not only did I grieve for so many years over his death, but I placed my children in your hands! You're lucky no harm has come to them because of you."

Before Frances Lorraine could move, Julian accosted her. "Who else knew about this?"

An idea popped into her head. "Shaun. Shaun knew and insisted on keeping the truth from you. He felt you couldn't handle it. You're a weak pathetic fool, Julian, and everybody knows it."

Julian was devastated. How could Shaun? He had promised no more lies. They were going to make a clean start. They were going to trust each other. He couldn't lose Shaun on top of everything else. He covered his face with his hands. Red-eyed, he looked up at Frances Lorraine. He had never taken her seriously. He considered her a messenger of sorts until now. How could he fault her for merely telling him the truth? Only now it dawned on him that she set out to hurt people. He realized that she needed to be stopped. The others had failed, so now he was going to be the one to have to do it. His methods were different from theirs. Pilot and Dennis connived to set traps to catch her. Shaun was too young and hotheaded. Sooner or later she would get careless and Julian would be waiting. She had too little respect for him to consider him a threat. "Leave," he said. "Both of you. And don't come back. I'm going to get a lock for the door."

After the two women left, Julian went out to the short front porch. It would be so easy to go away to flee the pain . . . leave it all behind. The pain was so strong. He couldn't stand it. He knew that sooner or later it would wear him down and paralyze him. All the compulsion to fight back would be exhausted. He had so much pain that he no longer recognized the source. A breeze in his face distracted him. He remembered another time. He looked up into the trees. Squirrels were scampering about, working hard to provide themselves with food and shelter. What a simple life. The breeze refreshed him. Now, a few years later, he realized that their lives were not so simple. They competed with each other for food. The strongest squirrels hoarded all the food for themselves and their young ones. The weaker ones starved and became sick and were devoured by predators.

It would be so easy to leave the problems behind. Anything to get rid of this pain.

He saw a familiar figure come down the quarters road. A faint smile came to his face. It was the man with auburn hair, wearing faded jeans and a cotton-knit shirt. He waited for him to come up on the porch. He hugged him in his lean tanned arms. "You don't know how much I've missed you."

The two separated. Adam swallowed, and stuttered, "I-I wasn't sure you wanted me. It didn't seem so . . ."

"I'm sorry," Julian said, his eyes welling up in tears. "I haven't been myself in some time. Will you forgive me?"

Adam nodded. Julian pulled him close again.

"I need you," Julian said in desperation. "I find it hard to go on each day. My doctor used to tell me 'one day at a time and it will all start to make sense.' I need some help."

Adam nodded.

"Will you stay with me a couple days?" Julian pleaded. "I'm spending time with Billy's family. It helps with everything. They will be grateful if you stay. It will give you a chance to get to know them. It would mean the world to me. I feel they are my family. We've suffered a tremendous loss. It's good not to be alone. As much as things hurt, it's not so bad with them here."

"I'll stay," Adam agreed. "Let me go home and get some belongings, then I'll be back."

Julian nodded. "Adam, can you take the baby to his mother? It can't be good for him here. She'll be glad to have him."

Adam nodded. "I'll be back before too long."

# – 33 –

"Albert, you and I need to have a word," Dennis remarked as the man from St. Louis got out of the car with the rest of the family. They had been at the hospital all night. They had persuaded Shaun to come home with them. Carmen's parents were due in sometime today and they were going to be frantic over their son. Shaun would need to be rested.

"As you can see, we are all exhausted beyond belief. Can't it wait?" Albert complained. They were in the backyard behind the big house. The others went into the house.

"Albert, I'm prepared to throw a tantrum if I must. Now let's talk!" Dennis ordered.

"Here?" Albert said with a frown.

"Not unless you want to run the risk of others hearing what I have to say," Dennis retorted.

Albert paused a moment then relented. He wouldn't be able to dissuade this man. Especially when the kill was in sight. "Okay. What do you want?"

"You rented that car that pushed Carmen off the road and killed Billy," Dennis accused him.

Albert saw no reason to deny it. "It's true," he replied, bowing his head. "It was an accident."

"I know," Dennis said. "Still . . ."

Albert saw from the corner of his eye that Candace was getting out of Frances Lorraine's white car. She started up the walk to the big house. "Can't you pin it on her like you did the last one?"

Dennis had a bad taste in his mouth. "I guess you figured that out," he stated. "I only did it to save your brother . . . and Billy."

"Everyone knows about it," Albert exclaimed. "It didn't take a rocket scientist to figure it out. She killed in cold blood; I didn't. I'm not a murderer."

"That's not what your son's going to believe, Albert," Dennis said.

"Dennis, as much as I really hate to do this, I'm begging you not to divulge this to Shaun. I take back every little disparaging comment about your degenerate lifestyle. I promise to try to lift you up from your depravity." Albert continued, "Please, Dennis. I'll never live to see a jail cell if Shaun finds out. My brother will see that I die a slow death if he finds out I killed his friend."

"Albert, why did you come here?" Dennis said, taking a different tack.

A solemn look came over Albert's face. "I wanted to make up with Shaun. I no longer want to be enemies with my son. My daughter . . . his sister has been urging me these last few years to find some common ground with him."

"If I let this go, Albert, you are going to have to do better than that," Dennis stated.

"You mean, you're willing to consider it?" Albert replied with surprise. "Thank you, Dennis. I'll do what you ask."

"You're going to have to insist on an audience with Shaun. You won't take no for an answer," Dennis began. "Once you get the chance to speak with him . . . I'll be there with the two of you; you are going to say how much you love him. That you regretted from the moment you disowned him that you made a mistake, but were too proud to admit it. You are going to say that you've been tormented for years over all the terrible things you did to him as a child. You are going to say how proud you are of him and his accomplishments. . . . No, you are going to say, how much you love his lifestyle, that you've seen the light. You are going to say how much you're looking forward to meeting Carmen when he gets better and accept him into your family. You are going to go overboard. You're going to offer to throw a wedding for the two of them and invite everyone you know." Dennis fished for some more demands. When he couldn't think of any, he said, "That's all for now. Don't worry, I'm going to make a list for you to memorize."

Albert was dumbstruck. "I don't know if I can do all that."

"It's either that or die a torturous death," Dennis threatened. "Come on, Albert. I'm putting myself on the line here. It's my neck. I'm just trying to make something good come from this mess."

"Who else knows of this?" Albert asked, cocking an eye at Dennis.

"Just you and me," Dennis replied. "However, if I should somehow die a tragic death, there is another individual who will have the pieces to put it together. Your secret is safe with him."

"I can find out who he is," Albert threatened.

"Albert, I'm warning you," Dennis sneered. "I've set a few traps along the way. Your secret is safe as long as I stay healthy."

Albert shrugged. "I wasn't going to do anything. The terms seem acceptable. When can we move on this?"

"When things with Carmen settle down. The longer he lives, the better his chances," Dennis answered.

Albert looked grave. "He needs to regain consciousness soon if he's going to make it without too much brain damage. He's going to need a lot of plastic surgery."

"Albert, if he does make it, you run the risk of him identifying you," Dennis warned. "I'm risking everything for you."

Albert nodded. "Everything will work out fine."


Sunday came and there had been little change in Carmen's condition. Dennis decided to skip church. "I'm just so exhausted," he told Pilot. Most of the others were excused. Jeffrey understood. If the past few days were not stressful enough, the next several would be the test. Dennis was going to explain to his two boyfriends that he had not been up front with them. No doubt he would be forced to choose. A short fling or two might be understood, but affairs spanning many months might not be forgiven so easily.

Typically, he looked forward to seeing Simon. Today, he had a sense of dread. It could be the last time he spent time with Simon, or things could go to another level. Dennis just didn't know.

As usual when Simon came to pick Dennis up, they went to his farm and went straight to bed. Why make excuses? This was where they both wanted to be.

"Dance for me," Dennis ordered. Simon climbed on top of the cedar chest that sat at the foot of the bed, which came up to about the same height as the mattress. He started to sway his hips side to side in languid motions. Dennis lay back on the bed with his head propped up on two pillows and his hands cradling his neck. He watched. One article of clothing after another dropped. Simon drifted into another world as he stripped off every piece of clothing. Dennis sought to follow him, getting lost in every movement.

When Simon stopped dancing, Dennis said, "How about a rubdown?" He turned over onto his stomach. "Then I'll give you one."

Simon shrugged as he climbed onto Dennis's body. "You need it."

With gentle care, Simon undressed the man with broad shoulders.

They made gentle and tender love, different from their usual rough tumble. Simon could sense the need in his partner. He didn't think to ask Dennis what was bothering him. He figured the man would say something if he wanted to.

When it was time for Simon to tend to the animals, Dennis tagged along as he had countless times. He tugged on Simon with more affection than usual. The man with silk-smooth flesh thought it strange. It was their habit to roughhouse through his chores, taking occasional time-outs to wrestle in a pile of hay.

On their walk back to the house, Dennis started to explain his somber mood.

"Simon, I have to tell you something."

Simon waited for the man to continue without much expression.

"Through most of the time that we've been seeing each other, I've been seeing someone else at the same time," Dennis explained.

Simon nodded.

"I know I should have said something sooner. I guess I've been selfish."

Simon didn't give a response.

Dennis felt uncomfortable. He wished his friend would say something. Simon didn't express his feelings, but lashing out, or tears, anything would be better than the silent treatment. "Don't you have anything to say about it?"

Simon shrugged. "I don't expect you to hang with just me. After all, you are a man. I never knew one to be satisfied with just one. And just as long as you don't give me that bug you were telling me about."

"But you're a man, Simon," Dennis protested. "I feel like I know your every move. Why don't you go out on me?"

Simon shook his head. "Dennis, I'm a simple man. I get what I need and don't think much beyond that. I've haven't had an urge to go looking elsewhere. If something came up, maybe it would have happened. I don't know."

Dennis moved to another subject. "You know I'll probably go back East to live after awhile. You must have thought about that."

"I kind of figured I could go with you," Simon explained. "I'd lease out the farm and rent the house. I could go to Washington with you and work in one of those garden centers."

Dennis nodded, considering this option.

Then Simon bowed his head. "But I guess you wouldn't want me to be around your friends. I guess I'd be an embarrassment to you."

Dennis said with surprise, "Not at all, Simon. I'd be proud to have you with me. I'm sure you would be the most handsome man any of my friends had ever seen. They would be green with envy that you belonged to me." He sighed. "The other man is Jeffrey Martin. Do you know who he is?"

Simon nodded. "Well, why don't you bring him here? I'll treat him right. The three of us could get along fine."

Dennis knew Jeffrey would never go for this idea. He wasn't sure he could either.

"I'd want you to myself," Dennis replied. "Besides, I know the doctor would never go for it. He most likely is going to drop me as soon as I tell him about you."

Simon looked confused. "I don't see why he should object. Why can't things stay as they are? What's the fuss about?"

Dennis shook his head. "I wish more of the world thought like you do, Simon. We would all get along much better."

Simon didn't say anything for a few moments. "Come with me. I want to show you something."

Dennis followed, as they headed toward the woods. The mood didn't seem right for a tryst. He trusted Simon. Despite what the younger man thought, he was bright in ways other than those involving textbooks. He was wise, instinctive. The man didn't speak much, but his words and actions broadcast volumes.

In the deep woods, they came to a small stream. In a bend edged with a pile of large rocks, water collected in a quiet pool. Simon pointed to a nearby tree. "Look up there. Don't make any sound," he said in his most gentle voice.

Dennis saw a beautiful peacock. He had forgotten that they were common in this part of the country. "Wow," he marveled. "I've only seen them in cages at petting zoos. You knew he'd be here?"

Simon nodded. "That is you sitting on that branch," he muttered. "You are next to him. You couldn't tell the two of you apart."

Dennis chuckled in disbelief. Then he remembered that Julian had said something similar. He pondered the thought for a few moments. "Why do you say that? You are the pretty one. I could never hold a candle to you."

"You are the same," was all he said. He walked behind the tree where the bird was perched. Somehow, he knew this would propel the bird to drop from the branch to the stream bank. When the peacock saw his reflection in the pool, he opened up his tail feathers in a brilliant display. "There you go," Simon said. "When others come, you are at your best and most beautiful. You are no good stuck on a farm like this one. You must be in a crowd where others can recognize you. You think you don't have beauty, but you are mistaken. You walk like you are beautiful and that's just the same."

"I'm not sure that's so good."

Simon shrugged. "I like being with you. I'm sure others feel the same. We watch where you go and wonder what you are going to do next."

Dennis replied, "I want to stay the night with you and spend the day with you tomorrow. I promise I won't get in your way. I just want to watch you."

"Then you'll be on your way," Simon stated.

Dennis knew he meant for good. "That may not be the case, Simon. I have to work through a few things first. I promise I won't be long. I won't keep you or Jeffrey in suspense for long."

"We'll make the best of tomorrow," Simon replied.

"Simon . . ." Dennis started.

"Dennis, I'm not a smart doctor like he is," Simon said, looking at his friend. The peacock had folded its feathers and gone away. "He is more your kind. I'm a country boy who lives on a farm. You could never be happy with just me. If you have to make a choice, I guess it's best that it's him." He motioned for Dennis to come along with him. They said very little to each other the next day or two, as a sense of melancholy had descended on both of them. Still, they remained close and gave each other more affection than usual. Perhaps this was good-bye.

# – 34 –

A few days later, Adam returned home with a sack of dirty laundry.

"I guess that's one way of getting you home," his wife, Nancy, said with a grin. "When the laundry gives out, you realize it's time to come home. Do you want something to eat?"

"No," Adam replied. "A glass of sweet tea might be nice, thank you." He set the sack on the kitchen table of their country house. It was similar to the one Jeffrey owned. The couple had planned to build a bigger house when it was needed, but the children never came.

Nancy wore a white cotton dress with a red-checkered apron tied around her waist. She was a slender woman of medium height with long straw-colored hair tied neatly in a bun behind her head. She was tired, for she had spent the morning at church with the women's leadership.

Adam sat on the edge of the table. "I know I should have called a couple of days ago. I'm sorry if I worried you. It was inconsiderate of me."

"No need to say I'm sorry," she said as she placed a glass of iced tea next to him. "I've become accustomed to it over the years."

"Still . . ." Adam protested as he took a drink.

"I've got other matters to discuss with you, Adam, besides your being tardy arriving home," Nancy replied in a more serious tone. She sat on the sturdy table across from Adam. "I want a divorce."

"What!" Adam exclaimed in disbelief. "What are you talking about?" He had a look of shock on his face as he examined hers for the truth of her words.

"Adam, we haven't been husband and wife for years," Nancy said. "I can't remember the last time we were close. We are two ships that pass in the night. We hardly acknowledge each other. I need a husband who loves me."

"I'll change," Adam replied quickly. "I'll make it up to you."

"No, Adam, you won't," Nancy said. "I'm not Emily Pilot. I can't sit by and watch my husband with someone else. We've never discussed your relationship with her husband, but I'm not strong like she is. I need someone to take care of me."

"Nancy, please. What about the church?" Adam asked worriedly. "They'll never accept this."

"Adam, we've done our part," Nancy replied. "We've raised countless elders and leaders in the church and sent them off to start new churches. The leadership here in town is strong. The women I've worked with are committed. It's my time now to start thinking of myself. I've earned it after all these years. I've been a selfless wife and leader in the church. Now, I'm moving on."

"What do you mean?" Adam replied, coming unglued for one of the few times in his life. "Where will you go?"

"I'm going upstate to work with some men and women up there to revive some dead churches," she explained. "I'm forty-two years old, Adam. I've wanted children. The doctor has told me time and again that I'm fully capable of mothering a child . . . many children."

"God hasn't seen fit . . ." Adam started.

"I think the problem is with you, Adam," Nancy explained. "God has been wise in keeping us from having children. If I join with a man in the next year or so, maybe I'll still be able to have a couple babies before it's too late. My flow is still strong. It's possible."

"Nancy, I won't be able to stay here," Adam said. "The elders will never have me as their leader if my wife has divorced me. One of the basic premises of being a pastor is how we conduct our home life. I should have been more considerate." He swallowed. "I'll give up Julian to make our marriage work. I'll be the model husband. We can adopt children. We should have done that years ago."

"I'd still have half a man," she said. She placed her hand on his. "Adam, I feel so at peace with my decision. I'm going through with it. I don't know what you are going to do. I know you'll think of something." She got up to go into her bedroom. Adam could see that she had already started to gather things.

"When will you be leaving?" he asked, following her.

"In the next day or so," she replied, folding some clothes and placing them in her suitcase. "I'm going to tell folks I'm going upstate for a while to check on some work going on there. It will be the truth. I will leave it to you to explain things at your leisure. Don't wait too long. Word of our divorce will circulate down to this parish."

"Nancy, is there any way I can convince you to take more time to consider this?" Adam pleaded. "Perhaps we can get some counseling from one of the other elders."

"That may be a good idea, Adam," Nancy concurred. "It may do you a world of good. However, I'm still leaving you. I suggest you accept this, so you can make some choices in your life."

Adam was perplexed. For the first time in his life, he felt fragmented and didn't have the answers. He was going to need several days of prayer and meditation. Julian would be fine with Old Bill's family. He knew that Adam would have pressing matters relating to his church duties. "I'm going to my cabin," he said to Nancy. "I guess this is good-bye. I'll take food and clothes with me as soon as I launder them. I won't be back for several days."

Nancy nodded. She expected as much. "Good-bye, Adam."


Dennis approached Jeffrey's house with a great deal of apprehension. He was upset after his time with Simon. Despite what the young stud thought, it still wasn't a done deal that things were over for the two of them. He didn't want to be here. He'd rather find somewhere to sulk for a few days. However, he had promised Simon a quick resolution, so he pressed forward as he rapped on the kitchen door.

Jeffrey sought to give him more than the perfunctory peck on the lips. Dennis forced himself to comply. He wasn't feeling amorous or even affectionate. "We need to have a talk," he said. He wondered why he wasn't concerned for Jeffrey's feelings just yet. He felt guilty for feeling angry.

But as he walked into the house, he took one look at Jeffrey and melted. He was close to tears. The doctor gave him a look of adoration that couldn't be equaled. *Why does this man love me so?* Dennis looked at the floor. "Let's sit down," he said. He took Jeffrey's hands in his own as they sat in adjacent chairs in the living room.

"You're going away again," Jeffrey guessed with a smile. "I promise to take it better this time around. Do you know for how long?"

Dennis shook his head in amazement. "You've matured so much in these months," he said. "You're improving so much in these kinds of relationships. I wish I could say the same about me. I've behaved badly toward you."

"We've been through this," Jeffrey said, moving his hand to Dennis's cheek. "I know now that you'll be back. I won't be so difficult."

Dennis shook his head again, giving a wan smile. He couldn't bear to look into that angelic face, because he knew if he did, he would falter. "That's not it," he replied. "It's something else."

"What can it possibly be that has you so distressed?" Jeffrey asked. "Of course. How insensitive of me. I heard that the Pilots are going through a rough time now. Of course it has to affect you. I'm sorry."

"Listen carefully," Dennis said, "and try not to interrupt, because this is going to be next to impossible for me."

Jeffrey nodded. He was starting to feel concerned.

Dennis took Jeffrey's hands in his own. "I know that I haven't told you this before, but I love you. I have for some time, but I felt too guilty to say it with words."

"I know you do," Jeffrey said, failing to keep from interrupting. "I've known it even without you saying it."

"Well," Dennis started again, placing a finger on his boyfriend's lips, "I've been . . . uh . . . I've been . . ." He was losing his resolve. Why couldn't it be like Simon said? Why did things have to change? Nobody was complaining.

"Go on," Jeffrey prodded. "It can't be that bad."

Dennis frowned. "Do you know Simon Potter?"

Jeffrey thought for a moment. Why did the name ring a bell? Being a doctor, he felt he should know everyone in town. "I can't place him."

"Well, he's a farmer on the other side of the parish," Dennis explained. "He's kind of removed from everyone else as he tends to keep to himself."

"Oh yes," Jeffrey said, remembering the face. Then he thought for a moment. "I've seen him outside after church a time or two . . . most peculiar that he didn't come in for services."

"Well . . . he was waiting for me," Dennis said. "After I would see you off, I'd take off with him. It started during our first breakup . . . really before anything got started between us."

"What started?" Jeffrey replied, not grasping the truth.

"Jeffrey, for much of the time that I've been together with you . . . I've been together with Simon as well . . . in the same way," Dennis said, looking Jeffrey in the face with a nervous grimace.

"You can't be serious," Jeffrey said, getting to his feet. "There's just no way."

"I'm afraid there is," Dennis said. "I'm sorry for not coming clean with you sooner . . ."

"You are serious!" Jeffrey shouted. "Why are you doing this? How can you be so cruel? I've trusted you like nobody before. You've known of my trust issues . . . my religious morals. . . . Dennis, how could you!"

Dennis stood up. "I'm coming clean now. I know I have to make a choice. You both deserve better than me. I'm only hoping that one of you will have me."

"Get out!" Jeffrey cried, pointing toward the door. "I don't ever want to see you again." He rushed to the door and opened it for Dennis to exit.

Dennis walked over the threshold. He turned around to find one of the men he loved crying into his fist. "Jeffrey, I know I don't have any right to say this, but if I leave this time, it will be for good. You will have made that choice."

After a pause, Jeffrey moved a few steps toward Dennis and drew him into a tight and desperate embrace. "Choose me," he whispered softly. His sobs quieted. "Please, choose me," he pleaded.


It was midweek, so the church stood empty as Adam walked down the aisle of the sanctuary. He chose the front pew to sit in. He hoped that being in God's house would bring him closer to Him. The answers were not coming to him in his cabin. Instead, he just got more frustrated and agitated. He had broken down countless times now . . . yes, real tears. The first in many years.

*Answers . . . please, answers, God,* Adam prayed. He noted that someone had sat down next to him.

"Hello," Adam said, trying to hide his sorrow.

"Hi," Shaun replied.

"What brings you here?" Adam asked between sniffles.

"I thought God might listen to me more here than in the hospital," Shaun replied. "Still no change in Carmen. At least he's not getting worse."

Adam nodded.

"Deep down, I think I knew I'd feel better coming here," Shaun confessed. "It's peaceful here. I wanted to feel that."

Adam nodded, with another sniffle. "Me too. I wanted to feel peaceful."

Shaun slouched back in the pew and looked over at Adam. He could tell the man was distressed about something. It was weird seeing him in this state. Adam had always seemed like a pillar of strength and dependability . . . just as though he didn't have problems like everybody else. He just thought that God always took special care of him, so that he would have the strength to help other people. He felt warm to the bottom of his heart, as he understood now that Adam was human like everybody else.

"How are things?" Shaun asked.

"Okay," Adam replied.

Shaun nodded and looked toward the big cross pasted on the altar.

"You are going to know sooner or later," Adam said in a heavy voice. "Nancy is divorcing me."

Shaun nodded. "Oh."

"You don't seem surprised," Adam snorted. "I guess I haven't been fooling anybody. My marriage has been in turmoil and I failed to do anything about it. Everyone must know."

"It's not what I expected to hear," Shaun admitted, "but I knew something was troubling you." After a pause he added, "As far as everyone else knowing, I'm not sure. Sometimes folks see only what they're willing to see. You shouldn't worry so much about that."

"But as the pastor of this church, I have to, Shaun," Adam replied. "All my sheep look up to me as the ultimate moral authority."

Shaun didn't try to disagree with him. He only wanted the man to feel better.

"Look how I've treated you over these past few years, Shaun," Adam said. "I've done you wrong . . . all in the name of preserving the church. I knew I could do something to help your uncle and you get along better, but I didn't. I hope you will forgive me someday."

Shaun nodded. How could it be so easy? For years he had hoped to be included in Uncle Julian's and his lover's life. All the bitterness drained away at once.

"I love your uncle, Shaun," Adam admitted. "He's given me so much support through the years. The success of the church has so much to do with him. He's been a true life partner. He's grown so much in that time. He's starting to reach out to me when he's in more pain than he can endure. That's not easy for him. You should have been included in all this."

"Maybe the church will understand about the divorce," Shaun offered. He didn't agree with the way Adam lived his life, but he suspected that the preacher had done the best anybody could do, given the situation.

Adam shook his head. He started to sniffle again. "No. There's nothing for me here anymore. I'm finished. The elders will expel me soon enough."

Shaun thought for a few moments. "You know, you always said in your preaching that God may close one door so another can be opened. You've gone as far as to say that He may close three doors, just so one could be opened."

Adam agreed. "Yes, I've said that and now I'm being put to the test."

"What are you thinking?" Shaun asked with curiosity.

"I've been thinking on how I can build on some of my past successes. Again, I ended up with you, Shaun. I thought about the times your uncle, you, and I built the youth center in town and how it's spurred a sense of community in this parish. I'm thinking of doing some ministry along those lines."

"Sounds good." Shaun nodded. "Maybe I can help some. We had a lot of fun together a few years ago."

"Well," Adam forged on, "I'm thinking I'm going to make a career of it. I'm going to leave this parish and go to the inner city and start an afterschool and weekend program for urban teenagers. There has been success in taking teens off the streets after school and nighttimes and then doing things like intramural sports. They're occupied with something they like doing instead of mischief out on the streets. There's a lot of talk about it."

"Where do you want to go?" Shaun asked softly.

"Philadelphia, Pennsylvania," Adam replied.

"What about Uncle Julian?" Shaun replied. "You can't just leave him. He needs you more than ever now."

"That's what's been tormenting me so," Adam admitted. "I can't stay here, Shaun. I'll go crazy in this parish. I have to minister. I can no longer do it here. I don't know what I'm going to do about your uncle. Before I can help him, I have to take care of myself. I'd be no good to him otherwise."

"I wish you'd talk to him about your decision to leave," Shaun said. "I wish you could wait before you break the news to him. Maybe there is something the two of you could work out."

"You know he'll never leave this place, Shaun," Adam said. "He's said over and over that this is his place. He has no intention of ever leaving."

"Just talk to him," Shaun prodded. "My uncle will know what to do."


Dennis and Julian were sitting on the edge of the front porch, under its protection of the hot afternoon sun. Julian sensed that his friend had a lot on his mind, so he drew him away from the rest of the activity in the big house so that they could talk.

"Well, Simon wants things to stay as they are. He doesn't care what I do with Jeffrey, just as long as I make time for him," Dennis explained.

"That sounds ideal," Julian said hopefully.

"Jeffrey would never go for that," Dennis said.

"Sounds like Jeffrey's a drag," Julian replied. He had already made up his mind who Dennis should stick with.

"It's not just Jeffrey," Dennis said defeatedly. "I can't go on with both of them. My libido is having a ball now, but how much longer can it last? It's not only that—I don't work that way. I'm a one-woman man . . . or something like that . . . for gay guys. I want to just settle down with one guy."

"So what are you going to do?" Julian asked. The suspense was killing him. He couldn't read which way Dennis was leaning.

"Well, Simon is just so easy to be with. I absolutely adore him. He's devoted to me and we get along so well. The sex is incredible. I thought it would cool down, but it just keeps getting better. He could come back East with me. Jeffrey won't do that. He's anchored here. The chemistry is just so good with Simon," Dennis explained.

"So you've decided on Simon." Julian was pleased.

"Well, on the other hand, Jeffrey's a good catch. I have more in common with him than with Simon. We share the same interests. We have intelligent conversations. That is important to me. The sex is passable, but he's learning and starting to keep up with me. He's also devoted to me. We have disagreements . . . well, we have heated arguments . . . usually about something I did or didn't do. He keeps me honest," Dennis said.

"But he won't go back East with you," Julian reminded him.

"I've been thinking," Dennis said with a frown. "I'm not so sure I want to go back there. Everyone is dying there, Julian. Maybe here I'll be safe from it. I'm getting too mature for my roller-coaster career back there. After my last case, I've had a lot of offers. Simon and I could live comfortably. On the other hand, I'll find some way to screw that up like I always do. In Louisiana, I could work for the Pilots and your interests." He paused a few moments. "There are so many options to think about."

"Yet you've decided," Julian replied. "I can tell."

"Yes, I have," Dennis agreed. "I'm going to stay in Louisiana . . . for good. I won't be going back East."

"Okay, but with which boyfriend?" Julian pressed.

"As much as I love Simon, I can't live with him, Julian. We are different in enough ways that neither of us could be happy for long. I can't be trapped on a farm. I need friends. Despite all of Jeffrey's faults and quirks, I think he's right for me. He's trying so hard to grow up. It's true he doesn't have the wisdom that Simon does, but he's learning. He likes people. It's going to be hard for me to live in the country. Jeffrey will be good at getting me out and doing things."

"I have to admit I'm disappointed," Julian admitted. "Even though Simon has said less than two words to me, I like him. The two of you move well together. He's right, Dennis. You move with the grace of a peacock. You draw so much attention without recognizing it yet you thrive on it."

Dennis wasn't used to the analogy, but maybe it was true. He had been called worse things in his life.

"I don't know if this is such a good idea, Dennis," Shaun complained.

"Come on. He's waiting for you on the front porch," Dennis said, beckoning. "I've sent everyone away. There's nobody left in the big house except the three of us. Well, Leah's close by if you want her here."

"I do," Shaun said, feeling comforted knowing that his sister would be present. Then he turned and faced Dennis in the foyer just before he stepped onto the porch. "Do we really have to? I don't see what good it'll do."

"I promise it will be worth it," Dennis assured him. "He's going to be the perfect gentleman. He wants to make amends, Shaun. Let's just see what he has to say."

Albert watched his son and friend come out onto the porch. He looked closely at Shaun's clothing to make sure there wasn't a hidden pistol. He couldn't help but feel responsible for what he had created. Shaun was a finished product now. Despite Albert's attempts to mold him, he saw a young adult who possessed just enough masculinity to be called a man. Shaun was clean-shaven, without a trace of peach fuzz on his chin. His clothing clung to his wiry frame and didn't reveal an inch more flesh than necessary. *I thought homosexuals couldn't wait to get out of their clothes,* Albert thought. Maybe he had done something right by his boy.

"Shaun, I just want to say how proud I am of you," Albert started.

Dennis gave Albert a dirty look. They hadn't even gotten through the pleasantries yet. He didn't want Albert's speech to sound too rehearsed.

"Yes," Dennis interrupted. "He's handling Carmen's situation well." Then he added, "Albert, I understand you've been at the hospital all morning."

Shaun had a look of surprise on his face. "You have?"

"Yes, I wanted to check on things," Albert said, clearing his throat.

"You did?" Shaun replied with skepticism.

"Yes, Albert has been at the hospital while you've been sleeping just in case there had been any changes," Dennis added.

"You have?" Shaun asked. "Why?"

Albert cleared his throat again. "Well, Shaun, I could see how much that young . . . *man* . . . means to you. I knew you'd probably like somebody from the family to be there at all times, so when all the others left, I took it upon myself to be there."

Shaun was having trouble believing his father. "Why are you here?" he asked.

"Shaun, I know I haven't been around these past few years," Albert stated. The men remained standing on the porch. Sweat started to bead on Albert's forehead. Even though it was spring, it was humid and hot for a man wearing a dark suit. He wrung his hands while he searched for words. Had he forgotten his speech? He spoke before groups all the time. Why was it so difficult now? Without a gun, this kid was harmless.

Dennis nodded to prompt Albert to continue. "Like I said earlier, Shaun, I am so proud of you. You've done well in your young life despite . . ."

Dennis shook his head once.

"Yes, despite having me as your father," Albert continued. "I mean, I was a terrible papa to you and did things to you that I will regret for the rest of my life. I want to say I'm sorry."

Shaun started to feel uneasy. He wanted to get this over with fast. "What's made you come to this? I have a hard time believing you. You're never wrong."

"I know. I know," Albert said, nodding. "It was Leah," he said, as she walked onto the porch as if on cue. "She has worked on me relentlessly until I could see the error of my ways. She reminds me often of your Grandma Elizabeth. Anyway, it's important to her that we make up. As you can see, I've never been able to refuse her. But she's right, Shaun. I need to at least try to make things right with you. I hope someday you'll forgive me."

"Is that all?" Shaun said, putting his hands in his pockets. "If it is, then you're forgiven. I need to go . . ."

Leah placed a hand on his arm to dissuade him from leaving and stood close to him. Feeling more secure, Shaun remained.

"Like I said earlier, Shaun," Albert began again. *Maybe if I say it fast it will all come out okay,* he thought. Despite the notion, the words that came out were slow, thick and deliberate. "I am so proud of you. Leah has kept me abreast of all the wonderful work you are doing for young people in your charities. I never took the time to get involved with those things. I just always give money to different nonprofits in an attempt to make them just go away. You, on the other hand, have made it your life's work. I've begun to see that you've grown up to be a successful young man. I admit that I don't understand many of your ways. I'm under the impression that your Uncle Julian still shares those ways, as does your good friend Dennis here. Well, maybe God is trying to tell me something, I'm thinking. I pushed away my only brother and then I pushed away my only son. As a man gets older, he realizes that he can only push so many people away. What I want to say, Shaun, is . . . is that I love you very much. You are a good man . . . in spite of having me as your father. From what I'm told, I have your Uncle Julian, your Aunt Emily, your Grandpapa Pilot, and your church minister to thank."

Shaun looked at his father with awe. "You mean all of this?"

Albert nodded.

"I don't think I'll be coming to St. Louis for holidays, but maybe it would be good for you to spend some time with your grandchildren."

"Grandchildren?" Albert replied.


Pilot went to the Lamond house to pay a visit to his wife. She was expecting him and was dressed with exquisite care. She was hoping for a hefty divorce settlement. They met out on the veranda.

She was waiting for him to say how nice she looked. Knowing this, he said, "You look very pretty as usual."

"Thank you," she replied, fanning herself. She knew that yellow was her color.

"Your partner in crime . . . your friend has left us," Pilot commented. "I expect that she has gone back to Europe. Will it be a while before we see her again?"

"Yes, things were getting a mite sticky for her here . . . and I don't mean the weather," Frances Lorraine concurred. "She's a free woman with a hefty change purse. She's not needed anymore."

"When is all this going to stop, Frances Lorraine? The family has told me to give you what you want."

"Has our little Julian had enough?" she purred.

"Our little Julian seems to have a good hold on himself," Pilot said. "You better watch out for him, dear. He may seem gentle to you, but he's a smart man and has amassed a great deal of wisdom through the years. You may have met your match."

Frances Lorraine dismissed the thought. "He was just the target. You all fawn over him so." Then she switched subjects. "So we are speaking settlement?"

"If you divorce me, you can kiss your election good-bye," Pilot retorted. "You'll no longer be the victim. Wouldn't it behoove you to stand by your man despite your . . . my wicked ways."

"The governor wants to marry me," Frances Lorraine said, fanning herself in quicker, longer strokes as if she was getting ready to have the vapors.

Pilot was silent. Frances Lorraine knew her husband well enough to know he was gathering all the facts and piecing them together. She also knew that he would present her with his final offer. He was calm and collected. Now he was putting his morals aside and thinking business without prejudices. She knew that she shouldn't interrupt.

"I know you don't want to marry the goat," Pilot replied. He held up his hand to stop her protest. "Come on, Frances Lorraine. If your own infidelities don't betray you, what about his? You won't be able to overcome his problems. They'll be linked to you. He will care less about your comings and goings. The best thing you can do is what you've already done. He's helped you politically. Now it's time to cast him aside. Let him worry about getting elected to the U.S. Senate.

Personally, I don't think he has a chance. Why be on a sinking ship?" She was getting ready to protest again. "Instead of promoting his lost cause, why not continue to ride your tide? You don't need him anymore. I know you promised him help, but I don't see you losing sleep reneging on your other deals. Just get elected."

"What's in it for you?" Frances Lorraine shot back.

"There may be a certain prestige for me to have a state senator as my wife," Pilot commented. "I'll give you my own stake in the family over ten to fifteen years. It will have to be in cash, no stock. If you invest wisely over the years, you will be a wealthy woman. That's the deal. No ownership of the farm. That's it, my dear. It's out of my hands. Emily and Julian will fight to the death to keep ownership in the family. So will Jack, Marge, and my other children. It's a cold world. They've decided they'll let Julian be sacrificed even if you're successful in running him into the ground."

Frances Lorraine mulled over these prospects.

"Take it, Frances Lorraine," Pilot urged.

*This will be fine for now,* she thought. She had other battles in her life right now other than the Pilots. She needed to get elected. "It will all be in writing, I suppose," she said in a sanguine tone.

*A couple days later.*

Julian was sitting on the front steps of the big house. Dennis came to join him. It was late afternoon after a bright sunny day. The weather had turned unseasonably cool with little humidity in the air. Julian didn't visit the cans much anymore. It was a useless place anyway. Everyone knew they could find him there if they wanted him for some reason. Sitting on the front steps was just as good. People wouldn't have to go far to find him.

"Hey," Dennis greeted him.

"What's up?" Julian replied.

"You're back up at the big house now?" Dennis inquired.

"Yeah, it was time," was all Julian said.

"I thought I'd give you everything I know about your parents. I'm giving it a rest for a while. I'm going to leave the last of the investiga-

tion to you. You can find things at your own pace," Dennis said. "I
know that you're more than capable."

Julian shrugged. "What do you have?" he asked.

"We know there were two babies born. I suspect you are baby
number two. Baby number one, Elizabeth's baby, died and we don't
know where the remains are. Shaun and I believe that baby number
two was born to Elizabeth's sister, who was christened with the name
Elizabeth. That's why Elizabeth Jones is on your birth certificate.
We'll call her Liz. We'll call the living Elizabeth "Emma" for now.
We believe Emma, Granny Smith, and Liz connived to produce an
offspring because Emma didn't believe she'd go full term with baby
one and wasn't sure she be able to conceive again. She went to Granny
Smith and begged for her help. It looked like Granny Smith smiled
with compassion upon Emma instead of dismissing her from the family. This was not the case. Granny Smith paid Liz handsomely to produce the heir she wanted. When the baby was born, she was to leave
and never come back. But here's the twist," Dennis added with excitement. "Granny Smith didn't slip Liz frozen semen from Bernard.
No. Unknown to all, she slipped Emma semen from her other son
Matt. Nobody knew she had it locked away in the Smith labs. Shaun
was able to confirm this, since he is now CEO of the conglomerate,
Smith Power. Granny Smith wanted a grandchild from her dead son
Matt and jumped at the opportunity to make him legitimate. She was
the only one that knew."

"So my biological parents are Elizabeth's . . . I mean Emma's sister
and my Uncle Matt?" Julian asked with a puzzled look.

"Well, it's all circumstantial," Dennis cautioned him. "Your job
will be to confirm these presumptions. You can do it at your leisure if
you want to."

Julian nodded. "That will mean finding Liz. That may be difficult
so many years later."

"It's your choice, my friend," Dennis said, getting to his feet. He
gave his friend a clasp on the shoulder. "Good luck."

A short time after Dennis left, Julian could see Adam walking up the front lawn. He smiled broadly at the sight of Adam's sparkling emerald eyes. He was glad to see him. He had enjoyed having Adam to himself for those few days down at the cottage. He made a pledge to himself to make more time for the pastor.

Adam eased to the steps next to Julian. They sat a few inches apart. They were not an affectionate couple except at times of intimacy. "You look good," Adam said.

"You look tired," Julian replied, looking ahead. "Church have you busy?"

"Not really," Adam replied, staring into his hands clasped between his knees. He turned his head and looked to Julian's face. "Julian, Nancy is leaving me," Adam said. "She's filing for divorce citing irreconcilable differences."

"I'm sorry, Adam," Julian said, meeting his gaze. "I know what it must be doing to you." He looked ahead once more.

"Julian, I'm leaving the parish," Adam said in a controlled tone. "I'm going to Philadelphia to start a program for urban teenage schoolchildren." He paused and swallowed. He felt a sudden thirst and licked his dry lips. "I'd like you to come with me," he said in a hoarse voice.

Julian pressed his lips together and looked his friend straight in the face. "When do you want us to leave?"

"You mean you'll come?" Adam said with disbelief.

Julian shrugged. "There's nothing here for me anymore," he said. He held his palms together between his knees. "Emily is taking Louis and Candy to Paris to live. She's just so sick, Adam. The climate is bad for her breathing here. She gets one infection after another. She's leaving the baby with me, so if you want me, it will have to be a package deal."

Adam was overwhelmed. "Why Paris?" he gasped. "Is the climate good for respiratory problems?"

"I don't know," Julian replied as he shook his head. "She seems to think so."

"I'm surprised at all of this," Adam said, sifting through all the information.

"I guess we've all done a lot of thinking over these past weeks," Julian said. "It's good," he added. "She will be near the three other children. We will all come back to the farm for holidays and summer breaks. I'll go overseas from time to time to see them. I guess she'll come with Louis, Candy, and maybe the other children to where we live from time to time."

"What about Shaun?" Adam said.

"I have a feeling things are going to be changing for Shaun," Julian said. "I think he'll be taking Carmen back to Boston when he's able to travel. I think he'll end up staying there to raise a family. That's what they both want. Carmen hates Louisiana. If Carmen comes around, Shaun will do whatever it takes to solidify their relationship. That means staying put in Boston and leaving Louisiana alone."

"What will Pilot do with the farm?" Adam asked. "He's aging and he knows it."

"I think little Marge is going to get her wish and get involved with big business. This may not be what she had in mind, but she'll be fine with it. Pilot, Jack, and she will be fine running things. Who knows? Maybe one of my children will come back here one day to run the farm." Julian turned back to Adam. "What about you?"

"I will want to leave soon," Adam said.

Julian studied him thoughtfully. "Why don't you go to Philadelphia and, when you're ready, find a place for Six, you, and me to live? When you're set up with your new career, we'll join you some time this summer. How's that sound?"

"Like a plan," Adam said as he kissed Julian's cheek. He started to rise but Julian stopped him.

"We have to work through a few things," Julian said. "I want to live openly as a gay couple with a child. No more closets."

"Okay," Adam replied. It seemed agreeable to him. "But it's just you and me. No relations outside our relationship."

"Of course." Julian nodded.

Shaun opened the screen door and paused there. When he didn't come over the threshold, Julian and Adam looked back at him. Shaun pursed his lips. "Oliver died a few minutes ago," he said. "Grandpapa

Pilot is with him now." He looked toward Adam. "He's waiting for you."

Adam went into the house. Shaun went and sat down next to Julian.

"Uncle Julian, I know this isn't the appropriate time, but I have to tell you something. I'm being selfish, but I don't want this hanging over me with everything else I'm dealing with. That Lorraine woman made a point of bringing that Candace lady to see me a couple of days ago to tell me that she had killed your lover, Lamond, a few years ago. I don't know what that means to you, but I thought I should tell you."

"I suspected as much," Julian mused.

"You know?" Shaun asked with interest.

"Yeah, she did the same thing to me, hoping to stir things up," Julian replied. "It worked to some degree, but that was so long ago. If anything, it helped me. I don't feel so guilty anymore."

"But she killed him," Shaun retorted. "Don't you want to get even? She caused you a great deal of pain."

"Perhaps some day," Julian shrugged. "I have a lot of other things on my mind than revenge. Despite the many bumps, life's been good to me through the years. I never realize that until I look back and see where I've come from."

"I hope I can say the same," Shaun said, turning solemn.

"How is Carmen?" Julian asked. "I'm planning a trip to the hospital. Maybe we can go together."

"They say he's getting better," Shaun said with relief. "He'll be coming out of the coma soon." Then Shaun began to get upset. "Uncle Julian, I know this sounds self-centered but I've been holding it inside and need to say it. What if he dies thinking that I cheated on him and didn't love him? Or what if he lives and I can't communicate to him that it's not true? I don't think I'll be able to forgive myself."

Julian placed an arm on Shaun's thigh and gave it a reassuring squeeze. "He'll be okay. Just watch."

Shaun bowed his head. "If he makes it, he's going to need a lot of plastic surgery. He's always been so concerned with his looks."

"You guys will be fine. I'm sure he'll wake up with you next to him and then he'll know how much you love him. Just think about it when you start to feel uneasy," Julian advised him. "I'll stay with you until he wakes up. How about that?"

"You're the greatest, Uncle Julian," Shaun said, resting his cheek against his uncle's shoulder.

Julian smiled with relief and pleasure. It was nice to be a hero.

# Epilogue

*Two years later.*

It was the noon hour on a beautiful spring day in Philadelphia. Julian peered through the blinds and studied the street from the window of his three-bedroom apartment where he lived with his partner and two-year-old son. The other bedroom was reserved for his nephew Shaun, who often came by to visit him from Boston for a night or two. The apartment was large. The front door opened into a little foyer, leading into a comfortable living room. Beyond this was a dining room and to the right the kitchen where Julian continued to develop his culinary skills. He managed to attend cooking school at the urging of his little family. A hallway led from the living room to the bedrooms and bathroom. Shaun's room was on the left. Beyond that was the bathroom. On the right was Julian and Adam's room. The back bedroom at the far end of the hall belonged to Six. Large windows lit the apartment in the kitchen, the dining room, Julian's bedroom, and Six's room, providing a view of the neighborhood street. There wasn't much traffic, which made a safe place for the neighborhood children to play. The city noises could be heard a block away. This was a far cry from the tranquil environment of the Louisiana sugarcane plantation where Julian had lived for twenty-plus years.

Julian was a househusband who worked from home. His six children had a vast trust fund, which he managed, taking many hours of the day to oversee. There was time to clean the flat and cook a few meals. He devoted himself to tending his youngest son and his partner. Adam worked with the neighborhood teenagers, finding activities for them to do to stay out of trouble. He was gone most of the day.

Julian was taking a break from his desk, which sat against the wall between the dining room and the kitchen. He had other things on his mind besides work.

Shaun came through the door while Julian was looking through the window shades. He had been expecting his nephew. He watched the traffic across the park on the other side of the street. "Hey," he said without looking over at Shaun.

Shaun was attuned to his uncle's moods. They were melancholy at times. Sometimes Uncle Julian said what was on his mind; at other times he kept his thoughts to himself. "Anything going on out there?" he asked.

Julian turned to face his nephew. "No," Julian sighed. "I was just thinking about Jesse. Today is his seventeenth birthday."

"Yeah, I know," Shaun replied. He had suspected that his uncle might be thinking of his eldest son.

"He's practically grown and I haven't seen him much in two years," Julian said. "He goes to summer camp, so I don't get to see him when school's out. At breaks he visits with friends and their families. I don't know my son anymore. I haven't spent but a few days with him in five years. He's usually too busy to see his mother and me when we go to visit the school. I don't know why I let him go. I've missed out on him growing up."

There was a knock at the door. Shaun hurried to answer it. A young man crossed the threshold and entered the living room. He stood close to six feet tall. His white-blond hair was buzz-cut and pasted heavily with mousse. He sported a lean frame and was slender like his mother. He hadn't finished filling out yet, because today was just his seventeenth birthday. His shoulders had medium breadth like his daddy's. He also had his daddy's brown eyes. However, he favored his mother.

Shaun looked over the young man. He hadn't seen him in a long time. Jesse had idolized Shaun just like the other children did when they were small. Jesse wore a tight blue plaid shirt with short sleeves rolled just below his armpits. His waist was narrow, secured with a wide black belt that seemed to be just for decoration, because his blue jeans looked like they were painted on his frame and didn't need any support from the leather strap. Shaun saw what looked like a log running from his zipper all the way to his hip. *Must be from Emily's side of the family,* Shaun thought. He said a little prayer of thanks that Carmen and he were not overly endowed. Jesse's jeans were snug down his legs and were tucked into a pair of black leather high-tops.

A look of joy came over Julian's face. He walked across the room to embrace his son. "This is the best birthday present I've ever had. . . . Even if it is *your* birthday." He held his son's upper arms. "Let me take a good look at you."

Shaun noted that Julian didn't seem to notice Jesse's provocative dress. If he did, he didn't seem to show it. No, his uncle was just glad to see his son.

"You look great!" Julian exclaimed. "Are they feeding you okay at school?"

"Yeah, Papa, just fine," Jesse replied with a grin. He seemed glad to see his daddy.

Julian gave him a sly look. "Papa? What happened to Daddy?" he asked, letting him go.

"Daddy is what kids say," Jesse explained. "You call your daddy Papa, so I figured I'd do the same."

Julian nodded. He wasn't concerned at the moment with his name. "Just don't stop calling your mama by her name. She'd be heartbroken."

Jesse nodded in agreement.

"Are you on break from school? You must be early," Julian said. His son had been doing well in school over the past couple of years; all A pluses. It had been a marked improvement. In the past, Jesse had lagged behind the other children when it came to grades. Nonetheless, he was their leader. All his siblings looked up to him.

"I tested out," Jesse explained. "I'm finished for good. I was ahead of the others, so they saw no reason to keep me. I'll be ready to graduate early if it's okay with you and Mama."

Julian nodded. "This way, you'll get a head start on college."

Jesse didn't say anything. Instead, he nodded toward Shaun. His cousin opened the door to the outside corridor. "There's someone I want you to meet," he said.

Julian looked on with curiosity. Adam came through the door holding the hand of a little boy who looked to be around Six's age.

Maybe a few months younger. He was blond like his father and was wearing a navy blue jump suit with shoulder straps.

"This is Seven," Jesse said, introducing the toddler. "Your first grandson."

## ABOUT THE AUTHOR

**James W. Ridout IV** lives in Washington, DC. He holds a master's degree in human resources from the University of Maryland in College Park and is the author of *Plantation Secrets*.